Praise for internationally bestselling author Harriet Evans

A Place for Us

"Each of the characters is distinct and sympathetic, and the tensions in the family are often treated with a comic touch even in the midst of tragedy. While a story with this many characters could have felt disjointed, here they are interwoven tightly to create a single, absorbing tapestry."
— *Kirkus Reviews*

"A brilliantly written story that will stay with you long after the last page."
— *Fabulous* (UK)

"Harriet Evans is a master at creating characters you feel like you know inside out, and wish you could meet in real life—we almost couldn't bear to leave them when we finished. An unputdownable thrill of a novel—you'll be racing to the end to find out the Winter family's deep, dark secret."
— *Heat* (UK)

"I was blissfully carried away by this intelligent . . . classy and superbly executed family saga."
— *Saga* (UK)

"Lovely and heart-warming, *A Place for Us* is a thoroughly readable novel filled with tragedy, love, and redemption."
— *Peterborough Telegraph* (UK)

"Fabulously gripping story."
— *Prima* (UK)

Not Without You

"The stories of Sophie and Eve take center stage here, providing a refreshing and absorbing depth and complexity. A fascinating look at the Hollywood machine of past and present and those who have struggled within it."
— *Booklist*

"The shallow LA of today is wittily satirized, and the more glamorous age of the '50s brilliantly recalled."
— *Sunday Mirror* (UK)

Happily Ever After

"If you've been suffering from chick-lit fatigue, this is the book to give you back the love."

—Heat (UK)

"This funny but thought-provoking book follows our heroine as she tries to find her way in a world tainted by her own cynicism. . . . An absolute must-read."

—Cosmopolitan (UK)

"Evans's stories are modern, absorbing, and compelling."

—Lovereading.co.uk

Love Always

"Evans keeps the reader turning pages to see what Natasha will do next because they will identify with a protagonist who strives to pick apart the lies in her life and piece together a truth."

—Publishers Weekly

"A poignant tale of self-discovery. . . . Wonderful."

—Marie Claire (UK)

"Written in the author's usual warm, witty style. . . . Perfect for a cozy night in."

—Cosmopolitan (UK)

"An effortless and deeply satisfying romantic tale."

—Glamour (UK)

I Remember You

"A satisfying summer read."

—Library Journal

"A compelling story complete with mystery, unearthed secrets, and longing for new adventures and old comforts."

—RT Book Reviews

"The perfect girly read."

—Cosmopolitan (UK)

"A fabulous feel-good love story of friendship lost and love regained."
—Woman & Home (UK)

The Love of Her Life

"A heart-tugging tale. . . . Peopled with well-rounded characters and compelling dilemmas, the story will have readers sighing, hoping, and finally smiling. A read both entertaining and emotional; tissues at hand highly recommended."
—*BookPage*

"A poignant twist on the usual tropes of chick lit."
—*Booklist*

"An unputdownable, gripping story of life, loss, and one girl's search for happiness."
—*Glamour* (UK)

"Brilliantly observed and emotionally charged throughout."
—*Daily Mirror* (UK)

A Hopeless Romantic

"A delicious romcom, surprisingly believable."
—*Marie Claire* (UK)

"Hard to resist."
—*Elle* (UK)

"Touching, engrossing, and convincing. . . . A rollicking ride of joy, disappointment, and self-discovery, which you'll want to devour in one sitting."
—*Daily Telegraph* (UK)

Going Home

"Fabulous. . . . I loved it."
—Sophie Kinsella

"A brilliant debut novel. . . . A delightful romantic comedy with self-effacing humor and witty dialogue."
—*RT Book Reviews*

"An engaging first-person recounting of a watershed six months in one young woman's life."
—*Booklist*

"A lovely, funny heart-warmer. . . . Evans's heightened comic style and loveable characters make it effortlessly readable."
—*Marie Claire* (UK)

ALSO BY HARRIET EVANS

Not Without You

Happily Ever After

Love Always

I Remember You

The Love of Her Life

A Hopeless Romantic

Going Home

HARRIET EVANS

A Place for Us

G

GALLERY BOOKS

New York   London   Toronto   Sydney   New Delhi

Gallery Books
An Imprint of Simon & Schuster, Inc.
1230 Avenue of the Americas
New York, NY 10020

Extract from *Dear Octopus* by Dodie Smith reproduced by kind permission of Laurence Fitch Ltd.

First Gallery Books trade paperback edition February 2016

GALLERY BOOKS and colophon are registered trademarks of Simon & Schuster, Inc.

For information about special discounts for bulk purchases, please contact Simon & Schuster Special Sales at 1-866-506-1949 or business@simonandschuster.com.

The Simon & Schuster Speakers Bureau can bring authors to your live event. For more information or to book an event, contact the Simon & Schuster Speakers Bureau at 1-866-248-3049 or visit our website at www.simonspeakers.com.

Manufactured in the United States of America

10 9 8 7 6 5 4 3 2 1

Library of Congress Cataloging-in-Publication Data

Evans, Harriet, 1974–
   A place for us / Harriet Evans. — First Gallery Books hardcover edition.
      pages ; cm
   1. Domestic fiction. I. Title.
   PR6105.V347P57 2015
   823'.92—dc23   2014021087

ISBN 978-1-4767-8678-0
ISBN 978-1-4767-9340-5 (pbk)
ISBN 978-1-4767-8679-7 (ebook)

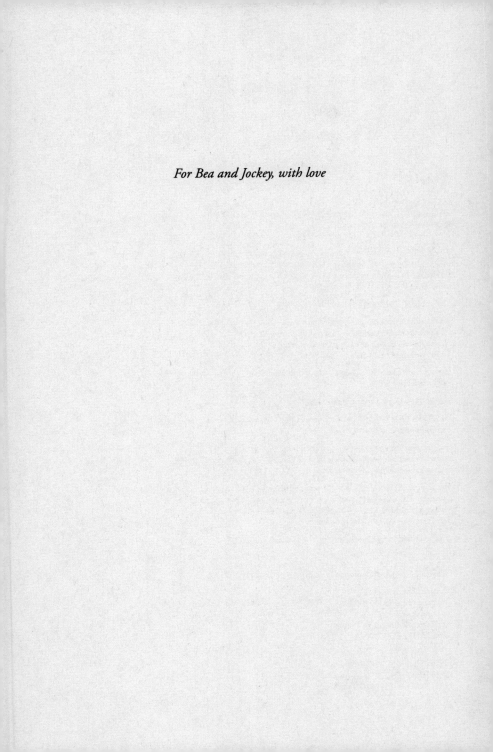

For Bea and Jockey, with love

PART ONE

The Invitation

The family—that dear octopus from whose tentacles we never quite escape, nor, in our inmost hearts, ever quite wish to.

—Dodie Smith, *Dear Octopus*

Martha

August 2012

THE DAY MARTHA Winter decided to tear apart her family began like any other day.

She woke early. She always did, but lately she couldn't sleep. This summer sometimes she'd been up and dressed by five: too much to think about. No point lying in bed, fretting.

On this particular morning she was awake at four thirty. As her eyes flew open and memory flooded her body, Martha knew her subconscious must understand the enormity of what she was about to do. She sat up and stretched, feeling the bones that ached, the prick of pain in her knee. Then she reached for her old silk peacock-feather-print dressing gown and quietly crossed the bedroom, as always stepping over the board that creaked, as always silently shutting the bedroom door behind her.

But David wasn't there. She could count on the fingers of both hands the nights they'd spent apart, and this was one. He'd gone to London to see about that exhibition, and Martha meant to put her plan into action today, before he came back, told her she was wrong.

In late August the sun still rose early over the hills above Winterfold, the heavy trees filtering the orange-rose light. *Soon*, they'd whisper, as the wind rushed through the leaves at night. *Soon we will dry up and die; we will all die sometime.* For it was the end of summer, and the Big Dipper was in the western sky. Already she could feel the chill in the evening air.

Was it because autumn was on its way? Or her eightieth birthday? What had prompted this desire to tell the truth? She thought perhaps it was this exhibition next year. *David Winter's War*, it was to be called. That was why he said he'd gone to London, to meet up with the gallery, go through his old sketches.

But Martha knew that was a lie. She knew David, and she knew when he was lying.

That was what had started this all off. Someone in a gallery in London deciding the time was right for a show like this, little knowing what damage they would do. So innocuous, thinking the past was dead and buried and couldn't hurt anyone. "Didn't David Winter do some rather good stuff on bombed-out London?" "David Winter? The Wilbur cartoonist?" "Absolutely." "Gosh, no idea, old chap. Where was he from?" "East End, I think. Could be interesting. Not just cartoon dogs and all that." "Good idea. I'll write and ask him." And then plans were laid and events put in motion, and slowly, inexorably, the truth would come out.

Martha made herself a pot of tea every morning, singing to herself. She liked to sing. She always used the same mug, Cornish pottery, blue and cream stripes, her gnarled fingers hooked round its scalding middle. She had time to drink tea now, gallons of the stuff, and she liked it strong. "Thrutchy," Dorcas had called it. A good Somerset word, that: Martha had learned it during the war. Evacuated out of Bermondsey aged seven in 1939—four kids in one room, where life or death was seemingly as random as swatting a fly or missing it—one day she'd simply been shoved onto a train and the next morning woken up in a strange house with a view of nothing but trees out of the window. She might as well have been on the moon. Martha had gone downstairs crying, and there she'd seen Dorcas, sitting at a table like this. "Cup of tea, my dear? Nice and thrutchy, it is."

A long time ago. Martha drained her first mug of tea, then spread her pens out, and the smooth creamy paper. Readying herself for the moment when she felt able to write.

So many years now in this gentle, honest house, every inch of it made with care, refashioned with love. They had been here for forty-five years. At first Martha had thought she'd never be able to take it on. It was a mess when they saw it: green paint covering the original Arts and Crafts wooden paneling, rotten floorboards, the garden one large compost heap of moldy brown mulch.

"I can't do this," she'd told David. "We don't have the money."

"I'll make the money, Em," he'd told her. "I'll find a way. We have to live here. It's a sign."

The children had bounced up and down, holding on to their parents' arms, little Florence like a monkey, gibbering with excitement, Bill peering out of windows, shouting, "There's a huge dead rat up here, and something's tried to eat it! Come up!" Even Daisy's face had lit up when she saw the space Wilbur would have to run around.

"But do you have the money?" she'd asked, worried. Daisy heard too much, Martha knew it.

And David had swept his daughter into his arms. "I'll make the money, little one. I'll make it. For a house like this, wouldn't it be worth it?"

Martha always remembered what Daisy said next. She'd struggled to be put down on the ground again, crossed her arms, and said, "Well, I don't like it here. It's too pretty. Come on, Wilbur."

She'd run off into the house again, and Martha and David had looked at each other and laughed.

"We have to live here," she'd said, feeling the bright sunshine on her head, the children shouting happily behind her.

David had smiled. "I can hardly believe it. Can you?"

"Shall we tell them why?"

Her husband had kissed her, and stroked her cheek. "No, I think not. Let's keep it our secret."

They had money now, of course, but not then. David was the creator of Wilbur the dog and Daisy, the little girl who thought she understood him. Every home had a Wilbur tea towel, pencil case, book of cartoon strips. But back then Wilbur was in the future and the Winters had nothing much, except each other. Only Martha and David knew what they'd gone through to get to the moment when they stood on the lawn that hot day in 1967 and decided they'd buy Winterfold.

She had forgotten nothing, nothing that had happened, before or afterward. The secrets every family acquires, some small—little indiscretions, tiny jokes. Some big, too big for her to bear anymore.

The morning sun was above the trees now. Martha moved around the kitchen, waiting for more tea to brew. She'd learned the art of patience long ago; learned that having babies slows you down, takes your dreams of your own career and slowly chips away at them. She had wanted to be an artist too, as much as her husband. But each pregnancy tied her firmly to her home; each night lying awake on her side, feeling the movement, back aching, breath short, and nothing to do but wait for the baby to come. And then you grew older and slower and those babies grew up and left you. You could hold them close but one day they would leave, as sure as the sun rising in the morning.

Bill was still here, she told herself, but he was different, not the man she'd thought he'd become. He was nearly eight when they moved to Winterfold. Daisy and Florence would spend all day out in the garden, or in the tree house in the woods, collecting friends, dirt, stories to tell. But Bill would usually remain inside, playing Meccano or Battleship, or reading his book. Occasionally he would come into the kitchen or the sitting room, his sweet, serious face hopeful: "Hello, Mother. Are you all right? Can I give you a hand with anything?"

And Martha, in the middle of mending a plug or stuffing up a mouse hole, for there was always something to do in this house, would smile, knowing what he knew: that Bill had saved up his visit to her, counting down the minutes, because he wanted to be with her all the time, but knew he couldn't. It was sissy, and Daisy already taunted him about it, not to mention the boys at school. So if she felt she could get away with it, Martha would give him a hug and something to do: washing up, chopping vegetables. Both of them pretending he didn't want to be there, that he was only trying to be helpful. Where was he now, that serious, brown-eyed boy who'd broken her heart with love every day?

At least he was still here. Her daughters weren't. After Bill came Daisy, and the moment they'd handed her to Martha that first time Martha had looked into her green eyes, just like her own, and known her. She could translate perfectly her furious, shifting expressions, her love of solitude, her little plans. Daisy was the only thing Martha and David had ever fundamentally disagreed about in six decades. People didn't understand her. But she'd proved them wrong, hadn't she?

"Daisy? Oh, yes, she's very well. We don't hear from her so much these days. She's very busy and the area she's in has extremely poor communication. She sends a message from time to time. But we're so proud of her." It was a neat little speech, she knew: Daisy had come good. Daisy wasn't who everyone thought she was. Whereas Florence . . . Martha often felt Florence was like a giraffe in a family of eels. She loved her, was so proud of her, in awe of her intellect and her passion and the way she'd become, against all the odds, spectacularly her own person—but sometimes Martha wished she wasn't so . . . *Florence*.

Bill, Daisy, Florence. Martha told herself she loved all her children equally, but in the secret part of herself she had a little rhyme: Bill was her first baby, Daisy was her first girl, and Florence was David's. She knew it sounded awful. But it kept coming back to her, this little rhyme. She'd find herself chanting it under her breath while she weeded the garden, walked into the village, brushed her teeth. Like a song stuck in her head, as though someone were playing it while she slept every night. She found she was terrified someone might look into her heart and see what she had done. But the time for secrets was over. It was coming. It was all coming to her, and soon it would all come out.

Would anyone want to come back after the truth was out? There was a set program of entertainment in place at Winterfold, which never varied in the detail. Their Christmas drinks party was the biggest night of the season for miles around: mulled wine served from a huge, two-foot-high pot on the Aga, Martha's famous gingerbread cut into stars and hung with ribbons on the huge Christmas tree, which stood in the sitting room by the French windows, as it had done for years and would continue to do. The Valentine's Day drinks, where the children handed round heart-shaped sandwiches and the guests drank too much sloe gin, and more than one amatory mistake had been made late at night walking back down to the village (the teenage Bill, alighting from the bus late one night returning from another party, swore he'd seen Mrs. Talbot from the post office kissing Mrs. Ackroyd, the landlady of the Green Man, on the other side of the bus shelter). Fireworks every year on Guy Fawkes Night, a hugely popular Easter egg hunt, and always a summer party in August, around which people planned their holidays: an awning on the lawn and paper lanterns stretching along the driveway.

Nothing changed, not even after the disastrous summer party of— was it 1978 or '79?—which had passed into local legend. The truth was no one knew why, or could have explained how, it was different at Martha and David's. Their house was lovely, the food was delicious, the company was always warm and fun. All Martha had ever wanted was to make it clear that you were welcome. Whoever you were. Whether you were the television actress who lived in the mansion at the top of the hill, or the postman who stopped to chat to Mr. Winter about cricket every day in summer. That there was no "gang." All she and David had ever wanted to do was to make a home, a place unlike their pasts. To give their children a childhood that would stay with them. To work hard together. Be happy.

A blackbird bounced through the herbs in her garden, acid-yellow beak pecking at the cocoa soil. He looked up with a bright, glassy-eyed stare at Martha as she sat by the window, pen poised, and she met his gaze until he darted into a hedge. She took another sip of tea, delaying for just a second. Savoring the final moments of stillness. For she knew that the moment she began to write, something would be set in motion, a time bomb waiting to go off. She would post the invitations and then the party would happen and she, Martha, would finally be able to tell them all what she had done. And it would never be the same after that.

A single tear dropped onto the worn kitchen table. She sat up straight, and said to herself, "Come on, old girl. It's time."

Carefully her pen scratched across the surface, lines crosshatching and curling till they formed something, a house, a long low house: the roof, the wooden buttresses, the old front door. Underneath, in her beautiful italic script, she wrote:

David & Martha Winter
request the pleasure of your company at
a party to celebrate Martha's 80th birthday

There will be an important announcement.
We ask that you please be there.

Drinks with friends Friday, 23rd November 2012, 7 p.m.
Family only lunch 1 p.m., Saturday, 24th November
Winterfold, Winter Stoke, Somerset
R.S.V.P.

David

It was a mistake. He shouldn't have come back.

David Winter sat alone in the corner of the pub, trying not to look as obviously out of place as he felt. Returning to the old neighborhood was one thing. Meeting here—he'd been crazy to suggest it, but he hadn't known where else to go. The old Lyons Corner House was a bank, the other old places round here all gone or so gentrified they weren't actual pubs anymore.

He flexed his aching hands and checked his watch again, blinking hard. Some days he felt better than others. And some days the black cloud felt as if it were swallowing him whole in its pillowing softness, so that he was ready to float away with it. He was so tired. All the time. Ready to lie down and go. And yet he couldn't, not yet.

Seventy years ago, when he was a boy, the Spanish Prisoners had been the roughest pub in the whole area, and that was saying something. They said the Ripper had drunk there, once upon a time. That a barmaid had been murdered and buried beneath the bar. The clichés weren't funny here, they were true. Every kind of Bill Sikes was to be found at the Spanish Prisoners—and Nancys too, women like his mother. There was nothing David didn't know about that, about dark corners, terrified women, fear that sank into your bones so deep you didn't know if you'd ever shake it off the rest of your life, ever be free of its shadow.

The Spanish Prisoners had stunk of tobacco, of piss and sweat, of mold and sewage and stout. There were men there who could recall sheep being driven down Islington High Street to Smithfield Market, who remembered the old Queen's death, who'd had sons killed in the Boer War. Davy Doolan had collected the pennies whenever his mother

11

played piano and waited to help her husband home. If he decided to come home, that was. The pub was a vast Georgian box on the outside, London stock brick, big windows, and it was a mystery how inside it was such a dark warren of a place. You had to be fearless, or dying of thirst, to go in there.

Now, in 2012, it was unrecognizable—a gleaming temple to the religion of coffee and microbreweries—and David wished his hands weren't so damned painful that he couldn't whip out a notebook there and then and start drawing. The wood shone, glass sparkled. The list of beers was as long as David's arm; he hadn't known where to begin, and in the end had plumped for an orange juice. The barman had a beard and tortoiseshell-frame glasses, and when he walked past after his shift ended, David had noticed, with his cartoonist's eye for detail, that he was wearing shorts, socks, and slip-on loafers, carrying a canvas printed bag. Before that, though, he'd presented David with a minuscule glass of hand-pressed Valencia orange juice and said politely, "Four pounds, please."

Four pounds for a glass of orange juice? He thought how Martha would laugh if she saw him, for the first time practically, balk at the expense of something. But Martha wasn't here, and he couldn't tell her about this. He had to carry on with this fiction for his visit to London. And he hated it, hated lying to his wife.

It wasn't entirely fiction: there was to be an exhibition of his early East End work. When the call came through, he had agreed, hadn't he? With a weary acceptance: time was running out. A fortnight after the gallery had rung him to suggest the idea, David had finally taken out the drawings, hidden away for decades in hard, cloth-backed folders in the cupboard in his study. He'd waited till Martha was out, gritted his teeth, and at first it had been fine. Then, suddenly, it had been too much, looking at them again, the weight of what he carried. He'd simply put his head on the desk and cried, like a little child. And he couldn't stop crying, had to tell Martha he was going to bed, another headache. He knew then, knew it meant he had to ring her up, beg her to see him again.

"Davy?" The tap on his arm made David jump; he looked up in shock. "Don't get up."

"Of course—" He struggled to stand, his breathing rapid, every gulp an effort. "Of course I will. Cassie, my dear." He put his hand on her shoulder.

They stared at each other, face-to-face after forty-four years.

She was the same height as he, tall for a woman; he'd loved that about her. And her eyes were cool and clear and gray, as if they saw through you and were laughing at you. Her ash-blond hair was smooth, carefully twisted up on her head. She wore no wedding ring. She looked . . . classy.

"You're still tall," he said. "Tall and slim and beautiful. I'd know you anywhere."

She fiddled with the belt of her coat, never taking her eyes off him. "I can't say the same about you, Davy. You look—well. I wouldn't have known you."

He gave a faint smile. "Let me get you a drink."

"No, Davy. I'll get it. You sit down."

She returned with a rum and Coke. "Five pound eighty! Five pound eighty, Davy, what a racket!"

Her rueful smile relaxed him. He pointed. "Four pounds, this was."

"The world's gone mad."

"Too right, Cassie."

There was an awkward pause; she took a sip of her drink. David cleared his throat. "So—you keeping well?"

"I'm all right, thanks."

"Where you living?"

"Flat off the Essex Road. I came back, you see."

"I'm glad," he said uncomfortably.

"It's not the same. Everyone's gone. It's bankers and lawyers round here mostly. Or younger people. I don't know anyone." Beneath her heavy fringe her eyes filled with tears. "Long way back to Muriel Street from where you are, isn't it?"

He nodded. He didn't belong here. He'd hoped he might walk around afterward, but fear haunted these streets for him, the way it always had. Suddenly he wished he was at home, sitting in his sunny study, the sound of Martha singing in the kitchen, Daisy and Florence playing in the garden. . . . He blinked. Daisy was gone, wasn't she? And Florence . . . Cat was still there, yes? No, Cat had gone too. They'd all gone.

"You got any more kids? I'm sorry. I don't know—anything about you." He gave an embarrassed half-laugh.

"You know I didn't want us to stay in touch," she said. "Look, we got our own lives. No. I haven't got any kids, Davy. We never had any, me and Terry." Her watery eyes were fixed on him again. "You understand what I mean."

His hand covered hers. "I do, Cassie."

"What I don't understand is why you wanted to see me," she said. "After all this time."

David shifted in his seat. "I'm dying," he said. He smiled at her, trying to ignore the pain that was always there. Her gray eyes widened.

"Davy. That true? Cancer?"

He loved the vowels. *Kainsa*. That London voice. He'd lost it deliberately, couldn't wait for it to melt away. "No. My heart." He clenched his fist, in and out, like the doctor had showed him. "The muscle's dying. It doesn't want to work anymore. One day I'll just—*phut*. Then that's it."

Her tears fell then, little black circles staining the newly waxed wood tables. "Oh, Davy."

He hadn't told Martha. Only his son, Bill, knew. As Cassie put her arms round him and drew his head onto her heaving shoulder, as she cried softly and silently, it occurred to David she was the only link he had to where he'd come from. He'd tried for years to put it away, to push forward toward the golden life he'd promised himself he and Martha deserved, only to be obsessively seeking it out again now. He thought of the meeting he'd had that morning with his gallery on Dover Street.

"I mean, there's a few I wonder if we need to show. Sensitivity and all that. Do we want to include this one?" Jeremy, the director of the gallery, had slid the watercolor, pen, and ink toward him.

David had looked at it and, as he always did with everything he drew, squeezed his arms against his sides, a little *aide-mémoire* to help him recall what it was, why he'd done it, how, what it had been like. In fact, he remembered the scene well, a bombed block of flats out in Limehouse. He'd walked there, the morning after a bad night. V-2 rockets had come to London when the war was almost over, and they were worse than the bombs of the Blitz. You only heard them flying toward you if you were out of their path. If they were headed right for you, you never knew until it was too late.

David hadn't slept much, since the bomb had hit their street. He'd dream about pulling Mum out of the wreckage, his sister too, running away with them somewhere safe. Not to the shelters but far away, out of the city, out where there were trees and no dead people, and no Dad coming at him, huge and black, stinking of stout and that smell men got.

He'd woken up early that morning. Walked and walked as he liked to do. He could walk for hours; no one was bothered where he was, after all. He'd gone along the canal to Limehouse, past the bombed-out warehouses, the abandoned boats, the muck. A girl asleep on a bench, lipstick smudged, greenish tweed skirt twisted around her legs. He wondered if she was one of those kinds of girls, and he'd have stopped to draw her but a policeman came past on a bicycle and shoved him along. He kept on walking, and walking, because John, a boy down the street, had told him there was a bad lot there.

The sketches he produced that morning of the scene in Victoria Court had become the painting he'd seen that morning, nearly seventy years later, in the white, hushed gallery in Mayfair. But he could still remember how it felt, all these years later. Women sobbing, hair coming loose from their scarves. Men dazed, picking through the rubble. It was very quiet, otherwise. There was one wall standing, against the road, and he'd squatted and sketched, a parody of a still-life scene of the corner of a room.

Flaps of yellow wallpaper printed with ribbons, fluttering in the morning breeze. The side of a cup, a packet of rice, a tin plate, blue paint scratched off. And a child's arm, probably a toddler's, the cotton sleeve of its shirt frayed where it had become detached from the body with the force of the explosion. The small pink fingers, curled up.

"Of course it stays in," he'd said.

Jeremy had hesitated. "David, I think it's wonderful. But it's very dark."

"War is very dark," David had said, the pain almost sending him under. "Either we do this or we don't. If you want cheeky urchins playing in rubble, forget it." He had bowed his head, remembering, remembering, and the other men were silent.

Now, as he hugged Cassie, he realized he didn't know her anymore, and that he had to do what he'd come here for. He sat back and patted her hand.

"Don't cry, dearest. Let me tell you why I wanted to meet."

She wiped her nose. "Fine. Make it good. You bastard, making me cry, after all these years. You're the one who ran out on me, Davy."

"Don't start that. Didn't I help you?"

"You saved my life," she said. "And my little girl's, later. I know it, I'll always know it. Davy . . ." She gave a big sigh. "I wish it was all different, don't you?"

"I don't know," he said. "Maybe. Maybe not. I'd never have gone to Winterfold if it hadn't been like this. I'd never have met Martha. And had the children."

"Give me their names, then? All of them?"

"Bill, he's the eldest."

"Where's he?"

"Oh, Bill never went far. Lives in the village, he's a GP. Pillar of the community, you might say. Married to a nice girl, Karen, much younger than him. Second marriage; he's got a grown-up daughter, Lucy. Then there's Daisy . . . she's—well, we don't see her so much anymore. She's in India. A charity worker. Very dedicated. Raises money for these schools in Kerala."

"Blimey. How often does she come home?"

"It's sad. She doesn't, really."

"Never?"

"Not for years now. She has a daughter, too. Cat. Lives in Paris. We raised her, after Daisy . . . left."

Cassie seemed fascinated by this. "She ran out on her own kid?"

"Yes. But . . . it's hard to explain Daisy. She was—she's difficult to understand. We're very proud of her."

It was such an easy lie, once you got used to it. He kept thinking of Daisy these days. Wondering what had gone wrong with her, whether it was his fault, something in his genes.

"And—the other one, Davy, so what's she called?"

"Florence. Florence is the baby. But she's very tall too."

Her eyes met his. "Just like her father."

"Just like her father, and we're very close. She's . . ." He hesitated. "Very academic. She's a professor, Cassie. Of art history. Lives in Florence."

"Lives in Florence and she's called Florence?"

He smiled. "It's true. She—"

16

A languorous waiter came over to ask them if they wanted food, and broke the spell. David looked at his watch and said no, and Cassie slid her wallet into her handbag. She clicked her tongue. "So tell me what you want."

David took a deep breath, ignoring the fluttering pain in his chest. "I want you to come to Winterfold. Meet them all. Before I die."

She laughed. It took him by surprise, a big belly laugh, a touch of hysteria, and it went on and on, until the fellow drinkers turned round to see what the two old people in the corner found to laugh about.

When she stopped laughing, she swallowed, and drained the rest of her rum and Coke.

"No," she said. "Absolutely not. You got your nice life down there, I got mine. That's the deal we made. I wish it were different but it's not. Forget about the past, Davy."

"But we need to straighten everything out. I want it all done before . . . I don't know how long I've got. It could be months, it could be years, but—"

She gripped his wrist, her eyes bright. "Davy, you always said I was cleverer than you. Didn't you? So listen to me. Leave the past alone. Forget you saw me. All right?"

"But doesn't family mean anything to you, anything at all?" David tried to hold on to her grip, but she pulled her hand away from him and stood up.

"Yes, my dear, it does. It means pain, and misery, and suffering, and you're mixed up with it enough. Take the time you've got and just enjoy it," she said, fixing her big bright scarf, not looking at him. Her voice wavered, but she finished firmly, "Let it be, Davy. God bless you, my love."

Karen

KAREN WINTER SAT at the counter while the girl in front of her held her fingers, scraping at her cuticles. Outside, rain fell steadily out of a metallic sky, turning the golden Bath stone a dirty sand. People hurried past the nail salon, the fogged-up windows blurring their figures into smears of dull color. Karen stared blankly up at the music channel on the screen above her head, eyes following the video, not registering any of it.

The invitation had arrived that morning, as she was on her way out. What did it mean? What the hell was Martha on about? Had she guessed? Was it a threat? Karen wasn't normally one for introspection: she acted first, thought later. When her stepdaughter, Lucy, stayed with them, she alternately drove Karen up the wall and made her laugh with her amateur dramatics, staying in bed till all hours, sighing over her phone, frantically texting, scribbling her every last thought into a book she called a journal, which Karen thought was pretty pretentious. Then she'd flop into the kitchen at midday and say she hadn't slept well because things were "on her mind." Karen, who was only ten years older than Lucy, always wanted to retort: *Can't you unload the dishwasher at the same time as having things on your mind?* Karen was a devotee of motivational self-help books and knew that the main principle of effective living as outlined in *The 7 Habits of Highly Effective People* was the Character Ethic. Lucy needed the Character Ethic. She, Karen, had it and—well, anyway.

She sighed. Coralie looked up. "Okay, miss?"

"Sure." Karen shrugged. The nail salon was warm, tiny, crowded; it hummed with the easy chatter of women in salons. She could hear snatches of conversation: Marks & Spencer was having a sale on clothes,

18

some child wouldn't eat pasta, someone was going to Minorca on a package deal. "Didn't sleep much last night," she added, for no particular reason.

"Oh dear. That's bad. Why?" Coralie slapped Karen's hands, slicking them with cream, and rubbed each one in turn.

Karen's fingers itched to scratch her own face, a habit of hers since she was little whenever she felt awkward. She inhaled slowly, watching Coralie deftly plumping the glossy blob of undercoat onto her nail. "Oh, family business."

"Oh. Family." Coralie coughed. "Huh."

Karen smiled. "My mother-in-law's having a party. Could do without it. You know?"

"Sure. I know." Coralie rolled her eyes. "Where do they live?"

"They're just south of here. It's called . . . Winterfold." She looked at Coralie, expecting her to recognize it, and then smiled. Why the hell should she? The way people said "Winterfold" in hushed tones, same as "the Queen" or "the National Trust." But the Winters were famous, they had a sort of sheen to them. Their parties were legendary, they knew everyone for miles around, and it was all because of Martha. She had a cupboard full of woolen blankets for picnics in summer, for God's sake. She made sloe gin, she pickled green tomatoes, she sewed bunting for birthdays. She remembered anniversaries, and brought round lasagnas to new parents. Didn't stop to coo, just handed it over and left. She didn't want to be your best friend; she just made you feel welcome and gave you a drink, and she listened.

Karen's only attempt to create something similar, her and Bill's New Year's Eve drinks party the previous year, had been a disaster. Susan Talbot, who ran the village shop–cum–post office, and therefore apparently had to be kept sweet otherwise she'd close it down and then Winter Stoke would be plunged back into the Middle Ages, had leaned too close over Karen's Swedish candle display, which she'd recreated from a magazine article, and Susan's hair had caught alight. It had ruined the atmosphere. Thirty people was too many in a house the size of theirs, and the smell of burned hair wouldn't leave, even after they opened all the doors and windows.

It was somehow symptomatic of her and Bill, she thought. They didn't "entertain" well. At least his daughter brought a bit of life into the house, even if she was messy and loud and bouncy, like Tigger. Lucy made Bill smile. People seemed to drop by when she was staying. She was the exact combination of her grandparents: warmth radiated off her like David; she could knock together a meal from baked potatoes and a packet of ham and turn it into a delicious little winter supper, and the wine would flow, noise and laughter flowering in the house like a desert after rain. . . . Karen had bought Susan vouchers for a proper salon experience at Toni & Guy by way of apology for the New Year's incident, and Susan had been deeply offended. Karen knew that if Lucy had been responsible for the Swedish candle disaster, she'd have had everyone laughing in seconds and more drinks flowing, and sent Susan Talbot home warm with attention and grateful for her free haircut.

Afterward, in bed, Karen had said angrily to Bill, "I'm sure your parents never have a sodding cock-up like that at one of their parties. It's just us."

Bill had laughed. "You weren't there for the Summer Party Disaster."

"What?"

"Oh, it was years ago. Our dog, Hadley . . ." He'd begun to smile, then said, "Actually, it was awful. But everyone stayed till three, in the rain. There was a conga, I seem to remember. Funny, isn't it?"

No, it wasn't funny. Karen, dying to know what had happened, had simply turned over and pretended to go to sleep. They'd had a party and it'd gone horribly wrong, but of course that was all part of the fun, wasn't it? Those Winters!

Maybe that was when the sinkhole started to form under their marriage, and no one saw it, of course. Karen hated herself for being mean about her in-laws, but she couldn't help it. Winterfold was only a house, for God's sake, not a cathedral. They were only a family.

"It's my mother-in-law's eightieth. They have a beautiful house," she told Coralie. "Near here. Yes . . . they're having a family party."

Coralie looked blank. "Fine. Why don't you want to go?"

Karen's cheeks twitched. "Because . . . we're so different. I don't fit in there." She didn't know Coralie's surname or where she lived, but it was easier to say it to her than to him. She'd been married to Bill for four years now, she knew every mole and freckle on his slim body, she knew how he liked his eggs done and what he meant when he said "Hmm" any one of fifteen ways, and yet she didn't know how to tell him that. *I don't fit in.*

"Fit in?"

Coralie's supple fingers pressed the tiny bones in Karen's hand. She jumped. "Like . . . I don't belong there. Oh, it doesn't matter."

"You feel stupid with them. I know." Coralie took the clear nail varnish off the rack, shook it. Karen stared at it.

"Something like that." She imagined the look on Martha's face if she could hear her. Did she know that was how Karen felt? Did Bill? Or his crazy sister, Florence the crackpot? Florence barely acknowledged Karen; it was as if she didn't exist. Karen laughed softly to herself. She remembered the first time she'd met Bill and he'd told her he had a sister who studied art history.

"Just . . . looks at paintings all day? For real? That's her *job*?"

"Yes, I'm afraid so," Bill had said, as if she'd said something funny, and she'd flushed. This quiet man who was—what?—ten years older than she, and yet so handsome in a strange way, so intriguing, polite. He'd been so easy to tease, back then. She'd wanted to talk to him just to hear his soft voice, see the light in his eyes when he looked at her. But she'd made a fool of herself, even that first time.

Funny to think of it now, really, the first time she'd met him. She remembered thinking: *This guy's a bit older than me but he could be the father of my kids.* She'd felt instantly, completely, as if she'd found someone safe, calm, funny, kind. But she'd got his age wrong: he was seventeen years older, almost old enough to be her dad. He had a twenty-year marriage behind him, and a teenage daughter. She'd got a lot of things wrong, hadn't she? And now she was paying, she supposed. Paying to not fit in.

Karen heard her phone buzz with a text message; she glanced down into her bag, hands trapped, then, with her heart racing, looked up again, trying to seem calm.

Suddenly she said, "Can I change my mind about my color? I don't want clear anymore."

"Fine. What color you want?"

Coralie gestured at the wall behind her, where the bottles of polish were stacked in multicolored rows, like sweets. Karen nodded. "Fifth Avenue, please. Third along from the end."

Coralie reached around and plucked the third bottle off the shelf, then checked the base. "Yes," she said, impressed. "Is Fifth Avenue. How you know that?"

"I just know." Karen shrugged.

"Bright, sexy red." Coralie pulled one of Karen's slim, tanned hands toward her, unscrewed the white lid. "You going out tonight?"

"No," said Karen. "We're staying in."

"Aha!" Coralie smiled. "You want to look good, huh? A night in with hubby."

"Something like that." Karen tried to smile.

Florence

"DEAR ME," FLORENCE Winter said, hurrying along the road, shoving the invitation back into her capacious yet overstuffed straw bag. "What does it mean?"

She felt upset. Out of the blue here it was, this extraordinary message slapping onto the cold stone tiles of her apartment floor while she was having her coffee. Years ago her brother, Bill, would joke that that was why she'd gone to study in Italy, to drink as much coffee as she liked. He didn't make that joke anymore—she'd lived there for twenty years. Besides, these days you had to search high and low for a decent *tabacchi*; everything in Florence was either Irish-themed pubs—the Italians were mad about them, perplexingly—or soulless *pizzerie* serving an ever-changing carousel of Japanese, American, French, and German tourists.

Nowadays Florence felt less disloyal about admitting that the worst tourists were often the English. They were either bellicose, obese, annoyed at being in this culturally heavy but entertainment-lite hole, or by contrast desperate to prove they were Italian, waving their arms around and saying *grazie mille* and *il conto, per favore*, as if that made them Italian, as if every waiter couldn't speak English like a native because that was the only way of getting ahead these days. It depressed her, either shame at her homeland or sadness at the world she inhabited. Florence the city, once the noble flower of the Renaissance, was becoming a ghost town, a history-theme-park shell filled with moving shoals of visitors, shepherded along by pink umbrellas and microphones. And still she loved it, with all her heart.

When she was a little girl, many years ago, she'd asked her father why they'd named her Florence.

"Because we went there on our honeymoon. We were so happy," David had told her solemnly. "I made your mother promise if we ever had a baby girl we'd call her Florence, to remind us every day how much in love we were."

"Why didn't you call Daisy that then? She came first."

Her father had laughed. "She wasn't a Florence. You were." And he'd kissed her on the head.

When Florence was a little girl, her birthday treat was to go up to London for the day with her father: he was her favorite person in the world. They always followed the same program. First to the National Gallery to look at the Italian Renaissance paintings, paying particular attention to her father's favorite, *The Annunciation* by Fra Filippo Lippi. Florence loved the story of the chaste monk who'd run off with the golden-haired nun, and she loved David's quiet, rapt expression as he gazed at the handsome angel with his thick curls, the graceful arc of Mary's bowed head as she received news of her destiny. "The most beautiful piece of art in the world," her father would say every time, visibly moved.

Then they would walk five minutes up to Jermyn Street and have lunch at the same old-fashioned English restaurant, Brights, where the waiters were all terribly ancient and formal, and the tablecloths snowy white linen. Florence always felt so grown-up, drinking a ginger beer out of a huge crystal goblet and eating a steak the size of her head, having proper conversations with her father. Not talking about Wilbur, for once; everyone always wanted to ask him about that silly dog. When she was out with Pa they always wanted to know if she was Daisy. Florence hated that, though not as much as Daisy would have, if she'd known.

She could ask him anything at those lunches, so they didn't talk about boring things like Daisy's moods or the girls at school or games. They'd talk about things he'd seen on his travels, because he'd been everywhere when he was younger.

"Before you married Ma and she had all of us."

"Ma came too. We were both artists, we wanted to see the world. Then we had all of you. And then we moved to Winterfold. We didn't want to go away much after that."

Florence didn't really understand why they'd moved to Winterfold, when they could have lived in London. She wanted to live in London, but whenever she asked her father about growing up there, she got the same response: "I never liked London very much."

He never talked directly about his childhood. Never said, "Your granny had blue eyes," or, "We lived on this or this road." Only oblique references to events that had happened to him. Florence worshiped her father and wanted to know everything possible about him, so she'd draw him out as much as she could. Hear about Mr. Wilson, the art teacher at school who'd let David stay late, given him construction paper and pastels to take home. The boy the next road over who was born without a nose—Pa swore it was true. The time one summer's morning he caught the train to Bath, then walked for hours until he saw Winterfold, how he'd promised to come back there one day. He loved walking, back then. He'd walk into town and go to concerts at the National Gallery during the war. All the paintings had been taken away, to a cave in Wales, but people played the piano there instead. Once, the air raid sirens sounded and he had to stay there for hours, hidden in the basement with all the others: local office workers, young lovers meeting at lunchtime, posh old men. Everyone was very scared; they sang songs, and one of the posh old men gave David a piece of fudge.

Years later, Florence was back at the National Gallery, giving an oft-delivered lecture to some students in front of Uccello's *Battle of San Romano*. Her mind wandered and she found herself working out that her father would have been really quite small during the Blitz, no more than nine or ten. The idea of him drifting freely around town at that age, in the middle of a war too, seemed appalling to her. When she'd mentioned it to him later on, he'd smiled. "I was grown-up for my age. You had a sheltered childhood, Flo."

"I'm glad," she'd said, never happier than when she was safely cocooned away with a book or several books, undisturbed by dogs or family or Daisy's special treatment.

And he'd said, "Well, that's good, isn't it?"

Florence sometimes wondered now if her childhood had been too sheltered. She was nearly fifty, and felt she should have a better grip on life; yet more and more it seemed to her that life was veering away from her, like a runaway train. The little girl who was too tall for her older sister's cast-offs, who only wanted to read and look at pictures, was now a professor employed at the British College of Art History in Florence, author of two books, contributor to several more, a visiting professor at the Courtauld Institute of Art in London, and an occasional voice on the radio: she'd been on Melvyn Bragg's *In Our Time* last year, only they'd cut most of what she'd said. (When Florence was nervous, she tended to ramble, and it was often impossible to prune the tangled mess of her original point.)

When she was alone in her apartment, writing or thinking on her own, everything was always clear. It was talking aloud, interacting with people that tripped her up: it was reality she found difficult.

When Florence had last been back in the UK in July, she had been invited to dinner at the house of her Courtauld colleague, Jim Buxton. Jim was an old boyfriend of hers from Oxford, still a good, dear friend. He was married to Amna, a professor of Islamic studies at University College London, who spent much of the year in far-flung places like Tashkent, spoke at least six different languages, and was, frankly, terrifying to Florence. They lived in Islington, not far from the center of town, but due to several mishaps including broken spectacles and a flapping boot sole, Florence arrived late and flustered. When Jim introduced her to the other guests, one of them—a well-known editor at Penguin called Susanna—half stood up, shook her hand, and said, "Oh, the *famous* Professor Winter! We heard you on the radio, talking about Masaccio. I agreed with you broadly, but for your interpretation of the *Expulsion of Adam and Eve*. It's simplistic to merely say that—oh!"

For Florence, still holding her cloth book bag, which passed for a handbag, had simply cut a deep bow (so that her change slid out of her pockets) and backed out of the room, the boot sole folding under and nearly tripping her up. She went to the downstairs bathroom and sat on the lavatory for five minutes. She knew she'd have to apologize when she emerged, could see enough to know that she should explain about the broken spectacles meaning she'd got on the wrong bus, and the unglued boot sole severely impeding her journey; but she couldn't ever work out a way to apologize gracefully for something so that the moment was forgotten.

When she emerged, they'd all gone into the dining room, so she'd taken her seat and the other guests pretty much ignored her, but Florence didn't mind. She almost preferred it that this Susanna person *thought* she was totally crackers, that they all did. It meant she didn't have to bother with entangling herself in social situations.

The next day she'd gone to see Jim in his office.

"I'm sorry about last night, Jim, about stowing away in your lav. I was in a bit of a flap when I arrived. So was my boot. Ho-ho."

And Jim had said with a smile, "Don't worry. Susanna's awful. It rather made the evening, I thought."

Yes, more and more this idea haunted her, the question she couldn't escape. What was that missing piece, the one she knew existed but couldn't ever see? What if she'd wasted the last twenty years staring at the same paintings, working on the same ideas, and coming to no worthwhile conclusions? Just shuffling opinions around and about from one journal to another book to yet another set of students, in the same way a banker got paid for moving money about? She loved Florence, but had she stayed here for one reason, and one reason only, for a man who barely cared if she was there or not?

No, she told herself in her more buoyant moments. He did care. He *did*.

Florence hurried over the Ponte Santa Trìnita, barely glancing at the tourists thronging the Ponte Vecchio, crammed with tiny shops like a pantomime set. She was able to block out the modern world, almost too effectively; if Lorenzo the Magnificent had appeared on horseback cantering over the bridge and asked in his best Renaissance Italian if she'd like to accompany him to his palazzo for some wild boar, Florence would not have been surprised.

She was so absorbed in imagining what Lorenzo de Medici would wear on a normal day out and about in the city—and he *did* go out and about, that was why he'd been such a great leader, truly *Il Magnifico*—that, as she turned the corner leading to the college, Florence wasn't looking where she was going. She felt herself trip on something and then stumble, hurtling to the ground with the curiously drunken sensation of lost gravity.

"*Attento!* Signora, please take care!" said an angry voice, one that set her heart thumping as she lay on the cobbles, arms and legs waving in the air like an upturned beetle's. "*É molto*— Oh, it's you. For God's sake, watch where you're going, can't you?"

Florence scrambled to her feet by herself, as Peter Connolly disentangled the leather straps of her bag from his leg with such force she nearly yelped. "Oh dear," she said, looking down at the ground. "Where are my glasses?"

"I've no idea." He was rubbing his foot, glaring coldly at her. "That bloody hurt, Florence. You—" He stopped, looking around.

The arriving students watched them curiously: Byronic, slightly eccentric, but still impressive Professor Connolly, the one who'd written the unlikely best-seller about the Renaissance that made the Medici into a bawdy soap opera, and got a BBC TV series at the same time—he was famous, their mums watched him! And that weird Professor Winter, mad hair awry, searching for her glasses. The plastic frames were cracked and frequently the sharp wire arms of the glasses slid out if she leaned forward, but she never even noticed. Someone had seen her singing Queen to herself the previous week as she walked past the Uffizi. Singing really loudly.

Florence's head was spinning. She looked at Peter, flustered, and pushed her hair out of her eyes. He was so different these days, ever since that damned book had come out and he'd started to listen to the siren call of Fame. All smart and stylish, in a televisually approved rumpled academic sort of way. So very far from the curly-haired, slightly hopeless man she'd once known and loved—loved so much that she—

"Here." Professor Connolly pulled her bag back up so it was slung over her shoulder and not hanging off her wrist.

"Ha-ha! Oh, unhand me, Professor Connolly!" Florence said loudly, putting her hand to her breast, and dropping several items on the ground in the process. She had thought this would sound hilarious, but as so often when some witticism came out of her mouth, it hung there in the air, sounding completely awful. She looked mad, as always, a crazy old hag whom no one had ever loved or could possibly ever in the future love, especially not Professor Connolly, to whom of all people she had once so hoped to cleave herself.

The professor bent down and picked something up off the curb.

"You dropped this." He glanced down nosily. "Nice invitation. Is this your family? Curious way of asking people to a party. What does that bit at the end mean?"

Florence gently took it out of his hand, biting her lip.

"Thank you. It's from my parents. I have no idea what it means. I'll have to go home for it, I suppose."

"Leaving Florence again, Florence?" He gave a small smile. "I must say, we are becoming practiced in the art of missing you." He rocked on his feet, and tipped his imaginary hat to her.

"Why, did you—did you need me for something, Pe—Professor?"

He gave her a look of complete astonishment. "Goodness, no. Why would you think that?"

Another slight, another little barb, but she was equal to it. She knew his little secret, and she was glad to carry it safe until such time as he felt the need to make use of her again. Florence bowed her head, as though she were a lady bidding farewell to a knight.

"Then, Peter, I must bid you farewell for now, yet not forever," she said, though this too came out all wrong. He had walked toward the revolving doors, not even saying good-bye. She hobbled toward the entrance, and as she did she glanced down at the invitation, and the strangeness of it struck her again. Ma wanted them all back.

Why? Was it Dad? Was it about Daisy?

And Florence suddenly realized, though she had not considered it until this very moment, that she knew why.

Joe

JOE THORNE LEANED his weight on the smooth oak bar, crossed his arms, and looked around him. Midmorning, midweek, he would have hoped the pub would be, well—not crowded exactly, but at least hosting a few old regulars with a pint, maybe a couple of early patrons for lunch. But no. The eponymous tree outside cast only gloom into the room. It was too early in the season for a roaring log fire. The bowls of sweetly salty pork crackling that Joe himself had roasted and stripped that morning stood on the bar, untouched. The barrels were full, the glasses gleaming.

And the place was empty.

Sheila Cowper, the landlady, appeared in the doorway of the snug. "Don't stand there with your arms folded, Joe," she said briskly, whipping him lightly with a tea towel. "No one'll want to come in if they look in and see you growling at them like an angry bear. Go and cut up that bread like I asked you an hour ago."

"Oh, what's the point?" said Joe gloomily, though he obeyed her, stomping back into his tiny kitchen.

He took a newly baked loaf of sourdough, weighing it in his hands. Joe loved bread, loved its smell, its texture. He loved the springy smoothness of newly formed dough, how you could thump the base of a freshly baked loaf, hard, and get a pleasing drumlike sound, how homemade bread had love and care baked into it, like a new life. Joe started cutting slim, even slices, his strong fingers working the knife. *Who am I making this for?* he found himself wondering. *What is the point?*

Six months ago Joe had left Yorkshire, Jamie, and home to come and work for Sheila. She'd spent fifteen years in London working as a manager in various restaurants and had returned home to Winter Stoke the previous year with some cash in her pocket, and the dream of rejuvenating the Oak Tree. She wanted to make it the best place to eat in Somerset, at the same time turning it back into a proper local pub. "Better than the Sportsman in Whitstable, better than the Star at Harome. I want it to get a Michelin star," she'd told him, and he'd found his heart beating faster. He believed this woman, and though he'd never met her before he was sure she could do it. And Joe, with his training and his track record, had been a shoo-in. At the interview he'd made her pork belly with fennel, accompanied by homemade char siu buns and a cabbage rémoulade, and sea-salted caramel threesome—ice cream with popcorn, toffee pot, and compote with marshmallows. He was a bit over sea-salted caramel himself, but it was all the rage, and he'd known from their phone conversation that she'd like it. Joe could pretty much tell what people wanted to eat.

It was because he trusted Sheila that he'd taken the job. He couldn't turn it down, it was too good an opportunity to miss and it was time to leave Yorkshire. If it wasn't for Jamie he'd have done it years ago. He'd been there all his life apart from his training. Yes, his restaurant had a Michelin star, but he'd learned all he was going to there. The head chef was a psychopath, the old cliché, and it was a joyless place to work, more about assemblage and timings than baking with care, making food with love. Joe cooked to make people happy, not to hear them faint with admiration over his use of nasturtiums in salads or sumac-flavored sorbets or any of the other silly things you had to do these days to be a "hot young chef," whatever that meant.

Joe didn't want any of that. He wanted to work in a place rooted in the community. He wanted to see old blokes chatting about their experiences in the war over a pint, to have lonely people come in for a read of the paper and a friendly face. A place for dates, anniversaries, weddings, funerals. Family. In his mind's eye he saw this happy group of punters round the bar, perhaps even singing songs of an evening, while Joe served up delicious, lovingly prepared meals, food that'd bring people together, make them happy. And Joe's food was the best there was. . . .

But it wasn't working out that way, not at all. Six months on, everyone still went to the Green Man at the other end of the high street. The Green Man had Sky Sports, velour carpets, and piles of cigarette butts by the door that no one ever seemed to sweep up. It served pickled onion crisps and rancid old pasties, and there was a fight most Saturdays. It was a dump. But it seemed that the residents of Winter Stoke and the surrounding countryside would rather take their chances there. The Oak had been closed for so long it was hard to change habits.

Sheila had a few months left, still, but if things hadn't picked up by Christmas she'd as good as told Joe they'd each be out of a job. She'd have to sell, and Joe would be cast out into the metaphorical snow, and he'd have to go back to his mother's in Pickering. The way things were going here, especially in the last couple of weeks, that didn't seem too bad a prospect. He missed home, his mum and sister, more than he'd thought he would. Most of all he missed Jamie.

Sometimes when Joe thought about Jamie he was almost ready to pack it in and drive back that night to Yorkshire. Like when he thought about his crazy, curly blond hair, the dark little smudges he got under his eyes when he was tired or upset, the little red birthmark above his lip, and the things he said that cracked Joe up. "I'm going to live on the moon when I'm older, Dad. You can come and visit me in the long whooshing tube I'll have built by then, all right?"

The more Joe tried not to think about his son, the worse he felt. He knew now that looking at pictures of him on his phone didn't bring him closer. Sometimes it just made him sadder. He was supposed to see him once a month, but often it didn't happen: Jemma had booked a holiday to Turkey, Jamie's best friend had a birthday party, a school outing would be getting back too late for Jamie to travel all the way down to Somerset, or for Joe to pick him up and take him to his mum's in Pickering, which was what he sometimes did. The thing was, Joe knew it wouldn't ever get better, because Jamie wouldn't ever live with him full-time, of course he wouldn't, he had to be with his mum. But Joe missed him, as though there were a clamp on his heart that made him wince when he thought about him, pepper in his nostrils that made his eyes water, dry bread in his throat that made him swallow, bow his head, say a prayer for him and whatever he was doing. Playing in break time? Drawing at one of those little tables, messing around with toy dinosaurs on the floor, dancing to "Telephone," that Lady Gaga song he'd made up all the actions to?

"Joe? Joe!" Sheila's voice penetrated his train of thought.

"I've nearly done it." Joe blinked, wiping his forehead on his arm. "Nearly there."

"No. Not that. Mrs. Winter's here for you."

He flinched, instantly recalled to the present. The knife slipped, and he pushed it away, against his knuckle. It fell onto his left hand, sliding across his finger and cutting open the flesh. Everything seemed to happen almost in slow motion: Joe felt and, most disturbing of all, saw the flash of hard white bone beneath, watched almost with disinterest as the long thick line suddenly turned red, and his hand started to throb, black-red blood gushing out—and there was so much of it, dripping crimson onto his kitchen whites.

Sheila yelped. "What's—oh, Joe, dear, what've you done?"

Joe held up his dripping finger. He wrapped a cloth around it. Now it really hurt. He smiled, feeling slightly stunned. "Stupid idiot. I'm sorry. You gave me a fright. Mrs. Winter . . . she's in the bar?"

"Sure, but it's okay, I'll tell her—"

"No." Joe tightened the knot on the cloth. "Don't turn away anyone who's come in, much less one of that lot." He followed Sheila into the pub.

"Hello, Joe," said Martha Winter. "Lovely to see you." She glanced down at the bloody cloth. "My goodness. What have you done to your finger?"

"Nothing. Perk of the job." The finger throbbed again, an aching thrum. "How can I help you?"

"You're sure you're all right?" He nodded, and she looked at him a little quizzically. "Well, I wanted to talk to you. I wondered if you'd be able to do the food for a party we're having in November. It's drinks on the Friday, so I'd need canapés for about fifty."

Her husky, accentless voice was soothing. "Right, then." Joe started mentally calculating how much canapés for fifty would cost. "I can do that."

Martha cleared her throat. "And then lunch on the Saturday." She paused. "That's the main event."

"How many on the Saturday?"

"Just family. Seven of us. I think."

The Winters were kind of famous round these parts. Joe had always imagined there were loads of them. He said curiously, "I thought there were more of you than that."

"There were, around twenty of us," Martha said. "But I've murdered them all and buried them in the garden."

"Makes the catering easier," Joe said, and they both smiled, shyly, at each other.

"David says you're a wonderful chef."

"He's a nice man." David Winter came in sometimes for a whiskey. Joe liked him a lot. He was one of the few people around here Joe had actually had a proper conversation with.

"He's a very nice man and he takes his food seriously."

"I know that," he said. "I've never seen someone eat a pie that fast."

A shadow crossed her smiling face; she said, "Anyway, he says I need to hire you right away for this party. He thinks you'll be off soon." She leaned forward on the bar with her elbows. "Give us a chance, won't you?"

Joe stiffened. "I never—I'm liking it very much here, Mrs. Winter."

"Don't go all formal on me again, will you?" she begged. "I only meant I know how hard it is. When I first came here I didn't know anyone. I was just a mouthy Cockney and I thought it was the back end of beyond. An awful place."

He didn't believe she'd ever been a Cockney. "You're from London?"

"Yes, Bermondsey. But when the war came I was evacuated, and . . ." She waved her hand. "Never mind. I know what you're going through. We're nice people round these parts. Give it time."

Joe's head spun, the finger throbbing so hard he felt it might suddenly burst. "Yes, of course." He tried to concentrate, and picked up a pen from the bar, holding it uselessly in his right hand. "I'd better do you a quote."

"You're left-handed? Oh dear, that's bad," she said. "So am I, so's David. All the best people are. My granddaughter Cat, too. She lives in Paris." She added, suddenly, "You'd like her. She's coming back for this party. At least, I hope she is. I haven't seen her for a very long time."

He tried to nod and winced; the pain was really bad. She was right. No. Left! It seemed funny suddenly. "That's nice for you. What were . . ." He blinked; a throb of exquisite pain from his finger ran through his body. "Excuse me."

"Joe, it does seem to be bleeding rather a lot," Martha said. She took his hand, and the feeling of skin, of her warm flesh holding his, was almost intoxicating. Her green eyes stared at him appraisingly, and he felt quite light-headed. "I think we'd better take you to Bill's office, just to be sure," she said.

"No, I don't want—uh, don't worry," Joe gripped the rail of the bar firmly in his strong hand, but everything was rocking suddenly. He swallowed. "I'll be right as rain, I just need to—"

Martha swam before him. The floor seemed to be rising up, his eyes unbearably heavy. Something was pressing down on his head, and as he sank down he saw her face, shaken out of its calm, her mouth open in a small O, before everything, slowly, went black.

Cat

ALWAYS LATE. ALWAYS needing to be somewhere else. Cat hurried out of the Marché, past the endless cyclamen in gaudy reds, the knotty geraniums with their fading flowers, the bushes with zesty, citrus-colored berries. Working at the flower market you were always aware of the changing seasons: every year she dreaded the arrival of winter, standing outside all day and slowly freezing to death. But in the first week of September it was still summer; the tourists were still jamming the tiny streets of the Île de la Cité, moving so slowly they might be zombies, heads down, eyes fixed on their phones.

Cat strode across the slim pedestrian bridge at the foot of Notre-Dame, weaving her way in and out of the crowds. The usual troupe of jazz musicians on the bridge was playing a wistful, lilting version of "There's a Small Hotel." She slowed down for a split second. It was one of Gran's favorite songs. She'd sing it in the evenings, wandering round the kitchen, mug of tea in hand. Gran was always singing.

"Hello, English girl!" one of the musicians called as she hurried past them. Cat rolled her eyes. All these years here and *English girl*, when her French was probably better than theirs. But in Paris you were Parisian, you were French, not that you went around yelling about it, that would be so very, very *outré*, but there were certain things, a particular finesse, an attitude to life . . . Cat consoled herself with the knowledge that she passed for French these days. She was slim, French-girl slim, not through effort: she just didn't eat very much. Her dark gray eyes were partly hidden by her treacly brown-black mane of hair. She was wearing the only expensive thing she owned, a pair of glossy red Lanvin ballet flats, which Olivier had bought her, back when things were still good between them.

36

She had tried to sell them on eBay a few months ago; she'd finally got so desperate she had to have the money, and it was ridiculous to have shoes worth £300 when she couldn't afford a sandwich at lunch. But there was an olive oil stain on one shoe, a remnant of a Luke-based accident, and the buyer had rejected them when Cat, eternally honest, had pointed this out. She was glad, for they were beautiful: a glossy coral red, they made her happy in a way she hadn't thought possible. Like all fashionistas, even lapsed ones, Cat despised the handbag culture, the stamping of labels on everything: *Look, my sunglasses say GUCCI in huge letters, therefore I must have money.* But looking down at these beautiful red shoes always made her smile, even if it was a particularly bad day and the smile merely a tiny one. It surprised—and cheered—her, to discover this capacity for pleasure still existed within her. She thought it must have been entirely stamped out.

Cat strode quickly along the main street of the Île Saint-Louis, her rangy frame weaving nimbly around the shuffling crowds gaping in at the windows of the *boulangerie*, the *fromagerie*. She could see them queuing up for Berthillon, the old-fashioned *glacier* with its gleaming marble tabletops. Cat loved Berthillon, she knew it was hopelessly touristy to do so, but sometimes when she was in particular need of a treat, when the fog settled over the two little islands and the bleakness of her situation seemed particularly acute, she would wish more than anything that she could just run over the bridge at lunchtime and order a tiny cup of molten black chocolate, served with yellow cream in a smooth little silver jug. But finances didn't stretch to that, hadn't for over a year now since Olivier's money stopped altogether.

She popped into the convenience shop around the corner from the apartment, to buy vermouth. It was eye-wateringly expensive—but this was the Île Saint-Louis, of course it was eye-wateringly expensive, and it was for Madame Poulain. *No expense spared* was very much Madame Poulain's motto, though she kept track of everything she gave Cat to the nearest cent, and nothing was bought for Madame Poulain that Cat might share. This was made very clear, always had been: Cat shopped at Lidl or Franprix. She smiled as she waited to pay, catching sight of the rows of Dijon mustard. That was why Paris was civilized, despite its many annoyances. In a tiny convenience store you could still find five different types of *moutarde de Dijon: mais bien sûr.*

"*Bonsoir, Madame.*"

"*Ah, bonsoir, Catherine. Ça va?*"

"*Ça va bien, merci, Madame. J'ai pris le vermouth. Je vous offre un verre?*"

"*Oui, oui.*" The old woman gave a great guffaw in her wingback chair as Cat gingerly put the tissue-wrapped bottle down on the great old sideboard. If she asked the question she most desperately wanted to right away, Madame Poulain would get angry. If she waited just a minute, she would be pleased.

Cat drew in a short breath, took a glass off the shelf, and said, "Your medicine, Madame—all's okay for me to pick it up tomorrow, yes?"

"Sure." Madame Poulain stubbed out her cigarette. "Tell them to check it this time. I'm sick of the wrong dosage. I am ill. It must be correct." She lit another cigarette. "Can you make me the drink before you run off again? I mean, of course I know you're so *terribly* busy but . . ."

"Sure," said Cat, trying not to smile. The first time she'd come to Madame Poulain's apartment, overlooking the Seine south toward the Latin Quarter, she had been overawed by the vast airy space, the wooden beams, the old shutters with their carved iron handles, the fretwork on the balcony. Then, as now, the only items on the old mahogany dresser (from Vichy, acquired in shady circumstances by her father, a coward and a traitor, about whom Madame Poulain was only able to speak by expectorating heavily into her ashtray afterward) were menthol cigarettes, an ashtray, and cough syrup. Which, Cat had often thought since, pretty neatly summed up her landlady.

"Was it busy today?" Madame Poulain stretched out in the chair, flexing her long, clawlike hands.

"The market was crowded. But we were not busy. Henri is worried."

"He should be worried. Now that this fool is in charge we are all doomed. That I should live to see socialism annihilated in this way. When I was a child we would have called that man a fascist. Ha!" Madame Poulain dissolved into a fit of coughing, which consumed her for some time. Cat fetched her a glass of water and poured her vermouth, all the while anxiously listening for other signs of life in the apartment. She could hear nothing.

Eventually Madame Poulain's hacking subsided and she shoved aside the proffered glass of water, grasping the vermouth. Cat passed her her pills and she swallowed each one laboriously after much sighing, followed by raspy gagging. It was the same every night, had been for these last three years. Olivier had hated Madame Poulain, the couple of times he'd met her. Said she was a fake, a phony. Her family were collaborators. How he knew this Cat had no idea, but Olivier's biggest *bête noire* was phonies. One of his many ironies.

Don't think about Olivier. One . . . two . . . three . . . Cat looked around the room, counting objects to distract herself. She knew what to do now. When Olivier barged into her thoughts as he did so often, she had a rotating carousel of images with which to distract herself, otherwise . . . otherwise she'd go mad, get so angry she'd smash something. She thought of Winterfold. The Christmas when she and Lucy had made the snowman with a beach-bucket-shaped head, covered in sand from the previous summer in Dorset. The walk into the village on an autumn day when the leaves were quince yellow. Her uncle Bill with the wastepaper basket on his head, trying to find his way from one end of the sitting room to the other. Sitting up in bed in her cozy, sunny room on summer mornings peering out of the window at the peach, violet, turquoise sunrise creeping over the hills behind the house. The patchwork cushion Gran had made her, her name in blue hexagons, and Lucy's rage that she didn't get one. "She lives here, she has everything!" she'd shouted. She was three years younger than Cat. It had seemed such a big gap sometimes; now it would be nothing at all, she supposed.

All these things she didn't know. What was Lucy like, still the same? Cat often wondered. She was going to be a famous writer and live in a turret, that was always her aim. Was Southpaw's leg still bad, and *did* Gran still sing all day, giving you that quick, catlike smile if you corrected her lyrics? And was the patchwork cushion still there? Resting on the old wicker chair, waiting for her to come back?

Yet it was all so clear to her. She remembered every creaking stair, every mark on every wooden pillar, every old, battered book on the shelf opposite the chair: *Ballet Shoes* next to *Harriet the Spy* and *The Story of Tracy Beaker*, a much-too-young birthday present from her father.

She had cut them all off, and now she couldn't go back. Years and years of feeling like this had changed her personality, she knew. She was a different Cat now, the one she had always secretly feared becoming. When a door banged these days, she jumped.

"How's Luke?" she asked finally, when Madame Poulain was more settled.

"Asleep. Curled up in the warmth. You spoil him. Like they always say, the English spoil their pets and ignore their children. He's your pet, hmm?"

Since Madame Poulain seemed to feed Luke on nothing but biscuits while Cat was at work, this was not something Cat felt equal to tackling at that moment. She could not risk an argument, any shift in the status quo. She was, as ever now the day was drawing to a close, so tired she felt she might slide onto the floor. She rubbed her face; it was a little sunburned, and suddenly she longed for winter. For crisp cool days, for cozy evenings inside, not this dried-out, strung-along warmth.

"I'm just going to go and check on him," she said, getting up. "Then I'll make you an omelet, yes?"

"Well . . ." To Madame Poulain, any display of concern for another living thing was a waste of cigarette-smoking time. "Go, then. And—oh, before that—your grandmother rang."

Cat turned round. Her heart started to thump, hard, in her chest. "Gran rang, here? Did she say why?"

"She wants to know why you have not replied to the invitation."

Cat cleared her throat. "I . . . what invitation?"

"I said that too. The French post. This man will break the country. I do not—"

"Madame Poulain, please"—Cat's desperation, just this once, nearly broke through—"has there been an invitation?"

"The strangest thing, today there it was. As I told your grandmother when she rang. And I said that I would pass it along to you, the moment you arrived home." Madame Poulain slid one bony hand down the side of the chair, like a child sitting on secrets. "They don't know, hmm? They don't know your little lie to them, do they?" She handed the creamy card to Cat, who held it between her fingers as though it were something magical.

"Not a lie . . ." she said in a faint voice. The address, in Martha's familiar elegant hand. It wasn't a lie when you simply hadn't told them, was it?

That writing: Cat knew it better than anyone's. Who else had written her those endless stories, dotted with jewellike, tiny illustrations? Who had stuffed notes into her lunchbox for Cat to find, sitting by herself underneath the scratched and slimy benches in the playground, chin resting on her scabbed knees?

Gran used to sit at the kitchen table every morning, teapot next to her, slim, poised frame perfectly still as she gazed out of the window into her garden, making plans for the day ahead, scribbling little ideas and plots and jokes onto her pad, and notes. These notes, which Cat would find hidden behind her sandwiches, she would usually scrunch up and throw away, embarrassed in case they'd find them again.

Your grandma writes you love notes?

You baby.

Your mum's a hippie, everyone knows that. She freaked out and ran away and that's why you have to live with your grandma!

Hippie! Hippie! Hippie! Cat's a hippie!

Memories, sensations, long-buried, threatened to wash over her. The envelope paper was thick, heavy, cold, and Cat's fingers trembled; she fumbled with the glue, wanting to tear it open, wanting to know what was inside and yet at the same time dreading its contents. Madame Poulain watched her, head curving around the wing of the chair like a gargoyle.

"The letter opener is on the dresser, Catherine. Don't tear. Don't be so foolish."

Oh, shut up, you hateful, awful, loathsome, vile, horrific old woman. Shut up or I will hurt you. I will smash your head in with your precious Sèvres vase and I'll watch you die and laugh as you do.

She was no longer shocked at how easily thoughts like this slid into her head. She read the invitation, the hand-drawn letters, the plea contained within them, and then looked up, staring at nothing, as the voices that screamed at her from rising to sleeping climbed to a fever pitch. Home to Winterfold. Could she even think about going, this time? What would she tell them about what had happened to her since she left England? How could she start? And how would she get there? She had

41

no money. She had not been able to afford a Métro *carnet* last week, let alone a Eurostar home. *Home.*

She let the card drop to the floor as her fingers twisted restlessly in her lap, and Madame Poulain took her silence for surrender. "I would love that omelet. If you are not going to check on Luke, why don't you make me one?"

"Yes, of course." *Everything is all right,* Cat said to herself, going into the kitchen, and when Madame Poulain gave a little grunt of curiosity, she realized she had said it out loud, in English. *Everything is all right.*

Lucy

"*LUCY!* THE MEETING. Are you coming?" Deborah called over her shoulder as she passed. The sound of her low voice, suddenly so alarmingly close by, as ever had the effect of freezing Lucy to her very marrow.

"Sure, sure. Just a minute."

Lucy hesitated, scribbled one more line in her notebook, then leaped up from her desk. *Don't sweat. Don't talk too much. You always talk too much, just shut up and don't say anything for once! Except when you have to. Then be brilliant and incisive. Like Katharine Graham. Or Nancy Mitford. Or Gran. Be like Gran.* Propelling herself forward in haste, Lucy collided against Lara, the newly promoted junior fashion writer, with a hard, deadening *thwack.* She ricocheted back toward her desk, catching her thigh on the sharp gray metal of her filing cabinet.

"Oh, please watch where you're going, okay, Lucy?" Lara didn't break stride, simply carried on walking, the corridor her own runway, her curious loping gait aping that of a catwalk model. She turned her head slightly and gestured downward. "These are new, you know? I could have been carrying a coffee."

Lucy, wincing with pain, looked at Lara's retreating feet, as she was supposed to. Of course Lara had the new high-tops exclusive to Liberty, which *Grazia* had featured this week. Of *course* she did: high-tops were everywhere. Lucy didn't think she could walk in them, but she'd probably have to get some. Sneakers with heels? What was the point of that? No point at all, it would be like putting tights on a giraffe. But after one year on the features desk at the *Daily News*, Lucy knew what to expect. The men didn't have to do anything, just show up in a crappy suit; but if you were a woman you had to follow each new trend obsessively. You'd never heard of BB cream and suddenly it was everywhere and if you didn't use it you might as well be saying "I hate myself and I am a loser." Lucy glanced anxiously down at her little blazer as Lara rounded the corner, tossing her blond hair, and disappeared. Was the cropped blazer over yet? Would anyone tell her if it was or would she suddenly be dragged outside, forced to rip it from her body and burn it in an oil drum, surrounded by a circle of angry, jeering fashion policewomen?

"*Lucy!*"

"Coming, I'm sorry, Deborah!" Lucy jogged along the corridor, ignoring the stabbing pain in her leg. Outside was a bright, blustery day, puffy clouds scudding over the churning Thames. She wished she were outside, walking in Embankment Gardens, maybe. Watching a blackbird pick at the soil. At Winterfold, the trees over the valley would be starting to turn. Pale green at first, barely noticeable. Then mustard yellow, then in a few weeks fiery orange, chili red, hot pink.

She hurried into the meeting area and sat down. The Topshop batik-print dress was slightly too small and cut into her legs—everything was slightly too small for Lucy. She stared at her chicken-skin thighs, wondering whether she should go down there this weekend, stay with Gran.

The invitation was stiff in her pocket, and she could feel it digging into her hip. Lucy had always thought she was up to speed with Gran's plans, but this had come out of the blue, that very morning. When she'd rung her dad to pump him for information, he'd been useless. Would Florence and Cat return for this strange-sounding party? Would Daisy?

Deborah cleared her throat and the others put down their phones. "Right—everyone here?" She scanned the room, eyes resting on Lucy, then looking away. "Wow, Betty, I love your scarf. Is it Stella McCartney?"

"Yes, it's so cute, isn't it? I love her palette."

The others cooed agreement, Lucy joining in late and halfheartedly with a blank, "Nice."

Exactly one year ago today, Lucy had joined the *Daily News* as features assistant. She'd spent the previous day, Sunday, in bed going through her finances, or rather lack of finances. This was the other thing she didn't understand about working here. She could barely pay for her rent, let alone scarves from Stella McCartney. How did the other girls afford it?

The bags from Marc Jacobs, the sandals from Christian Louboutin, the Ray-Bans? In an effort to keep up, last month Lucy had bought a pair of blue what were called "Rey Sans" sunglasses from a knockoff stall on Leicester Square, which she had worn triumphantly back to the office, only to be chided by Deborah for supporting fashion piracy.

"Lovely note of color, Betty. Very visual. Okay, let's crack on." Deborah cleared her throat and crossed her legs, brushing an imaginary speck of something off her long, slim calf. Lucy knew this was because she'd noted Lara's high-tops and had to let Lara know she eschewed high-tops (this was the one area Deborah and Lucy agreed on) in favor of heels—in this case, Jimmy Choo holographic leather with heels three inches high.

"Ideas meeting. It was shit last week, we got virtually nothing we can use." Her voice was toneless and low, and Lucy found herself as ever leaning slightly forward to hear what Deborah was saying. "I really hope you're all on better form this week. Trends and fashion first. *Stylist* has a great piece on autumn layering, what have we got?"

"What about color-blocking?" said Betty. "It's really hot right now. I saw these great pictures of Gwyneth Paltrow on the school run—"

"Great. Lucy, write it down."

"Winter coats," said Suzy, the deputy fashion editor. "There's some big statement pieces from—"

"No, done to death already, Suzy. Way too late for that." Deborah smoothed a strand of glossy, fine, black bobbed hair slowly between her fingers. Suzy's face froze, her mouth a tiny O. "What else?"

"Eyebrows," Lara said, as Suzy began tapping at her BlackBerry, muttering angrily. "They're massive? We could do a feature on how to do them properly. You know, eyebrow makeup, Cara Delevingne. Bushy is back. Throw away the tweezers. Lauren Hutton, Brooke Shields."

"That's good." Deborah clapped her hands briskly. "What else?"

Relieved, everyone started babbling. "Travel hot spots for 2013. Iran is going to be huge." "Sherry is back." "Grilled chicken is going to be a thing next year." "Butt lifts." "Foot jewelry." Lucy scribbled it all down, different words but the same ideas every week. It wasn't an ideas meeting, more like a random word generator. She often thought she could stand up and say, "Fossilized dinosaur bones hollowed into clogs will be massive in 2013," and they'd all nod, those identikit girls with their blond center partings and platinum-diamond-whose-fiancé-earns-the-most engagement rings, then look panicked they hadn't heard about dinosaur bone clogs.

"There's some stuff here." Deborah tapped at her phone again. "Thanks, everyone. Now, features. Did anyone have anything—"

"I had some ideas." Lucy heard her own voice, far too loud, too high, the words floating above the circle and hanging there. "I mean—sorry, Deborah. I interrupted you."

"Right. Of course." Deborah pursed her lips and leaned forward, as though confidentially imparting a secret. "Girls," she murmured. "It's one year today since Lucy joined the features desk. We had a talk last week and she mentioned she had some ideas. Didn't you, Lucy?"

This wasn't exactly a representation of their conversation, which had started with Lucy asking for a promotion or at least a pay raise, and ended with Deborah telling her that if she was 100 percent brutally honest, she didn't see Lucy's future in features.

Lucy had become used to that sad sense of alienation that defines office life in the early years of one's career, the gentle deflation of your hopes and dreams to workaday reality. She'd been a waitress, an envelope stuffer, a PA, a temp, and a junior reporter on the *Bristol Post* before being laid off, and now she was here, and she knew she was lucky, very lucky.

Southpaw had told her about the job. He still did a few cartoons a month for the *Daily News*, and when he did, the front cover had a huge blue rosette with "New Wilbur Inside!" in big gold letters, and the circulation rose each time by at least ten thousand copies. Lucy didn't want to think about how she'd got the job—she'd interviewed twice, supplied references, seen four different people, but she couldn't ever escape the lingering suspicion she was there because she was David Winter's granddaughter. She stuck out like a sore thumb, she knew it. Aside from her grandfather, she was unconnected to the things that mattered, completely separate from this strange world of trendy London where people operated at a higher level of consciousness than she did, a bit like Scientology. They knew about pop-ups and new margarita flavors and YOLO, while Lucy was rereading Frances Hodgson Burnett books and planning day trips to historic houses like Charleston, Chatsworth, and Highclere. In addition, and most damningly, she knew, she was a size ten. She was, to them, fat.

Her gaze shifting around the circle, from one expectant face to another, Lucy cleared her throat and opened her notebook. Trying to sound casual, she said, "What about a jokey piece on how to get more Twitter followers? I tweeted a photo of a dog jumping in the air on the beach, and about thirty more people followed me. But when I'm tweeting about that No More Page 3 campaign, no one pays any attention."

"That's a nice idea, Lucy. Very sad, though, because we ran something similar in August. I think you were on holiday."

There was a pause. Someone cleared her throat.

"Or . . . Top Tens. Top Ten on how to get over being dumped." A snigger. Lucy could feel a red flush starting on her breastbone, prickling up her neck. "I was dumped last year. It was awful. How you get over it. Because *He's Just Not That Into You* is a great book." She paused, feeling the red blotchy blush rise higher. "My stepmother gave it to me and I thought I'd hate it, but actually it was brilliant."

Lucy was sure that those weeks, after she found out Tom was seeing Amelia and everyone had known for months except her, had left her with a Pavlovian fear of her dad's new house. She'd go there every weekend and lie in bed crying until she felt like a zombie, face puffy, synapses vanished so that she was unable to hold a sensible conversation without either trailing off and staring across the room or weeping. One Saturday morning her stepmother, Karen, had left the book outside her bedroom door with a note: *Hope this helps. Karen.* As so often with Karen, Lucy was sure it was meant kindly, but at the time it didn't feel particularly kind.

Deborah's voice was icy. "No, not this time. Anything else?"

Betty laughed nervously—half in sympathy. Betty was nice, but the laugh was sad. The others crossed their legs, enjoying the show, Lucy knew it. She breathed in, then stared down at the list in the notebook.

Twitter followers. The dreaded number 267—how most people just have 267 followers.
Getting Dumped. Big feature about turning our lives around and seeing the positive.
Eyebrows. Why is there always one really long hair that you haven't noticed in your eyebrows?

And, at the bottom:

> *The invitation this morning. A piece about our family?*
>   *Something about Southpaw?*

"Well, eyebrows." She looked up. "Do you ever suddenly notice there's one really long eyebrow hair, about an inch long, and it'll suddenly waggle out of place and stick right up like . . . a pubic hair?"

In the silence that followed Lucy heard the rush of the air-conditioning vents, the clicking of someone's hard drive.

"I don't think that's . . . no," Deborah said. "Let's leave this. We're really looking for something a bit meatier than that." Lucy opened her mouth. "Okay, thanks, Lucy, was there anything else?" And, like the owner of a pet shop throwing a blanket over a squawking parrot, she turned to the rest of the group, and the meeting continued.

Back at her desk, Lucy tore out the page of her notebook. She stared at it, then angrily threw it in the bin. The line *A piece about our family?* seemed to burn into her eyes. She thought about going back to her damp, cold flat tonight, taking out the thick cream card, and propping it up on her desk in her bedroom. Those words, in Gran's beautiful blank script: "An important announcement."

What was it all about? What was going on there?

Lucy's heart ached, as it always did when she thought of Winterfold. It was home, though she'd never lived there; it was her weak spot. Winterfold was the happy place people talked about finding in psychobabble articles about mindful relaxation, which the *Daily News* ran at least once a week: "Go to your happy place." Lucy was always there, that was the trouble. Wondering when the air would start to smell of autumn, as it always did by half-term. The sloes thickening, ripe for picking in late October on the bushes by the river, that first frost, the hunter's moon.

When her parents divorced and sold the messy Victorian villa in Redland in Bristol where Lucy had grown up, she hadn't minded that much. When Cat was upset about Daisy, her mum, or worrying about some mean girl at school, or about life in general (Cat used to do that a lot), Lucy, the younger one, was the bracing dose of common sense. When her dad was at his lowest and she'd moved in with him for a few months after university, she'd held his hand, helped him paint the tiny almshouse he'd bought in the village, listened to him witter on about his patients, and watched *The Godfather* trilogy with him on a loop. She was all right when she was there, at Winterfold. It was the one place she felt truly safe, truly happy.

Lucy muttered something to herself, then stood up and walked over to the corner office. She knocked on the door.

"Yes?" Deborah looked up. "Oh. Lucy. Yes?"

"Can I have a word?"

"*Another* word?" Deborah pulled at one of her delicate gold cluster earrings.

Lucy ran a hand through her short messy curls. "Yes. I'm sorry about earlier. I've got an idea, though, a much better one. You told me to think big."

"This isn't about diets again, is it?"

Lucy had written a pitch last month called "The Myth of Diets: Why 85% of All Weight Lost Through Dieting Goes Back On After 6 Months." Deborah had practically choked on her soy latte. "Jesus, if people knew that was the truth, half our ad revenues would vanish. Are you mad? Women like reading about diets, okay?"

Feeling Deborah's coolly appraising gaze on her, Lucy sucked in her stomach. "It's not about diets. You know, that exhibition of South—of my grandfather's is opening next year. I want to write a piece about our family. I think—it might be interesting."

Deborah didn't sit up exactly, but she stopped gazing over Lucy's shoulder. "What kind of article?"

"Um—what it was like to grow up with my grandfather." She hoped she wasn't blushing. "How wonderful he is. Our family. The house. You know they live in this lovely house and—"

"I know about the house," Deborah said. "Yup. It'd make for some nice photos. This is a good idea, Lucy. Warm reminiscence. The *Daily News* family. 'As our beloved cartoonist celebrates X years in the business with an exhibition of landmark paintings showing our city at war, *Daily News* features assistant Lucy Winter tells us about life with the grandfather who created the nation's favorite cartoon strip.' She nodded. "I like it. All the family there? Any skeletons I should know about?"

"My mum's an herbalist called Clare who lives in Stokes Croft," Lucy said, deadpan. "In Bristol. So . . . I don't think so."

Deborah laughed, but she sounded a little impatient. "I mean your grandfather's family."

"Right." Now she had got this far, Lucy suddenly found she didn't know what to say. "My aunt Daisy—well, maybe it's not really a mystery."

"What about your aunt Daisy?" Deborah's tone was, for her, almost flippant.

"Uh—well, I'm never sure if it's serious or not. I've always thought it was a bit strange." She glanced at Deborah, feeling suddenly uneasy: was she really the right person to be talking to about this stuff? But it was too late now. "My aunt sort of . . . disappeared twenty, thirty years ago. Out of the blue. Left her baby with my grandparents when she was just five weeks old and took off."

"What do you mean, 'disappeared'? Did she die?"

"No. It's weird. I mean, she's still alive. My grandmother gets e-mails from her. Now and then."

"If your grandmother gets e-mails—where does she think she's gone, then?" There was a note of impatience in Deborah's voice. *What kind of family doesn't know where their own daughter is?*

Lucy tried to explain, but as she didn't really understand it herself, it was hard to know how to put it. "I think she was . . . always a bit difficult." She remembered having a teenage tantrum once about not being allowed to go to Katie Ellis's party and her dad yelling at her: "Oh, God, Lucy, don't be like *Daisy*," as if that was the worst thing a person could be. And Lucy had seen Daisy all of four times in her life. She didn't really know her. "She's very cool. Um—well, I think she got pregnant very young, and it was all a bit much for her?" Almost appealing to Deborah for her agreement, she held her hands slightly open, racking her brains for a way to try to explain it. "We don't talk about it, you know what families are like, the strangest things happen and people act like it's not even a big deal. Do you know what I mean?" Her shoulders slumped; of course not.

But Deborah said, "Oh, tell me about it. My mother never knew who her father was, grew up believing he was dead, in fact, and one evening she and my dad are sitting there—I'm at university by this point—and there's a knock at the door and there's this man and he says, 'Hi there, I'm your father, and I've been looking for you for ten years.'"

"What?" Lucy's eyes bulged. In the year she'd worked for her she'd learned nothing about Deborah, other than that she was from Dorking but said "near Guildford" and that she'd asked Lucy to order her loads of *Fifty Shades*–style erotica to take on holiday that summer. "Oh my goodness. What happened next?"

Deborah shook her head and crossed her legs briskly, as if she was regretting saying anything at all. "It's not important. I'm just saying, I agree, families are strange. Go on. What happened to—what's your aunt's name? Don't tell me. She was murdered?"

"Er—no. Daisy. She ran off to India to work in a children's school and my grandparents raised the baby. Cat, my cousin. And that's basically it. She stayed in India and lives there now. She helped build a school; I think she got some award for it. She's been back home four, five times since. Usually to ask for money." Lucy frowned at the clearest memory she had of her thin, wrinkly-tanned aunt Daisy, so pretty and exotic and strange, and yet familiar in the old safe surroundings of Winterfold. She'd come back for Dad's unexpected wedding to Karen (which took place so hastily, Lucy had been gloomily convinced that news of a pregnancy would come soon afterward, but no such announcement was ever made), and everyone was surprised to see her, Lucy remembered that much. She seemed to be permanently half there, half-eager to join in and yet always on the edge of leaving. She had a silver elephant she always carried in her pocket. And big green eyes, too big in her gaunt face; she really was the thinnest person Lucy had ever seen. She clearly had no idea how old Lucy was and kept asking her if she'd read *The Famous Five* and talking to her in a babyish voice. She had a row with Dad about money the day before the wedding. And she'd said something to Cat, Lucy was never sure what, but she found Cat crying afterward in her room, hugging her old cushion on the bed, almost inconsolable, and since then Cat had hardly been back, and Lucy missed her so much, though Cat had become so cool, so distant, she'd never dream of saying any of that to her.

"Daisy usually has some argument with my dad or my grandparents," she finished. "She leaves and says she's never coming home again."

"So she's broken off contact with all of you?"

"It's not really like that." Lucy didn't want to exaggerate. "She wasn't ever that close to Flo, my other aunt. Or Dad, I suppose. But she still e-mails Gran these days. It's strange because . . . we've always been a really happy family otherwise. It's like she came from somewhere different."

As she said this, she felt it was true that they had been a happy family once, but not now. Things were different, they were all sadder; she could not explain it.

Deborah's hands were pressed to her cheeks. "Well, you're right, that is interesting. An article about growing up with your grandfather, the lovely house . . . and then this about Daisy. Very meaty—yes. I suppose your grandfather wouldn't mind?" She looked like a cat, about to pounce on a mouse.

Lucy said carefully, "I didn't mean . . . I'm not sure I'd want to write about all of it."

"Why not? Lucy, don't be contrary."

"I was really thinking of a piece about our family, how jolly we are, what we get up to, Southpaw drawing us little pictures, you know?" Deborah's nostrils flared. "Look"—Lucy tried to sound firm—"my grandfather doesn't like people digging into his past. He wouldn't even let the man from the *Bath Chronicle* interview him about his new show. I don't think he's going to want you to publish an article about . . . Daisy and stuff."

Deborah's voice took on a gentler, honeyed tone. "Of course. Look, Lucy, you don't have to be sensationalist about it. There are plenty of people in situations like that: you know, unfinished business. And you never know, you might find out more about her and think how happy your grandparents would be. We've got two million readers, there must be someone who knows something." She cleared her throat delicately. "I'll be honest. I like you, Lucy. I want to help you. You know? I mean, don't you *want* to write it?"

"I could ask him," Lucy said hesitantly, trying to feel her way on this slippery ground. "We've got a family reunion coming up—I don't know if Daisy'll be there. It just feels a bit funny. . . ."

"Ask your grandparents. Or speak to her daughter. Though I don't know why you can't just e-mail your aunt yourself, ask her if she's coming back for the reunion. That'd make the perfect hook for the piece. Imagine it. You must have an address for her somewhere." The phone on Deborah's desk rang and she diverted it with a jab of one bony finger.

"When you were in here last week asking for a pay raise, you told me you were positive this was what you wanted to do. I'm not asking you to write some hatchet job on your family. I'm just saying, think about digging around a bit, seeing if there's something there."

Lucy nodded. "Okay."

"You can write, Lucy." Deborah shook her head so her hair fell into its perfect bobbed shape. She ruffled it with her fingers, and then put on some lip gloss. "You're good at pitching, you made me believe you wanted a job writing for a newspaper. You aren't there yet." She stood up, peculiarly gawky, and slung a long coat around her shoulders, rather like Cruella de Vil. "I have to go, I have lunch with Geordie. Think about it, Lucy. G'bye."

And she left, leaving Lucy alone in her large glass office, staring out of the window, wondering what she'd just got herself into. *You can write.* Lucy pulled out Gran's invitation, her mind racing. She had no idea what she'd do next, but she was sure about one thing: wherever Daisy was, she wasn't coming back for this party.

Daisy

March 1969

I HATE THIS house.

We have been here for a whole year now and I know I hate it. I am nearly eight and I am not stupid, though everyone seems to think I am, because I don't like reading stories like baby Florence, and I don't like hanging round the kitchen with Ma like Billy Lily. He hates it when I call him that!

When we first saw this house I didn't understand it would be only us living there. I said to Daddy: "But it's far too big! There's only five of us and the dogs!" They thought that was so funny, Daddy and Ma, like I'd said something jolly amusing. Grown-ups never understand that you mean what you say.

They showed us around the garden and Flo and Bill were awfully keen on it. Because of the space and the woods. But I *hate* it. I am scared out here. I wish we were back in Putney, where the houses are the same and everything is safe.

And it is too big for us, now we're in. Daddy is so pleased with himself because he could afford to buy it, because of him having no money and a sad childhood. I heard him saying that to Ma. I listen to them all the time, when they don't know I'm there. I know all about his dad and how his mummy died too. All the wood is painted green (in the house). There's mice and rats everywhere and Wilbur is terrible at catching them. He hides under the sideboard or once in the games cupboard in the sitting room when they appear. There's wasps, too, under the roof. No one else has spotted the wasps yet. And a huge garden. Ma is cross all the time. She wants to draw and she can't draw because she doesn't have time because of the mice and the dogs and dropping us at school and

54

making food and all of the housewife chores. Daddy is off in London having meetings and lunch with friends. He comes home late, he smiles, Ma hisses at him and she gets so cross. They shout but they also whisper things, and that's when I like listening, when they're in bed at night and they can't hear me pressed against the door.

Everything's different since we came here. And Florence is here. Since she came along everything's worse. We moved because of her. We had to leave Putney and our old house with the poppies and the corn wallpaper because of her. Everything was fine before she arrived. It was quiet and nice and I knew where we were, me and Bill, Daddy and Ma. Ma had time for me, for Wilbur. Now she's always cross.

The other thing is we don't have enough money to pay for the house. I worry about it all the time. I try to say it to Ma and Daddy: 'There's not enough money because you told me once Daddy gets £100 for a painting or a sketch and this house was £16,000.' And Ma doesn't have any money. She is from a poor family too, though not as poor as Daddy's. We don't see her family very much. There wasn't room for them in Putney to come and stay, but they stayed the night here last week and I hope they don't come again. Her sister speaks with a funny accent and she was mean to me. She told me to shut up when I wanted to talk some more about Wilbur. So before she went I put a piece of broken glass from the time I pretended Florence broke the mirror—well, I keep some of the pieces in my tree by the daisy bank at the back of the garden—and I put it in her handbag. So when she reaches in for her handkerchief she will slice her fingers. I hope she slices them right off.

So I have got three things that I want to do. One, move back to Park Street, Putney. Two, get rid of Florence. An accident like what happened to Janet, although that scares me, and I didn't mean for it to happen. Three, make everyone say that Wilbur is my special dog, not the family's. They can have Crispin as their family dog and Wilbur can be mine. I drew some pictures of him doing funny things, and I put them up in my room. The first one is of Wilbur hiding with the snakes and ladders in the cupboard when he sees a mouse. The second is him jumping up like a beanpole on the other side of the table when he sees food held in the air. He looks so funny. The third is him walking behind me down the hill to school. He does it every day and then he walks back up to Winterfold and sits with Ma and waits for me to come home. I love Wilbur more than anyone else in the whole world. He is a bit sandy, and he is a cross between a Labrador and a retriever, I think.

This is what I'm worried about most at the moment: just before the holidays, Janet Jordan at school laughed at him and said he was ugly and a mongrel. The next day Janet fell on the steps and hit her head and now she can't speak. At all.

I worry that I did that to Janet. I didn't make anything special happen like I do sometimes, but I thought a lot about it, I wanted her to die for being nasty to Wilbur. I really did. Sometimes I stare at things very very hard and I'm sure I move them just a bit with my thoughts, and I get so scared but I can't stop doing it. When I look at books late at night in the new room sometimes the colors jumble up and start to jump in front of my eyes like they're talking to me. And when I see myself in the mirror I think an evil person's talking to me, and sometimes he is. Then I think: *So what?* Janet wasn't nice, she laughed at me for being new and having a pinafore on, and she was nasty to other girls, but she started being nice when she saw my house was big. She deserved it.

When Wilbur's with me, though, it's all all right. They are saying they might put poison down for the rats, and if Wilbur ate it it would kill him, so he has to get used to sleeping in here, then. I like him being in here. I feel safe. We are friends. I draw him while he's lying there. I can't draw like Daddy but I try to match the way his back swishes in a curl, and how his legs fold under him so neatly. Wilbur is very clever as well as being a bit silly sometimes. Mrs. Goody says my drawings of him are very good, and I should hang them up in the classroom, but I don't want other people to see them and ooh and aah so I put them up in my room.

Daddy likes the drawings. "Well done, Daze," he says, looking at the picture of Wilbur in the games cupboard hiding from a rat. "Lovely idea, that. Very funny." But it's not funny at all, it's serious.

Joe

TEN DAYS AFTER his accident, Joe Thorne left the Oak Tree and, carefully carrying his package wrapped in brown paper under one arm, walked up to Winterfold. He couldn't help but be nervous. He'd mentioned he was doing this catering gig to a couple of people. "Ooh, up at the Winters', are you? That's good," Sheila had said. "Listen here, Bob, Joe's going up to Winterfold."

Bob, their one regular, had raised his eyebrows.

"Right, then," he'd said. And he'd almost looked impressed.

The early autumn sunshine was like misty gold, flooding the quiet streets as he strode past the war memorial and the post office. Susan Talbot, the postmistress, was standing in the doorway talking to her mother, Joan. Joe raised his bandaged hand at her and Susan smiled widely at him, waving enthusiastically. Joe felt bad about Susan. He wasn't sure why, just that she was always on at him. Last time she'd wanted him to lug some boxes around, then stay for a cup of tea, then the rest of it, and she'd gone a bit funny when, in the course of conversation (in truth, when she'd asked him outright), he'd said he wasn't really looking for a relationship. Not at the moment.

"No time for love?" Susan had said. "All work and no play . . ." She'd smiled brightly at him and he'd frowned, because he hated that look on her face like she was making the best of it. "You want to be careful, Joe, my dear. A good-looking chap like you, those lovely blue eyes and those cheekbones to die for, all going to waste! Someone should enjoy them. You can't just coop yourself up in that flat night after night on your own."

It had freaked him out, more than a little bit. The way she'd stared at him, as though she knew something.

Now he nodded at her in a friendly way and carried on, clutching the brown paper package under his arm so tightly that he gave a tiny moan as his finger throbbed once more.

Bill Winter was a good doctor. The nurse at the hospital in Bath where Joe had ended up that day told him Bill had saved his finger and maybe his whole hand—Joe thought that was a bit dramatic, but they'd said if blood poisoning had set in it'd have been serious. Who'd want a chef who couldn't use a knife, whisk a sauce, knead dough? What would he have done? He'd have lost his job here, that was for sure. He'd have had to do something else, become a bartender, maybe. Besides, he wanted to help Jemma out with money, even if she said she didn't need it, didn't need anything, as she kept telling him. Not now she was with Ian.

Jemma had canceled Jamie's last visit, a couple of weeks ago; something about *The Gruffalo* onstage and how he couldn't miss it, everyone in his class was going. Joe hadn't seen his son for two months. Jamie had been down to stay in late July, just after school holidays had started. It had been brilliant. They'd gone swimming in the river at Farleigh Hungerford. They'd camped out at Sheila's—Joe's rooms above the pub were tiny, and Sheila had a cottage with a long garden that stretched down to the woods, where you heard foxes fighting and owls hooting and the strange, rustling sound of unknown creatures nearby. They'd made a fire, Joe had cooked the Oak Tree's own delicious herby sausages and put them in his own rosemary and walnut bread rolls, slathered with mustard, and there the two of them had sat, out under the stars, munching away together, and Joe couldn't remember ever feeling this happy. He'd made Sheila some treacly, creamy truffles to say thanks for the garden loan. He and Jamie had made a box for them out of cardboard and decorated it—the felt-tip marks where they'd overshot the cardboard were still on his kitchen table—blue, orange, and green scribbles, made in a second; and now when Joe saw them every night, he felt the sharp pang of Jamie's absence. Sheila had cooed with delight when he gave her the box, the night after he'd got back from taking Jamie home to York.

"You shouldn't have, it was my pleasure, Joe. He's lovely. You must be very proud of him."

"I am," he'd said, swallowing hard. "Nothing to do with me, though."

"You're joking, aren't you? He's the spitting image of you, my dear, it's uncanny." Then she'd seen his expression. "Oh, Joe. I promise you, he is. And he's welcome anytime you want."

He would always love Sheila for saying that, but being here was taking him away from his son, more and more. This restaurant, two hundred and fifty miles away from his son. Why had he thought he could do it? Why was he screwing everything up here? Why wasn't he back in York, or even Leeds, or back with Mum in Pickering, helping her out?

Jemma and Ian were getting married next year, and though he honestly wished them well and was glad for Jemma that she could have all the manicures she wanted, Joe was the one left behind. He'd never been right for her. He'd never really understood why she'd come over to him in the first place. She'd been way out of his league. He'd only been in the club because one of the chefs was leaving. It was a footballer's place, and she was the kind of girl you saw with footballers.

Joe's sister, Michelle, had warned him off her. "She's trouble, Joe. She's after your money."

Joe had said quietly, "She knows I don't have any money."

"You're her cute bit of action on the side before she bags herself a millionaire, Joe," she told him. Michelle was a realist. "You don't understand women, okay? You're not that fat spotty kid with the knee-high socks and Mam's apron on making brownies anymore, right, love? You're . . . ugh." She'd closed her eyes and shuddered. "You're a good-looking lad, and you're nice, okay? All my friends are after you. So just use your head."

They'd only been dating a few months when Jemma told him she was pregnant. Joe was over the moon, but she wasn't. She was scared. He could see now that the game she was playing was to get herself some security, because she'd failed at school and her mum had nothing, and her dad, like his, was long gone. Jemma was like Michelle: she didn't have any qualifications, anything to give. The only thing she had was her body and her looks, and she'd used them to get him, someone who wouldn't hit her or cheat on her; but the moment she'd decided it'd be him, she'd realized she didn't really love him anyway. She was nearly five months gone by that point.

If they'd been older and wiser, maybe it could have worked. If he'd been mature enough to see how young and scared she really was and how a lot of the crap she pulled was because she was frightened and wanted to test him, maybe he'd have kept her. But she started going out again when Jamie was only a few weeks old, and coming back at all hours, and he was working all hours too, and they were shouting when they were together, her yelling at him because he was never around and didn't earn enough money, and the flat in Leeds was tiny and both of them were so tired all the time, they could only be vile to each other. She'd start shouting at him—completely wild, she'd get—and Joe would stare at his son, his tiny red wrinkled head, solemn mouth, beady black eyes that opened wide, the sudden smile when you picked him up. He'd wonder: Could Jamie hear the terrible things his mum and dad were saying to each other? Was it damaging him, making him believe the world was full of anger and sadness?

One day he'd got back from the restaurant at four in the morning, and they were gone. Just a note, and it said, *Sorry, Joe. I can't do this anymore. You can see Jamie whenever. J. x PS You were lovely.*

It was fine to start with. He saw Jamie every weekend, some weekdays, took him out and about, to the park, to the playgroup at the church hall. He loved kids, and the mums were always friendly; Joe loved it. Then Jemma moved to York and it got a bit harder to see Jamie, but it was still okay. Joe kept on working, head down, not living much, going on the occasional date, the odd pint with an old mate. Really, just waiting for his weekends with Jamie, time he could make into bricks, a substantial bulk of memory.

Then, at Jamie's third birthday party, there was Ian Sinclair, a lawyer. Jemma had cut his hair and he'd asked her out, and now he was here in her living room, snapping away with a massive expensive Nikon camera and his own present, a bright red sit-on truck for Jamie. Joe had turned up late with a Victoria sponge made by his mother, which Liddy had laboriously decorated all over with Smarties. It had got squashed on the bus. He'd stood at the back chatting to Jemma's neighbor Lisa, then tried to pick up Jamie but he'd wailed and screamed. Then he'd given him a bow and arrow set, and Jemma had practically stabbed him with it: "What the hell is he going to do with that, Joe? Walk down Museum Gardens and shoot something? Are you serious?"

Ian Sinclair had handed round a train-shaped cake and given the grown-ups each a fondant fancy, both of which he'd ordered in from Bettys. Joe's present was rolled up in its plastic bag, put down beside the sofa on the floor. On the way back from the bathroom Joe caught sight of his mum's squashed cake, abandoned untouched in the sterile, brand-new kitchen, buttery grease blotting the now-bent paper plates Liddy had carefully sandwiched it between. Joe ended up drinking too much with Lisa, the neighbor, then going back to her flat, where they had sex, he was sure—he couldn't ever remember and that made it worse somehow.

It got worse: the next day, as he was leaving, Jemma appeared on the pavement, shaking with rage.

"Things are changing, Joe. Okay?" She jabbed her finger on the window of Ian's jeep, which she used to drive Jamie to the child-minder's. "I'm sick of you hanging round like a dog that's lost its owner. He'll always be your son, don't you understand that?"

Joe could see Jamie, strapped into his car seat, watching his father, thumb in mouth, a little confused. His thick curls were stuck to his head; he still looked half-asleep. He reached forward and jabbed at the window with one small finger. "Dad?"

"Go and get your own life," Jemma hissed at Joe. "Seriously."

She was right, of course. But Joe didn't know what his own life looked like. His dad had left when he was five and Michelle was eight, and he'd come back lots at the start, then not at all. Derek Thorne was a liar and a gambler who took money off their mother, and once hit her when he was drunk. The worst thing was, Joe remembered him pretty well. He'd always thought he was a brilliant dad, till the moment he'd upped and left. Joe didn't know where he'd gone; his mum never wanted to talk about it, his sister hated him, and that was it. . . . It wasn't even dramatic. He'd just sort of faded away.

Now Joe saw that it could happen very easily. How careful he had to be, to maintain his amicable relationship with Jemma and Ian. Because the memories of his times with Jamie were growing more and more precious. *He* was Jamie's dad, not Ian, and nothing could change that. And he didn't want to be a dick about it; he wasn't some Fathers4Justice idiot. He didn't ever want to get in the way of Ian. Ian was the one who'd be there at night when he woke up, who'd hug Jamie when he was scared of monsters under the bed. He would do all that. . . .

Joe stopped halfway up the hill, breathing in the scent of fallen leaves, wood smoke, rain, and blinked back the sharp tears in his eyes. The memory of his son's wriggly, sturdy body against his when they hugged was exquisite pleasure mixed with aching pain in his heart. The smell of wood smoke in his hair, his head next to his father's in the tent at night that summer. His low, dry voice, the way he slept with his fists scrunched up tight—he'd always done that, ever since he was a baby. His gummy teeth, his babbling chatter about children at school, and how his best friend was a girl called Esme.

Joe knew he had to keep going, now he was in this situation. But he was already screwing it up, he felt. It was already maybe too late.

It was a ten-minute walk out to Winterfold. The lane grew steeper, winding up through the trees past the ruins of the old priory and then ending with a wooden gate, and there was the name of the house, carved into the low wall behind. *Winterfold.* Joe hesitated before unhooking the latch. Though he didn't care much about money or privilege, he found he was nervous, walking up the gravel drive, as though he were entering another world.

The trees were dry, the dark olive-green leaves burnished with bright yellow. The branches rustled softly as Joe looked up to see Winterfold in front of him. The front door was right at the center of an L, so the house seemed to hug you. The bottom half was golden-gray local Bath stone, sprinkled with white lichen, and it was topped by four great gables in wooden clapboard, two on either side, each with a dormer window, like eyes peering down. Wisteria twisted and turned along the edge of the lowest beam. Joe peered into one of the low leaded windows by the door, then jumped. Someone was moving around inside.

Joe went up to the great blackened oak door on which were carved intricate repeating patterns of berries and leaves. The knocker was in the shape of an owl. It stared at him, unblinking. He knocked firmly and stepped back, feeling like Jack coming to see the giant in his home.

He waited for what seemed like ages, then reached forward to knock again, and as the door opened he fell forward, almost lurching into Martha Winter's arms.

"Well. Hello, Joe. It's lovely to see you. How's your hand?"

"It's much better." He fumbled for the parcel under his arm. "I brought you something, actually. To thank you. They said if Dr. Winter hadn't acted so fast, I'd have lost the finger."

"Come inside." Martha unwrapped the bread, her fingertips running over the cracked, crusty surface. "Tiger bread—it's my favorite, did you know that? No? Well, it's very clever of you. Joe, I didn't want anything. Anyone would have done the same. It's my son you should be thanking."

"Yes," he said. "Of course."

"You haven't been here before, have you? It's lovely in the afternoons, when the sun starts to come over the hill."

Somehow she'd taken his coat off and it was hanging on the old carved row of hooks. He glanced left as they passed through the hall: a huge, light sitting room, lined with dark wooden cupboards, white-washed walls slit by black beams. The French windows were open and beyond them was the garden, a green mist splashed with reds, blues, and pinks.

"It's been a great summer for gardeners. All the rain. The tree house is practically pulp, but we don't have any children running around these days, sadly, so no use for it." Martha pushed open the kitchen door and he followed her. "I'm shutting the door behind us because David's in his study and he'll try to join us."

"Oh. Would that be so bad?"

"He's got a deadline. He loves being distracted and he'll hear you and come in." She ruffled her bob with her fingers. "Do sit down, Joe. Would you like some tea? I was going to make a pot. Have a piece of ginger-bread."

Martha pulled out a large, carved wooden armchair and slid a blue-and-white plate across the table toward him. Joe took a piece gratefully—he was hungry all the time since the accident, and wondered if it might be some kind of delayed shock. He watched as she moved around the roomy kitchen. Behind her a large pair of wooden doors was folded back, leading through to the wood-paneled dining room. A jam jar of hot pink and violet-blue sweet peas stood on the sideboard. Liddy grew sweet peas back at home, obsessively trailing them through the trellis on the wall outside their little cottage. Joe breathed in, smelling their rich, heady scent. He looked around the room as she made the tea, thinking he ought to say something. Show he was engaged, keen, up for this job.

"Is that Florence?" he said, pointing to a watercolor on the wall.

Martha looked up in delight. "Yes. We did it on our honeymoon. Both of us together."

"It's beautiful. I studied in Italy. My catering course—we were there for a term."

"My daughter lives in Florence," she said. "How wonderful. Where were you?"

"In a village, middle of nowhere in Tuscany. It was great. What's she doing there then?"

"She's an art history professor. Mostly at the British College, but she teaches over here too. She's very clever. Nothing like me. I studied art, but I'm no good at talking about it."

"You're an artist too?"

Martha folded her arms and looked down at her wedding ring. "Once, I suppose. David and I both had scholarships to the Slade. 'Those poor East Enders,' they used to call us. Terribly posh children from the Home Counties, and us. The girl I shared a bedsit with was called Felicity and her father was a brigadier. Golly, she did go on about him." She smiled, and her lips parted, enough to show the gap between her teeth. "Now you'd just look it up on your phone, I suppose, but then, I had no idea what a brigadier was. After about a month, I asked David what it meant. He was the one person I could ask."

"Did you know him from home?"

Martha suddenly snapped shut the recipe book next to her, and stood up. "No. Different parts of London. But I'd met him before. Once." Her voice changed. "Anyway, I don't paint anymore. Not really. When we moved here . . . everything else took over." She smiled, a little mechanically. "Here's your tea."

She doesn't like talking about herself either. "When you were doing it though . . . what kind of stuff did you paint?" He corrected himself. "Not stuff, sorry. Works."

Martha laughed at that. "'Works' sounds so grand, doesn't it? Oh, everything. I started off doing pastiches, watercolors, copying famous paintings. Used to sell them in Hyde Park on a Sunday. But latterly it was more . . . woodcuts. Prints. Nature and nurture." Sun flickered into the room, reflected off a plane high, high above, and her green eyes flashed hazel-gold. "But it was a long time ago. And having children isn't conducive to being the next Picasso, you know."

"So, you've two children then?"

"Three." She went over to the sink. "There's Daisy too. She's the middle one. She lives in India. Works for a charity—literacy and schools in Kerala."

Joe didn't say, *Wilbur and Daisy, I know all about her.* He somehow hadn't thought that little girl in the cartoons he'd devoured as a child was real. "India. That's exotic."

"Don't think it is, much, not with the work she does. But she's had some wonderful results out there." Martha washed an apple, splashing water everywhere. "Right. Do you want one of these?" He shook his head. "Then shall we draw up a list? I had a few ideas, just a couple of suggestions."

"Will she be there for your birthday?"

She stared at him blankly and sat down again. "Who?"

"Daisy? Your daughter?" Joe said nervously.

Martha started peeling the apple with a knife. "This is a tense moment." There was a silence as the silver cut through the shining green skin. "I like doing this in one perfect ribbon, and lately my skills are starting to slip." She added, almost as an afterthought, "Daisy won't be there, no."

"I'm sorry. I shouldn't have asked." Joe fumbled to take his notepad out of his pocket, embarrassed.

"No, it's fine. There's no big drama with Daisy. She's always been a bit—difficult. She had a baby very young, an affair with a boy she met in Africa, building wells, I think it was. Nice young boy." Martha screwed up her face as if trying to picture him. "Giles something. Isn't it terrible? Nice boy. Very Home Counties . . ."

She stopped as though recalling something. "Anyway. She's out in India now and she really has made a difference. The area where she helped build the school in Cherthala has equal attendance rates for girls and boys now, and last year we—she, I should say, she did it all—raised enough money to ensure that every school in the area is on the mains system for water. It'll save about five thousand lives a year. It's things like that—she's very driven, when she gets the idea in her head, you see."

"You know a lot about it." He was impressed.

"Well, we just—miss her. I'm interested in what interests her. And Cat—that's her daughter—it's sad, like I say." Her eyes were shining.

"She's never seen her baby? Not once?"

The spiral of skin fell on the table. Martha sliced the creamy naked apple. "Oh, a few times over the years. We raised Cat ourselves. Daisy's always seen her when . . . you know, when she comes back. She loves being here."

"When was the last time she came back?"

Martha looked thoughtful. "Oh . . . I'm not sure. Bill's wedding to Karen? That was four years ago. She was a little difficult. Daisy has the zeal of the convert, do you know anyone like that? It annoys some people. Her brother . . . her sister too, come to mention it. It's just . . ." She stopped. "Oh, nothing."

Intrigued, Joe said, "Go on. It's just what?"

Martha hesitated and looked over her shoulder toward the dining room, golden autumn light streaming in from the garden outside.

"It's just—oh, Joe, it's not the way you imagine they'll turn out when they're babies. When you hold them in your arms, that first time, and look at them. And you see what kind of person they are. Do you know what I mean?"

Joe nodded. He knew exactly. He could still remember the moment right after the birth, as Jemma lay back, exhausted, and the midwife turned round from the station by the bed and, like a magician performing a magic trick, handed him this bundle in a towel, which made a mewling sound, a bit like a persistent ring tone. *Waah. Waah. Waah.*

"Your son!" she'd said brightly. And he'd stared at his round, purple face, and the eyes had opened so briefly and fixed on something near Joe's face, and what had crossed Joe's mind was, *I know you. I know who you are.*

"Yes," he said after a moment. "I knew what he was like the first time I held him. Right then just by looking at him. Like I could see his soul."

"Exactly. That's all. It's not . . . it's not what I wanted for her." Martha paused and her green eyes filled with tears. She shrugged. "I'm sorry, Joe. I just miss her."

"I'm sure you do." Joe's heart went out to her. He sipped his tea and finished the cake and, for a few moments, they sat in companionable silence. He felt once again that strangely familiar sense of contentment in her presence. As if he'd known her for a long time.

"So, then," he said, putting down his mug. "I had a few ideas. Want to talk them over?"

"Sure," Martha said, brushing something off her cheek. She gave a quick smile. "I'm so glad you're doing this, Joe."

"Well, I'm glad to be doing it." He grinned almost shyly at her. "I thought for the family lunch on Saturday we'd do a big tapas selection, loads of dips and meats. Go up to the smokery on the Levels together and get some sausages, salmon, pâté, and the like. And then a suckling pig. Porchetta, fennel seeds, sage, a nice sort of event piece, and I can do loads of veg and all. Fruit salad and a big birthday cake for afters, and a huge cheese board, all as local as possible. How's that sound?"

"It sounds wonderful," she said. "I knew you'd get it." She reached out and patted his good hand. "My mouth's watering, just thinking about it. You can use herbs from our garden, that'd be a nice—" The door swung open behind them and she turned, half in irritation, half in amusement. "David, darling, it's been ten minutes! Can't you—oh, *Lucy!* Hello!"

"Hi, Gran!" A tall, curly-haired girl bounded into the room and threw her arms around Martha. "Oh, it's nice to be back. Where's Southpaw?"

"What are you doing here?" Martha stroked her hair.

"Sorry to surprise you, I only decided—oh, sorry again. Didn't realize you were with someone."

"I'm Joe," said Joe, standing up. "Nice to meet you."

"Lucy. Hi." She held out her hand, staring up at him, and he shook it. She had big hazel eyes, a creamy complexion, and a wide, generous smile. There was a gap between her teeth, like her grandmother's, and she blushed as she smiled at him, clamping one arm self-consciously over her chest.

"Oh, what a nice surprise," said Martha. She hugged her granddaughter again, and kissed the top of her head. "Lucy, Joe's the new chef at the Oak Tree. He's going to do the food for the party."

"How exciting!" Lucy said eagerly. "My stepmother can't stop going on about you. Says you're the best thing to happen to the village since she got there." She took some cake and sat down. "Mm. Gran, it's so great to be here."

"Right. Who's your stepmother?" Joe put another piece of gingerbread in his mouth.

"Well, I think she's got a crush on you, so watch out." Lucy was shoveling down cake with aplomb. "Karen Bromidge. D'you know who I mean? Thirties, small, looks like a kind of female Hitler in tight tops?"

"Lucy, don't be rude," said Martha. "Joe, are you all right?"

Joe was coughing, trying not to choke. "Bit . . ." He couldn't speak. "I—"

"Get him some water," Martha said.

Lucy jumped up, ran the tap, and handed him a glass and he tried to drink, breathing hard, feeling like an idiot. *Nice one.* She thumped him hard on the back and he spluttered, then sat down again.

Lucy wiped the crumbs off her face and turned to Martha. "So, Gran, what's the big idea?" she said. "With this party, I mean. I got the invite. You sent it to my old address, by the way."

"Darling, you keep moving. I don't have your new address. What was wrong with the old flat?"

"Domestic issues," Lucy said succinctly. "It was time."

"You were only there three months."

"This pigeon kept raping another pigeon on the roof outside."

"What?"

Lucy swallowed the last of the cake. "Every morning. This pigeon with a big fluffed-up neck would chase these other pigeons and they'd try to fly away and he'd fly after them. And I'd be lying in bed and there'd be this screaming cooing noise and I'd look out and feel really bad for the girl pigeons."

"It's the circle of life," Martha said. "Draw the curtains."

"There weren't any curtains." Martha buried her face in her hands and laughed. Lucy ignored her. "I'm living with Irene now. It's all right."

"Who's Irene?"

"Irene Huang? Irene from Alperton? Gran, you met her when we had lunch in Liberty. She's a fashion blogger. Allegedly. She's actually pretty annoying. She leaves these notes on the fridge about her cat and his distressed bowels and how I must not, repeat not, feed him anything myself."

"Lucy!" said Martha, as though she were eight. "No bowels talk, please."

Lucy shot her a look. "It's germane."

"It's not bloody germane to talk about some cat's guts."

"The cat's called Chairman Miaow. Now, that is germane. It's actually quite a great name. I was sucked in by the greatness of her cat's name and now it's too late."

"Why did you want to live with her? Apart from the cat?" Joe asked, trying to breathe steadily, though he could still feel exactly where the gingerbread had become stuck in his throat.

"She lives in Dalston. Dalston's the center of everything these days."

"Never heard of it," said Martha.

"It's East London," Joe told her. "Very trendy."

"Imagine the Greenwich Village of the fifties, today," Lucy said.

"Oh. Right. How's the job? Lucy works on the *Daily News*," Martha explained to Joe.

"The job?" Lucy said brightly. "It's great. Really great. Listen—I wanted to ask you something about it, in fact. Do you think—" There were footsteps in the hall; Joe saw how quickly Lucy flushed, and shrugged, saying quickly, "Actually, never mind," as the kitchen door banged open and David Winter stood on the threshold, holding the door back with his stick.

"Any chance of some tea, Em?"

"Of course." Joe saw Martha look at him. "What's up?"

"I'm having some trouble with Wilbur. Can you come and pretend to be chasing your tail?" He caught sight of Lucy and his face lit up. "Lucy, darling, hello! This is much better. Come into the study, I need you to run around in a circle." Lucy gave a throaty, delighted chuckle. "And Joe, wonderful! Hello there, sir. Are you here to talk about the plans for the party?"

"Hello, David." Joe stood up and shook his hand. He felt faint. "Yes. I think we've agreed on the menu."

David leaned against the table. "Well, that's marvelous. Now I shall take this piece of gingerbread and go back to my study. Lucy . . . ?"

"I need to ask Gran something." Lucy looked at her grandmother. "Can Joe do it?"

"Joe, please come and run around in a circle pretending to be a dog, won't you?" David said, smiling, and Joe thought again that you'd do anything to please a man with a smile like that.

"Of course."

"You know, it's easier to just show you on YouTube," he said, when they were in David's study.

"On YouTube?" David sat heavily back in his chair, breathing hard. Joe glanced at him. There were dark gray circles under his brown eyes. "That hadn't occurred to me. It's a terrific idea." He lay back a little and closed his eyes.

"You all right?"

"Bit tired, that's all. I don't sleep that well. I used to take sleeping pills. Can't anymore." He tapped his chest. "Dodgy ticker."

"I'm sorry." Joe moved round next to him behind the large oak desk and began typing on the old computer balanced precariously on the corner, next to sheets of paper, a large mug filled with pencils, and a pile of thrillers in a large, wobbling tower. David stared into space, his hands sitting idly on his lap. "This desk is a health and safety liability, David," Joe said, for want of something else to say. David's fame made him nervous. He wasn't like the footballers or *Big Brother* rejects who came into the restaurant back in Leeds and ordered Cristal and then sat there fiddling with their phones. He was someone Joe really admired, had done all his life, and it was weird . . . and strange. "You'd never be allowed to work in my kitchen."

"Ha," David said. "My life's work is in here. All our paperwork too. It's a mess, and one day someone will have to sort it all out. Hopefully not me." He sat up as Joe clicked on a video. "Look at that, eh. Marvelous. How did you know what kind of dog Wilbur was? That's the exact spit of him."

"I owned all your books, David," Joe said, embarrassed. "My uncle used to buy me the new one every Christmas. I knew Daisy and Wilbur better than I knew most of my family."

"Really?" David looked absolutely delighted. "That's wonderful! What was your uncle called?" He picked up a pencil, his thick red hands curling uselessly around it, until it slipped out of his grasp. "Damn it. My hands are bad today. Having terrible trouble doing anything."

"Alfred, and he's dead, so don't worry." Joe put his hand on the older man's trembling fingers, immensely touched. "David, everyone in my school had something from Wilbur."

"Oh, well. Isn't that terrific, though?"

"Yes." Joe grinned. "Now, I'll leave you to get on."

"No—oh, do stay and chat," David said sadly. "I hate being in here all on my own. Especially days like this."

"I'd best get back. Mrs. Winter wants you to do some work." Besides, Joe was already feeling he'd spent enough time in this house, getting into all their business. The way they pulled you in, all of them, without stopping to ask you if you wanted to—it was crazy, charming, discombobulating. His head was throbbing. "I've got to head back to the pub for evening service."

"Well, this is awful news," David said. "Absolutely ruddy awful." He plucked the gingerbread out of his jacket pocket. "I might eat this, then have a nap. Don't tell Martha. Deadline's later."

Joe left, shutting the door softly on David picking up his pencil again. He walked back toward the kitchen, and as he did he heard Martha's raised voice.

"No, Lucy. Absolutely not. I can't believe it. How dare they even ask you? How much has Southpaw done for them over the years?" There was a clank of something, a crack of china clashing. "Oh, damn it. I've a mind to ring them up, give them hell."

Joe hovered, not sure whether to go in; but he didn't want to eavesdrop.

"Please don't, Gran. It wasn't their idea, it was mine. Forget it."

"Your idea!" Martha laughed. "Lucy, after everything—absolutely not."

Lucy's voice was thick. "I wouldn't put anything in you didn't want, Gran. If it's a terrible idea, of course I'll leave it. I just wondered why I can't simply e-mail Daisy and ask her why she's—"

Martha's hissed reply was so soft Joe barely heard her. "It'd be a pretty bad idea, that's all." Then she added, as if she knew someone was outside, "Is that Joe, then?" Her voice was sharp. "What are you doing, hanging around listening to us bicker?"

"Sorry." Joe came in, scratching his head. Lucy was flushed. Martha put her hand on her soft hair, and stroked it.

"Forgive me, darling. I shouldn't have lost my rag. Joe, do you want some more tea? Or maybe a glass of wine? I could do with a glass of wine."

Joe looked at the clock. "I'd best be off soon. Let's just nail down the rest of the menu and then I'll go."

Lucy pushed her chair out. "I'll pop back to Dad's, dump my stuff. I'll see you back here for supper then, Gran? I'm sorry." Her eyes were still bright, feverish almost. She swallowed, then turned to Joe. "Someone rang you. Oh, and your phone kept buzzing, someone's texting you."

"Oh, that'll be my mum . . ." Joe began. Liddy texted him all the time. And then he looked down, saw the most recent text gleaming up at him before it faded away into black glass, and his mouth turned dry.

This is it, he thought. *I've been found out.*

See you later? I can get away.

But Lucy was staring fretfully at her grandmother, and he couldn't be sure if she'd read it or not. His finger throbbed as though darts of toxic poison were gushing into his body, and he braced himself, but all Lucy said was, "So, um. Maybe I'll see you at the pub sometime, I hope?"

"Absolutely," he said. "Come down whenever. Tell someone at the newspaper to come and review it. We need all the help we can get."

She stared at him thoughtfully. "Maybe I will. Thanks, Joe."

Lucy shrugged and picked up her bag. "I'd better get back to Dad," she said, and as she left, she threw a swift, secretive smile at Joe. He genuinely didn't know what it meant.

Florence

"*Pronto!*"

"Professor Lovell. You wanted to see me?"

George Lovell laid down his pen and gently placed the pads of his fingers together. He closed his eyes and inclined his head very slightly. "Yes. *Adesso, Signora.*"

Florence shut the door and sat down on one of the high-backed mahogany chairs which, common rumor had it, Professor Lovell had "liberated" from an abandoned palazzo near Fiesole. "In any case," she said, "I wanted to ask you if I may take some time off in November. Three days, I think."

"I take it this is not part of your work for the Courtauld?"

"No, holiday. I'm visiting my parents." Florence plunged her hands into the pockets of her skirt and smiled as engagingly as she could at him.

Professor Lovell sighed. His eyes rolled upward until he was staring at the tufty overhang of his brow. She watched him and wondered how he held that position, totally motionless, like an owl.

"George?" Florence said after a few moments. "Ah—George?"

"Florence. This, again. Again."

She was taken aback. "What again?"

"Going off in the middle of term."

"What?" Florence cast her mind around. "That? But that was two years ago, and it was an operation," she said. "I had a mole removed and it turned septic. You must remember."

"Yes, the famous mole on your back," said Professor Lovell, in a tone of voice that suggested he doubted the whole story.

"I got blood poisoning afterwards," Florence said in what she felt was a mild tone. "I nearly died."

"I think that's exaggerating it somewhat, isn't it?"

Florence crossed her hands in her lap. She knew Professor Lovell of old and there was no point in contradicting him. She could still see the nuns in the hospital round her bed as she drifted in and out of consciousness. She could hear them anxiously wondering in Italian about the *signora* and whether she was Catholic and would she like prayers said over her body, for surely she was not long for this world. "Again, I'm sorry about that." There was no arguing with George when he was like this. "It's my mother's eightieth birthday. I am owed the holiday, you know."

"Hmm." Professor Lovell nodded. "That's as may be. But, Professor Winter, Professor Connolly and I have been wondering." At Peter's name, Florence smiled privately, for merely hearing his name spoken in public felt like a luxury. "This was his idea, and perhaps it is appropriate to ask you now whether you would like to take some time off?"

Florence began to wonder whether George was losing his mind. "Well—that's what I was asking for. Yes. Three days in November."

"No, Florence." The professor's hand came down on the old desk. "I meant—a term or two. Give you some time to assess your options." He wouldn't meet her eye. "You're a busy woman, now you have this Courtauld job." He said the word "Courtauld" in the same way one might say "tumor" or "Nazi."

Florence stared at him, bewildered. "But, George—there's the paper on 'Benozzo and Identity' to finish for the conference in December, you can't have forgotten. And my book—I have a lot of reading to do on it. A lot."

Professor Lovell gave a sardonic laugh. "Your book? Of course."

"It's not the same level as Peter's, of course . . ." Florence began, and George smirked. *Of course not.* "But it's important nonetheless. And the spring lecture series—I really only want three days away next month, not two terms."

"Right." George Lovell sat back in his chair, hands on the armrests. There was a faint sheen of perspiration on his smooth, yellowing pate. "Florence . . . how do I explain this clearly? We think it's time for you to take a step back. This is not a demotion, nor is it age-related. But we need lecturers with a more diverse approach to complement our syllabus, and to that end—"

"*What?*"

"To that end," he repeated, ignoring her, "Professor Connolly has appointed Dr. Talitha Leafe to assist us in the art history faculty. I know the pair of you will work extremely well together. She's extremely talented, very enthusiastic—her specialties are Filippo Lippi and Benozzo Gozzoli—"

Florence felt like Alice, tumbled down a hole and out into a world that made no sense. "But—that's *my* specialty." She pointed above him. "Look! Look at the book behind you on the shelf! *Studies in Benozzo Gozzoli and Fra Filippo Lippi*, edited by Professor Florence Winter! That's why you employ *me*, George. You don't need this—Tabitha Leaf? *I'm*—"

"Talitha Leafe," George broke in. "Tally," he added, unnecessarily.

Florence narrowed her eyes, trying to think clearly. So this was it. She knew they couldn't fire her on account of her age, because last year they'd tried to get rid of Ruth Warboys, an excellent ancient history professor, and replace her with a twenty-four-year-old boy with slicked-back hair who had a Twitter account. Ruth had hired a lawyer and kicked them down the street, and the twenty-four-year-old had not been heard of again. Young blond WASP boys were right up Professor Lovell's alley, Florence knew: she and George had been at Oxford together, and she remembered the time he'd turned up for a formal hall with a black eye, the result of some misread signals from a fellow choral society member at Queen's College. George was peculiarly arrogant about his own chances. Florence had noticed that unattractive men often were.

But girls, girls like this Talitha—*Talitha?*—Leafe, that wasn't his area of interest. It just didn't add up.

"We have discussed this at length, Professor Connolly and I. And we also feel the burden of your extra work at the Courtauld, not to mention your penchant for traveling to conferences, as well as your . . . your *behavior*, well—it might all be compromising you a little." Professor Lovell shifted in his chair.

"My behavior?" Florence said, astonished.

"Come on, Florence. You must know what I mean by that."

"No, I don't." She screwed up her nose.

"You are a little—unpredictable. Particularly of late." George tapped his Adam's apple. "And you have become something of a talking point, with various insinuations . . . and so forth."

"Insinuations?" Florence could feel a watery sensation flooding her body, making her head spin. "Do elucidate, George, please. I'm afraid I have absolutely no idea what you mean."

Professor Lovell bared his teeth with a smile that didn't reach his eyes. "Come now, Florence. I'm afraid the facts about your workload speak for themselves." He added, in what was clearly supposed to be a kindly tone, "Perhaps you've simply taken too much on, my dear."

"What about Peter taking on too much?" she demanded. "Since the TV series and that book, he's never here. And he makes mistakes. I don't make mistakes. You can hardly castigate *me* when your head of department has taken it upon himself to become a media personality, George."

"That is an entirely different matter," squeaked George. "*The Queen of Beauty* is an enormous hit. The value to us of Peter being a . . . a . . . 'media personality,' as you put it, is incalculable."

"He didn't even get the date of the Bonfire of the Vanities right!" Florence said, trying to stop her voice from rising. "He was on some silly BBC breakfast program and he couldn't say when the most notorious event of the Renaissance took place!"

"A lapse," George said, irritated. "Live television, Florence. He got it right in the book, didn't he?"

"Of course he got it right in the book!" Florence shouted, and then stopped abruptly, and the two of them stared at each other, eyes wide.

Don't say it. Just leave it well alone. She bit her tongue.

"You may scorn it, but what Peter's doing is the future, Florence. Times are tough and your jetting off to London every two months to give up your best research to the Courtauld is not particularly collegiate, is it?"

As news of Florence's Courtauld appointment had come through, it emerged that Professor Lovell had applied for a similar post at the same time—but without success. His specialty—Holman Hunt—was out of fashion. Florence loathed Hunt, and found it rather satisfying that George couldn't understand why no one else was as interested as he in hyperrealistic, moralizing paintings of symbolic goats, fallen women, and ghastly pink and blue babies.

She could see very clearly what this was all about. They were scared of her, so the old boys' club was closing ranks. She reminded herself of what she did, in fact, know, the damage she could do if she just opened the hatch and gave her craziness full rein. She could hear the words forming.

You know I wrote most of Peter's book for him. You know if I were to tell anyone, it'd be a scandal big enough to close down the college.

And yet she couldn't do it. She wasn't brave enough. Was she? She wished she had a coffee. She always thought better after coffee. She sat silently, almost slumped in her high-backed chair, listening to George's reedy, precise voice.

"This isn't immediate. We'd want to see a change come January 2013. Dr. Leafe is getting married at Christmas, of course, and she starts here in the New Year. She would very much like to meet you, work out a way in which the two of you—"

Florence stood up abruptly. "Is that the time? I have to go. Do forgive me. I have a meeting with . . ." She stared up at the ceiling, trying to sound calm and steady. "Rat controllers. I have rats. Well, George, I shall consider what you say and get back to you."

Professor Lovell stuck his fat lower lip out. "I shall be in touch, if you are not."

Florence put one trembling hand on the door and took a deep breath. "Well, we shall talk anon, no doubt, though I warn you I intend to defend my own patch extremely vigorously. Incidentally, your desk has woodworm. Good-bye!"

She even managed a cheery nod as she exited.

She ran until she was out of breath. It was only when she reached the other side of the river that Florence stopped and realized she was shaking, head to toe. She disliked confrontation, almost as much as she disliked mice. She had eschewed teaching and become an academic for that very reason, only to find out too late that the world of academia was like fourteenth-century Florence, riven with internecine strife, internal politics, and wordless betrayal. Increasingly these days it reminded her of growing up with Daisy, where she didn't know the rules and couldn't work out when the attack would come. At least the Florentines occasionally massacred each other at Mass to clear the air. Much more straightforward than all this creeping aggression and stress, which ate away at her, like waiting for one of Daisy's little plots to explode.

Talitha Leafe. What kind of name was that? With a thrill, Florence wondered if this was a legitimate inquiry she could make of Peter.

"Oh, *Peter*," Florence said aloud, scuffing one worn shoe on the ancient cobbles. Every single moment of those few weeks that hot summer were imprinted in her mind like an album of holiday photos, one she could flick through whenever she cared to, which was often. And she always felt quite the woman of the world when thinking about him, about what had happened. She liked acting as though things were normal around him, in front of other people especially. The idea that people might be gossiping about them thrilled her. *Professor Winter and Professor Connolly? Oh, yes. Apparently they had a fling a few summers ago. He was mad about her, I heard.* Yes, that was how she wanted people to think of her. Florence Winter: dashing, mysterious woman of letters, academic, passionate lover, brainy, vital woman of today.

Something touched her leg; Florence jumped, then realized it was her finger. Her skirt had a hole in the pocket. She scraped her nail on her naked skin. Her legs were hairy; she couldn't remember the last time she'd shaved them. Say if she were to meet Peter, right here, walking down the street, as had happened that Tuesday in January. He'd been on his way to dinner with friends in the Oltrarno. Niccolò and Francesca, she'd remembered their names, looked up their address.

Say they got talking, then she asked him up for a glass of wine. They'd sit on the roof terrace, a tiny space no bigger than a picnic blanket, looking out at the Torre Guelfa and the Arno. Say they laughed about George and his peccadilloes, the way they used to before Peter started freezing her out, treating her like she was an embarrassment. Say then that he put his hand on her knee as she said something funny, and laughed. "Oh, Flo." He always used to call her Flo, and it reminded her of home. "I miss you. D'you miss me?"

"Sometimes," she'd say, smiling just a little archly at him; she didn't want to seem girlish.

And say he simply took her hand and pulled her into the bedroom, peeling off her clothes one by one, and say they made love in the warm, terra-cotta–colored chamber, the sound of the evening bells in the distance, the sheets rumpled, their faces rosy and glowing with pleasure. . . . Say it were to happen, well, he wouldn't care, would he? He hadn't cared before. It had been so lovely, like that. . . .

Florence peered up at the blue sky, framed by the black, shadowed buildings, her hands pressed to her burning red face, a secret smile playing on her lips.

Someone laughed, and she looked up, almost surprised. Two spinsterish tourists, British, she knew it, were staring at her. She hurried on.

Florence lived on the top floor of an old palace, now divided into apartments, on the Via dei Sapiti. Her apartment had once been a prince's chamber, and when she'd moved in ten years ago there had been several old pieces of furniture that no one had ever claimed and of which Giuliana, her landlady, professed to know nothing. Florence liked to think they might have been there for centuries; that perhaps some scheming nobleman had hidden letters in the wedding chest, or a knife under the great wooden chair.

She closed the huge wooden door on the outside world, feeling quite light-headed. She needed coffee, that was it. She wandered into the tiny kitchen. It had a plug-in gas ring, an espresso maker, some dusty packages of pasta and tomato purée, and a vigorous, thickly scented basil plant flourishing, against all odds, on the windowsill. Like the Boccaccio story of Isabella and the pot of basil, which, alas, always reminded her of yet another awful Holman Hunt painting. It was so typical of someone like George. How could you live here, among this great art, and still admire Holman Hunt?

Florence set the battered Bialetti on the gas ring, and flung open the warped doors that led out to the terrace. She breathed in, as the golden evening sun fell on her tired face. She could hear children playing in the street outside.

It was moments like this that she realized how much she loved it here. The sun, the smells, the feeling of being alive, of possibility. When she'd first arrived on a sabbatical, twenty years ago now, she hadn't intended to stay. But her brain worked here, like being plugged into the right socket. How she longed for Italy when she was back in England, where the damp and the gray seeped into her bones and made her feel wet, woolly, soggy. She didn't want to end up like Dad, clawlike hands, pale and gasping for sunshine, or like Ma, shut up, closed off. It was here she had discovered who she was.

Waiting for the coffeemaker to boil, Florence put the books she'd brought home on her desk, staring at the frieze of *The Procession of the Magi*, which she'd Blu-Tacked up there herself many years ago. She shivered suddenly, thinking about her meeting with George. Florence was no good with instant reaction; she needed to go away and sift through the data presented to her.

Think about it later, she told herself. She'd leave if she had to. Why was she staying here at this second-rate college, humiliated by men who weren't her intellectual equals? Why did she care so much?

But she knew the answer. Peter. She would always stay while he was here and she thought he might, one day, need her again. Sometimes she wondered if she'd deliberately made him into the engine that kept her pushing along, and now it was too late to admit she was wrong. Florence stared at the pictures she'd pinned up, scanning them for something, some message. Her eye fell upon the only one in a frame—the reproduction of her father's favorite painting, *The Annunciation* by Fra Filippo Lippi, which they'd visited every year for her birthday. She gazed at the angel's calm, beautiful face. Something important, buried deep in her consciousness, was tapping at the edges of her weary brain. A thought, a memory, something that needed to be salvaged. She looked at the boy again, at the shaft of light on Mary's womb.

What's going on?

The coffeepot rattled on the gas ring, the black liquid bursting like oil from the funnel. Florence poured the coffee, and as she took the first scalding sip the doorbell rang, so shrill and unexpected she jumped, and the cup trembled, spilling half the contents onto the floor.

"Bugger," Florence said under her breath. She went over to the door, frowning; her fairly eccentric landlady had a habit of waiting until Florence had been back for half an hour, then stomping upstairs, demanding a translation of something, an explanation of something else, an argument with someone.

But it wasn't Giuliana, and as she opened the door her face froze.

"Florence. Hello. I thought you'd be in."

"Peter?" Florence clutched the door. Had she conjured him up by thinking about him? Was he real? "What are you doing here?" And she smiled, her eyes lighting up.

"I had to see you," he said. "Can I come inside?"

She knew him so well, every inch of him committed to memory for years now through intensive recall and daydreaming. It was often a surprise to her, as now, to note that he was wearing something she didn't recognize. Florence smiled at him as she held the door open, noting the squeak of his new shoes, the faint scent of aftershave. He had made an effort.

"I was just having some coffee."

"Of course you were." He gave a little smile.

She blushed; he knew her better than anyone, she knew it.

Peter cleared his throat. "I wanted to talk to you, Florence. Have you got anything to drink? I mean, some wine?"

"Absolutely." Florence shoved her hands in her pockets, to stop herself fidgeting, and went into the kitchen. "A lovely Garganega, delicious, just like the one we—"

Just like the bottle we had at Da Gemma that evening, when you had the lamb and I had veal. We did drink an awful lot, then we argued about Uccello and kissed afterward for the first time, and you were wearing that tie with the tiny fleurs-de-lis on it, and I had the blue sundress on.

"Sounds delicious. Thanks, Flo, old girl. Listen, I'm sorry to burst in on you like this. . . ." Peter followed her into the kitchen. He hesitated. "God, I haven't been here for a long time. Lovely place you have. As they say."

He gave a little snort and she did too, almost unable to believe this was happening, that this was real time, instead of some elaborate fantasy she had constructed. *It's not, is it? Am I completely crackers?*

Part of her wasn't sure she should trust him. But she also knew he still felt something for her. She was sure of it. And even if he slapped her now, or told her he'd been married for ten years and wanted her to be godparent to his child, even if he urinated on the floor, she could still say that he'd been here, still have some fresh memories to add to that photo album in her head. In fact, she thought wildly as she ushered him out onto the tiny terrace with a soft push on his back, nothing she owned or thought or had meant as much to her as this, this moment right here.

Peter sat down, folding his gangly limbs into the chair. Florence watched him. Though his mind was the most precise she had ever come across, his body, like hers, seemed constantly to take him by surprise. She put the scratched old tumblers down on the rickety table, and handed him a bowl of olives. He took one, chewed it, threw the pit over into the street.

"Bloody tourists," he said, as the babble of Japanese from below momentarily stopped.

Florence handed him a glass. "*Salute*," she said.

"*Salute*," he answered, and he clinked his glass to hers. "To you. Good to see you, Flo."

"And you, Peter. We're quite the strangers these days."

"I looked for you yesterday. I wanted to ask you about an inscription in Santa Maria Novella."

"Oh? You should have called me." She wanted to sound beatific, happy, self-contained, a woman with her own life yet who would always, always be waiting for him.

"Yes. Perhaps I should have."

There was silence then. Florence stuck her finger through the hole in her pocket again, arched her back, and wondered if she could quickly excuse herself to shave her legs. *Always be prepared.* Her brother, Bill the Boy Scout, lived by this motto and had tried to impress it upon his chaotic sisters, to little effect.

The bells from over the way rang out, a loud metallic clamor. The sound of a police car faded away in the distance. She breathed in the warm, petrolic, pine scent of evening.

"I miss you, Peter," she said eventually. "I'm sorry. I know there's other things going on, but . . . I do. I wish—"

And she reached out to touch his arm.

It was as though she had flicked a switch. Peter jerked his head up and swiveled toward her. "This is what I mean, Florence. That's why I need to talk to you. It's got to stop."

"Talk to me . . . about what?"

"You. *You* . . . and me. This lunatic idea you have that there is something between us." His jowly face was suddenly taut, and he jabbed a forefinger at her. "The hints, the insinuations you've been making to people. I know you told the chap from the Harvard Institute we'd had an affair. Dear God, Florence! And the Renaissance studies seminar group. One of them asked me if it was true. I tell you, I will sue you for slander if this goes on."

Florence tugged at her hair, hanging on either side of her cheeks. "I—what?"

"Do you deny it?"

"I have never told anyone, *anyone*, about our relationship. Peter, how could you?"

Peter's voice dripped scorn. "It *wasn't* a relationship." He downed the rest of the wine in one gulp. "Florence, it was three nights. Four years ago. Don't be ridiculous. That's not a relationship."

"Four," Florence said, her voice shaking. "It was four nights. And you said—you said you loved me."

"No! I *didn't*!" Peter stood up, his face red with fury. "When will you give up this pathetic fantasy of yours, Florence? I know what you do. You hint and you nod your head and smile, you say these half sentences, and you make people believe it was something."

"I have never done that!"

He wiped his mouth, looking at her with disgust. "Florence, you told Angela that you'd seen my bedroom, but that you obviously couldn't say any more than that. You told Giovanni that we'd discussed getting *married*! But that you weren't keen and he wasn't to mention it! I get a phone call from him asking me if it's true! You *have* to stop this, it's . . ." He searched around, shaking his head. "It's—it's rubbish! We had three—okay, okay, *four* nights. That's it. Understand?"

There was a terrible silence. "You d-d-*did* say you loved me," Florence said after a pause, her voice breaking.

Peter leaned over her. A white spot of spittle glistened on his lip. "One sentence said after too much wine against four years of total indifference? You're building a case against me based on *that*? Doesn't hold up,

Florence." He waved his long, thin hands at her. "Don't you mind how damned tragic it makes you look?"

Florence stood up, as though she were stretching. She took a deep breath, and patted his arm. "Peter. Don't be horrible," she said. She needed to recast herself. Needed to know this was going to be all right when he left. "I'm sorry I've made you angry. Obviously some people have . . . got the wrong end of the stick, taken things I've said out of context." She peeked down at him, then pushed her glasses along her nose. "Now. What was it you wanted to discuss? Or was that the nub of it?"

"That—yes. And, well, there was something else. It is linked. It's all linked, as you will agree," Peter said rather grandly, but he glanced at her uncertainly and Florence knew she had the power back, if only momentarily. He was scared of females, that indefinite group of humans with breasts and hormones and bleeding.

"Well, have some more wine," she said, turning back into the kitchen. She picked up the bottle.

"For God's sake, Florence," Peter said. His heavy brows suddenly shook with rage. "Are you actually taking any of this in? Don't twist this all to suit your ideas for once. Just listen."

"Gosh, Peter, how cross you are," she said, trying to keep her voice light, but suddenly she was afraid. "Why are you being like this, is it b-because you're a big star these days? And you don't want to be reminded of your past mistakes? Mistakes, Peter. You have made mistakes, haven't you?"

"What does that mean?" He looked up warily.

They'd never discussed what she'd done for him. Florence bit her tongue, but she was too upset now, and she couldn't stop the words pouring out.

"You know what it means. Remind me . . . how many weeks did *The Queen of Beauty* spend at number one?"

"Shut up."

"How much have your publishers offered you for your next book?" The questions flew out of her, bitterly, eagerly. "What did you tell them when they said they wanted the next book to be *just as good as the last book*? Did you tell them you'd have to ask *me* to write another one? Did you tell them that?"

"I don't know what you're talking about," he hissed, his eyes widening, his face going pale under his tan.

She laughed. She felt quite mad, and really didn't care anymore.

"Jim asked me if I'd written it, you know. Out of the blue."

"Jim?"

"Jim Buxton. At the Courtauld."

"Oh, come off it. The man's a liar. And an idiot. What Jim Buxton knows about the Renaissance you could write on a matchstick."

"He knows me. He said he could tell it was my writing, not yours."

"That's because he wants to sleep with you, I expect. He's always been eccentric." He looked at her with disgust, and she almost laughed; it was cartoonish, his revulsion toward her.

"Jim's not—" Florence wrapped her long arms around her body. "Nevertheless, he specifically asked me if I'd written any of it. Someone gave it to him for Christmas—he wanted me to understand he hadn't bought it himself. I thought that was quite funny. He said the writing style is quite obviously mine, if you're aware of my other work."

Peter Connolly laughed. "You're pathetic."

"No, Peter, I'm not," Florence told him smartly. She was feeling almost confident again. He couldn't push her around . . . he had to see how much he meant to her now, that she was willing to subjugate herself totally to his needs, already had done. "You owe me so much, Peter, but you see, I don't mind." She walked toward him; had she judged this right? "I like it like that." She stared up into his face, at the dark, clever eyes, the drooping mouth.

"Oh, God," he said.

"I know," Florence replied. "We're even now, don't you see? Darling, I'll do anything for you."

He pushed her away. Actually shoved her, hard, in the breastbone, repelling her like a force field, and Florence stumbled, catching hold of the rusty railings. "God." The revulsion on his face was horrible to see. "You don't understand, do you? You don't get it."

"What?" she said.

"What? I'm getting married in a few weeks. Didn't George tell you? Because before Tally arrives we'll need to reorganize the department, and you and I need to discuss how best to do that." His voice took on a beseeching tone. "Listen, we worked well together in the past . . . which is why I thought a one- or maybe two-term sabbatical might be the answer for you. To get you and Tally both used to the situation."

"Tally," Florence said blankly.

"Dr. Talitha Leafe. George said he'd told you."

"You're marrying *her*?"

"Yes. Once again." Peter glanced at her wearily. He jangled his keys in his jacket pocket as if to say, *When will this be dealt with? When can I leave?*

"You can't," she heard herself say.

"What?"

There was that voice again, pushing her, like a finger jabbing in the back when one is standing on the edge of the precipice. "If you marry her . . . I'll—I'll tell everyone I wrote *Queen of Beauty*. I'll sue you, Peter. And the publishers."

"You wouldn't." He sat back and laughed. As if he was so confident of his position at the top of the tree, and she some grubby little minion in the shadows. "Don't be silly. Listen, Tally's at the Sorbonne at the moment. You'll meet her soon. You just need to get used to the idea, understand that some of your responsibilities will change. . . . After our marriage she'll move to Florence, and of course George has very kindly done his best to be accommodating, and that means—" He broke off. "Florence? Florence?"

For Florence had walked through the apartment to the huge old door. She turned and looked at him.

She opened the door, Peter staring at her all the while.

"No. You can't treat me like that," she said clearly. "Not anymore."

"Oh, come on, you can't run off like you always do—" Peter began, getting up, exasperated, but Florence went out, slamming the door behind her so hard that the whole building seemed to shake. She ran downstairs, past old Signor Antonini and his little wife, past Giuliana, wailing loudly in her kitchen to Italian pop. She ran through the old palazzo door, down the street, the balls of her feet bare on the hard old cobbles, her hands deep in her pockets, hair flying behind her. She passed out of the Porta Romana, the ancient gate south of the city. The sun had set now, and the heavens swelled into a deep lavender-blue, clouds above her, gold stars pricking at the velvet sky.

• • •

As she ran the old memory resurfaced: the day Daisy had pinned her up against the wall and told her where she'd come from. Whispered this filthy, awful stream of stories into Florence's small head, lies about their dad, about the Winters, about everything Florence believed in.

Florence had run away then too, through the woods at the front of the house that covered the hill and led down to the village. She'd tripped on the brambles twined into the trees, torn gashes in her spindly legs, but kept on going. She'd ended up at the church and sat in the graveyard, hiding behind one of the angels guarding the grave of a child who'd died years ago. She was nine. She'd never been this far away from home on her own before, and she didn't know how to get back.

It was Dad who'd found her, much later that evening, feet drawn up under her chin, little voice piping out Gilbert and Sullivan songs to keep her teeth from chattering in the cold spring dusk. He'd crouched down, inky hand leaning on the angel.

"What have we got here, eh? Is that my little Flo?" His voice was light but a bit strained. "Darling, we've been looking for you, you know. Mustn't run off like that."

Florence had stared at the lichen blooming on the old stone. "Daisy said you're not my mum and dad."

David had stopped stroking her hair and looked down at her. "She said what?"

"She said you're not my mum and dad, that my real mum and dad didn't want me, and that's why I'm here, and I'm not like any of the rest of you."

David had shuffled closer to her, sideways, like a crab, then put his arm round her thin shoulders. "Darling. Did you believe her? Is that why you ran off?"

Florence had nodded.

He'd been silent then, and Florence was terrified, more afraid than at any time with Daisy. That he was going to say, *Yes, it's true, I'm not your daddy.*

She could still remember that feeling now. The black hole of fear that the one person in the world she loved more than anyone else would be taken away from her. That Daisy would win, that she'd have been right.

Her father had pulled her head close to his. She could hear him breathing fast. She held her breath. *Please. Please don't let it happen. Please . . .*

But after a while he simply whispered in her ear, "That's rubbish. You know you're much more my daughter than she is." Then he sat back a little. "Don't tell anyone your old dad said that, hmm?"

"Oh, no," Florence said, giving a little secret smile, still looking down, but when she stole a glance up at him shortly after, she saw he was smiling too. Then he held out his hand. "Come back with me? Ma's made a lemon cake and she's been so worried about you. We all have."

She stood up, brushing the fresh black earth off her pinafore, her tights. "Not Daisy. She hates me."

"Wilbur's just died, she's sad about that. Let's be kind to her, though. She doesn't have what we have." It was the only time he acknowledged it really, and she always remembered it. "Come on. It's time to go home, Flo."

They trudged back up the road to Winterfold, and as they reached the drive her father had said, "Let's keep this to ourselves, shall we? You pretend to Daisy she never said anything. And if she does ever say something, tell her to come and see me and I'll set her right."

There was a tone in his voice then, and she nodded. When Dad was angry he was scary, really frightening. Florence wondered if he ever said something to Daisy, because she left Florence alone for a month or two, until the next time, the wasps' nest, which nearly killed Florence, and which she knew she couldn't ever actually pin on Daisy. Daisy wasn't stupid. She'd always known exactly when to pounce.

Eventually Florence stopped running. She collapsed onto a graffitied bench in an old square filled with bashed-up cars, staring at the cobbles below her. There was no one this time to come and pick her up, to tell her it was all a lie. No one who'd say, "They're all wrong and you're right."

She knew her dad hadn't told her the truth. She didn't know how or why, just knew. Daisy was never wrong about things like that, and when she'd pinched Florence's arm and said, "You were a bastard orphan and no one wanted you, little sister, so they picked you off the scrap heap, otherwise you'd have been kept in a home," Florence knew she was right. She didn't know how she'd found out: Daisy knew how to get into secret drawers, how to hear private conversations, how to twist and turn situations to get what she wanted from them.

It struck Florence then, sitting on this bench surrounded by empty Peroni bottles and cigarette butts, the night's chill cooling her sweating limbs, that it was all the same now. She'd been fooling herself again.

She wondered when she could go back to the flat, if Peter would still be there. She wondered how long it had been coming, this realization that despite how she liked to run away, she'd got it all wrong. How long she'd been kidding herself about her life here, about living away from home. And as she sat with her head in her hands, she wondered if she'd always known that at some point, she'd have to go home and face the truth again. What came next she didn't know.

Karen

"Hello, love. Sorry I'm late. How are you?"

"Oh, hello, Bill." Karen didn't look up from the couch where she was reading a magazine, or pretending to read. She raised an eyebrow and turned a page. "How was your day?"

She didn't need to watch to see his little ritual every evening. She knew it off by heart. The way he carefully wound his scarf once around the banister. Always just once. He'd take off his coat, thumb precisely flicking the buttons out, one-two-three in a row. A little shake before deftly hanging it up with one finger. Then the clearing of the throat and a rub of the hands. That hopeful, kind look on his face.

He wore that expression now. "Good, thanks, my love. I'm sorry I'm late. Mrs. Dawlish . . . she's very shaky since the fall. I paid her a quick visit to drop off the pills and ended up staying on for a cup of tea. And—how about you?"

"Crap. Annoying." Karen ran one finger over the bridge of her nose up to her forehead.

"I'm sorry to hear that." Bill picked up the post on the hall table, thumbing carefully through it. She watched him in silence.

Their marriage was based on silence these days. More and more. What they didn't say was everything, and what they did, inconsequential.

After a minute or so Bill looked up from his credit card statement, his brow furrowed. She could tell he was trying to remember what she'd said, pick up the thread, carry on with the steps of the dance. "So, what's up? Is it work?"

Karen shrugged. "They're announcing the layoffs next month."

His eyes flickered briefly to meet her gaze. "Are you worried? Surely not. Your review was great, wasn't it?"

She wasn't in the mood for him to be right. "That was four months ago, Bill. It's a big company. Things change fast. You don't—" She pressed her hands to her cheeks. "Never mind." She sounded hysterical, she knew. Sometimes she felt as though she was going mad with it all. "I can feel a headache coming on. I might go out for some fresh air in a bit. I said I'd pop round Susan's birthday card."

"Oh, right." He dropped the little pile of his post onto the bureau and stood behind her, then tweaked one of the cushions on the sofa. "That's nice."

"What's nice?" Karen had picked up the magazine again.

"You. Seeing Susan. I'm glad you two are friends again."

"After I set fire to her hair, you mean?"

"Well, it's nice you have a friend in the village."

She threw him a glance of amused contempt. "You make it sound like it's a real achievement."

Bill went into the kitchen. "I didn't mean it like that." He never picked a fight, and it drove her insane. She really wanted him to tell her to shut the hell up and stop being such a cow. To grab her by the shoulders, kiss her, and tell her she was in need of a good seeing-to. To sweep the damned letters off the stupid hall table and push up her skirt, bending her over the immaculate cream Next sofa, until they collapsed on the floor, tangled, smiling, his hair ruffled, their warm bodies flushed with the sensation of nakedness. She wanted to see the man she'd fallen in love with, the sweetly awkward, fastidious, and kind man who was late for their first date because he'd stopped to help a young mother whose car had broken down by the A36. Who lived to be useful to others, who made himself indispensable, who chuckled with hilarity like a toddler being tickled when he spoke to his daughter, who used to look at Karen as though she were a goddess come to life before his very eyes. Everything was always all right when Bill was in the room.

She blinked, staring into nothing, and then followed him into the kitchen.

"How was your day?" she said, guilt making her attentive. She smoothed her hand over his close-cropped hair.

Bill was rubbing his eyes, tired. "Oh, all right. I had Dorothy in again. She's in a bad way. Oh, I bumped into Kathy, she said she'd had Mum's invitation to the drinks on the Friday. Everyone seems excited about there being a party at Winterfold again. Very nice."

Karen went over to the fridge. "Supper's ready, in fact. Want a glass of wine?"

Bill shook his head. "A cup of tea'd be nice first."

"I'm not making tea. I'm opening wine."

"Right, I'll put the kettle on, then," he said imperturbably.

Karen poured herself a drink, her mind already running through the list she kept at the front of her thoughts. She had an early start tomorrow, 8:00 a.m. train from Bristol to Birmingham for a conference. Suit hanging in spare room. Sandwiches for train. Presentation locked and loaded on laptop. Rick's notes typed up—her boss e-mailed her all the time, and you had to transcribe it to make sure you'd got everything he'd said. Rick was exacting, to say the least, but Karen liked order. And she liked a challenge, relished it, in fact. Lisa, her best friend back home in Formby, was always saying Karen was born to have children.

"You're the most organized person I know," she'd said, last time Karen was back home. "You'd deal with the—Megan, leave it, okay? You'd deal with not being able to take your eye off them, getting everything ready in the morning, knowing how to get one into the bath and give the other his tea. *No! Niall!* You stop that, you little monster. I've had enough of you, I'm telling you. Honestly, Karen, you'd be great. . . . Any plans?"

Any plans? Any plans? She perfectly recalled Lisa's intense, slightly cultish expression, the one all mothers assume with childless people, like they *have* to understand exactly what it's like because they can have no concept of how wonderful and natural and fulfilling it is. She'd left soon after. But the truth was that what she couldn't forget, what she found more disturbing, was the warmth created by the mess and haphazardness of Lisa's life. Her bungalow near the sea, overflowing with broken toys and discarded clothing. Awful childish paintings stuck all over the place. Silly magnets on the fridge, "World's Best Mum" and all of that. But it was a home, a safe, welcoming place; and as Karen set the little dining table, she looked around at the life she had created with Bill. She couldn't see how any number of armless dolls and pieces of Lego would make their cottage feel like home.

Karen's parents had divorced when she was ten. She and her mother were both neat freaks, and enjoyed nothing more than having a really good go at the oven. After her mother had been to Winterfold for the first time, just before Karen and Bill's marriage, Mrs. Bromidge had grabbed Karen's arm on the way home.

"That fireplace!" she'd said. "Doesn't it drive them up the wall? All those ashes? It's summer, they don't need to keep it burning—why don't they get a nice fire effect? Or get gas?"

Her daughter couldn't help but agree. Karen often thought the difference between her world and the Winters' was that she believed in gas fires and much of the time at Winterfold seemed to be spent lighting or replenishing the fire in the huge hearth of the sitting room. But she didn't say that to her mother. She had to be loyal to this strange family she'd chosen to enter. She made sure Bill's house had a gas fire, though.

New Cottages was a row of four almshouses down from the church, one of which Bill had bought after his divorce. A couple of months before their wedding Karen had, with Bill's agreement, had the place redecorated so it felt a bit more modern, a bit less like the home of people who wore nylon nighties and smelled of Yardley English Lavender perfume. She'd moved those possessions of hers that weren't already there over from her single girl's flat in Bristol. There wasn't really room for them. It was a tiny house. That first night, over Chinese takeout and some white wine, sitting on a blanket on the new cream carpet because the new sofa hadn't arrived yet, Bill had said, "If something or someone else comes along, well—we'll have to think about scaling up, won't we!"

He'd said it in that Bill way—gently joking, with a puckered brow, so that she could never quite tell how serious he was about it. And when, a year and a half later, she'd mentioned it—"I've not been on the Pill for nearly a year, Bill, isn't it strange nothing's happening?"—he'd just smiled and said, "It'll take a while, I think. You're thirty-three, but I'm old. I'm fifty!" That was what he'd kept on saying. *It'll take a while.* Eventually, as with so many things in their marriage, she'd given up. He was so closed-up, like a clam, like his mother. Karen liked Martha, always had. But she didn't know her. She just knew that behind that cool exterior there was something there, some secret storm. But did Martha ever show it? Course not.

She was getting more and more frustrated, trying anything to get a rise out of him. When, a year ago, Karen had thrown a tea mug at him and the splintering china cut his ankles, Bill had said, "That was a bit dangerous, Karen. Maybe don't do it again." Six months ago, she'd stormed out, after a row about something so stupid she couldn't even remember it now. She hadn't come back till morning. He hadn't texted her until lunchtime.

Do you know where the torch is?

Why was he like this? How could he be so passive? It drove Karen mad. At first she'd tried to change him. Lately, she'd simply stopped trying.

They had dinner in silence, opposite each other at the tiny table. Bill ate methodically, lining up each morsel of food like a balancing act; Karen sometimes found it hypnotic. When the watery garlic butter burst through the meat of the chicken Kiev and landed on his napkin and not his shirt, she was almost disappointed.

She was silent because she'd got used to it. Before, she'd chattered away. Now it was less effort, less disappointing, to just sit there and eat. Like those couples you saw on holiday, sitting there with nothing to say to each other. She'd think things instead. Wonder about this or that, her mind racing, her heart pounding at how bad she could be if she pushed herself. It surprised her, she'd never thought she was the kind to have an overactive imagination; and she was in the middle of a mental conversation with him about their sex life when suddenly she heard Bill say, out of nowhere, "I wonder if Daisy'll come to this thing."

Karen blinked. "What thing?"

Bill speared a single pea with one tine of his fork. "Ma's party. Wonder if she'll even remember it's her own mother's eightieth birthday."

Karen didn't know quite what to say. "Course she will, she wouldn't forget a thing like that. Anyway, your mum's asked you to all be there, hasn't she? That odd invitation and everything."

"I'm not sure. It's typical Ma. It's her strange sense of humor."

Karen wasn't sure about that. She had the feeling it was more than having a slightly idiosyncratic sense of humor. "Okay, then. Well, I'm sure she'll be there."

Bill opened his mouth, then shut it, then said slowly, "You don't know Daisy."

He wants to talk about it. "Well, I know what you lot say about her. Or rather don't say about her. She obviously loves your mum, even if you and Florence don't like her much."

"Of course I like her. She's my sister."

"That's not the same thing."

Bill sighed. "I mean . . . there's something there. Despite everything she's done, I still love her. We're family."

"What exactly did she do, though?"

He shrugged, a classic boy's slump of the shoulders. "Nothing. She just isn't very . . ." He mashed a clump of peas against his knife. "She's mean."

A bark of laughter escaped Karen. "Mean! What, she used to hide your things and call you Smelly? That's no excuse, Bill!"

"She called me Lily," he said, staring at the plate. "Billy Lily. 'Cause she was Daisy Violet and Florence's middle name's Rose, and she said I was the biggest girl of all." He rubbed his eyes. "But you're right, it's silly. She didn't do anything terrible—"

"I thought she stole the Girl Guides' money from the bring-and-buy stall at the church fête and spent it on pot?"

"Oh, yeah." Bill was stroking the bridge of his nose. "How d'you know that?"

"Sources." She tapped her nose. "Lucy told me."

"How does *she* know that?"

"Your daughter knows everything," Karen said. "And she told me Daisy nearly set the barn on fire smoking a joint with some guy from the village when she was back from traveling."

He stared at her for a second, almost visibly debating whether to have the conversation or not. "Well, I have to say she was a bit of a druggie before she took off. And she did stuff. I've often wondered . . ." He stopped.

"Wondered what?"

"It sounds rather hysterical if you say it out loud, I'm afraid. Events beyond my control. Although now she's turned into this angelic figure who saves orphans and raises all this money, we're not allowed to criticize her." He laughed. "Don't mention that to Ma, will you?"

"You lot are crazy," Karen said, piling the plates together with a crash and almost throwing them onto the breakfast bar, which connected them with the kitchen. "Why don't you ever talk about it? I mean, why did she leave in the first place? She never sees Cat. It's mad." She could hear the Mersey in her voice, coming out the more she spoke. "And Cat's mad too, while we're at it. Over in Paris and won't let anyone visit her, like she's a leper or something."

"That's not true. Cat comes home." She knew Bill was very fond of his niece. "She's just busy, that's all."

"She works in a flower market, how's that busy? She used to be some amazing fashion journalist mixing with all these designers and all sorts, and now she's selling potted plants, Bill." She knew she sounded cruel, but just for once she wanted to shake him out of his quiet, repressed complacency. "She hasn't been home for more than three years. Don't you have to wonder what that's about?"

But her husband merely shrugged. "She had that chap, Olivier, he sounded like bad news. He went off to Marseilles. Had a dog, Luke. Left the dog behind, left Cat to look after him, from what Ma said. The whole thing was a bad business, poor old Cat." Bill poured himself another glass of wine. "He was a nasty piece of work."

Karen found she wanted to scream. "What does that mean? Was he abusive? What did she need to get over?"

"I don't know, Karen," Bill said, and he looked sad. "I feel rotten, that's the truth. Haven't been in touch. Things just slide, don't they?" He rubbed his forehead, staring blankly at the tablecloth. "Did I tell you about Lucy?" He didn't wait for her answer. "She wants to write some article about it for the paper. 'David Winter's Family Secrets,' something like that."

Karen took a moment to digest this. "That's what it'll be called?"

He hesitated; she saw the sadness in his face and felt a sharp pain in her heart. "You know what these newspapers are like; they've learned nothing. They love picking over the bones of . . . things."

Karen felt herself shivering in the warm room and gave herself a little shake, as Bill leaned forward on his crossed arms. "I don't want to say no to her, but I'm not sure about it. I don't think it's a good idea, raking it all up. It'll just upset Ma."

"You say things like that, but I never really know what you mean, Bill," Karen said. "Raking what up?" She wished she could keep that note of impatience out of her voice. "Daisy's selfish, if you ask me. So's Cat. They could come back and they don't. As for Florence, she's in another world. And Lucy—it's about time she got on with her career. She's always saying she wants to be a writer, make it big and all that, and she does nothing about it." Bill and Lucy's closeness annoyed her now, as it always did when she got cross with Bill, and she wanted to hurt him. The way they laughed at the same stuff, the way his eyes lit up at a clipping she'd send him or a postcard or a cartoon from the *New Yorker*. Lucy had lived with him after the divorce, and their closeness excluded Karen. Lucy was full of life, a breath of fresh air, too big and clumsy for their small house. Karen wasn't part of their world, and she tried not to let it get to her, but sometimes it crawled out: a nasty, spiteful, childish desire to hurt. "You're the only one who seems to care about your parents. The way things are at the moment just leaves you shouldering everything down here."

"I'm not shouldering anything." He smiled sadly. "I like being here. I like popping in on Ma and Pa. I'm not like the girls. I'm the boring one. I like a quiet life."

Their eyes met and they stared at each other across the small table. There was a short silence. Karen knew she'd ruined the evening now; perhaps this was the moment to go. She stood up and crossed her arms. "I'm sorry. I'm tired and it's been a long day. I'm working too hard. Do you mind if I pop out now, drop that card off?"

Bill stayed in his seat, looking down at the grain of the wood.

"Bill?"

After a moment he said, "It's Susan, is it?"

Her voice trembled. "Yes, it is."

He glanced at her. "Give her my love."

"I will . . . I will." Karen turned away, putting her coat on.

"I've been thinking." Bill sat back slowly. "Maybe you need a break. After the party. Maybe we should go to Italy. Florence—we could see Florence. Or Venice. A mini-break in December, before Christmas. Karen? What do you think?"

Her heart was thumping so loud in her chest Karen felt sure he must be able to hear it. She rummaged in her pockets, then reached for her keys, buying time.

"Sure."

He got up and came over to her. "I know things haven't been—I know things are difficult." She nodded, slowly raising her chin so she was looking straight into his eyes. Her husband. His brown eyes, so solemn, so sweet and kind. A pang of memory shot through her like a comet streaking through the darkness, reminding her that she hadn't been wrong, that there had been something there once. "We deserve a break, both of us. We could get some practice making that baby," he said softly, as if it were a secret.

Karen put her hands up to his and they were both still, forearms touching. She breathed in, then out, slowly, trying to suppress the wave of nausea that threatened to sweep over her. *You're a doctor,* she wanted to shout. *Haven't you noticed it's been more than three years and nothing's happening in that department?*

Instead she shook her head.

"Maybe."

"Oh." He gave a small laugh, and his fingers grasped hers. They were warm: Bill was always warm. "Maybe's better than nothing, I suppose."

Karen said, "I'd better go. Susan'll be—"

"I know," he said. "I think I'll probably be asleep when you get back. Long day."

"Sure. Sure . . ."

Karen picked up the card so carefully propped up on the hall table— more post—and opened the door. Bill said softly under his breath, "Night, then." And as she walked hastily away, shivering in the sharp autumn night, Karen knew she should feel free, but she couldn't.

Cat

Cat—

*I cannot look after Luke that weekend in November. Luke is not
my problem anymore. You made that clear when you took him
away from me. You can't now have it both ways.*

*If you go and see Didier at Bar Georges in the eleventh he will
give you the envelope I meant to give you. Something to help you
in it. I think you will find it beneficial.*

Olivier

CAT READ THE e-mail and slammed the laptop shut so hard the corrugated plastic roofing of the stall rattled in the rain. Water dripped off
the roof and onto the edges of the ornamental lavenders, the sunny mari-
golds and geraniums. Tourists huddled miserably against the birdcages
crammed with brightly colored canaries who sang all day, an incessant
cheeping that filled the air but which Cat had long ago stopped hearing.

She didn't have time to go see Didier. But she had to. He'd got her,
again. She had to get back to Winterfold, and the price of the train ticket
was, these days, beyond her reach. But even the thought of going back to
the eleventh arrondissement made her angry and afraid. It was the idea
that Olivier still had the power to drag her back to her old life.

Once Cat had lived not far from the eleventh, before she met Olivier,
and if she could have seen herself now she'd have been astonished at
whom she would become. She had had a year of unemployment sprinkled with gardening jobs after university, until the magical day when

101

she'd heard she'd got the job as editorial assistant on *Women's Wear Daily*. It came after months of job applications, which had severely tested Cat, shy at the best of times, violently full of self-doubt and lanky awkwardness at the worst. When the letter arrived at Winterfold (she'd kept that letter, the one that brought her here; it seemed so quaint now, a *letter*) offering her the position, Cat had jumped up and down in the hallway, then clung to her grandmother, almost hoping Martha might beg her not to go. Even though all Cat had ever wanted to do was live in Paris and this job was more than she could ever dare to hope for, it still seemed too hard, too much to have to leave this place where she felt so safe, where she had been, she thought, so happy. She'd been away, to university in London, though that had been nothing really but extended periods where she always knew she was coming back to Winterfold. This was different. She was twenty-two, and this was the beginning of real life.

"I don't want to leave you both. I don't want to . . . do a runner. Like Daisy." Saying her mother's name was always strange. The *D* sang out like a bell, and she felt as though strangers might turn and stare: "Oh . . . it's *that* girl. Daisy Winter's daughter. Wonder how *she'll* turn out."

But her grandmother had been surprisingly firm.

"You're not your mother, darling. You're nothing like her. Besides, you're not some recluse who's never left home. You've spent three years in London, you've got a degree, and we're so proud of you, darling girl. But I think this is the right thing to do. Don't be afraid of going. Just make sure you come back."

"Of course I'll come back. . . ." Cat had laughed, and she remembered that bit, how ridiculous it had seemed that she might not return to Winterfold, but at the same time she knew her grandmother was right. Her friends were all getting jobs, moving on; it was time for her to do the same.

She arrived in Paris in the spring of 2004, a little unsure, already homesick. She found an apartment not far from Café Georges, on a little *cité* behind boulevard Voltaire. She had four window boxes, which she carefully tended, one tea trunk from home that stood in as a coffee table, an IKEA bed, a chest of drawers her grandmother and Uncle Bill brought over a fortnight later in the car, two hat stands from a market in Abbesses with wire strung between them for use as an open wardrobe, and a set of ten wooden hangers stamped *Dior*, acquired the same day. She loved playing house, her first proper grown-up home. It made her feel independent for the first time in her life.

Her bare, beautiful flat was usually unoccupied, though. She was either in the office or out with her boss, taking notes at meetings with designers, visiting studios for private views, or, during the biannual Fashion Week, dashing from show to show, sitting in the back row with the other penniless fashionistas, scribbling notes and trying to learn as much as she could. Her favorite part of her job, though, was calling on the individual ateliers and watching the stout, middle-aged Parisian seamstresses who had worked at Dior for years, seeing their flying fingers sewing the hundredth sequin of a thousand onto a shimmering, glittering fishtail train, pinning a tiny tuck-seam on a model's silk shirt, sliding butter-thick velvet through their machines, tidying, smoothing, finishing, their quick fingers transforming an inert piece of fabric into something magical.

Cat grew to find the world of fashion ridiculous, but never this, the beating heart of the business. It was why she had always loved gardening with her grandmother, for she already knew that creating a beautiful vision to be enjoyed by others meant hard work behind the scenes. Everything had to be perfect, even a seam that no one would see, because if it was to be done it must be worth doing. Her grandmother had always said there was only one rule to gardening: "The more care you take, the greater the reward you'll reap."

She sent Martha regular updates, letters and then e-mails. At first, Cat hardly went back, maybe because she loved the place too well, and a clean break seemed better than constantly revisiting; then, as her life in Paris took root, the trips home became even more infrequent. In the beginning, Martha had come to visit once a year; that had been wonderful. They'd shopped in Galeries Lafayette, walked in the Parc Monceau, strolled through the Marais.

Her grandmother had asked Cat once, as they wandered by the Seine, looking at the vintage prints and books for sale: "Are you happy? Do you like it here? You know you can always come back, don't you?"

Cat had simply said, "Yes, darling Gran. I love it here. It . . . it fits."

Martha had said nothing, just smiled, but Cat had seen tears in her eyes, and thought she must be thinking about Daisy. Out of the ashes of nothing except her grandparents' love and her grandmother's insistence that Cat must make something of herself, she had fashioned this life, and when she told Martha that it fitted her, she knew it was true.

Then she met Olivier.

One sultry June day, in a *boulangerie* around the corner from her apartment. So Parisian, so romantic. "We met in a *boulangerie* in Paris," she told the girls in the office, smiling, her cheeks rosy with shy happiness. "Olivier was buying croissants, I was buying Poilâne, we picked up the wrong bags—*voilà*." Appearances could be deceptive—Olivier didn't eat bread, it transpired; he had been collecting the pastries for a friend. She only wondered when it was all over who the friend was. A girl, waiting in bed for him while he picked up someone else. He had said, "I like your dress, English girl," and Cat had turned to give him a sharp, colloquial put-down, and been arrested by his tousled black hair, his brown eyes, his beautiful pink mouth with the amused smile playing about it. He was a jazz trumpeter, played every week at the Sunset, and had his own group. They were trying to make it work. He was good, she could just tell.

She was ashamed—or a little proud, she didn't know afterward which—to recall that they had slept together that very day. Yes, he had taken her out for coffee, and she had said she would buy him a glass of wine that evening, and so after work they had met in a little bar behind the Palais-Royal, in a cellar that was supposed to be part of Richelieu's old palace. They had each ordered a kir and picked at a plate of *saucisson* and cornichons, and after two drinks he had simply said, "I do not want to drink anymore. Will you come home with me?"

His apartment was tiny, the shutters flung open, the sound of people carousing, arguing, singing floating up from the street below all night, as they came together in a way she had never known she needed before. Cat was organized, controlled: she feared more than anything else being like her long-lost mother, a woman who had so little clue of how to live her own life she had had to leave everyone behind, go to the other side of the world to help people worse off than she was.

So at first she was horrified to discover, three years after moving to Paris and establishing her life so beautifully, that everything had collapsed like a pile of cards. That Olivier's strong, smooth hands, cupping her breasts and moving along her arms till his fingers twined with hers, his knee pushed between her legs, his lips on her neck, his words in her ear . . . filthy wet words that made her moan; that all this could quite simply unman her—unwoman, in fact, although she had never felt more womanly, never felt so sensuous and sexy in her life. The rest of that summer was forever in her mind an ache between her legs, where she wanted him inside her all the time. She grew pale and stringy: while her workmates were tanned from holidays, the sea, the outdoors, Cat was inside with Olivier, whole weekends lost in a haze of sex, sleeping, eating, the whole cycle over again. She was so happy, she felt like a new person, reborn here in Paris with him. He had not known her as the spotty, awkward, thin teenager, the girl without a mother. He only saw her as the person she had remade herself into, and he loved that person, or so he said, and so she loved him for it, even though all the time she kept wondering, *When will he find me out?*

Afterward she would look back and see how short a time the happiness had actually lasted. By winter the signs were all there, but she chose to ignore them. It made her sick, how stupid she had been. What was crazy was how long she'd let it go on.

How foolish she'd been, she saw that now, too. In the New Year she'd given up her flat, moved in with Olivier. She had gone home for Bill's wedding in 2008. To everyone's sly inquiries and Lucy's open enthusiasm about this mysterious boyfriend, Cat was noncommittal. And they didn't ask more. She had been a low-key, sardonic person for so long now that her lack of cozy tidbits about life with her French boyfriend didn't surprise anyone. "Typical you," her aunt Flo had said. "You always were a dark horse, Cat."

But I'm not, Cat had wanted to tell them. *I think I've made a terrible mistake.*

At the reception back at Winterfold, after the curious wedding in the Guildhall, she was trying to text Olivier, wondering what he'd want her to say. She felt something gripping her arm, and she jumped. It was her mother; it was Daisy.

Cat looked down at Daisy's tiny, skeletal fingers pressing into her arm.

"I'm just trying to send this text." She was short. She hated this, being here, feeling so out of place.

Daisy had leaned forward, skull-like face mirroring Cat's.

"Don't try to pretend I'm not your mother, Catherine. We're the same. I know it. I see it in you. We're exactly the same, so stop thinking you're better than me. You're not."

The scent of lilies in the cool dining room; Karen's white dress, flashing in her peripheral vision; the hot sun outside, beating down on the yellowing grass. Her mother's voice, hoarse and silvery. "I know what you're like, Cat. Stop fighting it and get on with it."

Cat had removed Daisy's fingers from her arm. She'd leaned back, away from her thin, awful face. "If I'm like you, God help me too," she'd said, and walked toward the open door.

That was the last time she'd seen her. Cat went back to Paris knowing she couldn't ever tell any of them what was really going on. She just had to make the best of it, because she was lucky, wasn't she? It was wonderful, wasn't it? She had such high expectations, because of her mother, because of everything, and she should just stop being so difficult, as Olivier said, and shut up.

And it was such a boring cliché. The gradual change, so that within months she had gone from glorious certainty in his love to absolute certainty that he despised her and that he was right to. The sudden absences, the unexplained behavior, the hours she'd spend waiting for him, only to have him turn up angry at her because he said she'd gone to the wrong place. She lost all confidence in her ability to make decisions. How often, when evening fell and she grew hungry, had she stood dithering in the hall about whether to start cooking for him? Was he nearly there, would he want some food? Or would he be back hours later and shout at her for letting his meal go cold? "How the fuck am I supposed to eat this—this shit, Catherine? You're so selfish, you couldn't wait another hour? What, okay, an hour and a half? So I met some friends—they're important contacts—I'm supposed to rush home because if I don't I'm not allowed any supper?" He always made it sound like he was right, and she always ended up apologizing.

They acquired a dog, a wire fox terrier called Luke, after Olivier's English grandfather, a soldier who'd stayed on in Brittany. When Cat laughed at this—naming your pet after your grandfather seemed to her a crazy thing to do—Olivier slammed out of the apartment and didn't come back till the following morning. At first he was obsessed with Luke, as though he were a son, or a new best friend—taking him for walks in the Tuileries Gardens, even once to a gig, where Luke sat obediently on a chair next to his trumpet case, Olivier exclaiming with pleasure when Luke did *un caca* on the parquet floor—but soon, as Cat was realizing, as with everything in Olivier's life, the obsession waned, to be replaced with disinterest, annoyance, and then downright contempt. Luke, still not quite a year old, did not understand why, when he trotted over to his master and stared hopefully at him, he was ignored or batted away with one big, hairy hand. "*Vas-y! Vas-y,* you stupid dog."

It was through Luke that Cat started to realize what a mistake she'd made, but it was longer still before she saw that it wasn't her mistake— that he had hoodwinked her. She was worthless to him except as a pretty plaything; and once that bored him, she—like Luke—was of no use. On the day that changed everything, she had coffee with Véronique, an old, very dear friend from work. They had once been almost the same: girls with long brown hair and fringes who giggled together over male models at the shows and saw each other into cabs after one too many glasses of champagne; they had struggled up flights of stairs with each other's boxes, moving into tiny apartments; they had slept on each other's couches and shared lunches. But these days Véronique was al- most a parody of everything Cat should have become. She had worked at *Women's Wear Daily* and was now at *Vogue.* She had shiny, glossy hair, patent-leather Marni sandals, a black Paul and Joe chiffon top finished off with a tailored pink blazer, and matching baby-pink nails. Cat, who barely cared what she looked like these last few months, was in dirty jeans, pulled-back ponytail, and blue Breton-striped top. She couldn't be bothered to dress. She felt sick all the time, a tight nausea at the back of her throat, she wasn't hungry, and she couldn't sleep.

"What the hell is wrong with you?" Véronique had said immediately. When Cat had tried to explain, she'd shrugged her shoulders in horror. "Why are you still there? Leave, for God's sake, Catherine! This man is . . . he's killing you slowly. What if you have children with him?"

A tear had run slowly down Cat's cheek. She brushed it away.

"I know," she said. "I had a miscarriage six months ago. He was glad. I was too, after a while, and now . . ." She started crying, pressing the heels of her hands into her eyes, rocking forward and backward, uncaring of who might see her.

After a while she said, "Sometimes I wish he'd hit me. To prove it. Maybe I deserve it."

Véronique had leaned back as if she'd been hit herself, and there was a silence.

She didn't leave him that day, nor that week; but once the words were out, it became something tangible. The look on Véronique's face—complete bewilderment, pity, a tiny flicker of disdain was the closest Cat could come to describing it—was almost a wake-up call: the two of them had once been so close, not just in temperament but in stages of life.

When it was all over Cat could see how lucky she had been. She had got out before he'd sucked her further in. She had nothing else, and so much water had flowed under the bridge, the many bridges, that she could not now, ever, ring up her grandmother and explain. Martha, who had been so proud of Cat, who had raised her to be like herself, not like her mother.

The last time Cat had seen Martha was before Christmas a year ago, when she came over for lunch and to do some Christmas shopping and "to see you, darling, because I feel I don't know anything about your life now."

They met in Abbesses and ate *confit de canard* in a dark red bistro with views over the city. It was very different this time. There was so much Cat couldn't tell her grandmother now. Something huge had happened to her, and somewhere along the way that had meant cutting everyone else out to try to cope with it.

Cat said as little about herself as she could. They walked around the shops in a desultory way, time dragging, until the hour abruptly came for Martha to leave if she was to make her train, and then she was gone. But Cat couldn't help but keep with her the gloved hand on her arm. The whisper in her ear: "We're always here when you need us, darling. Never forget that."

Then the desire to blurt it all out had nearly overwhelmed Cat. To sob on her grandmother's shoulder, tell her about Olivier, about Luke, Madame Poulain, about how she had nothing, how she sometimes missed lunch, how she had taken two pieces of bread off the table in the bistro for later. How she was doing everything wrong and couldn't just change one thing, needed to start again completely to have any hope of unpicking the tangled threads of her life.

But at the fatal moment Martha had gently, for a split second, looked away, then at her watch, and—

"I must go, darling. Are you sure you're all right? Tell me, you will always tell me, won't you?"

"Yes, yes." She had kissed her grandmother again, saw the tiny chink of light closing. "Please don't worry about me. How can anyone be unhappy, living here?"

The scudding December clouds, the twinkling fairy lights golden in the gathering gloom, the soaring towers of Notre-Dame, the honk of the *bateau-mouche* below as Cat watched Martha hurrying toward the Métro . . . She turned for home, alone again, knowing that something had changed. Too much time had passed. She could never really go back. This was her life, whether she had chosen it or not.

The following afternoon, Cat opened the door of the Bar Georges, just off the rue de Charonne. Despite her misgivings about returning, she liked the eleventh; real Parisians lived there, families—it reminded her of a happier time in her life. She checked her watch, always making sure she wouldn't be late for Luke. Forty minutes. Twenty minutes here, twenty to get back.

She waved hello to Didier, the owner, and took a seat at the bar.

"*Ça va, Catherine?*" Didier was polishing coffee cups, and expressed no surprise at seeing her after three years. "*Un café?*"

"*Non, merci.*" Cat spoke in French. "Didier, I had an e-mail from Olivier yesterday. He said you have an envelope for me."

Didier nodded. "Yes." He carried on polishing the cups.

"Well . . . can I have it?" Cat said, trying not to sound impatient.

"He's pretty sad, Catherine," said Didier. "You have been very cold."

Cat closed her eyes very slowly. "Huh-uh," she said. She nodded. *Don't get cross.* She pictured herself rolling up into a tiny ball like a wood louse, no part of herself visible or vulnerable. *Think of what you have to do.*

Didier reached under the cold white marble bar. He produced a square brown envelope. Cat stared at it; it was thick. "This is it?" she said, but she knew the answer. Her name was on the front, the handwriting she knew so well.

"Yes."

"So, you saw him?" Cat asked.

"I was down in Marseilles for the jazz festival. He asked me if I could help. I was glad to." Didier slid the envelope across to her.

Cat didn't know whether to open it in front of Didier or not, though her hands were shaking. In the end, she stood up and, clutching the envelope, waved it in front of him. "*Merci, Didier. Au revoir.*"

"You don't care how he is?"

She stopped and turned. "Olivier?" She wanted to laugh. "Um—yes, of course. Does he care? About us?"

"Of course he cares," Didier said, looking faintly disgusted. "How can you say that?"

"Evidence suggests otherwise."

"You are the one who left him."

Cat stood perfectly still. "I was pregnant," she said.

"Yes, and—"

She cut across him. "He nearly broke me." She said it very quietly, so quietly she wondered if Didier would hear. "He would have done the same to—to Luke."

"He loved that boy. Like he loved that dog, and you—"

Cat shook her head. "No, this is wrong, you are wrong," she said. Already she was terrified that Olivier was here somewhere, that he'd demand to see Luke, that he'd follow her home like before, that this was a trap. "He chose his name. I let him call him after his stupid dog, don't you see how crazy that was? Don't you see I'd have done anything to keep the peace? To stop him. . . ." And it didn't matter now, it didn't matter at all; but when she thought of any of it, it made her remember how low she had been. She had to leave. She had to get out of here, get back to her son now. She waved the envelope. "*Au revoir.*"

"*C'est pour Luke,*" she heard him call as she banged the door behind her, stepping out onto the narrow street.

Fingers fumbling, Cat pulled open the sticky glue, tearing into the thick paper. She felt ridiculous, desperate as she was, standing on the street unable to wait until she got home. Her hands touched something smooth, not crinkly and rough as she'd expected. She pulled out . . . a piece of cardboard. Thick, corrugated, plump cardboard, with a heart drawn on it in a wobbling line of Biro, arrows shooting out of it, dripping with blood.

Underneath he'd written:

YOU DID THIS. I HOPE YOU ARE HAPPY.

Her first reaction was to laugh. How pathetic. Then anger gripped her, anger that he could yank her around like this, like a dog on a lead. She could hear him laughing at her now. She looked up and around, as if expecting to see his dark face leering out at her from an upstairs window. He'd always loved "practical" jokes, tricking people. He was laughing at her stupidity, at how she thought she was free but she wasn't, because she'd still drop everything to collect a package from him.

She was like a dog, like a whipped dog; that's what he'd called her the day after Luke had run away, out into the street, never to be seen again. The old Luke. "You're my dog now," he'd said, and he'd gripped her by the throat and pushed bread into her mouth until she'd gagged and managed to break free.

Cat threw the cardboard into the gutter.

The voices in her head, calling out for her to do something stupid, go back to Didier and scream at him that his friend was a beast, that he had made her like this, that he had ruined any chance he had with his son, were rising again. With a supreme effort of self-control, she ignored them. She scuffed her shoes on the dirty streets, feeling with every scrape on the ground that she was somehow wiping Olivier from her feet. When she reached the Métro, she banged open the plastic ticket barrier and walked downstairs onto the platform, hugged herself, pulling the thin cardigan around herself so no one else could see she was shaking.

After all that, she was early. She knew where she'd find them, just before the Pont Marie in the little Jardin Albert Schweitzer. As she approached, Simone, the mother of Luke's friend François, looked up from her magazine.

"*Bonjour, Catherine.*"

Cat nodded, smiling. "*Merci beaucoup, Simone.*"

Simone smiled a little stiffly. She was one of the many people to whom Cat owed a huge debt, one she would never be able to repay.

Using up their goodwill when Madame Poulain's was exhausted. Relying on the kindness of strangers, people to whom she could never fully explain her situation.

"Maman!" She looked up at the sound of his voice, the thudding steps, the feeling of hurtling toward happiness that was always, always the best part of her day. "Mum, Mum, Maman!"

He threw himself into her arms, her little Luke. His thick dark hair, his hard little body, his babbling chat, his sweet, high-pitched voice, caught between English and French all the time, as she was.

He was hers, all hers. And he was all that mattered.

"Maman, Josef eat a snail last week! He eat a snail!"

She wrapped her arms around him as tightly as she could, brushed her lips on his forehead. "Ate."

"Ate. Can we have pasta for tea?"

At the memory of her sad self standing on the pavement scrabbling to open an envelope that wasn't full of money but a patronizing pawn in Olivier's little game, suddenly Cat felt something lifting up and away, and floating out over the road, out to the Seine, away with the churning river. Something that made her feel free. She said good-bye to Simone, and she and Luke crossed the road toward the bridge that would take them back across to the island. She clutched Luke's hand, so tightly that he shook her arm.

Everything was getting better. She saw it now. It could be good again, one day. She kissed his hand. It was a victory of sorts, for someone who'd had the fight knocked out of her a while ago.

THAT EVENING, CAT crept quietly out of the *chambre de bonne* and downstairs to the kitchen. Madame Poulain was out playing bridge, as she was every Tuesday evening; it was the one time of the week Cat had to herself. Free from the little room she shared with her son, sweltering in summer, freezing in winter; free from Madame Poulain's vermouth-soaked ramblings; free from the back-aching work when she had to stay late at the market. Sometimes she watched boxed sets that Henri lent her—she was very into *Game of Thrones* at the moment—but it was strange, watching episode after episode of *Spiral* or *The Wire* on your own. Usually she read. She made herself an omelet and salad and ate in a daze, staring out the window at the dark of the Seine and the glistening lights of the Left Bank. Not really thinking; just letting her whirling brain slow down a little.

Then she curled up in the big armchair with a glass of wine and a green Penguin paperback she'd been given by one of the booksellers on the riverbank, a nice old chap she said good morning to whenever she crossed the bridge. More and more she found herself drawn to the novels of her childhood, the books that filled the upstairs shelves at Winterfold: Edmund Crispin, Georgette Heyer, Mary Stewart.

Cat was utterly absorbed when the phone rang, and she looked at the screen with annoyance: Henri was always ringing to check up on his mother.

But no. *Appel international.* International call.

"Allô?"

A hesitant voice down the line: "Cat? Oh, hello, Cat!"

Cat paused, her wineglass halfway to her mouth. No one ever called her on Madame Poulain's landline.

"Who's this?"

"It's Lucy. Oh good. Your mobile was switched off. I didn't even know if this number would work. I'm sorry, are you in the middle of something?"

Lucy's voice, the same as always: how could she not have recognized it straight away? Cat put the book down and said cautiously, "No, it's lovely to hear from you. How—how are you?"

"Good, good. Thanks." Lucy hesitated. "I think I'm living round the corner from BO Bee Man, though. That was partly why I rang, actually."

"No way."

"Way. He's got the T-shirt and everything."

Incredulous, and yet wanting to believe it true more than anything, Cat asked, "Is it black and yellow?"

"Sure is."

BO Bee Man was a regular fixture of their seaside holidays in Dorset. He appeared on the beach at midday, clad always in black jogging bottoms, a black baseball cap, a black and yellow bumblebee-style T-shirt, and big black specs. He was about three hundred fifty pounds and walked very slowly up and down the promenade. Lucy once claimed she'd seen him weeing on a chained-up dog, but Cat never believed this. Lucy was a bit of a fantasist.

Cat snuggled tighter into the chair. "That is so random. Where do you see him?"

"On the way into work. He's got massive foam headphones. He listens to Bon Jovi and Guns N' Roses at full blast."

At that, Cat couldn't help but laugh, the tightness in her throat releasing just a little. "Please, *please* take a photo of him," she said. "You have to."

"I'll try to catch him unawares. He usually walks past while I'm going down the Kingsland Road."

"Dalston? What on earth are you doing round there, Luce?"

"Well, I live there," Lucy said. "It's lovely."

"Get away. Dalston was like murder row when I lived in London."

"How long have you been away?" Lucy said, sounding cross. "Eight years? Dalston's like . . . it's the new Hoxton."

"Don't I feel stupid," Cat said mildly.

There was a pause.

"Listen," Lucy said, sounding embarrassed, "I won't keep you. I just wanted to know if you're coming back for Gran's thing next month."

"Um—I hope so." Cat hesitated.

"Oh."

Cat could hear the disappointment in Lucy's voice, and she knew how much it must have meant for her to ring, and how much she missed her, and she said, "I'm coming, yeah. Absolutely. I just need to book my ticket and—sort out a few things."

"Oh, right!" She sounded so pleased, and Cat felt the warmth of being wanted, loved even, running through her veins. "That's so great."

"Thanks!" Cat said, almost gratefully. Then she added curiously, "Um, what was that strange stuff on the invite about, do you know?"

"Not sure." There was a small silence. Cat wished there were a button she could press, to take her straight into the groove she and Lucy had once had, the easiness that seemed to pick up where they'd left off every time: holidays, bank holidays, Christmas. Clare, Lucy's mother, was often away, and then Bill took Lucy to stay at Winterfold. Every summer there was Dorset as well, a cottage of an old friend of their grandparents on Studland Bay. They had so much fun, that was the thing. They were both only children and, though there were a few years between them, they loved being together, were more like sisters than cousins for a while. Lucy, bold and imaginative, invented the plays they put on and the songs they sang. Cat could make anything, headdresses for a story about Greek gods, bushy leafy tails for *The Lion, the Witch, and the Wardrobe*, and the one time when she really got in trouble: the summer of Cutting Up Her Mother's Dresses for Dolls' Clothes.

Martha had been furious—alarmingly, frighteningly furious—when she came into Cat and Lucy's room just after the school holidays had begun and found them crouched over Daisy's frocks, fixing pieces of fabric together with David's huge industrial-size stapler. Cat had never seen her grandmother upset like that. The lines of her grandmother's sculpted, delicate features were drawn into a rictus of rage: nostrils flared, thin eyebrows arched, teeth bared, like a hissing, angry cat.

"This was her room. She left those dresses for you, Cat. When she left. You remember?"

"Course I don't remember. I was a month old."

"Don't be cheeky." She'd thought her grandmother might slap her. "She left them for *you*, she said they weren't to be shared with anyone else, and she certainly didn't mean for you to ruin them. How—how *could* you?" Martha had picked up the curved scraps of useless fabric in handfuls, letting them fall through her fingers. "The only things, the *only* things she gave you, she wanted to be yours, and you've ruined them. I can't—no, I can't."

Glassy pools of tears wobbled in her cold eyes, and she had turned and walked out.

Cat had had to stay in her room for the rest of the day and night, alone, while Lucy slept in her father's room on the floor. The long Laura Ashley seventies floral robes like a medieval princess might wear, the demure violet velvet sheath, the white lace confirmation dress, the printed silk sundresses, all in little pieces, were taken away and Cat never saw them again. The holidays passed as they always did, in a constant carousel of silly voices, funny dances, hidden treasure, songs they changed the lyrics to and sang over and over.

But something changed then too. The result of the episode with the ruined dresses was that Cat never really talked to her grandmother about her mum anymore.

After a pause, Lucy said, "If I'm totally honest? Things are a bit weird down there. That invitation's only part of it."

Fear clawed at Cat's stomach as she said, "I thought it sounded a bit odd. The way it was worded."

Lucy paused. "Well, Gran must have something to tell us all, mustn't she?"

"Is she okay?"

"I think she is. I mean, she's going to be eighty." Lucy drew in her breath. "I think Southpaw's a bit crook these days."

"Really? How? What's wrong? What's he . . ." But the words died in her mouth. *Come home and see for yourself.*

"It's not about him, really."

"What's it about?" Cat said. She tried to keep her tone level, but she thought she might be shaking. She couldn't tell. She was scared, though. Lucy was like the gate back into Winterfold, into a world Cat had to keep shut out.

Lucy took a deep, ragged breath. "Oh, Cat, I don't know. The more I think about it all . . . maybe I shouldn't say."

She sounded miserable, and Cat felt a rush of sympathy for her.

"Hey, Luce," she said. "Don't tell me if you don't want."

"It's about my dad. Dad and Karen. I'm worried about him. Well, about her, really."

"What do you mean?"

"Something's going on." Lucy clicked her tongue. "I think—I heard her on the phone, last time I was down. Talking to someone. She's having an affair, I'm sure."

"Oh, no, Luce." Cat put down her drink. "Really? Could it have been your dad?"

"Dad was in the bath. Singing along to *The Gondoliers*. And I know it wasn't him. You could just . . . tell." Lucy's voice grew distant. "She sounded really excited. Happy. She hasn't sounded like that for ages. . . . Oh, poor Dad. I knew she'd do him wrong," Lucy said angrily. "I bloody knew it, the moment I met her."

"I liked Karen," Cat said. "Can't you—talk to her? Maybe you've got the wrong end of the stick. Do you have any idea who it might be?"

"No," said Lucy. "I thought it might be this guy Rick at work; she's always going on about him."

"Who is he?"

"Her boss. And she said something about giving him HR problems with his work . . . how she didn't want him to get into trouble because of her. In this awful flirty voice. Yuck. It probably is him, you know . . . he's a creep. But—oh, I don't know." She gave a big swallowing sound. "Just . . . I don't know what to do. And I feel as though if I could just talk to Dad, gently explain it . . ."

"Sometimes there isn't anything you can do, Luce," Cat said. "You've always worried too much about your dad. He'll be fine."

It was the truth and, as so often with the truth spoken aloud, it hung in the air like a sign written by a skywriter. They were both silent.

"You're right," Lucy muttered. "Look, I'm sorry. I didn't mean to ring you up and pour my guts out to you, you know, Cat. I just wanted to ask if you were coming back. And, you know, say hi and everything. How's . . ." She hesitated. "How's life?"

"It's good. How's things with you?"

"All right. I can't complain." Lucy sounded flat. "It's fine. I'm lucky to have a job, I keep telling myself that. And, yeah. You know. Flat has mice and my flatmate's cat won't catch them. Love life's a disaster. Except for this guy who's just started at the pub, you'd love him, I've already got a huge crush on him." Lucy talked when she was nervous, Cat knew.

"He works at a pub in Dalston? Is he a hipster? Moustache? Weird rolled-up trousers?"

"No, Cat! The Oak, in Winter Stoke! Joe, he's the new chef. He's won a Michelin star before. He's gorgeous. And . . . shy. So shy you can't get him to say a word. He's got these dark blue eyes, and they look at you like—"

Cat interrupted. "The Oak? The grottiest pub in the world? Why's he working there?"

"It's been completely done up. It's sad, though; no one's going there. I've told Joe I'll get Jereboam Tugendhat to review it. He's the food critic at the *Daily News* and he's got a crush on me. Or rather, he's an old perv who likes taking young women out to lunch. I said I'd go with him in early December, that's the next slot he's got free. If he starts wrestling with my jeans, I'll have Dad on speed dial and he can come and duff him up."

Cat smiled, though she couldn't imagine her lovely uncle Bill dashing into a pub and punching someone's lights out. "Are you going to ask Joe out?"

Lucy gave a shout of embarrassment. "Not likely! He'd never go for me. I mean, he's really nice to me and all, but he's very sad. He misses his son. He's got a son. He doesn't say much either, that's the trouble. Anyway, enough of him, I'll keep you posted. Maybe I *should* ask him out . . . don't know. So, how are things with you, Cat?" she said, not drawing breath. "I wish I'd called you sooner. It's been too long. You know—"

"Oh," Cat said hastily, "thanks. Things are good." She knew how to deflect. Give just enough information away so they didn't think to ask about the important things she kept secret. "It's still really warm. I love it here this time of year, fewer tourists, and Madame Poulain is better when the summer's over."

"You and that crazy old woman, it's so funny. I never understand it."

"Oh, I like to keep myself mysterious, Luce. I'm really a spy."

"Ha! That's funny. . . . Actually, it is funny you should say that. 'Cause I do want to ask you something for an article."

"So you're writing stuff for them, then? That's great."

"Just this, so far. I have to actually produce something first." Lucy stopped. "Maybe it can wait till you're back next month. You're busy."

Cat took another sip of wine. "No, go on. I'm not doing anything."

"Well . . . okay. I want to ask you about your mum."

Cat said, "What about my mum?"

There was a silence, and she could hear Lucy, who never had an un-expressed thought, working out what to say next. "Don't know if the phone's the best way to do it."

She's still so young, Cat thought to herself. *How can she be only three and a bit years younger than me? I feel like an old, old woman.*

"I'm writing an article about Daisy and—oh, hold on, that's my other phone." There was a muffled rustling sound, and Cat stared intently at the wall opposite, squeezing her toes and blinking as if she expected something else to happen, as if the saying of her mother's name might invoke some spirit. She put her hand on her breastbone. *Come on,* she said to herself, exhaling through the pain of it, the stress of the long day, of the con-stant battle to keep body and soul together, for herself, for Luke. But she couldn't think about her son now, no. She couldn't think about how much she feared she was simply repeating the mistakes of the past, that she was her mother, that she had become that person, just as Daisy had predicted.

"Are you still there?" Lucy's voice hissed. "That was Irene. God, she's annoying. My flatmate, she's got this cat and—"

Cat interrupted. "You're writing an article about my . . . mum?" It was one of the peculiarities of having seen your mother just four times in your life that Cat never knew how she should refer to Daisy. "Mother" was too Victorian, "Mum" too . . . too like someone who was your actual mum, which she definitely wasn't.

"Well, I offered to do something on Southpaw at work for this exhibi-tion of his, and then they heard about Daisy and they got all interested in that. The whole Daisy and Wilbur thing and where she's gone. And . . . look, I thought I should ask you what you think before I go any further. If you'd talk about it . . . what it was like, having her as your mother."

Cat had been told many times by well-meaning teachers and family friends that she was a lucky girl to be living in this beautiful house with her grandparents, surrounded by people who loved her. But she didn't have a mum. And it was little things that reminded her of it. It was rub-bish, that saying: "You can't miss what you don't have"—because she did miss it, all the time, in loads of tiny different ways. Like when she saw Tamsin Wallis being kissed by her mum after Sports Day. On the field below the church that the vicar let them use every year. She remembered it clearly: Tamsin and Cat together, hand in hand, running over to her mum. Shouting "Red Team won! We won!" And Tamsin's mother, smiling so hard, her spiky blond hair sticking up, her green earrings bobbing, her arms stretched so wide she could have caught fifteen Tamsins up. But she didn't, just one. Cat was left standing to the side, panting, while Julie Wallis gave her daughter a big hug, and then pushed her hair aside, kissed the dome of Tamsin's tanned forehead as if she was the most precious thing in the world to her, which she was.

Now Cat could see it. Now she understood it. Then, it only bewildered her, when she went over and asked for the same from Julie Wallis, who stared at her sadly, then gave her a little kiss. "Of course, Cat." A tight small hug, a quick little lip brush, a pat on the back.

"What do you think?"

Cat realized the phone was slipping out of her hand as she gazed unseeingly out into the night. She heard the sound of a door opening, then clicking shut: dread sound.

"What do I think about what?"

"Don't you wonder where she is?" Lucy's voice was loud down the crackling line. "And how weird it is she never comes back?"

Cat could hear Madame Poulain coming up the stairs.

"What a stupid question," she said, sounding much harsher than she meant. "She was my mother." She corrected herself. "She *is* my mother, I can't change that, but that doesn't mean I don't think about it. Or that I want to talk about it to you so you can put it in some newspaper."

"Oh, Cat. Listen, I only wanted to know—"

Cat held up her hand as if her cousin could see her. Rage bubbled through her. "You're a real little gannet, aren't you? Grubbing around in stuff that's not your business. You never get in touch, never ask me how I am; now you pop up, all friendly, because you want something from me."

"That's rubbish, Cat! You never e-mail. This—I was glad to have an excuse to ring you." Lucy's voice throbbed. "You've cut us all off, just like your mum, so don't make out I'm the one who's betraying the family in some way."

"There's a reason I don't come back. You don't understand—"

And the door opened with a bang; Madame Poulain flung her ancient purple umbrella on the floor. "*Les idiots!*"

Cat realized she was shaking. "Grow up, Lucy," she said, not caring how mean she sounded. "Just grow up. I think I'd better go now. Bye."

She slammed the phone back in its cradle, instantly regretting the words, and turned away, trying to stop the painful tears squeezing the corners of her tired eyes.

"Can I have a tea, please, Catherine?" Madame Poulain dropped her coat on the floor and flopped onto her chair. "Don't use those glasses, I'm worried you'll break them. A tea? Thank you so much."

Cat set her shoulders, rubbed her eyes briefly. "Of course, Madame," she said. "I hope you had a good evening?" She looked at her watch. Ten more minutes of fake conversation, then she could go upstairs, go to bed, lie down next to Luke and watch his warm, soft body on the cot next to hers, rising and falling with each breath. Wait for sleep to wash over her, until gray morning slid into the tiny room and the whole thing began again.

As Cat made the tea, she prayed she wouldn't dream about her mother. She used to have those dreams: Daisy running toward her on the beach in Dorset, hair flying behind her. She'd hold Cat tightly and whisper into her ear, "I'm sorry. I'm back now and I'm never going away again. You're my little girl, no one else's." She even knew where they'd live too—the tiny old schoolmistress's cottage next to the church, a gingerbread house with a thatched roof and roses round the door. Big enough for two, no one else.

Martha

MARTHA ALWAYS ENJOYED planning for Halloween, even though now there was no one really to celebrate it with; very few trick-or-treaters these days, what with the children having grown up and the village increasingly full of second homes. When the children were small, they'd had a famous party; Halloween was a novelty then, an American import, but now it was ubiquitous. She'd had a Chamber of Horrors, where the children had to put on blindfolds and be escorted round by her. They were made to feel various ghoulish treasures: a slice of lemon stuck over a bottle, which, when the guest inserted a cautious finger into the neck of the bottle, felt exactly like a dead man's eye socket; ghostly noises, rustling sounds made with newspaper; and a real skeleton David had acquired for life drawing—one dangled it in front of the blind victims, letting them feel the bones.

The children always screamed, always got hysterical, and then always ate huge amounts of chili con carne served with a golden cornmeal top, and baked potatoes and cheese. For months the anticipation was rife in the village: what new horror would Mrs. Winter have for them? Eight-year-olds would cluster around her when she walked into Winter Stoke. "Mrs. Winter, is it true you found a head on a spike?" "Is it true you got a dead wolf and you're going to stuff it?" "Is it true you captured a ghost, and you've got it upstairs in a room?"

"Yes," she'd always answer gravely, and they'd shriek with wriggling delight and rush away. "Oh, it's even worse this year!"

She'd carried on doing the party with Cat and Lucy: Lucy loved it, but Cat got genuinely scared, the only one of all of them who did. Years before that, Daisy had loved it, of course. Halloween was her favorite time of year.

It wasn't the same today, but Martha still kept an old plastic cauldron filled with sweets from the petrol station by the door in case anyone came, and this year she was rewarded: Poppy and Zach, the vicar's children, came around about six, she dressed up as Hermione Granger, he as some kind of amorphous zombie, his metallic silver and red face paint striped flesh-colored by the rain. Martha was vaguely amused: the austere, Victorian-era vicar who'd been here when they had first moved in hadn't allowed his grandchildren to celebrate Halloween—it was pagan, not suitable in this quiet, traditional village that had changed so little over the years. Kathy's children were delightful, well brought up and hopping with sugar and excitement. They said thank you very nicely for her sweets, as well they might; Martha never undercatered.

The rain was just starting again as she closed the door on them, smiling at their hoarse-with-excitement howls. As they ran away toward their waiting father, Martha shivered. She went into the empty drawing room and bent down, stiffly thrusting another log onto the fire. Resin crackled; something spluttered, and a ball of golden sparks leaped up, scattering over the great hearth. She stumbled back in shock, nearly catching her foot on the guard, and stood still for a moment, listening to the faint screams of the children echoing down the twisting dark lane, the eerie strength of the crackling wood, the sound of the wind at the windows. The clocks had gone back the previous Sunday, and now they were properly into winter. It had been a nasty autumn: wet, wild, sharp with sudden cold. Hurtful, as if to say, *Season of mists? What kind of sentimental idiot are you?*

Her old tutor at art college, Mr. McIntyre, had always made them sketch in winter, saying the bleakness was good for their artistic souls. He liked poetry and had made them read various poets, and often quoted John Donne: "Whither, as to the bed's-feet, life is shrunk." Life had shrunk. Well, if it was to come, let it come. She had nothing to fear now, she kept telling herself. This thing she had been dragging around for so long would be gone soon.

She tried to concentrate only on the positive: her family would be together, everyone here once again. Florence was coming back, Karen and Bill and Lucy all together again, and of course, her darling Cat— nearly four years away.

It was that falsely jovial, strange lunch with Cat the previous year in Paris that had made Martha realize that she had to change something. Cat needed her; so did Bill, and Florence, and Lucy, and—oh, all of them. Once they had been close, because of her. She'd kept them all together, like an invisible silk thread, binding herself to them, around them. But these last few years they weren't really a family anymore, and once they had been. Years had passed and changed them, and she knew she was the only one who could make it right again, and this was what the lunch would do. Beyond November 24 she saw nothing. She had no idea what the future after this might hold.

She didn't realize that she had fallen into a reverie, staring into the heart of the fire, but a sound across the hallway made her jump. A cry of pain.

"David?" Martha went into the study.

"It's nothing." Her husband was leaning heavily on his desk, one fist pressing down on a mass of crumpled papers, standing in a curious position. He was facing the blank wall, away from the window.

"What's up?" Martha said in the doorway, unsure whether he wanted her to enter or not.

"Damn it," David said. In profile he looked terrible: lines of pain deep as hatching etched around his mouth, across his sunken brow. As he stood in this strange spot, turned toward the wall, she saw him clearly for the first time in a long while and, with a dart of fear, noticed how thin, how gray he was. "It's nothing. Just the damn hands again—I get so tired, darling. I'm sorry."

"They're awfully swollen." She looked at him. "Worse than ever. Oh, my sweet."

"I can't do it." It came out as a sob. "They need something by Friday. Said I'd post it to them tomorrow."

"It doesn't matter. They'll understand."

"They won't." He closed his eyes slowly. "It's over, Em. That article they want Lucy to write—it's a stab in the back. They're looking for any reason to get rid of me."

"Darling, she's not writing it anymore. I asked her not to. She rang me yesterday. Said she's spoken to Cat and she doesn't think it's a very tactful piece to write. You mustn't worry about that. You really mustn't."

"Oh, but that's not fair. Poor Luce, she deserves a break."

Martha couldn't help but laugh. "Oh, my love. You're too kind. Forget about those vultures at the newspaper too. It doesn't matter, does it?" She stared at the scratchy sketch on the paper in front of him, and glanced at his kind, dark eyes, so full of pain, so sad. "It's been a good long run at it. You can't keep killing yourself trying to get them two cartoons a week. It's not fair. It's not—"

"Please, Em," he said. "Just once more. Just this once."

It was something in his voice, and in the hypnotic sound of the rain thrumming outside, enclosing them alone together around the green lamp under which lay a piece of creamy-white paper, glowing in the dark of the study.

Martha swallowed. "This is the last time, darling. It's gone on too long. It's not fair on you, anyway. It's killing you. You're ill because you push yourself like this and, David, you really don't need to."

"I'm dying anyway," David said harshly.

"You're not. Not until I say you are."

He smiled. "Maybe working keeps me sane. Stops me thinking."

Martha bowed her head and sat down at the desk, picked up the steel-nib fountain pen, and began to draw. She didn't need to ask him what he had in mind; after more than fifty years of marriage, she didn't need to be told.

David lowered himself into the chair opposite, looking over her shoulder as she carried on, sketching out swift, certain strokes.

"Thank you," he said. "My dear. What would I have done without you all these years?"

"You too, David." She looked up and reached out her hand. "Look what you've done for me."

"If people knew . . ."

"I think that's true of most families," she said. "Everyone has their secrets. We've had this place. We've had each other, and the children. . . ."

"But, Em, don't you think that's the trouble with it all?" She looked up, startled. "We've spent so long saying it has to be worth it, and I'm—I'm not sure whether it was." With great effort, David pulled

125

himself out of the low chair and walked over to the window, looking out into the darkness, the silver rain dripping like a curtain over the bare branches of overhanging wisteria. "You do everything. You've kept us all together these years, my darling, and I've done nothing. Nothing except—"

"Stop that." Her voice rang out, louder than she meant it to. "Stop talking like that, David. Of course it was worth it. You dragged yourself out of that life, you saved yourself, and Cassie—you brought me back here again. You brought in money. You gave me our babies. You made me grateful, every day of my life."

"Cassie . . ." He was still staring out the window. "She doesn't want to see me. Any of us."

"What?"

He ignored her. "Look what happened. Look how it turned out. All these lies we've told along the way. Look at us, we're miserable."

"We're not." She slammed her hand on the desk. "We're old and tired, and it's winter, and we have had some sadnesses to deal with. It'll be Christmas soon and all of this will be forgotten. You'll be happy again. I promise."

"I don't know." He looked so defeated, suddenly old, and she could feel her heart aching as she looked at him.

"David. You've made me so happy. You've made millions of people happy. I didn't do that." She laid down the pen, pinched the bridge of her nose, breathed in. "I'm no good at being spontaneous and carefree and making a mess and not caring what happens. You are. You always were. That's why people love you."

They were very still in the study, the only sounds the water outside and the moan in the chimney behind her.

"You had other things to do," David said. His face was gray. "You've done everything else." The final word sounded like a sob. "Darling, darling girl. I don't know what I'd do without you. Oh, Em."

She stretched across the desk to take his hand. His rigid, swollen fingers were immobile in her small, warm hand. She pressed his palm with the pad of her thumb. They stared at each other, David looking down, his breathing labored, and after a few moments Martha picked up the pen again and began drawing. He watched her.

"You're going to tell them about Daisy, aren't you?"

126

The figures were coming to life on the paper: a little girl dancing, a crazed, happy dog, and still she did not stop.

"Martha?"

"Yes," she said quietly. "I'll tell them then."

"That she's dead? Everything?"

She started, and the pen snagged on an invisible bump; the paper tore just a little, the ink bleeding out, black on white.

"Not everything," she said after a pause, and resumed her work.

PART TWO

The Party

Now, my bonny lad, you are *mine*! And we'll see if one tree won't grow as crooked as another, with the same wind to twist it!

—Emily Brontë, *Wuthering Heights*

Daisy

August 1973

WILBUR IS DEAD. We buried him last night, in the Daisy Bank. And I'm the only one who cares.

He was old, that's what Mr. Barrow the vet said, but I don't think that's a reason for him to just die. Plenty of people are old, like Mrs. White in the village who has—wait for it—white hairs on her chin. She is ninety-five, as she tells everyone every chance she gets. Stupid woman. Wilbur was the same age as me (I am twelve, in October). He wasn't old.

Ma was nice. She helped me bury him. We dug a big hole and wrapped him up, and we sang "Abide with Me." We burned candles. There were moths fluttering around in the evening light.

But the others weren't nice. Bill said it was stupid, a funeral for a dog, and he went to play guns in the wood. I always think this is funny because he's on his own—who does he hide from and who does he shoot? And when I crept up on him afterward and fired one of his blanks, he jolly nearly peed his pants. I think he might have.

And Florence said she didn't like Wilbur because Wilbur used to jump up and scare her and she didn't want to come. She watched out of the window in our room. Scared, stupid little pig. PIG.

And Pa? Pa was away in London for the night. Ma rang him to tell him. He didn't even care. Ma didn't say that, she said, "Oh, Dad is very sad. He says to send his love." But I know he didn't. Pa doesn't love me. He loves Florence, sort of loves Bill, but mainly Florence, because she likes paintings and she's a really vile little sneak, a swot, and the worst word I can think of and I'm not writing it down.

And Pa doesn't like me because he thinks I make trouble. I DON'T. I *gave him the idea for Wilbur* and he just doesn't care. All these years

Wilbur has been with us, our family mainstay and support (I got that in a book about awful lives of kitchen maids in Victorian times), and my family doesn't care enough to come and watch him be buried, just me and Ma. Pa stole my ideas off me too. He knows what he did, he knows about my stories about Wilbur. And that's why he's famous now and he still didn't come.

It's not even all of that, it's that I think Wilbur understood me and I understood him. Because he was shaggy and clumsy (not like me, I'm not like that, I'm very careful about everything) and he was enthusiastic about everything, so sometimes he scared people but he was only being friendly. I think people who don't understand that about dogs are stupid.

Florence, I am writing your name down on my list I am keeping. I wish you would die. If Wilbur's dead, you should definitely be dead too.

Florence doesn't belong here. She's not even one of us. Look at her. And look at me.

There is a wasps' nest in our room, underneath the roof. We used to have them when we first moved in, and now they're back. Last year there was a nest in the barn and Joseph, the gardener, was stung really badly. He had to go to the hospital. I haven't told anyone about this one. The art of war isn't Bill's stupid, stupid plastic gun with the babyish paper cartridges, it is planning.

I lie in bed at night and I can hear them humming in the eaves. It's the wooden gables they like. Wasps like wood. Sometimes it's very faint, but sometimes it seems to get louder, as though they will burst out of the back of the nest into my room. It keeps me awake. It scares me, but I like being scared too. I like the rushing feeling. I hate being bored. Really I hate it more than anything else.

I am going to make a list and plan out my life about what I want to do when I grow up. I can't wait to be a grown-up. I hate being here.

1. I will leave Winterfold, as soon as I can.
2. I will be rich.
3. I will have a husband. No children, I don't want any children.
4. People will be sorry when they have been horrible to me.
5. I won't come back, not even to see Ma.
6. I will be famous and everyone will have heard of me and be sorry they weren't nicer to me.

7. Florence, Verity, other girls at school who are my friends and then annoy me or won't talk to me anymore, I will pay them back for it.
8. I will have another dog and I will call him Wilbur.
9. I will make everyone see the truth about Florence.

But to do that I have to tell her the truth first of all. What I know . . . how little she knows. You see, yesterday I heard Ma and Pa arguing. In their room. I stood outside listening quite blatantly, as I knew I could quite simply say, "I'm on my way to the bathroom," if they caught me.

What they said needs some thinking about, as I am not sure I actually entirely understand it.

They don't argue like they used to when we came here. I think they have got used to this house and us all being here, but I haven't.

Ma said, "You said, when Florence came, you'd look out for her."

Pa said, "I am. You need to as well, Em. You said you'd send Daisy away to school if she didn't start behaving."

Ma said, "I don't want to. You of all people should know why."

That's exactly what they said, and I know two things. Florence is from somewhere else, and Pa wants to send me away.

I don't mean to be naughty, it just happens. I get bored, or angry, or I don't understand something, and then suddenly there's a broken glass, a smashed blackboard, someone crying. I want to feel remorse but I don't. Does Pa feel remorse, for Wilbur? Remorse is what Miss Tooth said I should feel when I flushed Verity's head down the lavatory after school. Verity is a coward, she screamed and cried. I don't cry. Verity's mother came to Winterfold and shouted at my mother. She said I wasn't ever to go to Verity's house again. I don't care about that. Verity lives in a nasty house, she doesn't have color television, and her father smells of BO. I hated going there for tea.

I sit in our room. It's the corner of the house. I can see Bill and Flo, playing some stupid game with Hadley, the new dog, and Bill's old swords in the meadow by the Daisy Bank, my Daisy Bank, mine mine. They should have asked me because it's my place and they're not allowed to play there, especially now that Wilbur is buried there. Everyone has one place for themselves. That's my place, my place where I can go. Flo is always in our room when I want to be by myself. She shouldn't be there too. I can see them there and it makes me very very very very angry. I can see Ma in the garden deadheading the roses, with a scarf in her hair. It's a pretty scarf.

There's two more things I know: Hadley is dangerous. His father was destroyed for fighting. He has bitten people before. I don't like him. They got him when they found out Wilbur was dying.

And I can see the wasps, flying into the eaves. Just casually, one at a time, and they're building up their nest till there's more of them, up till one day when they'll blow the house apart.

I hate it here. I wish I could run away. Ma is always asking me why I don't feel sorry. It's not a thing I can feel. I wish I could, I wish I was like them, but I'm not. I have always known it.

Florence

Dear Professor Lovell,

It is with great sadness that I write you this letter. But since it has
been made clear to me that my position at the British College is
under threat, and in the <u>most pernicious of circumstances</u>, I am
compelled to act.

My subject is nothing less than the most serious of academic
crimes. <u>Plagiarism.</u>

I am writing to set down before you in detail the charge that I
bring against our colleague Professor Peter Connolly. Namely that his
book The Queen of Beauty: War, Sex, Art, and God in Renaissance
Florence (a number one best-seller, translated into fifteen languages)
contains whole sections of work written by, but uncredited to, me.
I would estimate roughly 75 percent of the book is mine.

Please see the attached, a facsimile of a sample chapter on
Medici portraiture with my notes to Professor Connolly written
on the page. The original is in a safe place and can be examined
by you at any time. My colleague Professor Jim Buxton of the
Courtauld Institute is prepared to stand as expert witness should
these proceedings come to court. Believe me, it is extremely
painful for me even to contemplate betraying the man I once

"Flo? Florence, don't you want some tea?"

"I'm just coming!"

"It's getting cold!"

"Honestly, Mother! I'll be with you as soon as possible."

Florence smiled even as she heard herself—she'd be fifty next year, but it was funny how after only a day at home one reverted to type. Arching her back, she waggled her head, feeling the click of several bones in her neck and shoulders. She blinked intensely and stared at the screen, then deleted the last sentence. Then she typed:

> *I once thought Professor Connolly the finest of men, but he is no more than—*

No. Don't give them anything on paper.

> *Believe me, Professor Lovell, I raise this accusation reluctantly. It is only the fact that my job and reputation are being impugned by you and Professor Connolly—*

No. Too bitter, sounded like a revenge attack. And she wasn't bitter, was she?

> *I look forward to hearing from you. You will see that I am copying this letter to my colleagues at the Courtauld Institute, as well as Professor Connolly's literary agent and his publishers.*
>
> > *Yours sincerely,*
> > *Professor Florence Winter, DPhil (Oxon.)*

She saved the document, and opened her e-mails.

It was strange, working at her father's desk. There were his drawings littering the floor, the walls, scraps of ideas in his shaky hand pinned to the corkboard behind her, yellowing postcards and notes from friends and admirers. There was even a watermarked framed letter from 10 Downing Street; they all knew it off by heart. While the ancient Internet cable grumbled into action, Florence turned round to read it again.

Dear Mr. Winter,

The Prime Minister very much enjoyed your cartoon in yesterday's Daily News, *featuring Daisy and Wilbur throwing eggs at a*

*protester. He is a great admirer of your work and asks me to pass
on his very best wishes to you.*

Yours, etc.

And then a totally unreadable squiggle beneath. A letter meaning
nothing—why had he enjoyed the cartoon? "Bland, bland," David had
said, and he'd had it framed as an *aide-mémoire*—that was why he did
the work, to keep sharp, to stop himself from becoming bland. "Yours,
etc." had become a saying with all of them. A shorthand for glibness.

Coming home this time felt different. She'd e-mailed Daisy last
week before she left. Signed it "Yours, etc." Of course, she hadn't heard
anything back. On the flight, Florence had begun to wonder why she
was coming home at all, why she couldn't have just got out of it. Now
that she was here, she knew something was brewing. Her mother was
on edge—not that she'd ever confide in Florence. But Pa was so distant,
wrapped up in his own thoughts, smiling as he listened to her talk but
in a way that made her feel like a little girl again, chattering about something she'd read in a book.

She opened her e-mails, clicking her tongue with disdain at the attempt by one of her students to ask for another extension. No means no,
Camilla, Florence typed briskly. I don't care when ski season starts. I expect
the essay in by Friday at the latest. FW and pressed send. In haste, and wanting to be finished, she almost missed the e-mail nestling below it.

From: Daisy Winter
To: Florence Winter

Tue, Nov 20, 2012 at 11:30 PM

Flo,

Thanks for asking but I won't be coming back for the reunion dinner.
It's complicated. Ma will explain why. Hope all's good with you in Italy.

D x

Florence's heart skipped several beats. She peered forward, as if by
getting closer to the pixilation on the screen she would glean further

information about her sister. Where, why, who? *Daisy, Daisy, give me your answer do.*

Six years ago, two years before Bill's wedding, she'd come back. Some fund-raising mission. She could only pay a flying visit to Winterfold, one night. Florence had scrambled to get there; luckily she'd been going to Manchester for a conference anyway. She didn't know why she was so keen to see her older sister, who'd tormented her throughout their childhood, but she was—curious, was that it? Did she want Daisy's approval?

And Daisy was impressive when she talked about it—had all the facts to hand about literacy and clean water and female education. She made Florence, as ever, feel rather inadequate. She'd received a medal, though she didn't really like to talk about it (Martha brought it up). She'd been traveling a little, to see other projects. She said she'd come back for Christmas, hopefully she'd see Cat again?

In the end she couldn't come back over Christmas, she'd said, because the school was open over New Year. She sent paper lanterns in the post, folded cream and red paper stars with tiny star-shaped holes that let the light through. Martha had hung them in the dining room on Christmas Day and they all drank a toast to Daisy, come good at last. No one said as much, but that was what they thought.

So when she returned that summer, two years later, for Bill and Karen's wedding, Florence was looking forward to seeing her again, hoping that perhaps things might continue on the same positive footing. She was happier than she'd ever been, her brief affair with Peter Connolly at its height, and for the first time she felt the universe liked her. That she wasn't the freak everyone said she must be behind her back. Daisy too—she wasn't the cruel child who Florence sometimes, in her darkest moments, had thought might kill her. She was her sister! Her family! She was wrong, of course.

"Have you had your hair cut since I last saw you, Flo? Don't think you can have, can you?" she'd said, running a caressing hand through Florence's strawberry-brown and gray bob so that Florence stepped back in alarm. (She'd forgotten her sister had always had rather invasive body language, hugging people she didn't know when she was little, stroking the teacher's arm at the nativity play, clasping Dr. Philips a little too tightly when he bandaged up Florence's arm after an accident with a frayed swing rope.)

The gulf was too wide for Florence to reach across to her sister. She seemed odd. At breakfast the morning after the wedding, she was restless, shifting in her seat, constantly on the verge of speaking, long skinny fingers spearing holes in the bread roll on her plate. She ate nothing. Their father was due to go into the hospital that day for a long-scheduled knee operation, and when Martha asked whether Florence could drive him in, Florence had had to explain, regretfully, that she'd be leaving after lunch for London, a conference on Piero della Francesca that began that evening. It was Jim Buxton's conference, and she had to attend. She tried to explain this, to find out if she might see Daisy in London again before she left, but Daisy, with the older sister's contempt for any achievement of the younger, gave a small laugh.

"You are funny, Flo. Enjoy the conference. Good for you! I'm out of here soon; I won't see you again. I have to raise some money for actual problems. You know, like wells so people can drink. And drainage so they don't, you know, *die*." She'd blown her a kiss, careless, and got up and left the kitchen, slammed the door of her room, stayed there all day. That was the last time Florence had seen her.

As she stared at Daisy's e-mail, Florence picked at her fingers, puckering her brow as she reread the e-mail into meaninglessness. *It's complicated.*

"Flo! Your crumpet's almost cold!" The heavy door swung open and Florence's head jerked up guiltily. Martha paused on the threshold. "What are you doing?"

"Nothing—nothing! Just—doing some work. Checking e-mails."

Her mother's eyes narrowed and she plunged her hands into the pockets of the faded blue artist's smock she wore around the house. "Are you, now? Good-oh."

"There. Just one more thing."

Florence pressed delete, and the opening word, "Flo," collapsed before her eyes as the e-mail was sucked into the virtual trash can. Watching it, Florence was reminded of the plastic crisp packets the three of them used to toast over the campfire, watching them warp and shrink. They used them as tokens, and whoever had the most usually got their way. She remembered trying to explain this to some girl at school. *We camp in the woods in summer and we have tokens shrunk from crisp packets. The person with the most tokens given to them by the others in thanks for actions performed gets to be the king or queen for the day.*

As with so many aspects of Winter family life, this was met with blank incomprehension by outsiders.

"What are you smiling about?" Martha said. Her voice was light, but Florence thought she looked peculiarly unnatural somehow, leaning against the door and watching her daughter.

"Just thinking about camping in the garden and the shrunken crisp packets." Florence stood up. "It's funny, being back this time. I keep remembering things I've forgotten. Maybe . . . maybe it's winter," she finished lamely, looking outside at the driving rain. "What a nasty day."

"Yes, awful. There's so much water on the road you can't pass the lane in some places. Even this high up. Joe had dreadful trouble getting here this morning. He had to leave the car outside."

"Joe?"

"Joe Thorne. He's the chef who's doing the catering on Friday and Saturday. He's awfully nice. Come and meet him and have some tea." She tucked her arm into her daughter's. "You've been working so hard since you got back here."

"Yes, well. Something rather strange has come up at the college."

Martha stopped. "What's that?"

"A—oh, plagiarism, I'm afraid. It might end up in court," Florence said. The words sounded fantastical, spoken out loud. She was doing this. Wasn't she? Would she actually dare to send that letter to George Lovell? Seal it up, post it?

"Court? It's not anything to do with you, is it?" Martha patted Florence's hand. "You never needed to steal anything, did you? Look! Florence is here!" she called out as they entered the kitchen.

The kitchen was neater than usual, and Florence looked around and realized it must be the mark of a professional chef. Stacks of canapés in rows were laid out on the countertops amidst the everyday gentle chaos, while Radio 3 blared out slightly too loudly in the corner (Martha was a little deaf, but refused to admit it). Her father sat in his chair doing the crossword, chewing his pencil, one swollen hand resting on his lap.

"Hello, darling," he said with pleasure as Florence came in. "You finished with the world of academia for today?"

She put her hand on his shoulder and sat down next to him. "Yes. Thanks, Dad, I'm sorry to crowd you out of your study like that. Just a few things I had to . . . get to."

David tapped her arm. "Don't chew your hair, darling. What's up?"

It's just us. His smile was warm. Florence took a deep breath.

"Oh, Dad. I—"

The back door banged open and a tall, dark man came in. "Shit. I—I mean, sugar. The—ah, can I just squeeze past you, please?" He reached behind Florence, unhooked the Aga door, and took out a tray of tiny blind-baked tartlet cases, egg-yolk yellow like sunflowers; he flicked them onto a cooling rack, then slid another tray from the counter in and shut the door. "Sorry about that. Minute longer, they'd have burned." He wiped his hand on his apron. "Hello, I'm Joe. You must be Daisy."

There was a short silence.

"I'm Florence." She shook his hand quickly. "I—um, I'm the—I'm Florence. Yes."

Blood rushed into Joe's face. "I'm so sorry. I forgot. It's Florence." He whispered to himself, "*Florence.*"

"It's fine, there's too many of us, don't worry," Florence said. "Nice to meet you. Ma's so pleased with what you've been doing."

"Have a cup of tea, Joe," David said, pushing the teapot toward him. "Martha's made some of her gingerbread. You'll like it. Even you, a professional chef. Sit down."

"I've had it before and it was delicious." Joe grabbed a mug off one of the hooks on the dresser, then pulled out a chair. "I really am sorry," he said, handing the plate to David, then Florence. "I know you're Florence, you're the one who lives in Italy and you know everything about art."

"Sort of," Florence said, embarrassed. She was long used to being lined up next to her local-hero brother and feline, exotic sister and told by strangers or her parents' friends, "Oh, now, you must be Florence. I hear you're the brains of the family!" or once, memorably, "You've changed so much, dear. Oh, well," by an old newspaper editor, just after he'd said to Daisy, "My dear, you're ravishing. Have you ever thought of being a model?" So she changed the subject. "You live here, don't you? Have you met the others?"

"Yes . . . most of them," Joe said. "Your brother—he sewed up my finger after I sliced it open a couple of months ago. Did a fine job." He held up his hand and Florence stared at it, impressed.

"Good grief, that looks nasty."

"Would have been a disaster for me if it hadn't been done well. I—I owe him a lot." He gulped back the rest of his tea and stood up. "Look, I have to get to the shops to pick up a couple of things I've forgotten. It was great to meet you, Florence."

And he left, without even waving good-bye. Martha followed him out.

"Funny bloke," said Florence, taking a sip of tea. "Is he always like that?"

"Like what?"

"Shifty," she said. "Like he's just nicked your wallet, Pa."

David was fiddling with the jar of pencils that always stood on the table. "Don't be a snob, Flo. I think he feels uncomfortable here. For some reason."

"I'm not being a snob!" Florence said. "He was pretty odd, that's all. Like he thought we were about to arrest him or something."

Her father put his hand over one eye, then sat back in his chair and said quietly, "Oh, don't ask me. These days I just draw and have naps."

"You?" she said cheerily, though she watched the way he squinted, as if he couldn't make her out. "Hardly!"

"I can't afford to do anything else, my darling."

Florence gave him a sharp look. "What does that mean?"

"What I say." He wouldn't look at her.

"Pa," she said, her heart thumping, "are you all right? You don't look all right."

David laughed and sat up a little. "Charming child."

"Sorry. I mean, since I've been back. You . . . you look rather gray."

His face cleared. "Not really, that's the honest truth."

Florence took a deep breath. "Oh." She could feel her throat thickening, tears swimming into her eyes. "How bad is it?"

David took his daughter's hand and kissed it. "Do you remember when we'd go to the National Gallery for your birthday?"

"Of course," she said, alarmed that he'd think she'd ever forget.

"I'd like to take you back down to London sometime."

"Yes, Pa, I'd love that. We can look at *The Annunciation*, have lunch.

Have a steak, go for a walk in Green Park, visit that cheese shop you like. . . ." She spoke almost frantically.

They were alone in the warm, cluttered kitchen. He smiled. "'The most beautiful representation of motherhood in Western art. Mary is every woman, alive or dead, at that moment.'"

"I wrote that," Florence said, surprised.

"I know you did," said her father. He glanced up as Martha walked past the kitchen window, carrying a basket from the garden. She waved at Florence, shielding her head from the rain with her hand, and smiling. Joe Thorne climbed into his car, said something to Martha, then slammed the door. They could hear the engine, stalling and revving again as, having reached the bottom of the drive, he turned around in the circular area in the front of the house.

"This might be the only chance we get," David said urgently, his voice soft. She had to lean toward him to hear. "Listen to me. I love you all, but I love you in a way I didn't the other two. You know that, don't you? Always a special place for you. You are my golden girl. I saved you."

"Pa?" Florence shook her head, her mouth dry. She peered into his glazed eyes. "I don't understand. What are you talking about?"

"You must promise me you'll always remember I told you that. You were my favorite. Shouldn't say that. You'll understand one day. I'm so proud of you, my darling."

"It's absolutely bucketing down out here!" she heard her mother call from outside. Florence didn't move. She stared into her father's eyes, squeezed his hand gently. "Dad—I wish you'd tell me what you mean."

"Soon," he said, nodding, and he was smiling, and the smile was what made her want to cry. "Very soon."

Outside, Joe drove down the drive. In a blur Florence heard Martha call loudly, "Good-bye!"

It happened in slow motion. Florence looked up and saw, through the blur of rain, her mother wave, then drop the basket and shout, her hands pressed to her cheeks. Then the crash, the sound of splintering glass, someone screaming, someone shouting. Then, silence.

They stood up, Florence and David, struggling from his chair, in time to see a slim figure, hair flying, running down the drive.

"Oh, God," said Florence. "What—"

The figure was screaming, "Luke! Luke! Oh, my God, darling, *Luke!*"

There was a shattering crunch as Florence dropped her mug of tea on the floor, and stared through the window.

A little boy stood in front of them, thumb in his wide-open mouth, face purple with yelling, and blood dripping from his forehead. He screamed, pulling at his black hair, smearing blood across his wet cheeks.

Behind him a woman came running toward him, her mouth also wide open, her eyes wide, white, wild. She caught him in her arms and he buckled to the ground, still wailing with pain.

"Luke!" she screamed, turning this way, that way, then crying out as she caught sight of them, framed in the window. "Gran! Southpaw! Help me, Luke's, he's . . . he's hurt." And she buried her face in his, sobbing and stroking his hair.

Cat

SHE WAS AHEAD of herself, for once. For once! A miracle. The Eurostar had been on time. She had picked up the car without incident, though it was slightly unnerving, getting into a completely strange car when she hadn't driven for years, let alone on the left-hand side, strapping Luke in, and then setting off along the Euston Road, easily one of the busiest roads in London. Thankfully, the Wednesday afternoon traffic was thin and she drove through the drizzling rain with almost a light heart. When they got to Richmond, she turned on the radio, sang along to a Blondie song, "One Way or Another." *One way or another*. She was coming home. And even though she hadn't planned it like this, she had Luke with her, and perhaps, really, that was wonderful.

"What will we see, Maman? Will we see the tiger who came to tea?"

Luke was incredibly excited. He had never been to London, to England, never been away from France. He still didn't properly understand that he was half-English, despite what she told him every night as she stroked his hair and soothed him to sleep in their little room. He was too little to understand that you could be from another country, too.

Once they were on the motorway, he dozed, and a couple of times she turned around to check on him. His cheeks were flushed, his mouth in a pout; there was a scratch on his forehead, a line of little beaded scabs, the result of some convoluted dispute with Benoit over a ball at the nursery. He was here. Her son was here, with her.

The week before she was supposed to go, one night in their room when Cat was sitting up in her bed engrossed in a Ngaio Marsh, she suddenly heard a noise, and Luke's small hand burrowed under his duvet, out toward the edge of the bed, and found her hand. "I want to come with you."

"What?"

"To England."

"Oh, Luke," she'd said. The idea he might want to hadn't ever occurred to her, so busy was she planning, controlling everything to make his life as safe and warm as possible. "Don't you want to stay with Josef? It's only two nights. It'll be fun."

"I want to see the Queen. And I want to see the paper dogs."

"The dogs Southpaw drew me, darling?" The words caught in her throat.

"The ones in the frame. I want to see them." The little voice was clear in the darkness.

In the end, as big decisions often are, it was a simple choice to make. Why on earth wouldn't she take him? He wasn't four yet, he didn't need a ticket. When she rang to confirm this, the operator told her they were offering discounted transfers to a train the day before, as her train was overbooked. Gleefully, Cat said yes. She would get to Winterfold early and give them a real surprise, introduce her son, her secret, beloved, precious little boy, to her grandmother and grandfather. She would tell the truth at last. And somehow, the element of surprising them a day early took away the terror of reality. The fact that she didn't know where her mother was. The reason for this birthday lunch. And most of all, the fact that she had had this child, kept him a secret from her family for three years.

When she found she was pregnant, she was at the lowest point she'd been able to go. Olivier had stopped telling her what to wear or lashing out at her in rage, driving her into a corner of fear so great she tiptoed around him, making him even more vicious, contemptuous of her. Now he openly despised her. He barely came home by then, and when he did, brought people back with him, musicians, artists, philosophers—it made Cat feel very bourgeois that she didn't understand how one could be in one's late twenties and have a job as a philosopher. They stayed up long into the night, talking, playing music, drinking beers, banging out rhythms on Cat's old trunk–cum–coffee table. She never joined them.

She had a new job now, at the flower stall in the market on the edge of the Île de la Cité, and it meant getting up early. It paid virtually nothing, but she'd taken it because she didn't know what else she could do, and Olivier had made it clear he didn't want her hanging round the house during the day when he was sleeping off the excesses of the night before. She liked it, too, except that the hours were long, the pay small, and the weather sometimes tough. But it wasn't a career. At night she would come home, exhausted, and fall into bed praying that she wouldn't be called upon to see the others he brought back with them, ridiculed as the "fat English girl who lives with me. She's pathetic, like my dog, panting and following me through the place."

She heard him once, fucking a girl on the sofa, a lithe, smooth, ginger-haired thing of about eighteen who smiled patronizingly at her in the morning and offered her a coffee as Cat staggered blearily out of bed in her baggy T-shirt and into the shower. After that she started wearing earplugs. She didn't really know what else to do. She had no spine, she had no will, no energy to fight.

She had had a miscarriage six months previously, and had gone straight back on the Pill. When she missed a period she thought nothing of it; she wasn't regular, her body was behaving in strange ways. When another month went by and she eventually did a test, she was astonished: how could this relationship, this awful toxic mess of humiliation and unhappiness, have created something? Olivier did not want children, he had made that clear the last time. She didn't admit it to herself for a week or so, thinking perhaps it would go away, or that she would make the decision to get rid of it.

Cat had thrown herself into her relationship with Olivier thinking it would provide her with something she'd never had before: her own home, her own unit; and so it was ironic that it was finding out she was pregnant with his child that gave her the strength to break it off. She knew, though, if she was going to do it, she had to have thought it through. She had to carry on as though, to everyone else, everything was normal. Her grandmother came to visit; she told her nothing. She went out for drinks with Véronique, and said nothing. Here the seeds of secrecy were sown.

By the time she told Olivier, her exit plan was worked out. Her new boss at the flower stall, Henri, was always complaining about his elderly mother. Madame Poulain, it had been decided, needed a lodger, but she was so difficult it was impossible to persuade the procession of live-in helps to stay. It was not too arduous, so why was it so hard? She needed someone to help with her shopping, to collect her prescription, and to make sure she took her pills. (She had had cancer and she now had a heart condition, and diabetes and osteoporosis. In the years to come, Cat often had to remind herself of this, that for all Madame Poulain's faults, she really had not been well.) She needed someone to sit with her of an evening, an old-fashioned companion. No, she did not mind a baby. There was a *chambre de bonne*, a tiny room on the top floor, and the infant would be out of the way there, and an excellent public nursery was just across the river. All would be well. To Cat, desperate, it seemed like good luck from a movie or a fairy story; she didn't consider how it might actually work.

So, when she was around four months pregnant and starting to show, one beautiful spring day when Paris was coming alive with green and the trees were bursting with blossom, she packed up everything she owned in the coffee-table trunk; she kissed Luke the dog good-bye, her tears dropping onto his kinked, soft fur, stroked his ears, and hugged him close to her; and then she left. She didn't tell Olivier where she was going, just said she was leaving. A week later, an *avocat*, a lawyer wife of someone with whom she'd worked at *Women's Wear Daily*, a specialist in family law, had written to Olivier, explaining that Catherine Winter was pregnant and that he was the father and would be required to pay her child support.

She never received a penny, nor did she want to, but it did the trick: she turned from being a person of interest to Olivier—albeit briefly, although it was always dangerous—into a sad bitch who was trying to get money out of him, thus allowing him to be the wronged party. The one mistake she made was in the naming of the baby. A couple of months after she moved out (and long after Luke the dog had run away, never to be seen again), Olivier, deciding to toy with her, somehow managed to blame Luke's disappearance on her, demanding that he choose the name if the baby was a boy. He picked Luke. Some sad way of reminding her of his ownership of her? What else could it be?

But in the grand scheme of things, Cat didn't care. She liked the name Luke and she had loved the other Luke. She simply couldn't get upset about Olivier's games anymore, or so she told herself. When Luke was a year old, Olivier moved to Marseilles. He saw his son a few times, peripatetically, if he was in town. He'd bring Luke presents—a stuffed wicker elephant that took up a corner of the tiny bedroom, some jazz records, once a pair of shoes, which were too small, though new.

Cat wanted Luke to know he had a father, and to know that his father loved him. And so she had to let Olivier see Luke when he was in town. On the last visit, when he was three hours late, unshaven, smelling rank and unwashed, Luke had stared at him and said, "You stink!" Then laughed. "Stinky."

She'd seen Olivier's eyes narrowing, the precursor to his anger. The little quiver of the bottom lip. The tone of his voice when he said, "Don't say that again." And she was afraid for her son, afraid of what loving his father might do to him.

Luke sometimes asked, "Why doesn't my father live nearby?" But he never said anything else, and their strange but safe little life continued, high up in the tiny back bedroom on the Île-Saint-Louis, the days she took one at a time turning into weeks, then months, and now her baby was three.

She'd found that, since becoming a mother, she thought ceaselessly about her own mother. Cat knew where her father was—he was a charity worker living in Kent, with three children and a wife called Marie. He'd always kept in touch, assiduously enough to remove any sense of mystery about himself, and whenever she met him Cat found herself wondering how on earth she could be related to him. Winterfold was where she came from, not from this nice, kind, mild rangy man who wore wireless frames and had hair that stuck up in tufts.

When Cat had been nine, he'd taken her to the pantomime in Bath ("I think you should call me Giles, don't you agree, Catherine?"), as a special Christmas treat. He had talked all through their pizza about world hunger, then sat cross-armed and perplexed through the pantomime, hissing at Cat when she shot her hand up to go onstage. ("No, Catherine, honestly—I think you'd better not. You are in my care, after all. . . . Is that okay? I'm awfully sorry. . . .") Cat had sunk down in her chair furiously, watching with envy as a little girl called Penelope and not her was chosen, then shot out of a joke cannon on a seesaw by Lionel Blair. Giles had refused to buy a program or an ice cream, and then forgotten where he'd parked the car. Cat had come back and told her grandmother she thought he looked like an owl, but most of all he was very dreary.

She'd seen him since, lunches in London, and when she was at university she'd even stayed with him in Kent, but it was that encounter she remembered most clearly and about which she often felt guilty; it occurred to her when she had Luke that it must have been quite a thing for Giles, leaving his (then very small) three children with his wife, a few days before Christmas, to drive from Kent to Somerset to take a cross little girl out for an expensive treat. She liked him for sending Christmas cards, for the fact that he'd always been clear about where he was ("Dear Catherine, This is to let you know we have moved, should you need to contact me. We are all well. Emma is . . .").

She could contact Giles if she wanted, but she didn't really want to. No, it was her mother who haunted her, who filled her dreams. All through the hot sweltering summer before Luke was born, Cat lay in her new little bedroom and thought about Daisy, tried to piece together what she knew about her. The only concrete evidence she had was the clothes her mother had left when she walked out, nearly thirty years ago. A dress for every year, every occasion, and she'd hung them all up in a row and just walked out of the house and kept on walking, and that had been that. "Not to be shared"—somehow Cat felt sorry for her mother, so desperate that Cat should have her own things. She didn't understand that by leaving her like this she had ensured her daughter would have nothing but her own things. When Lucy came to stay, Cat was so keen to share her toys that often Lucy, bored, would wander off into the garden: "I don't care about your Sindy house, Cat. I want to play with this stick." It was what had led Cat to cut up her mother's dresses for dolls' clothes, that fateful day. It seemed such a waste, having them hanging there, unworn. *She* wasn't ever going to wear them, no fear of that.

When she gave birth to Luke, at l'Hôpital Pitié-Salpêtrière, he was very small and they took him to the baby unit and kept him in an incubator. Cat was in a ward on the floor below. She couldn't sleep, and so she walked the corridors at night slowly in her new bright yellow dressing gown, stomach still distended, very sore, feeling like a waddling duck. On the third day her hormones kicked in, and a male nurse found her sobbing brokenly into a wall, helpless with tiredness, with worry about this tiny baby who was so small she could hold him with one hand, about why she wasn't producing enough milk to feed him, with how she would get him home from the hospital, about the horrible, dark, nasty world he had come into and how she couldn't protect him from it.

The nurse sat her down on a plastic chair in the squeaky-clean corridor, the only sound the faint mewl of babies in the room next door. He patted her hand as she cried, tears dropping like rain on the shining floor.

"Take it day by day," he told her, and she only realized afterward that he had spoken in English. "Just day by day. Do not worry about the future. Do not worry about the past. Think of the day and what you have to do to get through, and it will be okay."

And that's what she did. Every day. When she thought about the future, how Luke couldn't possibly grow up in a tiny room with his mother, how she had no money, how she had to tell her grandparents one day, how she had let all of this happen and screwed it up . . . when the walls of her life started to crowd too closely in on her, Cat focused on the immediate present. *Get to the bank. Buy more vermouth for Madame Poulain. Put aside twenty euros a week for Luke's new shoes. Breathe. Just . . . breathe.*

One day, she would like to try to pull herself out of this life. Start a gardening business, everything from window boxes for busy people to full-on self-sufficiency vegetable gardens. But how could she when she wasn't self-sufficient herself? Once, Cat had been a dynamic person, but that person was long gone and she did not know if she could find that Cat again, dust her down, put her on like a dress from Daisy's wardrobe that she used to wear, before they were cut up.

When they got to Stonehenge, Cat woke Luke up, and they got out of the car. Luke was fascinated, standing as close as he could get to the stones behind the wire fence, staring intently around even as the drizzling rain misted everything in front of them.

"Where are they from, the stones?"

Cat screwed up her eyes. Being relatively close to her school, Stonehenge had cropped up frequently in day trips, but she could remember very little about it.

"That's a good question. No idea."

"They are very big." Luke peered at one of the signs. "I can't read."

"I think they put them on rollers and pulled them along." He looked unconvinced. "And I have a feeling they're from Wales. Somewhere like that. They weigh about two tons each." So she did remember. They stared up at the huge monoliths—she'd forgotten quite how big they actually were. "Good, isn't it?" She turned to him eagerly, smiling as he nodded and grinned.

They drove across vast, empty Salisbury Plain. She pointed out the mysterious hillocks and mounds, graves of buried kings, the empty tanks used for army training that hugged the narrow lay-bys, the sheep huddled on the hillsides, and Luke stared out of the window, his nose and one finger pressed cold-cream white against the glass.

As they started the slow but steady climb toward Winter Stoke, Cat felt sick, dizzy, tired, adrenaline swamping her body so that she thought she might simply pass out at the wheel. She had been trying to downplay it in her mind, as though this wasn't the most important moment of her life since Luke was born. Coming back. Maybe even to see her mother again, for ever since her phone conversation with Lucy she felt sure this was about Daisy in some strange way. Whatever this was, there was no hiding anymore. She had to keep reminding herself it was a good thing. Yet she was terrified.

Her thirteenth birthday! How could she have forgotten it? Yet there it suddenly was, then the highlight of her—as she saw it—dreary life. December 1995. They went to Pizza Hut in Bath—Gran, Southpaw, five of her best friends, Lucy too—then to the cinema to see *Goldeneye*. Lucy wasn't allowed to, being too young. She went back early to Winterfold with Gran in a right grump. Cat, Liza, Rachel, Victoria, and—who else was there? How awful that she couldn't remember—they all came home to Winterfold for a sleepover, and Martha let them have half a glass of champagne each. Gran had the right idea about birthdays. They were giggly and emotional with excitement, and they stayed up late listening to Take That and crying about Robbie leaving, and as they were going to sleep Rachel, who was the really cool one, said, "Wow, Cat, I'm really jealous of you, living here. Your gran is amazing." Only she sort of muttered it into the bedclothes so Cat was never sure if the others heard; but she had heard it, and she smiled in the darkness. She could still remember how it made her feel, the idea that this random girl—God knows what had happened to her—the idea that anyone would be jealous of her; it was a childishly lovely feeling.

The rain was still falling, soft yet heavy outside. Luke turned away from the window, sucking his thumb noisily, occasionally whispering to himself in French. At one point he called out, "Mum! Maman! *Le grand cheval blanc! Le cheval!*"

"Shh," she said, because he often had nightmares about lions and very big zebras, and she thought this was another one. "It's okay, there's no white horse, darling."

"Yes, yes, there is, Maman! *Look!*"

She turned swiftly and saw him pointing out the passenger seat window, and she corrected her steering and looked to one side, remembering at the same time that, of course, there were white horses everywhere round here. On the hillside, a tiny horse, prancing in the distance, bone white stamped into the green.

"Of course, I'm sorry. I'm stupid. They have them round here."

"*Why*, though, Mummy? Maman?" Luke demanded.

"No idea. I'm sorry. I should have—we'll get a book while we're here. A book of British history. It'll explain about Stonehenge too. You'll be able to show everyone at school we've seen it. And the Westbury white horse." Westbury—of course—where had that come from?

Memory led her further back as they drew closer to Winterfold. The hedgerows would be full of sloes now, the river Frome, below the house, swollen with autumn rains. The lichen silvery gray, the last of the autumn leaves on the roads, acid yellow and deep red. "It's close. We're very near, Luke." They drove along the vertiginous lane leading up to Winterfold. "Mummy hasn't been here for ages," she said, preparing to turn into the drive, a hard ball in her throat. "You're going to meet—"

There was a loud smash and a huge force, like a great weight pushing on her chest, thrusting her back. Her neck tore with pain, and she cried out. The car spun round so fast she didn't know what was happening. She remembered only the door flying open, glass everywhere, Luke screaming, and the deep, harsh bell of the blaring horn. She climbed out of the car, dazed, fingers fumbling at Luke's car seat, clicking, while he screamed, and blood was pouring down his forehead, ribbons of red. Was this Winterfold, had she come home? Why was this house so different, the windows so big?

"Luke—"

He darted away from her as she set him on the ground, and then her legs buckled with shock and she fell to her knees. She stood up, shaking, and ran down the lane, as though in her dreams once more. She yelled his name, and when she reached the house she saw a little figure running ahead of her. Was that Luke? Who was it, was it her? There was blood on the gravel, she remembered the gravel; there was a tall man, covered in blood, holding him. It was Luke. Her grandparents were there. A woman was screaming, and the tall man turning to her and asking her something. But she couldn't hear him, and that's why she thought it must be a dream, because everything else went black.

Martha

THEY WERE LUCKY, the emergency switchboard operator said. An ambulance was just passing, on its way back from a non-urgent drop-off. Martha moved them inside, out of the rain, to wait. They gathered in the middle of the sitting room, Florence throwing a blanket and cushions haphazardly on the floor. Luke cried and cried, his mother too, nestling his dark head in her arms, her blue sweater covered in blood. Occasionally he would stare up at this room of adults, then close his eyes and cry again.

Martha watched, her jaw working with anxiety. Her mind wasn't functioning properly; she felt as though she had slammed into something herself. It was by now clear that Luke—this little person was called Luke, wasn't he? Hadn't Cat also had a *dog* named Luke?—was going to be all right. It was a scalp wound, but it was a nasty cut, and a nasty shock. It was *all* a shock. She peered at her granddaughter's face, so thin, grimy with mud, blood, and tears. This was Cat. Cat was a *mother*. Martha, who knew what she would be eating for supper two days ahead, who could grasp any idea, had not planned for this.

"What the hell were you doing?" Cat shielded her son's head and glared behind Martha at the doorway.

"I'm so, so sorry," Joe said, as he fell to his knees next to Luke. He rubbed his eyes, his voice hoarse. "I don't know how it happened. I just didn't see you as I was driving out and—"

"You're a bloody lunatic, you shouldn't be behind the wheel." Her voice throbbed. She kneeled and scooped Luke round so he was facing away from Joe, over her shoulder. Her cheeks each had a pink spot, bleeding out on her too-white skin. Martha remembered, when Cat was little, how passion used to take over her thin body, whether with anger or happiness. "I mean, what the hell were you thinking? Don't you say: 'Hmm, before I just reverse at twenty miles an hour down this drive and round a corner, I might actually turn my head and look?'"

Joe said quietly, "I wasn't concentrating. My mind wasn't there. It's no excuse."

Cat shot him a look of pity tinged with disgust. Joe squatted beside her, twisting his fingers around and around. He squeezed Luke's shoulder gently and said quietly, "Hey, little mate. I'm so sorry. You're going to be all right."

Cat stared up at him, her gray eyes icy with fury. "Get away from him. Leave us alone."

Luke wriggled in her arms and turned round. "What did you do with the car dat was so bad, because you hurt my head when you did it." He hiccuped, with a little sob. "It hurt my head and . . . *Maman, je ne comprends pas pourquoi nous sommes ici.*"

His mother squeezed him even more tightly against her. "It's okay, sweet boy. The ambulance is on its way, they're going to—" As she spoke, a siren sounded and flashing lights bounced off the walls of the sitting room. Luke stiffened in alarm.

"It's all right, Luke," Joe said. "Promise. Some nice people are here and they're going to look at your head, and I'll give you a cake afterward."

"Stop talking to him," Cat said, standing up, lifting Luke with her and wincing slightly. "Just fuck off, why don't you?"

"Cat," Martha said.

"Sorry, Gran." Cat's hair flew into her eyes as she turned to her grandmother. She pushed it away with one hand, tangling it into a cloud. "But he nearly killed us. He shouldn't be—"

"Cat, I can't say enough how sorry I am." Joe backed up against the French windows as she passed by him, and they heard the ambulance sirens coming up the hill. Martha paused as she saw a police car turning into the drive.

"They always send the police if it's a road accident," David said, reassuring, in her ear. "He's going to be fine, Em. Don't worry."

She wanted to pivot around then and take him in her arms, kiss his worn cheek, stroke his hot, thick hands. He was always behind her.

"She's really back," she said, "isn't she?"

"Yes, she is," David said, watching Joe going up to the young policeman who climbed out of the car. He pointed at his bumper, shaking his head, jabbing his finger to his chest. "Poor Joe. That poor lad."

Later, when Jan and Toby, the paramedics, had gone, bearing biscuits and a thermos of tea, leaving Luke with a little line of neat stitches below his hairline, and the police had taken cursory statements from everyone and walked around Joe's car several times, then left too, Joe came up to Martha in the hallway, aimlessly brushing fluffy dust off a painting frame.

"I've given them a statement. I've told them Cat's insurance mustn't be affected. I've put the samosas in the larder and the little cakes. What else can I do Martha?"

"Just go, Joe," Martha said, looking at him. "Unless you want another cup of tea?" He shook his head, and she knew he wanted to be anywhere but here. "Go and get some rest. Leave the car here and walk home, the fresh air'll do you good." Cat appeared in the hallway, arms folded. Martha patted Joe's shoulder. "You look done in, my dear. I'll call you if they need you. I'm sure they won't."

"I need to do the rest of the pastry cases. I'll bake them at home." He didn't look at Cat. "Mrs. Winter, once again—"

"It was an accident, Joe, please. Of course it was. You look absolutely done in, you know."

"Thanks." He gave a faint glimmer of a smile. "Not sleeping that well at the moment. I've got a lot on my mind. I blame myself for what happened. I've had some news that has been a bit of a shock—but it's no excuse."

Martha looked at him with concern. There was something about Joe that reminded her of a small boy. Those sad eyes, that jaw that was so firm, clamped shut for most of the time. The awkward, shy way he had of explaining things, the way his smile, when it came, was like a bear hug—it wrapped you in its warmth. "Is everything okay?"

"Yes." He pulled the keys off the dresser and Cat stood up, darting out of his way as though he'd hit her. "I'd best be off. Leave you to it. I'll bring up the . . . should I come back tomorrow?"

Martha gave a sharp laugh. "You'd bloody better, Joe! Come on, it was an accident. Wasn't it, Cat?"

Cat stared at the floor. "Sure."

Martha opened the door and watched him wandering down the lane, almost like a robot.

"Bye," she called, but he didn't hear her. "He's gone now."

"Good riddance," Cat muttered. Martha shut the door and turned, her hand on the latch, looking thoughtful.

"Who was dat?" said Luke, appearing from the living room.

"Yeah," Cat said. "Who *was* that idiot?"

"The chef. He's doing the catering for this weekend. You poor thing. You'd have liked him, if you'd met him in different circumstances."

"I doubt it." Cat kissed Luke on the head. "Darling Gran. I'm so— this isn't how I wanted to come back. It was supposed to be a lovely surprise." She gave a small, tentative smile. "I'm sorry. About all of this."

Martha reached forward and touched her granddaughter's cheek. Her smooth, rose-pale cheek. Then she stroked Luke's head, feeling the thick hair, the shape of his skull. Her great-grandchild, his head in her hands. She closed her eyes briefly as the enormity of the moment threatened to overwhelm her, then steeled herself.

"Don't ever, ever be sorry, my darling. Let's get a cup of tea for ourselves. Florence? Can you put the kettle on? And get the cake tin. It's in the larder by the tea bags."

"You painted it!" Cat exclaimed, following her grandmother into the kitchen. Her face was pale, but she was smiling. She gave Luke a big hug and pulled him onto her knee. "Oh, the blue chair's still there. And the bowl of limes . . . Oh, goodness. Luke, this is where Mummy used to live."

Luke nodded, looking around him and chewing his thumb, with a kind of dazed fascination mixed with extreme fatigue. Martha couldn't stop staring at him. He was her great-grandson.

"It used to be orangey, now it's sort of wattle and daub, isn't it? Very trendy," Cat said.

Martha laughed. "It hadn't been painted since I did it myself when we moved in. Florence was four and she stuck her foot in the paint tin, I remember. Orange footprints everywhere."

"Really?" Florence said. "Oh dear, I'm sorry. Did I really?"

"I'm afraid so, and it took forever to get off your foot, too. But you did make pretty foot-shaped flowers on the tiles over there." She pointed. "This time I got someone in to do it. Very lazy." She moved toward Luke and stroked his cheek softly with one finger. "And how are you feeling, Luke? You were very brave."

"Yes, I was," said Luke. "I wanted to cry. But look at this." He tapped his head purposefully, then frowned and burst into tears again. "It hurts!" he wailed. "Maman . . ." And he began to babble away in French, and Martha did not understand him.

David, who had been standing by the doorway, held out his hand. "Luke, come with me, little one. I have something to show you. And there's cake in my study too."

Luke looked up at his great-grandfather questioningly, then nodded and ran over to him. He took his hand, and as they disappeared, followed by Florence, Cat sank down into Southpaw's carved wooden chair and stared into space.

"He'll draw him a little Wilbur cartoon about it, won't he?"

Martha thought of the last time David had tried to draw Wilbur, a pathetic, grotesque parody of the dog he used to scribble in one-two-three-four-five seconds for an eager child or an enthralled fan.

"He'll think of something, I'm sure."

"I can't believe it," Cat said. "I still can't believe . . . we're here." She squared her slim shoulders and said quietly, "Gran, you must want to know what happened. Why I didn't—tell you about Luke. Who he is, and all that."

"Well, I can guess he's your son, and his father had black hair, that's about it," Martha said. "What I want to know is why you didn't tell me."

Cat said something so faint Martha couldn't hear.

Martha leaned in. "I'm a little deaf. Say it again."

She said, very softly, "I lost myself."

"What do you mean?"

"It sounds so . . . stupid, saying it out loud." Cat said. "My friend Véronique calls it the mist. Like I got caught in it, couldn't see out of it."

Martha stood up and fetched the old teapot. She plucked the mugs off the dresser behind Cat as the door opened and Florence came in.

"There you two are. Pa's having a great time with Luke, you know. I'm going to make some coffee. Cat, love, coffee for you?"

Martha nodded approvingly at her, and handed Cat the mugs.

"I'll stick to tea. Oh, these old friends," Cat said, looking at them. "The Silver Jubilee, the hedgehog wearing glasses . . . Leeds Castle . . ." Martha saw tears falling onto the wooden table.

"Why are you crying, darling?" she said, stroking her granddaughter's shoulders.

Cat bent forward, her head in her hands, and cried as though her heart was breaking, softly, sobs thrumming through her, rocking backward and forward. It was a good minute or so before she could speak. Florence tactfully busied herself at the sink with some washing up, while Martha sat beside her granddaughter, waiting till she raised her head. Suddenly she felt enormously guilty. She had done this. She had created this.

Then, quite clearly, she heard Daisy's voice.

She has to know, Ma. You have to explain what you've done.

It was so distinct that she turned round. But no one was there. Martha shrugged, batting the invisible away. She gripped Cat's heaving shoulder.

"Darling, tell me what's wrong. Tell me why you're crying. Then I can help you."

Cat looked up and said softly, "Everything is wrong. I shouldn't have come home. Seeing the mugs and Southpaw's sketches on the wall, and the owl on the door—I—I can't go back there, knowing that now."

"Knowing what?"

"How much I hate it. I can't . . . we can't do it anymore."

She pressed her fingers to her face.

"You can stay here," Martha said. "You and little Luke." Her breath caught in her throat. "You don't have to go back."

Cat laughed. "We can't stay here."

"Yes, you can." She whispered it in her ear. "Darling, you're home. You don't ever have to leave again."

Only after she said it did she remember to whom she'd said it before, and why.

Lucy

THE DOORBELL RANG, ferociously, at 7:00 a.m. Lucy tried to ignore it, as she did most mornings; then she sighed and let out a low growl of irritation, rolled out of bed, and stamped down the hall. The rain had stopped, and as she opened the door a sharp wintry breeze flew into the damp flat.

"Package." The grim-faced courier held out a box and a tiny Black-Berry, screen hopelessly scratched. "Please sign." Lucy drew a straight line, wondering if there was a piece to be written about signatures on courier deliveries, because she'd never once managed to sign something on one of the screens that even closely approximated her name. The courier walked away without a word—they always acted as though she'd kept them waiting ten minutes, not ten seconds—and Lucy slammed the door, slightly louder than she should have.

"Post for you, Irene," she growled, throwing the box outside her flat-mate's closed door. Irene was an obsessive eBayer and at least once a day, usually more often, some piece of vintage fashion would arrive in Am-hurst Road, ready to be exclaimed over, photographed, blogged about. Lucy really didn't understand how Irene could afford any of it, but she didn't want to be hauled away to prison as an accessory to identity fraud so she assumed a position of *ask no questions*, and longed for the day when she had a place of her own.

Lucy started making herself some coffee, then remembered she was trying not to drink coffee because of that article she'd read about how every cup shortened your life by 3.5 minutes. So she made herself some hot water with a slice of lemon, which was what Lara had at the start of each day, as she liked to inform the office in her blaring foghorn voice.

"It's amazing, it's really cleansing. It means you're not hungry for break-fast."

She said it every morning.

The flat was on the ground floor of a chilly Victorian house in the heart of Hackney. Lucy's room was much bigger than Irene's, and soon after Lucy moved in she'd understood why Irene had chosen the other. Lucy's was freezing, even in summer. It faced northeast and the sun never quite reached the huge, draft-magnetic, grimy gray bay window. It smelled vaguely of cats and damp; Irene's room, however, smelled of cleaning products, plastic synthetic packaging materials, and Gucci Envy.

Snuggling back under the still-warm duvet with her hot water and lemon, Lucy pulled her laptop up onto the bed and waited for it to power up, gazing vacantly at the black screen. She wished she could shake this feeling of dread that seemed to have settled on her lately, like a cloud somewhere just above her head. She couldn't work out what was causing it.

It wasn't just the foreboding she felt when she thought about Gran's invitation, or her wild, panicked eyes when Lucy had asked her about that damned article. She wished she'd never mentioned it to Deborah. It wasn't just Southpaw's frail face and swollen hands, either. This time tomorrow she'd be in her dad and Karen's house. Karen would have bought croissants from Marks & Spencer. Dad would have something to show her; he always did. Some funny book, some article from a newspaper he'd cut out. And Karen . . . she'd be there, sipping coffee, just . . . staring at them.

It was always the same; but the last time she'd been back, nearly two weeks ago, she'd *known* something was going on between them. Was it true? Had Dad found something out? Karen was snappy, not eating anything. Dad was behaving strangely too. That kind, friendly, Dad-style jollity she knew so well was turned up several notches. He only did that when he was feeling panicked: the more worried he was, the more sprightly he became. She'd lived with it for years. As a child, Lucy had always known if her mother was particularly bonkers or feeling spiteful when she got up in the morning. Dad would be making French toast in the kitchen, singing Gilbert and Sullivan at the top of his voice. *Every-thing's fine here! Nothing to see!*

"So, all was good up at Winterfold," Lucy had said. "Gran says the preparations are going well. She's polished all the silver."

"Oh, yes!" Dad had said. "More coffee, Karen? The party, hey! It's going to be great."

Karen had looked up from her magazine. "No, thanks." She'd pushed her plate away, the croissant virtually untouched. "I'm not feeling that well, actually."

"Oh dear," Bill had said, and then, "Poor old thing. You've been working so hard lately, haven't you?"

Lucy saw her father watching Karen, and she didn't quite understand the look in his eyes, and was discomfited. "Yes, much too hard," Karen said. She arched her back and stood up, then said, too casually, "I keep meaning to tell you, by the way. I'll be at the lunch, of course, but the drinks on the Friday night—I'm not sure I'll be able to make them. There's a conference call with the States at six thirty that day—"

"Oh, no!" Lucy, ever the Pollyanna, cried. "Can't you tell them it's important?"

Karen was standing in the doorway. She rubbed her eyes, then looked over at her husband. "I have, several times. Rick won't listen. I'll be there the next day."

"But how sad you have to miss the drinks—those parties of Gran and Southpaw's are the best," said Lucy, who literally could imagine nothing better than a family gathering at Winterfold, the house full of people and light and laughter.

Her father said nothing throughout this. Then he got up too, went over to the sink, and rinsed out the cafetière. "That's a real shame, Karen," he said, and started humming.

And I am right and you are right and all is right as right can be!

Lucy took a sip of her hot water, grimacing. The lemon was bitter, the water lukewarm in the chill of her room. The truth was, she couldn't bear the idea of upsetting her dad. He'd been like a sad old dog after he split up with her mum, padding around his new house in the village in his slippers, trying to invite people over for weird things like Korean barbecue night. Karen had been good for him. And—Lucy forced herself to admit it—she liked her.

Karen was fun, when she didn't have that awkward look in her eyes. She liked *X Factor* and popcorn films; she could recite *The Proposal* and

The Holiday off by heart but, like Lucy, she hated *Love Actually*, said it was way too saccharine, which was exactly what Lucy thought. And she was so clever, she had this amazing job. Lucy had once heard her on the phone to her boss, and Karen had said about fifteen things Lucy didn't even understand as sentences, let alone pieces of actual information. She'd been good for Dad. She'd relaxed him, while Lucy's mother, Clare, had wound him up with her intense moodiness and obsession with fads: tai chi, womb rebirth, Bikram yoga. Lucy had grown up with it and she'd seen how hard it was for him. Karen didn't take, take, take all the time, she just let him be himself; and in the beginning you could tell she just thought he was wonderful, looked at him like he was the voice of wisdom. Lucy sometimes felt Dad labored under a yoke of Winter-ishness. Pretending everything was okay when it wasn't, keeping the mood of the room upbeat, happy, when it wasn't. He wanted the approval of his parents more than anything, and because he was nearby, handy, undramatic, he never seemed to get it. Which was stupid, Lucy thought. He was the best dad ever, and he was an amazing doctor, nothing too trivial for him. He cared about people: look at old Mr. Dill's housemaid's knee, which had got so bad he couldn't walk. Dad went and saw him every day for two weeks and took him soup and just let him talk. Or Joe Thorne's finger: Joe had told Lucy in the pub last week that he'd have lost it, if it wasn't for her dad. No career, nothing. He'd saved that awful man Gerald Lang's life at the disastrous summer party, which had passed into Winter folklore. And there was the time he waded into the river and pulled out Tugie, Gran and Southpaw's final dog, who was obsessed with finding otters, while Lucy and Lucy's then boyfriend, Tom, just looked on blankly.

Tom said afterward, "I would have gone in but I really didn't want to cramp your dad's style. I think he needed that."

Yeah, right, Lucy had wanted to say. *You're a twenty-five-year-old ex-rower who runs every day. My dad is nearing fifty and his knees click when he walks. Sure, that was really nice of you.*

Oh, why hadn't she done anything?

A sound along the corridor, of creaking floorboards and mewling, suggested Irene was awake and about to come out to feed Chairman Miaow. Lucy snapped out of her reverie, looking around her. It was seven thirty-two. She ought to get up, get in the shower first, be at work early, ahead of the game, so when Deborah asked her for the fourth time what was happening with that article about Southpaw, she'd be able to say, "I'm sorry. I still need to dig around a little more. Work out what angle to take. But I've had this idea for a piece on the Kardashians. The Oscars. Rihanna. Jennifer Aniston and her secret heartbreak."

She'd rung her grandmother and told her she wasn't going to do it anymore, and she'd meant it. Lucy's conversation with Cat had shaken her, not just because Cat was so . . . vicious. It was more than that. For the last few weeks Lucy had been buying time so she could decide whether she really should just give up the whole thing or carry on digging a little further, for her own sake, if no one else's. Even if she never showed the article to another living soul, she felt she had to write it: because something wasn't right, that was for sure.

She scrolled quickly through her e-mails. The usual morning inbox junk. Discounts from the Outnet, celebrity gossip updates, a new pub around the corner from her was opening a microbrewery called the Dalston Hopster—even Lucy could see that the lack of irony in that was almost appalling.

She almost missed the e-mail from her mother, sent late the previous night, and Lucy's shoulders tensed in anticipation as she opened it.

Hi Darling

I'm off to India tomorrow, just to remind you. I find it hard to be in the country with the celebrations taking place this weekend. I feel excluded by your grandparents. This is a source of sadness to me.

In answer to your question, I have been in touch with Daisy myself. I wanted some advice on traveling alone, especially through Delhi. I have tried to contact her several times with no reply. I did remember, however, that she used another name when she went to Kerala: Daisy Doolan. Read this because even though it's four years old I think it is very interesting.

https://bitly.com/perssonch

She didn't tell your grandparents she'd been booted out, did she? What's happened to her, then? I'll let you know if she replies.

I'm away until the week before Christmas. Raymond has my
schedule and the details of the ashram if you need to contact me in
an emergency. Take care, darling, be well, be full of light and love.

Clare xx

Who was Raymond? Typical Mum. Lucy clicked on the link, and as
she read slowly, her eyes opened wide, her jaw dropped.
"No," she said to herself. "She wouldn't do that. That's not right."

Charity worker fired, sent home in disgrace

Local residents profess themselves shocked and saddened by
the exit from the Sunshine Children's School of Daisy Doolan
from the United Kingdom, who has done so much to aid school
attendance and prosperity in this area and was rewarded only
recently with a medal from the mayor (see picture). In 1983
when Miss Doolan arrived in Cherthala, literacy was already
high but attendance was low and poverty was great. She
raised 2 million rupees toward the building of the new school
for girls and, as we know, five pupils have gone on to Bombay
University to study a diverse range of subjects. Miss Doolan is
said by the school's principal to have been embezzling money
up to the sum of 1 million rupees over five years. She has been
dismissed and police are anxious to trace her whereabouts.
One colleague said she had left and gone back to England.

Cat

By Friday, it felt as though she had been at home for months. Had she really been away all that time? The only difference was that first night in the upstairs bathroom, unchanged after all these years, same William Morris peacock wallpaper, same pig-shaped tooth mug, handle missing. Same carpet, same dust-encrusted bottles of ancient Body Shop Ice Blue Shampoo and Grapefruit Shower Gel. She'd stared at her reflection, tired, strung-out after a long day, and nearly screamed at the truth that only old, familiar mirrors give you. She'd thought: *I look like her. I look* exactly *like her.*

That first night, Cat slept as though she'd been drugged; Luke too. It was the first night they'd been in different rooms, and she was still worried that the cut on his head might wake him up; but the thought of putting him into his own room—that alone made coming home worthwhile. When she checked on him, he was fast asleep, arms flung outward as if he was running to hug someone, duvet tangled around his feet, cheeks flushed.

It was so strange, how easy it was to slip back into life here. As if it had been waiting for her, and her son, to come back into it. Easy, and terrifying at the same time. Had she changed? Was she a different person? Were they? She couldn't help asking herself this, as the day of the birthday lunch grew nearer, and then it was Friday.

"Apples, milk for Luke, trash bags. I'll be home in time for lunch. Luke?" She looked around. "Luke?"

"He's with Southpaw." Florence appeared in the kitchen, where Cat and her grandmother were sitting, and poured herself some more coffee. "They're making something together. They're covered in paint." She shrugged. "It looks like a dragon."

Cat stood up. "It's so great. I've never seen him like this. He's shy around men."

"Your grandfather is a childish man in many ways," Martha said, smiling. She stood up slowly. "Get some lemons, will you? Oh, and can you do me a favor?"

"Sure." Cat hunted around in her purse, hoping against hope she might find some more English money in there.

"Can you pop into the Oak Tree and tell Joe I've found the extra champagne glasses in the attic and he doesn't need to bring any more up?"

"Oh, right. Sure."

If Martha registered Cat's hesitation, she didn't comment. She reached for a chocolate biscuit. "Have this, darling, you're far too thin. Take your time. Lunch is all ready and Luke's fine."

As she strode away from the house, down the hill to the village, Cat swung her arms in front of her, breathing in the damp, mulchy air. Luke *was* fine, in fact more than fine. Since he'd been here he hadn't stopped talking, a sort of French-English babble that he sang to himself as he ran around the sitting room, picking books off the shelves that lined the walls, asking Southpaw a hundred questions. His great-aunt Florence, too—he seemed fascinated by her and what she knew about things. "Why is your hair so messy?" he'd asked—only he said "*messeee*"—the night before at dinner, and Florence had simply thrown her head back and roared with laughter.

Recalling it now, his pleasure at Florence's glee, the whole family together and the lightness of it, how silly it was, gave Cat a sharp pain in her chest. No matter how often she said to herself, "It's just for the weekend, enjoy it," she knew now that one of the reasons she'd never wanted to come back was simply that a part of her had always known she'd find it almost impossible, once she was here, to leave again.

To have been that person in Paris with that life seemed unreal, out here on this beautiful day, with the curling lane rolling away from her, the village in the distance, the gentle hue of ginger-brown leaves still dusting the tops of the trees. The sky was a clean gray-blue, wisps of cloud like lines of cotton wool. She breathed in again, clearing her mind. "Three more days," she said to herself as she turned off and headed through the woods, her feet following the same old path across the stream she'd always taken. "Forget about everything else. Be like Luke. Enjoy it."

. . .

It was a little after twelve when Cat entered the pub with her shopping, cheeks flushed from the crisp damp wind whistling through the village. The door banged behind her and the lady behind the bar looked up, as did the only other people there, a couple in the corner who then, after a brief pause, fell back into conversation.

"How can I help you?" said the landlady.

Cat stared. "Sheila? It's Cat! Winter! I heard you were back in Winter Stoke. Gosh, hello!"

Sheila stared back; then her eyes widened and she clapped her hands together. "Well, I never. Cat, my dear! Come here, give me a kiss." She hugged Cat. "Well, I heard you were coming back for this party, but I didn't think it'd be true. You here to see Joe about tonight?"

"Oh—" Cat began.

But Sheila said firmly, "He's nearly free anyway. *Joe!*" she called sharply.

Cat's heart sank as the man in the far corner turned round and, seeing her, scrambled to his feet. The woman he was with stood up quickly. "Cat!" she said brightly.

Cat froze. "Karen? Karen!" She'd seen her only once, and so long ago that it took Cat a moment to recognize her. She looked at her, and then at Joe. "How are you?"

"I'm really well, Cat. It's great to have you back. I know they're all so pleased you've made it."

Cat thought Karen didn't look well at all. She had yellow shadows under her eyes and she'd obviously been crying. She wrapped her shapeless black cardigan defensively around her, and Cat, trying not to let her mind run ahead, smiled at her in a friendly way.

"Oh, thanks." All she could think was, *Poor Lucy was right*, and she wished her cousin were there, wished their last words hadn't been angry ones. She laid a hand on the bar and gestured to Joe. "Hi. I didn't mean to interrupt. Gran wanted me to give you a message."

Joe glanced at Karen, who said, "I was just in to talk to Joe about your grandmother's cake, actually! Bill's sorting it out this end, and we've had—oh, we've had a lot of fun with it, haven't we . . . Joe?" she ended, as though she weren't quite sure of his name.

Cat nodded. She glanced at Joe, and their eyes met.

He looked awful, she thought, even worse than he had on Wednesday. Maybe he just looked like that all the time. She remembered Lucy saying he was gorgeous, dark blue eyes, all of that. To Cat he looked like a man pushed almost past endurance. His face was gray and he hadn't shaved. Black stubble prickled his jaw, and his eyes were bloodshot.

He rubbed his chin. "How's your little lad?" he said. "And the car—it's all sorted with the rental company? You'll let me know what I need to do?"

"Yes, thanks. And—Luke's fine. Thank you."

"I wanted to give you something for him, actually. I haven't—"

"Honestly, it's fine." Cat cleared her throat. "Listen, I won't keep you. I just wanted to let you know Gran doesn't need the extra champagne glasses. She found the others in the attic."

He nodded, still staring at her, but didn't say anything. "Is that okay?" she said after a few seconds.

"Joe," Sheila said sharply. "Answer her."

He jumped. "Sure. That's great. Thank you for letting me know. You must have enough on."

"Me? I'm fine," Cat said. "Seriously, are you all right? You look like you're coming down with something."

"I'll be off, then," Karen said chirpily to no one in particular. "See you—all later then. Bye! Thanks for the drink, Joe."

The door slammed heavily behind her. Joe flinched, then shook his head. "I—sorry. I'm just tired."

Sheila said, "He's not been sleeping. It's this party, is it, Joe?"

"Something like that." Joe gave a small smile. His phone buzzed with a text, but he slid it straight into his pocket, then looked up at her. "Can I get you a drink?"

Despite herself, Cat suddenly felt sorry for him. He seemed totally alone, standing by the bar, his wide shoulders drooping, his jaw clamped so tight it was almost as though he were smiling. But this was the man who'd written off his own car and caused thousands of pounds worth of damage to her rental car, to say nothing of nearly killing her son in the process. And Karen—what was he up to, huddled away with Bill's wife in the middle of the day?

"No. Thank you. So you know Karen, do you?" she asked, a little too bluntly.

"Yes." Joe picked up a beer mat, cracking the hard cardboard apart between his fingers. "She's been kind to me since I came here."

"Yes," she said uncertainly. "Course."

"It's strange. Moving far away from your—your family, not knowing anyone." He stared out the windows at the gray sky. "When you want to belong. And you don't. I'm grateful to her."

Cat, who had expected some glib reply, frowned. "Yes. Of—course."

He shook his head as though recalling himself to the present. "Look, I got Luke this book anyway. I meant to drop it off today. Jamie loved it when he was his age."

He disappeared behind the bar, and pulled a package out from beside the till. Dust rose up in the air, and it seemed horribly symbolic, falling there in the deserted pub.

"Oh . . ." Cat said, embarrassed. "You didn't need to."

"No, but I wanted to. Jamie and I read it all the time." He handed her a paper bag, and she slid a long, slim volume out of it, and looked dubiously at the front cover.

"*Stick Man*," Cat read. "Right. 'From the author of *The Gruffalo*.' It looks great. Thank you. Never heard of *The Gruffalo*, but I'm sure it's a good one."

Joe said softly, "Sorry. You've never heard of *The Gruffalo*?"

"No. Um . . ." She didn't want to be rude. "I'm sure it's a really good book. Looks great."

"You have never heard of *The Gruffalo*?" He repeated this. "Seriously." He looked around him. "Are you joking? Maybe it's got another name in France. Look at the back. There's a picture of the Gruffalo."

Cat, feeling annoyed, turned the book over. "No. Sorry. There are lots of children's books, anyway, and—"

"I think it's really weird you've never heard of *The Gruffalo*, that's all. What kind of a country is it you live in that doesn't have *The Gruffalo*?"

"So you've said." Cat put the book back in its bag.

"Let me give you some context," Joe told her. "It's like not having heard of Winnie-the-Pooh."

"That's rubbish."

"It is," he said insistently. "It really is."

"Well, I'll read him *Stick Man* tonight. Thanks."

"Stick Man's an idiot, basically, always nearly getting burned on a fire or carried away by a bird. *The Gruffalo*, that's what you want. It's double bluff, it's genius." He looked at her. "Look. I'll give you my copy."

"You've got your own copy? *That's* a bit weird, isn't it?"

He grinned suddenly, and his face changed. "That came out wrong. I mean for when Jamie comes to stay. My son. You can borrow it while you're here for the weekend. I'll bring it up sometime."

"This evening. The drinks."

"Yes." He stopped. "Of course. Look, I'd best get on. If that's all?"

"Oh, yes." She suddenly felt foolish, in the way. "Thanks again for this. Um—see you later." She raised her hand to Sheila: "Lovely to see you again, Sheila," and made to leave.

"Hey," Joe called out. "Cat, listen. I'm sorry, again."

Cat turned. "Are you talking to me?"

"Yes." Joe gripped his hair. "I'm really sorry. I feel worse and worse, every time I think about his little face. Believe me, I'm so glad he's okay. It was so bloody stupid." He stared at the floor.

Sheila had gone into the back and there was no one else in the pub. Cat crossed her arms. "Well, it was an accident. Wasn't it?" she said, gently smiling, but he looked at her seriously.

"Of course it was, Cat."

"I was joking," Cat said. "I don't actually think you were trying to murder us."

"Right." Again he scratched at his scalp. "I don't even understand when people are making jokes anymore. This morning the guy from the brewery went 'Boo' to me and I nearly punched him in the face."

She laughed. "You must have a lot on, with this party."

"That's about all we have on. This place isn't keeping me busy. So the party, yes, I want it to be right. Impress everyone so they start coming here. It's—yeah, I suppose it's been on my mind a lot."

She watched him. "Is there anything I can do?"

He gave a shy smile. "Just say 'ooh' and 'ahh' when the food comes out and make out you've never eaten anything so delicious before. That's what you can do."

Cat laughed. "Okay. Well, Gran says it's going to be amazing. She doesn't lie."

"You live in Paris, though; you're a tough person to please."

"Believe me, I'm not. I can't wait for a proper posh meal. I live on frozen foods and the odd croissant." *And Henri and Madame Poulain's leftovers, and once I ate a baguette someone left untouched on a bench in the Tuileries Gardens. Basically, I don't eat much because we live on eighty euros a week. And then people compliment me on how slim I am.*

"Well, I hope you enjoy tonight. And lunch tomorrow. It's very important to your gran that it's all perfect," Joe said, moving behind the bar.

She watched him, his easy strength as he lifted a crate of tonic bottles out of the way, almost like he could flick them with his finger. "Thank you," she said, trying not to sound defensive. "I think I know what it's about, though." She gave him a piercing look. "It's pretty obvious, isn't it, when you think about it?"

He stopped unloading the bottles and their eyes met again. Cat had the strangest feeling whenever she looked at him. As if she knew him from somewhere.

"Whatever. She's very glad you're back. She's missed you. And your granddad. He's not been well, has he?"

She shook her head, her heart pumping. "I—I don't know."

"He's a lovely man. Been wondering about him lately; wanted to ask someone in the family if he was okay."

"You could always have asked Karen," she said lightly.

There was a silence. "Yes," Joe said slowly. He bowed his head slightly, and their eyes locked again. "Look, Cat—"

What would have happened next Cat didn't know, but the door opened again. "Hello, Joe. Well, hello there, Cat!"

Cat turned round. "Hello," she said warily. A plumpish woman, older than she, around forty, with sandy cropped hair and a big smile, plumped herself down next to Cat, who racked her brains wildly. Who was this?

"What can I do for you, Susan?" Joe said. Cat threw him a grateful glance.

"Anything you want, Joe, you know that!" Susan said, and gave an awkward titter. Joe smiled tightly. *Susan . . .* Cat racked her brains. *Susan Talbot. Post office. George and Joan Talbot's daughter.*

She put her hand on Susan's arm. "Hello, Susan. Lovely to see you."

"And you, my dear." Susan chuckled, her eyes twitching in a slightly disconcerting way. "I'm looking forward to the party tonight. You'll all be there. It's all anyone's talking about. Have to work out what I'm going to wear!" She gave a matronly, arch smile and grinned at Cat, folding her arms below her big bosom. "I came in to get a bottle to take up with me tonight. You can help me with that, can't you, Joe?"

Joe nodded and bent down, taking out three different bottles. "Of course. One of these any good?"

"You don't need to bring anything tonight," Cat told Susan, who was watching Joe with a look in her eye that Cat didn't like. Susan had always been crazy. One of many tightly furled memories began to roll out in Cat's brain. When they'd been at school, Susan had accused one of the teachers of being a pervert, and he'd been sacked. It hadn't been true.

"No, no! I wouldn't hear of it! I want to do my bit, you're all like family to me! The Winters!" Susan took out her purse, looking at Joe from under her thick black eyelashes, so at odds with her blond complexion.

Cat caught Joe's eye briefly. "Okay, well, I'd better be getting back." She picked up the bag again. "See you later, both of you. And, er"—she smiled at Joe—"thanks again. So, I'll get started on this. We'll look forward to the other one. *The Gruffle*."

"Something like that," he said, and she wasn't sure if he was joking or not.

She left him dealing with Susan and strode home back up the hill, wishing Lucy would hurry up and arrive. She was less and less sure of everything the longer she was here.

Karen

"I'M DISAPPOINTED NOT to be going. Honest, Bill."

Karen sat at the foot of the stairs, watching Bill pull his coat on, and trying to catch his eye.

He buttoned his coat. Still not looking at her, he said, "I'm sure you are."

"It's just . . ." She tugged the dressing gown tightly around her. "I still feel really rotten. Think it's best I stay in bed after my call's done. Rest up for tomorrow. I'll definitely be there, tomorrow."

Bill didn't say anything. He went to open the door, one hand resting on the frame so it was still closed. She swallowed, tasting metal in her mouth, feeling weak, wishing he'd speak. These last few days . . . just waiting for him to say something. Because she knew.

"Okay?" she said. "Are you listening to me?"

"Lucy's already up there. I'd better go. Good-bye, Karen," he said.

"Look, Bill, I told you weeks ago I wouldn't be able to come, and I'm sorry, I wish I could. So—you go, give them all my love, I'll see them tomorrow, yes?"

He met her imploring gaze then and she thought he was smiling because he agreed with her. For a brief, blissful couple of seconds she thought the world was right again, and then he held open the door and said, "I think it's best you don't come tomorrow, Karen. I think you know that, too."

Cold air was rushing into the stuffy house. "What do you mean? Of course I'm coming."

"Karen, don't treat me as though I'm stupid. I'm not stupid."

Karen stayed where she was, afraid to move. "I don't understand."

178

"Yes, you do. Karen, I know all about you and him."

The door was wide open; people walked past, looking into the house.

"Hello, Bill! Oh, Karen! See you up there, will we?"

Bill turned with military precision, hand on the door again. "Evening, Clover. On my way up. See you soon." Then he closed the door and came toward Karen. He towered above her, sitting at the foot of the stairs. "I've known about it for weeks."

Karen swallowed. "Who told you?"

"That's—that's all you've got to say to me?" His voice was thick with anger and, she realized, emotion. But Bill never got emotional. "You're sleeping with someone, and all you care about is how I found out? Susan Talbot told me, that's who. Came in last month to show me her verruca." He gave an angry laugh. "Halfway through she said there was something she thought I *had* to know." His voice was cracking and she looked away, unable to bear the look on his face. All the seeds she'd sown, everything she'd done, it was all coming out now . . . and she had to take it. Nothing to do but sit here and accept it. "That's how I found out my wife is—is . . ." Bill covered his face with his hands. "Sleeping with someone be-be-behind my back. Susan Talbot with her sock off whispering secrets into my ear." He turned and stared at the empty bookcase, breathing heavily.

"It's not—" Karen began. It was all clichés, wasn't it? *It's not what you think.* How could she explain to him what it was? She'd slept with someone else, been doing it for months. Those were the facts.

I love you. And I know you don't love me. That's why.

She stood up, ignoring the wave of nausea that crashed over her. Holding on to the banister, she said, "Yes. It is true."

"Thank you," said Bill. Almost as though he was pleased to be proved right. "And is she right? Tell me who it is."

"Bill—"

"*Tell me who the hell it is, Karen!*"

Karen backed away so she was standing on the other side of the sofa, hugging herself.

Bill said, "I'm not going to hit you. Don't be ridiculous. Just say it. Say his name."

"Joe," she whispered. "It's Joe Thorne."

"I knew it." Bill bowed his head. "The . . . my God. I thought we had something. I know we've had our problems, I know we're different, but I thought you loved me."

"I do," Karen said quietly. "Bill, I've always loved you. But you don't love me. You don't have room for me. I realized that a while ago."

It was as though he hadn't heard her. "How long's it been going on?"

"It's not—it's not 'going on.'" She folded her hands together. "It was only a few times, the last time was September, and then he—he broke it off. When he found out I was married."

The night I said I was dropping off Susan's birthday card, in fact.

Your daughter happened to mention to him that she had a stepmother called Karen Bromidge, when they were both at Winterfold. He hadn't realized before then. So you can thank Lucy. Thanks, Lucy!

"He broke it off, not you." Bill looked at the ground. "He—oh, God, Karen."

"I never meant—I wasn't looking to—oh, Bill." She knew how lame that sounded. "We're similar. He's a good man."

"A good man! Karen, your sense of good and bad is pretty questionable, if you don't mind me saying."

"He—" Her eyes were full of tears. *A good man like you.* "He understands . . . oh, things." But she couldn't throw anything back at him, not now. "He understands what it's like, here."

"What, the awful life you both lead in this beautiful village, you with your lovely home and nice job? My heart bleeds." Bill's eyes were dark with anger. "You've always thought you're too good for us lot, Karen. That's the truth, isn't it?"

She laughed, crossing her arms. "What on earth are you on about? That's bloody rubbish. If anything, it's the other way round, Bill. I'm the one who's not good enough for the rest of you, and don't you love letting me know."

Bill shook his head. "You haven't got a clue. You think you're always right. Your point of view and no one else's. I've watched you give that bored little sneer when my family does something, if Lucy's a bit too eager or Ma talks about the garden or something."

"I don't!" It was getting away from her, all of this.

"You do. You only see Flo as eccentric." Bill's voice was quiet. "She's wonderful underneath, the funniest person I know, but you've never bothered to find out. You think we're all snobs, but you're the one who can't get past the fact she doesn't use conditioner and she doesn't care about manicures. That makes you the snob, Karen." Bill's face was pink. "And if we talk about a book we've read or cinema or anything remotely cultured, I've seen you, Karen. With the big sigh as if you think we're all a bunch of idiots. You think anyone who's interested in anything intellectual is a loser."

"No, Bill," she said, not wanting to sound spiteful, unable to help it. "I suppose just for once it'd be nice if someone didn't want to talk about books or paintings or Radio Four. Just for once."

"Ma and Pa had nothing when they were growing up. It's what they're interested in. Don't exaggerate."

"I'm not. I'm bloody not." Her voice shook.

Bill said angrily, "So in that case, I guess a man who cooks chicken and chips for a living's about your level then, isn't he?"

"He's a proper chef, you—you—idiot! And at least we'd talk about things! We'd laugh about things! We didn't sit there in silence doing nothing, saying nothing, night after night! He was there for me, when you're always out, Mr. Dill this, Mrs. Cooper that, Bill. You see your father at least twice a week, just when I'm back from work—"

His face got that pinched look she knew so well. "Pa finds the evenings hardest. Especially if Ma's out. You don't understand."

"Because you never tell me anything!" Karen's voice broke. "You love being needed, Bill. But I'm right here. *I* need you, I'm your wife. . . ."

She covered her face with her hands, furious with herself for crying, having not intended to.

For their third date, they'd driven over to the beach at Clevedon and sat on the beautiful old pier eating sandwiches he'd made, which tasted really strange. He'd pulled a blanket from his car and spread it over her knees. It had been chilly. They were silent a lot of the time, just smiling at each other.

Then he'd said, "I've been practicing chicken Kiev sandwiches all week. You—you—when we were talking last week, you mentioned it was your favorite meal when you were a little girl. I don't know how successful they've been, though."

And Karen had looked away from the gray sea, the endless white sky, and the wheeling seagulls at the quiet, neat man next to her, and they'd smiled at each other, and he'd taken her hand in his, under the blanket. "I feel like a pensioner," she'd said happily.

"Well, for the first time in a long while, I don't," he'd replied, and leaned over and kissed her, very calmly, and his hand squeezed hers tightly as he did. He'd stroked her cheek and said, "You're the most beautiful thing I've ever seen, do you know that?"

Karen, who knew she was a good prospect with her full bling, favorite Karen Millen dress, heels, and handbag combination on, had believed he thought it was true. She understood him, their world together. And then . . . then the doubts had set in, the loneliness, the need for attention, which had been her downfall. But she wasn't a child for wanting it, was she? For wanting someone to laugh with, talk to?

She scratched at her cheeks furiously, staring at him, remembering it all. This was it, maybe forever.

After a long pause, Bill said, "I can't believe how wrong I was about you."

She swallowed back a sob. "It's not just me, Bill. You're so distant. All the time, these days. You're shutting me out."

He paced back and forth, two steps here, then there. "I've had a lot on my mind lately." She stared up at him. "Nothing to do with you. It's—" He rubbed his eyes.

"Bill, tell me. Can't you tell me? Is it about this lunch tomorrow? Your mother's announcement?"

"It's not her. It's Pa." He rocked on his feet like a tired small boy. "Anyway, that's not what this is about, Karen. Don't try to turn this round."

"I'm not doing that, Bill," she said. She tried to think of the best way of making him see that this was exactly what she was talking about. "I'm not. You are. It's like a sinkhole's opened up, right under our marriage. Been growing bigger and bigger for ages. I can see it. You can't. You've just blocked your eyes to it. To me. To how far apart we've grown. I—I don't know how else to put it."

He blinked and said quietly, "Is it over, then? With him? With us?"

"It's over with him." She swallowed, praying she wouldn't start gagging, or worse. "I think it is." How could she finish this, how could she tell him the rest of it?

"Oh, no, he ended it? You poor thing." His voice dripped contempt, and it was horrible. Bill never teased, or was cutting. He was always gentle. "Well, I'd love to stay, but I'm already late. I'll leave you to nurse your bruised ego. Maybe eat a few chocolates and watch a sad film, eh?" He clenched his fists. "Damn you, Karen! Now, of all times. Why did you have to—"

"It wasn't my choice. None of this is my choice." She scratched her face again, feeling the ribbons of pain on her skin.

"Don't act like it's all a big surprise. You knew I knew. I've been watching you these last few days. You're like a cornered rat."

"I am," she said frankly, and she saw the look of surprise in his eyes. "I am, I'm trapped, Bill. Sit down. I have to talk to you properly. There's something else you need to know."

Daisy

January 1983

SHE IS STILL sleeping. If I just carry on maybe she'll stay asleep. I don't think it's sleep like adults sleep. It's a furious pause. Fists screwed up. Angry nasty little face wrinkled. Horrible bent knees and long feet curled against the cradle in these nappies I can't get right. The pin is blunt and I keep forcing it through the damn nappy and then pricking her.

I can see clearly, then I can't. I can feel calm, then I can't. I am worried I will hurt her. I don't think she'd notice, that's what I tell myself. She is so tiny, so cross and small, she doesn't open her eyes except to stare, not focusing on anything. I don't want her to love me, I never did this for that. I could have got rid of her. I just wish she'd look at me.

Sometimes when I've tried to feed her and I can't, and I've given her some other milk and she won't drink it, I lie in bed crying very quietly so they won't hear, and she cries and cries too. She falls asleep eventually and I stare at her, small and red, splayed across my tummy. Her mouth flutters open like a butterfly. She's so tiny. She felt massive inside me and now she's just so small.

I hate it here. I always did, and now I'm trapped. They think it's the making of me. I hate their condescension. Billy Lily at Christmas: "Be the making of you, everyone should have a baby, Daisy!" What does he know about it? That disgusting self-centered hippie he's going out with, she's completely wrong for him and that's obvious, but everyone's so pleased Bill finally has a girlfriend they don't care she's as ugly as sin, completely rude and stupid too. I really hate her.

And Florence. I can't even talk about Florence. I crawl with revulsion; I think I might be allergic to her. Whatever it is in my head, there's something there that reacts whenever I have to go near her. I hate how obvious she is. She doesn't . . . understand anything. I actually think she might be mentally disabled. I read an article about it. She is brilliant, I know, you all keep telling me, I know. But she is totally incapable of having a conversation. She can't even say hello without making fifteen different noises afterward and pushing her glasses around her face. I hate her. I'm quite calm about it.

She was there at Christmas, poking this baby, stroking her face like some pervert, cooing over her. I want to say: *You don't belong here, Florence. You aren't part of this family. Why don't you just get out?*

But I'm the one who doesn't belong. I can tell that's what they all think. They don't really get the fact that I'm the one who belongs here, and she doesn't. So I have to go.

This thing here—I've thought about plonking her on Giles's doorstep. But I know he's terrified his girlfriend will find out we fucked. Straight after we'd done it, he said: "That was a mistake." Nice, huh? Rolled off me and started sweating in the tent. I could hear the hyenas outside, screeching and mating.

I didn't say anything. Just turned over and pretended to sleep. I remember the mattress was scratchy and a little piece of horsehair kept poking me in the neck all night. It kept me awake, burrowing into me, but I couldn't pull it out when I looked for it. And all that night this thing was taking root inside me, swallowing me up.

I'd done it before: with boys in the village like Len the farmer's boy or that man who came up to drop off Daddy's page proofs, a long drippy thing he was, a bit like Giles, now I come to think of it. I think I got too sure of myself, because Gerald Lang from up at the Hall really hurt me. If you act confident they love it, they're so scared. I'd tell them to meet me in the woods, then be waiting with my panties off and let them touch me there, and then they'd want to do it, even if they didn't, if you know what I mean? Because they'd think it wasn't manly to say no. I think men are pathetic. But Gerald didn't like it that he couldn't do it properly the first time.

He said could he meet me again. I said yes. So we met at the back of the woods again and this time he was different, he kicked me, he bit my breasts and then he shoved up inside me, and I really did hurt for days and days, and I bled afterwards. He kept doing it after I'd shouted and when I bit him he bit me back. He told me I was a stupid cunt, kept

185

saying it. I couldn't stop him. I just said: "You're hurting me." Over and over.

The weird thing is he liked that.

So what is strange is: when he'd finished it, he stopped and was all normal again, and then he said: "That'll teach you a lesson, girlie."

Girlie. We'd grown up together. I was six months older than him, in fact. *Girlie.*

The next week I saw him in the street, and now I think about it, four or so years later, I realize it was rape, it was. And he waved. "Hello, Daisy, old girl, how are you?"

I don't understand the world, the way it works. More and more.

I think it is all part of the lessons I've learned. The one lesson that was wrong was Giles. It's lonely out there, dangerous too. During the day I was a hero; at night I was scared and didn't know where to go. I thought it'd be good to do it again with someone who wasn't rough. And Giles wasn't rough, he was a drippy, sloppy mush of a man. Like a cold wet plate of boiled spinach. I thought it'd be nothing, and instead look what it did to me.

I don't see why I should give her a name. I don't want to give her anything, then she won't have any connection with me, and really? It'll be much easier that way.

Ma and Dad are treading on eggshells around me; they'll believe anything I say. If I say she's hungry, they try to pretend it's all right that she cries for hours because they don't want to interrupt Daisy when she might be doing something useful for once.

Actually I'm arranging the clothes in the wardrobe, bit by bit. All my favorite dresses, all together for once. It's childish, but it *was* childish, how I had to give everything to Florence, to Caroline in the village, to everyone. I never had my own things. I never came anywhere except in the middle, people squeezing me on both sides.

It'll be light soon. She's crying again and I can't feed her. I keep trying and it's agony. They keep saying it'll get better, but it doesn't. I don't understand any of this, why this is in the world and what I should do. I know now she'd be better off without me. I look at her in the cradle. She is so furious. Her mouth is a wide, wide O. Purple, her face is purple.

She smells. If I put this towel over her, she's muffled and I really can't hear her.

It's quite nice, the sound blocked out.

I'm sitting on the edge of the bed rocking the cradle. If she'll just shut up, I'll take the towel off.

She's quiet now. I lift the towel away. You know, it's strange, she's crying, but I don't hear it anymore.

I look at my daughter's face as if it's the first time. Who are you? Who are you, little baby? Did you really come out of me? I know she did, and I know she needs me, and the idea of that makes me start to cry again. Her face has changed, even in the night. She looks like Ma.

I realize how bad it is. How bad I've got. I can't stay here and I know it now, it's just being brave enough to leave.

So I write the note. These clothes are for her.

I look down at her in the cradle, and I touch her cheek. It's very, very soft. I think I'll always remember how it felt even when I don't remember how everything else felt these awful last few weeks.

I know when I shut the door behind me I won't be a mother anymore. I can hitch to London, and Gary has said he'll save me the ticket. I wish it wasn't so easy to be like this, sometimes.

I look at her as she sleeps. Bye-bye, little girl. I'm sorry you're part of me. The thing I hope most for you is that you grow up to be absolutely nothing like me.

Lucy

EVERYONE AGREED THE Winters threw the best parties. Even though it might be, as tonight was, a cold evening, a swirling mist eddying along the lanes and roads, the kind of night that made you want to stay in, curl up on the sofa with a glass of wine, no one who was invited to Winterfold ever did.

It was a treat to make the journey up the hill to the house, and this time the arriving guests knew Martha had outdone herself. The sound of Ella Fitzgerald and babbled conversation floated out down the lane. Colored plastic lanterns hung from the branches and hedgerows as you turned into the drive, and golden light poured from the windows into the drizzle. The front door was propped open, and inside one of the vicar's children took your coat, and someone else—Martha, elegant as ever in a midnight-blue and gold shot taffeta jacket, her dark green eyes smiling at you; or maybe clever, striking Florence, bright as a peacock in green and purple silk, smiling and chatting; or taciturn but friendly Dr. Winter, Bill, who'd always looked after you so well, listened understandingly to your complaints about arthritis or your fears about cancer or your worries about your husband—one of them gave you a kiss and a glass of champagne, in a way that made you feel truly welcomed. You were ushered out of the cold into the cheery sitting room, where the fire leaped in the great inglenook hearth lined with pretty blue-and-white tiles, and someone else offered you a tray stacked high with delicious-looking canapés. As the first, chalky-sharp gulp of champagne bubbled through you, you glanced round and saw an attractive, dark girl leaning against the wall, and David smiling next to her—was that really Cat, the prodigal granddaughter returned from Paris? And as you inhaled the atmosphere, of light in the winter's dark, warmth and security, you felt the sense of being pulled into the center of something, a place you wanted to be.

The village was out in force. Kathy, the vicar, was over there, Sheila from the pub; even nervous new parents Tom and Clover, the pair always referred to as "that sweet young couple in the village," had got a babysitter for once, Tom's hair standing on end, Clover flushed and sweet in a dress that showed too much of her large breasts. The Range Rovers, who never came to anything in the village, were there. That pompous ass Gerald Lang, of Stoke Hall, and his wife, Patricia, who hadn't been to a Winterfold party for years, after what had happened to Gerald—even *they* were there. The biggest coup was the actress from the ITV cop drama and her director husband, who lived in the really big house farther up the hill and never came to anything. But they, like you, were simply guests in this lovely home, enjoying themselves, and you all had something in common, which was that a tiny part of you wished you could live there, become part of the family, have this life for yourself.

Though increasingly, you felt, the Winters had their problems these days. You knew Daisy wasn't to be spoken of, and the other daughter was, really, increasingly batty, wasn't she? And why was the son's new wife, a cold fish, mysteriously absent? Susan Talbot had been spreading rumors all week about Karen, and as you mingled more you discovered that Cat had returned with a *son*, whom she'd apparently kept secret. And Bill was drinking too much, and Lucy, his daughter, talked too much, and dear old David—he looked pretty done in, didn't he? Not well at all—and the birthday girl, Martha, wasn't herself, it couldn't be denied, distracted and mechanical in her responses to you, as though she were somewhere else entirely.

But though all of these things were true, when that nice Joe Thorne appeared, an hour or so into the party, carrying a birthday cake blazing with so many candles he seemed to be carrying a halo of fire and everyone sang "Happy Birthday," Martha's face, bathed in the glow of the fire and the champagne and the atmosphere, seemed then to be lit from within with some emotion. And you felt sure that, though of course things weren't easy for anyone, no matter how it looked from the outside, the Winters must, indeed, know themselves to be a lucky family.

. . .

Just as Lucy finished handing round another spread of canapés, she saw Cat shushing a reluctant Luke out of the room and off to bed. Cat turned and raised her eyes at Lucy, mouthing: *This is really weird.*

Lucy had to admit it was. Kind of unreal, a dream, or a scene from a film, not as she'd expected, and she rubbed her eyes. It had been a long day. Cat had a son. Karen wasn't here. Everything else seemed unchanged: the twinkling lights and the Clarice Cliff platters worn with years of sausage rolls and washing up, the old lead crystal flutes, the same faces of people she had known all her life, some bent with age, the children dashing around through people's legs, Gran talking intently to Kathy, the vicar—she looked tired; Lucy thought she must be knackered. The punch bowl on the side, the fire burning—but everything felt different this time. As she stood still and looked around the room, she wished she could go away now and quickly scribble it all down so she'd remember, beset by the sense of her world spinning, getting faster and faster, like a carousel before the music suddenly stops.

"Hello, old thing." Florence put her hand on Lucy's shoulder. "Haven't spoken a word to you all evening. How are you, darling?"

Lucy kissed her aunt, shaking herself out of her haze of thoughts. "I'm fine. Listen, have you seen Joe?"

"Handsome Joe?" Florence grinned. "He is awfully nice."

"Oh . . ." Lucy could feel herself blushing. "Don't be embarrassing. I need to tell him something. Hey, that purple and green is fantastic on you, Flo. You should wear colors more often. You look like Cleopatra."

Florence threw back her head and laughed. "You do talk rubbish." But she looked pleased, and there was an undeniable glow about her this evening. "I'm feeling pretty chipper, I have to say."

"How so?"

Florence drained her drink. "Lucy, well—I've been putting my house in order."

"That sounds vague." The sound of rattling glass sounded in the corner and, glancing over her aunt's shoulder, Lucy could see her father trying to push an empty champagne flute onto a tray, making too much noise.

"Yes, it does, doesn't it? But I've righted a wrong. Took rather a lot of courage to do it. No going back now."

One of the things Lucy loved about Florence was that she didn't seem to care about things that, to Lucy, were so important. "Flo, you're being very mysterious."

"Someone betrayed me. Sounds dramatic, but it's true." Her face clouded, and she looked frightened, very young suddenly. "I've been a total fool. I've decided I'm not going to put up with it anymore. God. I hope I haven't made a huge mistake."

"What have you done?" Lucy said.

"I've done something for myself," Florence said. "I'll tell you about it sometime. You might even be able to help me, in fact."

"How so?"

"Well . . ." Florence bit her lip. "I don't want to say too much at the moment. Maybe I'll be calling on your journalistic connections at some point. My niece, the Fleet Street rising star."

"Oh, I'm really not that," Lucy said frankly. "I couldn't—"

Someone shoved against her and Lucy jolted her glass, spilling champagne. She turned to find her father, swaying slightly, fiddling with his phone.

"Hello there, Dad," Lucy said. He glanced at her and grunted. "Good party, isn't it?"

She handed her father a tray of tiny Florentines. Bill looked at them and then at her, as if trying to remember why he was there. His eyes were slightly glazed.

"You all right, William?" Florence gestured to her brother, and Lucy realized she, too, was not exactly sober. "Look at those freckles. Do you remember in the summer we used to join the dots all over your body with one of Dad's ink pens? When he was bigger he'd try to fight us off, but Daisy was always stronger, wasn't she, Bill?"

Bill shrugged. "She was freakishly strong."

"Your sisters were stronger than you?" Lucy said.

"We were." Florence laughed.

"Oh, I'm the joke of the family, aren't I?" Bill said. "Big joke. That's me."

"Oh, Bill, no, I only meant she—" Florence began, but he interrupted heavily.

"Listen, Flo, I might head off. Not feeling so good and tomorrow'll be a long day."

"I'll come with you," Lucy said.

"No, you stay here, why don't you?" Bill squeezed his daughter's shoulder. "Think Gran could do with the help. Anyway, like I said, Karen's not well, I said, didn't I? You can sleep in Cat's room, can't you? Stay here, that's best."

Lucy gripped his arm. "Oh." She said softly, "What's up, Dad? Everything okay?"

Bill said, "It's fine, love." He blinked and swayed a little. "I shouldn't drink. I can't take it."

"You can't," Lucy said. "Remember my birthday?"

"Well, that." Her father stopped. "Was different. That bar was very loud. I distinctly said just singles, and she kept giving me triple gins and tonics."

"Rubbish," said Lucy. She looked to her aunt for support, but Florence had wandered off. "Dad—I'll come home with you."

"No," her father said roughly. "I said, stay here."

"I just meant I'll walk you home," Lucy said, feeling tears prick her eyes. "Make sure you're all right. I won't come in—"

A voice behind them said, "Any more champagne over here?" and both Lucy and her father turned.

"Oh, hello," Lucy said, smiling. "Dad, it's Joe." She nudged his arm and beamed at Joe, who was staring at them both, bottle in hand, frozen in place. She pulled at her floral shirtdress awkwardly, wishing it weren't so tight. "I—I—"

"Do I want more champagne?" her father interrupted, his voice a little too loud. "Is that what you're asking?"

Lucy ignored her father. She said brightly, "I've got some good news, anyway. Keep forgetting to tell you. I'm sure I've got our restaurant guy to agree to review the Oak Tree. He says December the seventh, and . . ." She trailed off, and looked at Joe and then at her father, on either side of her, staring at each other.

"I hope you rot in hell for what you've done," Bill said softly to Joe. He slammed his glass down on the table, where it rocked drunkenly from side to side, knocking over an empty plastic cup. Joe swept it up deftly in one hand as Bill strode out of the room, looking at no one, head down. There was a murmuring ripple of surprise around them as the heavy front door slammed shut.

It's starting, Lucy thought. She turned back to Joe, a polite smile fixed on her face, and when she saw his expression she knew. In that moment, she saw it perfectly clearly, almost everything. How could she have been so blind? Of course. He was looking at her intently, something like rage and anger written all over his face. He didn't even look ashamed, standing there holding the champagne bottle and the empty glass. Suddenly Lucy wished that everyone would leave, that this was over. At once it seemed unbearably fake, all of it. And what she wanted now was the truth. She knew it now. That was why they were all there, all of them.

Cat

"So you're back, dear, for how long?"

"I hear you have a . . . son, how old is he?"

"And you're still working at the . . . plant stall, then?"

"It must be wonderful to live in Paris, dear."

"Your grandmother's always talking about you, dear, she must be so pleased you're here."

Hiding in the loo off the freezing-cold cloakroom, Cat wondered how long she could actually stay there. Until someone banged on the door, maybe? She wished she'd brought a glass with her, but she'd already drunk too much. Maybe she needed something to eat. Those canapés were delicious—Joe Thorne might have nearly killed her son and written off her rental car, but he knew how to make pastry, and Cat, like any self-respecting Parisian, took pastry seriously.

She hadn't realized how hard it would be, this bit of coming back. Two days here and she was used to the shock of the familiar, but that was before the party. After an hour of questioning, of pecked cheeks and beady eyes, Cat was ready to hide upstairs. She'd never had Lucy's ebullience; if someone asked Lucy something she didn't want to answer—like Clover, that mumsy airhead from the village: "Do you have a boyfriend yet, Lucy?" (Cat got the feeling Clover was the kind of person who asked that question a lot)—Lucy just diverted attention: "Oh, no chance, not at the moment. Are you watching *X Factor* or *Strictly Come Dancing*? I'm *Strictly* this year."

Cat simply didn't know how to do it. So when Patricia Lang, who was very grand, fixed her with a stare and said, "Why haven't you been back for so long, dear?" Cat had felt herself flushing with irritation. She had never liked Mrs. Lang, and she loathed her husband, Gerald, who'd always reminded her of a kind of red-faced bullfrog. She remembered him of old. He gave her the creeps.

"Y'very like y'mother," he'd slurred once after midnight Mass, to which he'd turned up obviously drunk, and then he'd slid his large, meaty hand across her ribs and stomach, as if he were measuring her for size. Cat, then thirteen, had dodged out of the way, grabbed his arm, and bitten him, hard, on the fleshy ball of his palm, then kicked him in the shin. Then, surprised and slightly alarmed at the violence of her own behavior, had left him, hobbling and swearing softly in the porch, and run all the way home in the dark. She'd never told anyone.

He must be fifty or sixty now, but Cat realized she still loathed him. Wasn't it funny, these people you didn't think about for years? She'd looked round for him: Gran always said vaguely that it was no wonder he mostly never came to any of their parties after what had happened to him here, but could never be drawn on exactly what that was. Almost like it was a joke. She supposed he was a joke, in a way, a nasty, aggressive man who didn't realize he was a dinosaur. His wife, however, was more beady than ever, and Cat honestly hadn't known what to say. She'd blushed even more and then excused herself, to go to the loo.

Bang-bang!! Cat jumped out of her skin.

"Hello? Anyone in there?"

Cat ran the tap and dried her hands. "Sorry, just coming."

Opening the door, she saw Clover's large, moonlike face hovering in wait for her.

"Oh, I'm so sorry. I didn't realize—I wasn't sure—that's why I knocked, there was silence for *such* a long time, you see, and I do need to—we've got a babysitter, and we have to get back to her! It's a rare night out for us!" She gave what Cat thought would be best described as a simpering smile and said, "How often do you get to go out, Cat? In Paris?"

Cat said, "Not much."

"Yes. Of course." Clover nodded as if Cat had enlightened her. "And Luke's father, he . . ."

Cat let the half question hang in the air. "He, yes."

"Ha, ha!" Clover laughed too loudly. "Oh, well, I think you're *very* brave. Tell me, did you breast-feed? Because I hear that in France breast-feeding is totally frowned on. It's such a shame. One of my parenting-group friends—"

"Great!" Cat said, patting her on the back. "Lovely to see you again, Clover. I'll let you get off, isn't it awful weather? Good-bye!"

As Clover retreated, muttering something about playdates, Mrs. Lang appeared from the kitchen doorway. "Hello again, dear. I was just saying to Gerald that I must find out from Cat if—"

Cat couldn't take it anymore. "Thank you! Excuse me, have to check on something outside for Gran." Recklessly she drained the glass of wine on the sideboard, opened the door, and escaped outside.

It was still raining, and the soft mist rolling off the lawn met the light from the house, fusing into a phosphorescent glow. Cat hurried around the terrace, past the living room and the silhouettes of the guests, framed by the windows like pictures in a children's book. She stopped and looked out across the valley. It was a black night, the rain blotting out the moon and stars.

I think you're very *brave.*

Cat had turned at the corner of the L by the kitchen and was wishing she had a cigarette for the first time in years when a low voice called out urgently, "Hey? Who's there?" She started, and her hands shot into her mouth.

"It's Cat. Who is this?"

"Cat. It's Joe."

Joe Thorne appeared from the darkness, and Cat pulled her fingers out of her mouth. "Oh, thank goodness." Relief and adrenaline and al-cohol made her sound almost ecstatically glad to see him. "What are you up to?"

He stamped his feet gently on the mossy ground. "Just wanted some fresh air. Thought it'd be okay to have a couple of minutes' break. The party's starting to wind down."

Cat came and stood next to him under the shelter of the porch. She said awkwardly, "You must be exhausted."

He nodded. "Yes. It's been a good night, though. I hope your grand-mother's enjoyed herself. I wanted her to be pleased."

"I know she is. Very pleased."

There was a small, awkward pause. The rain dripped softly onto the stones of the terrace.

"Luke absolutely loved *Stick Man*," she began. "And, er . . . I looked up *The Gruffalo*. It turns out I'm the only person who's never heard of it. I feel terrible."

"Maybe it's banned in France. Anticompetitive. Perhaps they have their own *Gruffalo* knockoff."

"I'm sure they have it. Sometimes I miss out on stuff, with Luke. It doesn't matter, we read every night and he loves it, but we don't . . ." She looked down. "Oh, well. We have a bit of a strange life there. That's why it's so lovely being here. Everyone together."

He crossed his arms. "Right." Out of the corner of her eye, Cat stole a glance at him. He always looked so serious, so weary. Suddenly she wasn't sure if she wanted another drink or was wishing she hadn't drunk the last one so quickly.

"This is your idea of hell, isn't it?" she said.

"No, not at all." He glanced back at the door. "I suppose family things make me . . ." He trailed off.

"You like *Game of Thrones*, don't you?" she said suddenly.

"How do you know that?"

"Saw the DVD in your bag yesterday when we were all in the kitchen."

"Please don't say *Game of Thrones* reminds you of your family. Oh, my God." He looked around in mock alarm. "Winterfell. Winterfold. Are you . . . the Starks? Are you the Lannisters? Oh, no. Don't be the Lannisters."

Cat put her hands over her mouth and laughed softly. "No. Don't be silly. I just mean you have to take it all with a pinch of salt. Family. Otherwise it's . . . it's too much."

He nodded. "Yes. Well, *Game of Thrones* aside, family gatherings like this do make me feel . . . um. Very sad."

She tried to help. "You miss home."

He laughed. "Fat chance. My mother texts me every fifteen minutes. 'Did you know Di Marsden got married? Did you hear Steve was on *Look North* with his rabbits?' No, Mam, I didn't. It's my son," he said abruptly. "It's him I miss."

"Of course. He's called Jamie, isn't he?"

"Yes."

"Where does he live?"

"In York, with his mum. That's a tactful way of asking the question, isn't it?"

"I've had practice, you can tell. When did you break up?" She stopped. "Sorry, I'm being nosy. You don't have to say."

Joe rubbed his fingers. She saw he had a long, thin new scar on his left hand. "I don't mind. He was one. Just a baby really." He was staring at the ground, and then his head snapped up and he said firmly, "She's with someone else now. A good guy. He can give Jamie everything he needs."

"You're still his dad."

"Yes. Of course I am. But maybe that stuff doesn't matter."

"It does." Cat moved away from him, retreating into the darkest corner of the porch. "It shouldn't matter, but it does. He's your family."

My mum's still my mum, she wanted to say, *part of me will always love her no matter what,* but she found it impossible. She rubbed her hands along her rib cage, as though comforting herself. "What I mean is, you can't replicate blood. He's your son—doesn't matter if for a few years you don't see him as much, he'll always be your son. Even if you're away, you can always come back."

"Like you did, you mean."

"Like I did. But it took a while."

Joe said quietly, "Suppose sometimes that must be hard."

Cat stamped her feet, moving farther into the darkness. *Don't be nice to me.* "I wasn't talking about me. I'm used to being on my own. I don't know my mum, or my dad really. Don't have any brothers or sisters. I just got on with it, I had to."

She wanted to bat him away as she'd done with Mrs. Lang, but he just said, "You've had a time of it, haven't you?" and his voice was so kind.

Her eyes swam with tears. "Oh, it's all right. That's the way it goes." Cat swallowed; she had to move things along. "Anyway, enough about me. Maybe she's better off without you."

"Who?"

"Your ex."

"I'm absolutely sure about that, Cat." Joe gave a grim laugh.

"I didn't mean it like that." Cat was mortified.

"I know what you meant. And it's true."

"I meant you weren't right for each other. No point in making each other unhappy."

"We did make each other unhappy. But I should have been able to push that all to the side and get on with it for Jamie's sake. He deserves two parents who . . . you know what I mean?"

"No," Cat said, shaking her head. "No, no. It's not true. There's no way it would have been good for me to stay with Luke's dad. Not good for me, not good for Luke."

There it was. Right there. The guilt, pushing down on her all these years, just lifting off her shoulders and floating away into the night. It was true, and she shrugged to see it go.

"It's funny, being on your own, though, isn't it?" His face turned toward hers. "You think you're okay, and then suddenly you realize how sunk into yourself you've got. You sit there brooding on all these things that don't really matter."

"You shouldn't, Joe, it's not good for you."

"I don't, not really. It's only evenings, bedtime. If I'm not working. I think about Jamie. I used to read him a story every night. Jemma didn't like reading him stories. I'd read him this book—over and over and over again he wanted it. *The Runaway Bunny*. I bet you've never heard of that one, either."

She shook her head. "No."

"I'd love to see what books you have in France. Honestly. *The Runaway Bunny* is great." His soft voice was warm in the darkness. "You know, it's about this bunny who—"

"Who runs away?"

"No. He sets up an investment bank. Yes, he runs away." He smiled, and she thought how different he looked when he smiled. It changed his face.

"So this bunny—"

"I hate stories like this," said Cat. "Will it make me cry?"

"Probably. It makes me cry. Every time."

"Why?"

"Because the bunny keeps saying, 'I'm going to run away and turn into a fish.' And the mummy bunny says, 'If you turn into a fish, I'll turn into a fisherman and catch you, because you're my little bunny.' So he says, 'If you turn into a fisherman, I'll turn into a rock, really high up,' so his mummy says she'll learn to be a mountain climber, and climb all the way up there . . . and you get the picture. Wherever the bunny goes, his mummy says, I'll always come and find you."

"Right," said Cat, embarrassed at how close to tears she was. She swallowed, then gave a half laugh. "This is stupid."

"Well, it is," Joe said. "But it made me cry every time. It still does because . . . he's my lad, you see? And he must sometimes want me, when he's scared, or someone's being cruel to him, and I'm not there, because I've left him behind. You know, I thought it was for the right reasons, give his mum and her boyfriend some space, make a new life for myself, and now I just think . . . what the hell am I doing here?"

"Oh, Joe. Don't say that."

He looked down. "When all you want to do is make people happy by cooking up some nice grub and trying to be a good person."

"I'm used to being on my own," she said briskly. "Believe me, I prefer it."

"Oh. Right," he said.

She laughed. "You sound disappointed."

He looked up quickly. "I—"

Blushing at her recklessness, Cat found herself shaking her head. "I wasn't . . . I didn't mean anything by it. Sorry."

He moved forward into the light, his figure casting a shadow over her face. Cat blinked in the darkness, tilting her head up toward him.

"Look. I should go," she said.

"Of course. Cat?" He was facing her.

"Yes?"

"I'm just glad we've cleared the air. I'm so sorry. I'm just glad . . . you don't hate me."

She could see his shadow behind him on the kitchen door.

"You?" Her heart was thumping in her chest. She could feel her head, clearer than it had been for months, years maybe. "Why would I hate you?"

"For—you know. The business with the car." Joe shook his head. "I— oh, well, I won't keep on about it," he said under his breath.

They were inches apart now. "I've forgiven you for that," Cat said, staring straight at him, and she took his hand. "Honestly."

"Don't," Joe said, but he didn't move away. "Cat—" He broke off, gazing at her.

Cat could feel his bones, his fingers squeezing hers, a sweet, oddly old-fashioned gesture, and they stayed like that, pressed against each other, shivering in the cold, their warm hands knotted together.

"I'm going to anyway." Cat closed her eyes, leaned forward, and kissed him.

His stubble brushed against her cheeks, his body against hers, solid and tall; but she was almost as tall as he. She kissed him first, but then she felt his hand gripping her shoulder, his tongue firm in her mouth. He pushed her against the wall of the house, and she pushed against him frantically, feeling his weight on her body, the taste of him, the sound of his breath heavy in her ear. . . .

Then suddenly, he broke away, shaking his head. "Sorry. No."

Cat laughed, her mouth still full of the taste of him. She felt drunk, reckless. "What?"

"No." He shook his head. "I shouldn't have. Don't."

He was staring at her as though he'd seen a ghost. "Fine." Anger rose within her. "What's your problem?"

"I—I shouldn't have done that. That's all."

Cat was sobering up rapidly. "Are you with someone?"

"No," he said. "Yes. I don't know."

"What on earth does that mean?"

He touched his fingers to his mouth, breathing hard. "It means I shouldn't have kissed you. That's what it means."

"*I* kissed *you*. I wanted to."

"I wanted you to. But I can't."

Cat put her hand on the wall of the house, steadying herself. "Karen," she said suddenly, seeing it clearly, the alcohol all at once like acid in her stomach. "Are you sleeping with Karen? Because Lucy told me she wondered if she might be . . . And when I saw you two in the pub I wondered if . . ." She trailed off. "Oh, God. Oh shit. Of course."

Joe reached for her hand. "Cat. It's complicated. I can't explain it."

She pulled away from him, laughing. "Wow! You really are a snake, aren't you? Here tonight, serving our drinks . . . chatting about children's books . . . sucking up to my grandparents. 'Oh, Joe's so wonderful.' And you're—you're sleeping with *Karen*?" she hissed. "You prick. What the hell are you doing here? My uncle, my cousin—why are you here? Why don't you just get out? Go away?"

"I wish I could." He shook his head. "I can't. Not yet."

"I really don't think anyone'll miss you."

"I'm thinking about it," he said quietly. "Honestly. Look—"

"Oh, God," Cat said again. She wiped her mouth on her sleeve. "I'm so stupid. I can't believe it."

"I should have stopped it. But you have no idea how much I wanted to kiss you."

Cat could feel her eyes burning with unshed tears. She turned away. "I'm going in. Don't *ever*—"

"*Shh.*" Joe gripped her arm, turning toward the garden, alert like an animal on the scent.

"Don't tell me to—" Cat began, but then she froze as his grip tightened, and she followed his gaze.

On the raised stone path beside the daisy bank and the vegetable patch, a figure appeared, hurrying quietly through the rain, making no sound. Instinctively, Cat and Joe shrank out of sight under the porch, watching as she came closer. The rain was relentless now, and it was impossible to see her clearly, until she rounded the edge of the vegetable patch and stopped. She turned back toward the dark woods.

"See you tomorrow, darling Daisy," she called faintly, and she blew a kiss into the night air.

Cat held her breath, and found herself reaching for Joe's hand again, warm, wet, and strong, before pulling away, just as Martha looked almost straight at them, her eyes glinting in the dark. Then she turned back toward the front of the house, and was gone.

Daisy

August 2008

I SHOULDN'T HAVE come back.

I didn't realize how much it would hurt.

I'm no good at being this person . . . oh, what kind of person is that, though? A sister who throws confetti and looks pleased for her brother. That's who.

So Bill marries again, and we all stand there and look happy. I find it bizarre, to be honest. I always thought he was either gay or just one of those celibate types, you know, you'd get them in detective novels, and our old vicar was like that. Just not the marrying kind, they used to say.

I'm not the marrying kind either, I suppose. Whenever I looked at Bill and that rat-faced girl who's got her grubby red claws into him, I wanted to laugh. It sounds so bloody silly, doesn't it, when people are scratching around in the dirt for food, or children are dying from insect bites in their thousands, or women are being raped and murdered on a daily basis with no one so much as raising an eyebrow, and here's this . . . civilized behavior in this Regency Guildhall on this sunny day. Everyone being respectable. My daughter is here. We smile and say, "Hello, how are you?" like we're distant cousins at a family reunion.

She looks nothing like me and I'm glad. She doesn't look like her father either, but Giles was a drip so that's a relief. She looks like Ma; good for her. Ma is getting old. Southpaw's knee is busted, he can barely walk, and he looks done in. Bill has finally reached middle age, which is what he's been lurching toward as fast as he can since he was a child. Florence: oh dear. Florence is exactly the same, but she keeps giggling and is wearing a floral Laura Ashley dress, which would be hilarious if it weren't so embarrassing. I suspect she's persuaded some idiot to screw her, and that's what her tragic bucktoothed grinning is all about.

Oh, God. I hate Bath, I hate being home and going down these paths again. I'm not this person. In Kerala I'm not this person, I'm just not. I get up in the morning and I know what needs doing, and no one looks at me and sniffs out the stench of years of disappointment and fear they all smell here when they come near me. Since I've been here I keep telling myself I'll be back in Cherthala soon and I just need more time to make things work. Then I remember what I did, and how I can't go back there again.

I'm so stupid, so fucking stupid. I wanted things, I wanted more than I had. A nicer place, nicer clothes, money for a car. A couple of treats for myself, maybe? And people said I deserved those things. And, to be honest, really honest? I did deserve them, after all I've done for them. But I was silly about it. I have a trusting nature. I let the wrong people in, and they betrayed me, you see. I have lost everything these last couple of months, and now there's nothing I'm good at, nothing I can do.

Catherine is very thin. She has shadows under her eyes and she smiles in this shy way, as if she doesn't know if she's allowed to enjoy something or not. She has just started living with a boyfriend in Paris and she has a job in fashion. Which is funny, because she seems to me to be a solitary person. I can't work her out. Never could. "Fashion doesn't seem to suit her," I said to Ma, and she only said, "That's a terrible pun, Daisy. Oh, darling, do you really not see why she's doing that job?"

Oh, darling. Course I don't, because I don't understand anything.

If I could only get some help, something to calm me down, something to make everything distant and fuzzy again. I hate the idea of marriage too, how it chains you to someone else and you stand up there and actually admit to it, in a room full of people who supposedly love you. But then I hate the fact that they think they have a claim on me too.

I'm very tired, to be honest. Very tired of it all. I don't think anyone understands, either. I shouldn't have come back.

When Karen threw the bouquet—awful plastic gerberas—Lucy caught it, jumping up like some plump puppy. Everyone laughed and clapped, Karen kissed Lucy, and everyone was saying, "Keep it in the family," and being jostled on the steps by the next lot of idiots going in to tie the knot. Well, I thought I might just walk off then. I went and stood by the entrance to some sports shop opposite. These little oiks inside staring at sneakers, they all turned when my family started cheering. I'm there in my smart dress, half in that world of light and confetti and smiling, half in this normal one, gray, sad, boring. The photographer lined them up, started shouting, "Immediate family, please." There they all were. Grinning, humming with something.

And no one looked for me, no one said, "Where's Daisy?" I stood back against the racks of sneakers and watched them all, and they didn't even notice I wasn't there.

That's when I realized they wouldn't notice if I went. I watched them all, and I wanted to hurt them, to make them feel just a bit of pain the way I feel it, to make them hate themselves the way I hate myself. Most of all I just wanted to feel nothing. To know it's all over.

Saturday, 24 November 2012

AT EXACTLY 1:00 p.m. the day after the party, Martha stood in the doorway of the sitting room and rang the gong.

"Please go through to lunch," she said, gesturing, and then she turned and walked through the kitchen, and the rest of the Winters followed her in silence. Cat was the last one out of the room. As she put her hand on Luke's shoulder, propelling him through the kitchen, she looked up to find Joe's steady gaze on her, his hands mechanically drying a metal bowl.

She stared back at him, her tired, slightly hungover brain clicking over and over. Suddenly she wished she could close the door on the rest of her family, seating themselves carefully at the long oak table, chairs scraping, murmuring quietly, quiet panic on their faces. They all knew something was coming, like a twister over the plains. Somewhere, someone was having a perfectly nice, normal Saturday, a trip to the shops, maybe playing in the garden with their children on this unseasonably sunny, golden day.

The heavy crystal champagne flutes sparkled in the gleaming autumn sun; the untouched champagne in the glasses glowed like honey in a jar. Plump, snowy linen napkins, glistening silver cutlery, and the ancient Wedgwood dinner service, bought after David's first Wilbur syndication deal. The pattern on the plates—blue and white trim, yellow and coral at the center—was vaguely Chinese, now worn to pastel, the china veined with a hundred tiny lines after years of family meals ladled onto it, of Christmas goose and baked potatoes on Bonfire Night and roast chicken on birthdays and fish pie on Fridays.

As she sat down, Cat noticed the great green vase of wintersweet at the center of the table, the sparky yellow flowers splashes of sunshine against the dark wood paneling. Her grandmother had taken her seat at the head of the table, facing down the room toward the kitchen doors. Southpaw was opposite her, staring down at his empty plate. Bill was unreadable, scanning the room. Florence was in her own world, it seemed, buttering the bread and pouring water, but there were bruised smudges below her eyes. Lucy was quiet, breaking bread. She looked scared and young. Next to Southpaw sat Karen. Cat thought how pretty she was without makeup, a grave, boyish kind of beauty at odds with her usual coral lipstick, her boxy suits, her determined manner. Her small hands raked her cheeks, the nails leaving streak marks on the pale skin. She started when Martha stood up, and Cat turned to see Joe in the doorway.

Martha tapped her glass. "Luke," she said, bending down a little, "Joe's going to take you to the living room. He's made you a special pie and chips. You can watch *Ratatouille* while we have lunch." Luke glanced at Cat, astonished that such a great bounty should befall him. Cat nodded, smiling, and kissed his dark hair as he bustled past her, hurrying to take Joe's hand.

As Joe's hand rested on the handle, their eyes met again, and then the sliding doors were closed. Cat could hear Luke chattering to Joe, their feet clattering over the old kitchen tiles. Then there was total silence.

"We will eat shortly," Martha said, and gestured to a giant rib of beef and bowls of vegetables, resting on the sideboard. She cleared her throat and shook her head, almost smiling. She leaned both hands on the table, shoulders hunched forward as she looked carefully at each of them from under her fringe.

"I have to tell you something, as you know. That's why I planned this . . . this birthday." Her mouth twisted. "It's a special birthday, you see. And it's time I was honest."

"No!"

They all jumped, as David's voice cried out from the other end of the table. "I don't want you doing this." A paunch of skin quivered under his chin, his agitated mouth working, chewing his cheeks, his lips. He was gaunt, white. "I've changed my mind."

Martha got up swiftly. She went over to him, squeezing Karen's shoulder lightly as she passed, and Karen flinched with shock.

"My love," Martha whispered in her husband's ear. "You can't. It's gone too far."

207

David's voice cracked. "I don't want you putting yourself in the line of fire. It's for me to do, not you, Em."

"No, it is for me to do," she said quietly. "For me." She held his hand. "My darlings. All I ever wanted was to give you all a home." Her gaze swept the table. "The thing is—I failed."

"That's rubbish, Ma," Bill said clearly, and Karen felt her heart clench.

"Is it?" His mother smiled at him. "My sweet boy. You're the only one who's still here." She held up her hand. "I just want you all to understand a bit more. Understand why I did what I did. I've been trying for so long to make everything perfect. You know I was evacuated during the war. To a family very much like this. To a house"—she smiled—"a lot like this. And before that I'd lived in Bermondsey with a dad who was never home and a mum who tried to raise us, and I didn't have shoes, I didn't have enough to eat, I had lice and rickets and—more wrong with me than right."

"Martha . . ." David looked up at her. "No, love."

"And then I met David, and he made everything seem possible." She watched her husband. "He did. We were from these gray worlds, both of us, and suddenly there was art, and music, and poetry, these things I'd never come across, and my mind worked when I approached them, it worked better than ever. There wasn't an opera I didn't know, a poem I couldn't recite; I lapped it all up, all of it. And when we got married, well, I gave up my idea of being an artist. I'm going to sit down again. I feel rather shaky."

Martha walked back to her chair, along the length of the room.

"Women weren't supposed to think we could have both, back then. Do the job we loved, have the family we wanted. And it's a shame, because I loved doing it." She lowered herself into her chair and stared blankly at the wintersweet. "I really did. But that was what happened, then. You were all so tiny, and you needed me so much. Especially you, Flo."

Florence looked down the table at her mother. "Why me?" she said sharply, and Lucy watched her face change, saw something there she'd never seen before. *What does she know?*

"You were a surprise to me, that's all," Martha said. "A lovely surprise. But that's not what I'm talking about. I promised myself, when I packed away the easel and the hundreds of brushes I'd scrimped and saved for over the years, that I'd make the perfect family instead. I think that's what everyone wants to do, isn't it? They want to build a home, to lift up the drawbridge and keep themselves and their children safe at night."

Karen gave a muffled sob, her fingers pressed against her lips. Lucy closed her eyes, hugging herself.

Martha looked out over the dining room to the garden. Poised, calm. She spoke as though reciting lines from a script. "I think we raised you well. I think we gave you everything, tried to keep you safe, to plant you in the world. But we tried so hard I think we went wrong, somewhere along the way. What seemed like small things grew and—they've over-taken us now." She looked at Florence. "We haven't been honest with you. All of you."

She drank from the flute in front of her. They heard her throat working, the liquid fizzing in the glass.

"It begins with Daisy. It ends with her too. I don't really know how to say it." She gave a small laugh, twisting her rings round her finger. "Funny, after all these years of planning—"

"Ma," Bill broke in, and his voice was hoarse. "Where is Daisy?"

Martha and David looked at each other, across their children, across the table.

"She's here," Martha said, after a pause. "Daisy's here."

There was a silence, heavy and pregnant with meaning.

"What do you mean?" Cat said after a few moments. "She's—here? Where—where is she?"

Martha looked desperately at her granddaughter. "Darling. I'm so sorry."

"Where is she?" Cat said again, turning her head.

Martha looked out at the sunny garden. In her clear, calm voice she said, "I buried her there. In the daisy bank. Because we planted it together when she was small, and she did like it there. We buried Wilbur there, too. And that's where I thought she'd like to be."

"*Buried?*" Florence said, her voice shaking, and Bill said, at the same time, "She's dead? She's . . . Daisy's . . ."

"Oh, no." Lucy heard her own voice. "No, Gran, you didn't."

But Martha said, "She killed herself. Here. A few years ago."

"I don't believe it," Karen murmured.

Bill dropped his knife onto his plate. There was a cracking sound.

"She didn't want anyone to know. She just wanted to disappear back into her life again, you see. Gradually fade and leave you all with the idea she . . . didn't exist anymore."

"What?" Florence shook her head. "Ma, you helped her? She did it . . . here?" She clenched and released her hands, resting on the old table, then reached over to take her father's hand.

But David did not react, just stared into space. A plump tear rolled down his cheek, in a straight, glistening silver line.

Cat didn't move, couldn't speak. Her grandmother tried to take her hand, but Cat sat back, hands tightly clasped together. She stared out again into the garden, at the daisy bank.

Martha said, "I repaid all the money. We gave it all back. And more. I have all the records. Daisy—did some good. She wasn't a . . ." Her smooth, calm face cracked. "She wasn't a bad person. She tried her best."

And Martha sank back into her chair again. Her veined hands clutched the tablecloth; she stared at them all, and then, with something like surprise on her face, she started crying.

Martha

August 2008

MARTHA HAD ONLY realized how bad things were when it was too late.

The day after Bill and Karen's marriage, Daisy said she didn't feel well. David had gone off in a taxi first thing for his long-awaited knee operation, the first return to normality after the half-romance of the peculiarly rigid wedding day.

"Don't let her push you around," he'd said as Martha had helped him into the car. "See you tomorrow. Okay?"

She'd kissed him. "I won't. She doesn't do that anymore, David, honestly."

He'd sighed and smiled. "You always let her play you, darling. Don't do it. Be Martha. Be strong."

Martha had brought Daisy a cup of tea, up to the old bedroom that had been first hers, then Cat's, and, since Cat had left first thing that morning, back to Paris and her new life, Daisy's once more. She had heard their awkward good-bye. "It was good to see you again, Catherine. . . . If you're ever in India, come and stay with me!" Daisy had said, and Cat, halfway to the car where Florence was waiting to drive her to London, had turned back.

"Oh, gosh." She took a step forward, and Martha's stomach lurched. "Really? I'd love to," Cat had said, her mouth opening into a smile, her eyes shining. "When can I come? Will I stay with you? Will we ride on some elephants?" Daisy looked at her, bemused, incredulous, a lazy half smile playing on her face. Then, flushing with anger, Cat had shaken her head. "I'm joking. You know, that's a very strange thing to say." Her face was ugly. "I'm not going to go to India to see you. You must know that by now, surely. That's all you have to say to me? You don't once ask

211

me how I am or what my life's like? Don't you care?" She shrugged her slim shoulders, as if the simplicity of the question was too painful for an answer. "Doesn't matter. Good-bye, Daisy." She looked up at the house, festooned with wisteria like a wedding garland. "Bye, house." Martha felt then that she was saying good-bye forever, and she was worried about Cat; and then, later, the moment was lost, after everything else, wasn't lodged in her mind. A rare slip, when she prided herself on always knowing when they needed her.

"You're the only person in this family I don't think I've tried to kill," Daisy said to her mother after Cat had left. She was sitting in bed with the cup of tea. Martha sat down on the bed.

"You do say some silly things," she said carefully, because Daisy never got hysterical. When she was born, she hadn't cried. A mewl as she came out, and then—nothing. The cottage hospital thought the baby might be ill, at first. Martha knew she wasn't, though. Just calm, taking it all in. Her daughter had stared up at Martha, her eyes dark pools like liquid mercury, open from the start, not like Bill. She was always calm on the surface, and you never knew what was coming next or what in particular had triggered it. One summer in Dorset, after she kicked over the sand castle he'd spent hours on the beach making, normally gentle Bill had hit her really hard, *smack* in the face. Of course, Martha and David had punished him, but not too severely. Daisy had done it deliberately, for no other reason than that he'd been praised by passersby, who'd admired its four towers and handcrafted crenellations, and he had—unusually for Bill—enjoyed basking in the limelight, just this once. After the smack, and Bill's being sent to bed with no supper, Martha was on edge for the rest of the summer. What would Daisy do to him? Because she knew by now that Daisy wasn't like Bill, who blustered and cried, or Florence, who became hysterical and clingy. She was different. She was . . . not like the rest of them, and that was all there was to it. She would sit very quietly and then leave, and you never knew what was going on behind those now moss-colored eyes, in that curious head of hers.

At first, they made something of a joke of it. "Daisy? Oh, she'll either kill us or become Queen," David used to say. But there were little things, little things Martha noticed about her daughter that started to make sense; and the more they made sense, the more Daisy frightened her. Florence, caught in her bedroom for ten minutes with the wasps' nest and the door apparently swollen shut with summer heat, and David running the chain saw, so that no one heard Florence's screams. And Florence's hysteria, the crazy things she'd said afterward, the lies about Daisy. It wasn't true! The cuts and bruises on her arms that Florence whined about to Martha, who, wanting Florence to grow up, wanting Daisy not to be bad, told her not to fuss about them. The Girl Guides' bring-and-buy sale where the money vanished, and then Daisy was expelled from school for smoking pot, four months later. Martha still thought she was the only one who'd connected the two. Because Daisy took her time, she knew it by then. Just before the Christmas after the sand castle incident, Bill slipped on the floor of the bathroom on some Johnson's baby oil and broke his ankle.

And it was then Martha realized she was too afraid to talk to David about it, in case he confirmed her worst fears. She didn't know if he felt the same way. Every morning as the Winters sat at the breakfast table eating porridge or toast, Florence singing Latin verbs in the background and swinging her stockinged legs as she told everyone cheerfully what her day at school held, Bill carefully explaining the principle behind the latest Apollo mission by drawing careful sketches on the table for his father, Martha would watch Daisy in the middle of it all, eating carefully, watching, listening, but never betraying what she thought. A black hole in the heart of the family. Afterward, clearing breakfast away, Martha would shake herself and laugh at her own dramatic tendencies. Ridiculous!

Only she had made her daughter, and when she looked at her, as she did that day in August, she knew her heart. She knew Daisy so well, because she'd seen her a few seconds after she was born, when they handed her to Martha, and the same expression was on her face then as it was now, forty-seven years later. Calm, like Martha—everyone said she was like Martha—but something else too. "She's a cool customer, this one," the sister had said, looking at Daisy, tightly swaddled in her mother's arms. "I've never seen a baby that didn't cry before."

"What's wrong, pet?" Martha said to Daisy now. It was nearly lunchtime. She wondered whether Daisy would eat lunch or stay up here.

"I need to talk to you about something," Daisy said. She fingered the blancmange-colored tassels of the tattered bedspread. "You won't like it."

Martha tensed her shoulders, just slightly. "Go on."

"I've not been very happy lately, you know that, don't you?"

"Yes," Martha said. "What's up? Something's up, I can tell."

Daisy shook her hair out of her face. Dark rings hung below her eyes. "I can't speak for long."

"Why?"

She swallowed. "Just can't." She put her hand on her mother's. "Look. I got fired last month. I'm back for good."

"Fired?" Martha was appalled. "Darling, how come?"

Daisy rubbed her eyes. "Long story. I stole some money. That's what they said, anyway. That's what they'll say if you ask them. But it's not true. I just borrowed bits from different bits. I'm the only one who knew where everything was. You see? It's fine." She pinched the tip of her nose. "But, yeah, it was for drugs. And—well, drugs."

Martha kept quite still, not knowing how to react. She sensed this was the truth. "Is that all?"

Daisy nodded. "Yep. I've screwed up again. It's a real shame, because it was the one thing I did. In my life. You know." She sounded almost cheerful. "That's how it is, I guess. Only got myself to blame. It's just I wish I could swap myself for someone else sometimes. Just . . . *be* someone else, sometimes."

A cloud passed over the window and Daisy looked up at her mother. *She's getting old.* Martha realized it then: her daughter was a middle-aged woman. Not a cruel, fascinating, beautiful little girl. She was past the age when anything she did could be put down to youth or inexperience, and it struck Martha like an arrow piercing her heart. She had made her like this. Hadn't she?

So she said what she'd always said, because she didn't know what else to say.

"You're a clever, talented girl," Martha said. "I'm so proud of you. You'll find something else, you can—"

"No," Daisy broke in, her voice harsh for once. "No. Look, I need your help."

"All right," said Martha cautiously. It was usually money. Historically it would be a situation with a teacher at school, and once it had been picking her up from a police station in Bristol, where she'd been found wandering the streets after forty-eight hours absent from home. But usually, these days, it was money.

"I've been up all night, thinking about it," Daisy said.

"I'm sure you have, darling. Are you sure you can't appeal? Go back and find—"

But she was cut off again. "Ma, it's too late for that. It's too late. They don't want me back."

"Can't you just try—"

"God, I hoped you'd understand. Listen. I'll probably be arrested if I go back to India, don't you realize that?"

"Oh." Martha closed her eyes briefly. "I see."

"I just need your help, one more time. I didn't sleep at all last night, going over it all. Can I have a couple of Southpaw's pills, the ones in the bathroom cabinet?"

David had been prescribed sleeping pills and painkillers to help with his knee, which had been causing him more and more pain in the run-up to the operation. "No, Daisy," Martha said firmly. "Absolutely not. I said last time was the final time. They're too strong."

"Okay, fine," Daisy said. She took another sip of tea, then lay back and closed her eyes. Martha's hand reached out to Daisy's wrist, and she encircled it with her brown fingers. She was hot to the touch. "I might have a sleep. Thanks, Ma. I won't want any lunch. Just leave me now."

She seemed to be almost asleep, even then. Martha went out, shutting the door behind her, and stood on the landing outside her daughter's room for a moment, listening to the quiet, hoping Daisy would find some peace. She knew she'd found the wedding tough. Martha knew that seeing Cat was hard on Daisy, much as she pretended it wasn't.

Martha shook her head, swallowing back tears, and, picking up the laundry basket outside Daisy's room, started folding up towels. She found herself humming a tune from *The Mikado* under her breath; it had been on the Proms the previous night as they were clearing up after the (modest) wedding breakfast. It had been a strange wedding, she thought; and her mind wandered. Thinking things over, trying to work out what was going on so she could act for the best. Karen's mother seemed nice— should they invite her down for the weekend in the autumn? Cat's life in

Paris troubled her somehow—did she need to talk to her about it? Florence's behavior was a little strange, but she seemed happy. Something was on her mind, something nestling there.

When Martha went to the bathroom five minutes later, she wondered if she'd hear Daisy snoring, as she was wont to. She even smiled at herself in the mirror while washing her hands. Perhaps Daisy was mellowing in her old age.

The prickling, uncertain feeling she could never entirely get rid of, that was what was bothering her, not her hip, not those headaches. . . . And suddenly, with a small cry Martha flung open the bathroom cabinet. But she knew what she'd see even before that. The sleeping pills were open, and the bottle was empty.

Martha pushed open the bathroom door, kicking the towels and sheets out of the way, stumbling as her foot caught on a pillowcase. She fell to the floor, crying out, and then she remembered she was alone: Florence had taken Cat to London, David was gone. Gone. She staggered toward Daisy's bedroom.

She knew before she opened the door what she would see. Daisy was lying on the bed, head pulled back, but she wasn't snoring. Her eyes were half-open, just like when she was a baby. Martha leaned over, her heart pounding so hard she couldn't hear anything else. She cried out her daughter's name, over and over. She shook her, but she didn't move.

Then she saw the note, in Daisy's neat, tiny handwriting, splashed with tea.

Dearest Ma,

Don't be sad. I'd already taken the pills when you came in. I'm glad I got to talk to you before I started to go to sleep. I have only done what I wanted to do. I know how to do it, too, I've been planning it for a while. One of the reasons the charity sacked me was drugs—heroin. Heroin, yes, I know. Some kind guy from an NGO got me hooked on the stuff a few years ago. You'd expect better from a charity worker, wouldn't you? But it's a good way to kill yourself if you know how to mix it, and with what. I've picked up a few things along the way, haven't I?

I'd run out of things to do, and I wasn't any good at any of the things I did do. Never was, we all know it, don't we. And I hate being back here. Dad's a fake, it reminds me every time what a fake he is. You know I hate how he's lied about everything. Where he comes from. Where Florence comes from. She's his bastard, isn't she? I know she isn't yours. I remember that summer you went away, and you came back with a baby, and we were supposed to believe it. He had an affair, didn't he? He lied to you. I know she's his, he loves her more than me, more than Bill, you can see it.

I get these bits of rage when I can't see straight and I want to—I don't know. Kill something, I suppose. I always felt I didn't belong here. But then, not anywhere. I tried so many places and I went as far away as I could and it's just I don't belong anywhere.

I can hear you singing "The Sun Whose Rays" as I write this, and I wish you sang more. You used to all the time and now I think you're sad. Thank you for saying you wouldn't give me the pills. It makes it much clearer, doesn't it?

Ma, can you bury me here, next to Wilbur? In the garden. Wilbur was my friend, and he was my idea.

Tired now. Please make sure Catherine okay? She

There it ended.

She stood in the hot bedroom and looked down at her daughter, face slack, limbs heavy, at rest at last.

Then Martha went into her bedroom and shut the door. She listened once again. Everything was silent. No one near, no one with her except Daisy. She sat on the edge of the bed, gazing out at her garden, at the neat rows of lettuce, the apple trees in the distant orchard. At the daisy bank, churned with mole holes. Then she stood up and crossed herself, though she had no idea why, or what it would do to help her, and she went outside to the shed and picked up a spade. *A time to be born, and a time to die, and I was there at both of them. I love you, Daisy, and I will hold you close now, the way I never could before.*

Martha had learned a lot from her years in the countryside during the war. She knew how to bury old folk and dead sheep, and she'd buried a few Winter dogs in her time. She'd buried Hadley by herself, after he'd been put down after the summer party when he attacked someone. You had to dig a hole so deep nothing else could get to it. And as she was working all that long day, she tried to feel nothing, and when Florence came back from her day trip to London, flushed and happy and obviously up to something, Martha told her Daisy had left.

"She got an e-mail from the orphanage about a grant that's come through," she said, sitting at the kitchen table, sipping the stone-cold cup of tea as if it connected her to something.

"So she just *left*?" Florence said. "My God, she really does take the biscuit. She didn't even say good-bye!"

"You know Daisy," said Martha. "It must have been important."

"That's rubbish. She was just sick of being here, that's all, and no one was paying her any attention. She never changes." Florence looked at her watch. "Well—I might just make a phone call!" Her face creased into a joyful smile. "I have some work to do."

Martha watched her bounce out of the room into David's study. She followed her and stood in the doorway. "You seem very jolly," Martha said.

"Oh . . . it's nothing really!" Florence said, her mouth twitching. Then she frowned. "Oh . . . Daisy's Yahoo is still open."

"What?"

"Her e-mail. Looks like . . ." Florence started clicking on the screen.

"Stop it," Martha said, realizing something. "Let me. She didn't have time, she had to leave fairly suddenly."

Florence, who was even more in another world than usual, stood up and started scanning the bookshelves, humming to herself.

"Why are you singing that?" Martha sat down at the computer. She stared at the screen. If she logged out of Daisy's e-mail, that was it—she'd never get back in again. This way . . .

"Singing what?"

" 'The Sun Whose Rays.' "

Florence turned round. "No idea. Were you playing it yesterday?"

Heart racing, blood thumping, Martha opened Daisy's account details. *You have about ten seconds. You have to appear calm. If you take too long, this will start to look suspicious.* My account. Reset password online. She clicked on the link. What is your mother's maiden name? What is your date of birth?

Martha swallowed. "I'm sorry you missed her," she said. She had never wanted anything more than she wanted Florence to go away for just a minute. "Love, can you put the kettle on?"

Florence gave her a curious glance but went into the kitchen, still humming. Martha changed the password to something she could remember, Daisy61, and closed down the application. When Florence returned, she stood up.

"I'd love some tea if you're making a pot," Florence said.

Martha stared at her. "I'm not, no. See you later."

She went upstairs smoothly, and locked Daisy's door.

The next morning, after Florence had left, Martha dragged her middle child down the twisting staircase, through the kitchen, and outside to the garden. Though she had been painfully thin in life, in death Daisy was heavy, and Martha was old, and she cried as she carried her, because it was undignified, and she had wanted it to be dignified, a proper end to the life of her baby, her baby girl whom she had somehow ruined, broken. She had favored her too much or too little; she didn't know, but Daisy had never been right, and now that she could finally do something that her daughter wanted for her, it ought to be done properly. In the afternoon sunshine she rolled Daisy into the black sheeting they used on the lawn, and bound her up with plastic ties. Sometimes she had to stop, sometimes pain overwhelmed her and she knelt beside her daughter, crying as quietly as she could; but then she would count to five. Stand up again, pretend she was doing something else. Something mundane.

All the time she was doing it, Martha had the unreal sense that someone would appear, would find out what she was doing, would stop her. But they didn't, and she was glad, because she knew it was what her daughter wanted. Before the last tie covered up Daisy's face, Martha steeled herself, stroked her daughter's forehead, then ran her finger along the bridge of her nose as she had done when Daisy was tiny, to get her to close her eyes and sleep. She covered the body over with earth, and replaced the turf as best she could, trusting that no one would go out there for months, maybe. David wouldn't be able to walk far when he came home, and no one else was in the garden these days. Cat was gone, and Bill had Karen, and Lucy was grown-up. It was just Martha, and Daisy.

On sunny days Martha went out to the daisy bank, and sometimes she talked to her. Mostly, she just sat there, quite still, keeping her company. She knew enough to know it was ridiculous to think Daisy would want to hear her prattling on about life. She hadn't cared when she was alive; she wouldn't care now. Somehow that made a kind of sense to Martha.

Martha

November 2012

IT WAS KAREN who broke the silence. She stood up, walked over to the sideboard, and poured Martha some red wine. "Here," she said, and then she crouched down beside her mother-in-law and handed her the glass. She pulled Martha's neatly pressed handkerchief out of her pocket and gave it to her, and Martha blew her nose, still crying, as Karen stroked her arm, her hand, the back of her neck. "There, there," Karen said softly. "It's all right. You did the right thing. You did the right thing."

The others watched her without moving, rooted to their seats as though by some kind of magic. Martha's sobs hung in the heavy, silent air, only the faintest rattle of chase-scene music from Luke's DVD echoing from the other side of the house.

Eventually Karen stood up again and went back to her seat. She spread her hands wide and, with a little laugh of strained near-hysteria, she said, "You know, someone has to say something eventually."

She turned to her husband, who wouldn't meet her glance. His eyes were full of tears.

"I gave her money," said Florence eventually. "For her school. Last year. *And* she e-mailed me," more loudly. "A couple of days ago, Ma. Was—was that you?"

Martha nodded.

"You were e-mailing us all?" Florence said hoarsely. "All that time?"

"Since . . . after Bill and Karen's wedding." Martha wiped her nose and stuffed the handkerchief in her pocket. "Not before. She did it all before."

"What happened to the money?" Bill said.

"That's what you care about?" Martha turned to him. "Honestly, Bill? I tell you this story and *that's* what you want to know?"

Bill said softly, "I was just wondering, that's all. Ma, it must have been quite a lot."

"The charity and the orphanage, they sacked her for stealing. I sent them the money back, in her name, to apologize. And then I kept on sending them money, as if it was from her, from all of us." Martha shrugged, her hands in her pockets. "I thought that's what she'd want."

"Daisy was out for herself—" Florence stopped. "I'm sorry." She wiped her nose on her sleeve, and looked from her father to her mother. "This is . . . Ma, this is crazy. Absolutely bloody crazy. Why didn't you tell anyone?"

Martha sat upright. This was the hardest bit of all. "I wanted people . . . to . . . to think well of her. She wasn't like you two. She found things difficult."

"I—" Florence exploded, her mouth open, but she closed it swiftly, shaking her head. "We all find things difficult, you know, Ma. That doesn't mean—you lie, and steal, and cheat, and abandon people, and hurt people, and . . ." Her voice broke. "That doesn't mean you do those things."

"I know," Martha said. "I know that." Her fingers touched her forehead, as if buying herself time. After a pause, she looked up at her eldest granddaughter. "Cat?"

Cat shook her head, her lips clamped together, grimacing. She covered her face with her hands. David reached out to her, stroked her arm.

"My dear girl," David said, his voice as faint as a whisper, but Cat said nothing.

"I don't know what to do," Bill said, almost conversationally. "I honestly don't know what we should do."

"Well, I think we should call the police." Florence looked around the table. "It's illegal, what you did, Ma, I'm sorry."

"Oh, don't, Florence," said Lucy, speaking for the first time.

Florence said, "But someone's going to find out sooner or later. We can't just leave her there."

"We can," said David. "You can bury someone on private ground."

"Not like this!" Florence blinked, her eyes bulging. "Bill, what is it? What's the term for it?"

"Disposing of a body and preventing lawful burial," Bill whispered.

"Exactly. It's illegal. You could go to prison. Why—what?" Florence burst out laughing. "This is crazy, it's just crazy. . . ."

Lucy turned to her left and pointed her finger at her aunt. "Oh, stop it," she said. "Have a heart, Florence, for God's sake. Stop it." Florence shook her head in disbelief and Lucy paused, trying to think through what they should do next, what happened now. "Does anyone know a lawyer? I think we need a lawyer."

Karen said, "I do."

Lucy nodded. "Great, Karen."

Bill looked at his wife across the table. "Who's that, then?"

But Karen looked sadly at her husband, and turned to Cat. "Cat, love. This is a big shock to us all, isn't it? Why don't you say something?"

Cat, who was staring down at nothing, shook her head. Eventually, very softly, she whispered, "I don't know what to say."

Bill shuffled his chair closer to his niece. He put his arm around her. "Cat, whatever it is that's happened, we're all here now, aren't we? It doesn't change the fact we're very glad you came back, and that you've brought Luke. He's part of our family, like you, me . . ." His eyes rested on Karen for a moment, then dropped down. The plate was broken where he'd dropped the knife on it. He pushed the two cracked pieces together carefully. "Daisy—she was wonderful, but she wasn't ever happy. Perhaps it's . . ." He trailed off.

"It's for the best?" Cat laughed. "I don't know." Her eyes filled with tears. "What was wrong with her? What's wrong with me?"

"Oh, sweetheart," Florence said wretchedly. "Nothing's wrong with you. You poor darling girl." She stood up. "I do think we have to call the police."

"No." Karen shook her head. "Let them alone for just a day or two. Then we'll decide."

Florence gave her a sharp look, but said nothing.

"Who made you the family spokesman all of a sudden?" Bill asked his wife.

"Don't, Bill," she said, brushing him aside with a tired gesture, so small and determined, right hand fiddling with her wedding and engagement rings, turning them over and over.

"Get out," he said suddenly. "You shouldn't be here."

Karen stared at him. "Really, Bill? Now?"

"You two. Not now," Martha said.

"Dad—" Lucy held out a placatory hand. "Not now, Dad, if you're going to—"

He turned to her and said, "Don't worry, Lucy sweetheart."

"But, Dad, please don't—"

"Lucy." His voice was hard. "Mind your own business."

"It *is* my business!" Lucy shouted, her voice cracking. "This is all my business, all our business."

"No," David cried weakly. "We mustn't turn on each other. We're a family, goddamn it. That's what I did it all for."

But his soft voice was drowned out by the sliding of the doors. Karen stood up and Bill turned back to her, grabbing her wrist.

"All I ever wanted was to make you happy, to make a home with you, our own home away from all this. And what have you done? Why are you here?"

"You're right. I shouldn't be here," Karen said. "I've never belonged here. It's a shame 'cause I thought I could, but you're right." Her voice rose, and she didn't see the two figures standing in the open doorway. "You're all so afraid of being honest with each other, telling the truth for once, being open about what's going on, and this is where it's got you!"

"You bloody *hypocrite!*" Bill shouted, and Martha watched in horror as her son's expression changed so that he looked quite wild. "She's pregnant, you know? Three months pregnant! And, you know, I'm not the father." He jabbed his hand behind him. "That idiot through there, Joe! *He's* the father, for God's sake, and yet I'm the one who's not been honest!"

Karen put one hand to her neck, rubbing it, her eyes huge in her small, white face. "Bill, I told you yesterday. It could be his, it might not be. I said I always thought because nothing happened for years . . ." She shook her head. "Not now. Let's not talk about it now, Bill."

"Why not?" Bill drew himself up, tall, his trembling lips pushed together. "Why can't we?"

"Dad, shut up," Lucy said. "Not now."

"Of course I couldn't talk about it to you," Karen said suddenly, tears glittering in her eyes. "Four years together, and nothing happened. I thought it must be me. You'd already had a kid. And I couldn't talk to you about it."

"No." He stared at her, agonized. "You could."

"Bill, I couldn't. I tried and I—you know I tried. You have time for everyone else, darling. Not me." The words stuck in her throat. "And the one time I didn't—I was reckless—I . . . the one time we didn't . . . Oh, God. This is a mess. I . . ."

Karen put her hands over her face and began to softly sob.

"Mum, I finished the movie," came a small voice. "I don't like it here anymore. I want to go home now."

Luke and Joe stood in the doorway as Karen pushed back her chair, which fell to the ground with a cracking thud, and ran past them, not even looking at Joe.

"Karen," Joe called in a low voice. "Where are you going? *Karen?*" He kept his hand on Luke's neck, propelling him toward his mother. Cat wrapped her arms around him and stared up at Joe.

"Go after her," she said. Joe nodded, and left the room, his heavy footsteps thudding through the house. Seconds later, they heard the front door slam.

At the other end of the room, Martha said, "I'll repay you all the money, of course."

"Don't be silly," Florence interrupted her. She stood up and went over to her mother. "Oh, Ma. You're very brave to have told us. I don't know—I don't know why she was like that."

Martha stared at her, and she put her hands to her cheeks. "Flo. Oh, Florence, darling, you . . ." Her face was drained of color, her eyes glassy. Her eyes darted toward David, then back to Florence. "I don't know why either, darling. That's families for you. I had to tell you, you understand that, don't you?"

Bill came and stood next to Florence. "Flo's right." He kissed his mother's head. "I'm sorry, Ma. I'm so sorry."

"I just wanted everything to be out in the open. I wanted us to be . . . happy again." She looked down the long table at her husband, and then screamed.

"David? *David!*"

Lucy, glancing at her grandfather, cried out. His head had fallen forward; his mouth was wide open.

"Oh, no. *No, no!*" Bill ran over to his father and fell to his knees. He loosened David's tie, patted his face. "Lucy, call an ambulance." Lucy ran out of the room. "Tell them it's urgent."

Martha had stumbled out of her chair, over to her husband. "Urgent," Bill shouted after his daughter, cradling David's head in his hands. "Tell them it's urgent." He turned to Cat, nodding at Luke. "Get him out of here."

Cat left, and the others stared at each other, blind panic on their faces. A weak afternoon winter sun shone into the stuffy room. "Help me," Bill said to Florence, and the two of them lifted their father gently, terribly carefully, out of his chair and placed him on the worn carpet.

His face was gray, his mouth turned down, as though in ghastly mockery of a clown. He said, "Violet's hat."

"What's he saying?" Martha moved closer.

"Violet. Bury me with my old hat."

"What?" Florence said, squeezing his head to her, as if by holding him tightly she might make it better. "What hat? The one on your door? Of course, Pa, darling, but don't be ridiculous." She swallowed, struggled to speak. "You're going to be all right."

He raised his hand to try to touch hers, but he was too weak.

"You're my girl," he said. "I'm so proud of you, Flo."

Then his head rolled away. Florence gently cradled it, brokenly whispering to him.

Five minutes later David died, his head in Florence's lap, his hands folded on his chest. Martha, kneeling on the floor beside him, saw a movement out the window. She looked up and caught sight of Cat in the garden, hand in hand with Luke, the shadow of the house falling over them. Suddenly they heard sirens, ringing out loudly in the lane leading to the house. They all looked up at each other, and then, instinctively, at Martha.

She took David's warm hand in hers and gently closed his eyes. They needed her to be in control. She was, she was completely in control.

"He's tired," she said, very calm. "He's resting. He's been tired for a while. Don't let them in, not just yet. It's going to be fine. He just needs a bit more time."

She could feel them all, all of them, staring at her. Then came the sound of the door knocker, thudding loudly through the still house.

PART THREE

The Past and the Present

Does the road wind up-hill all the way?
Yes, to the very end.
Will the day's journey take the whole long day?
From morn to night, my friend.

—Christina Rossetti, "Up-Hill"

Martha

ONE DAY, MANY years ago, Martha had had a premonition of death.

She'd never tried to explain it to anyone else: it sounded too unlikely. They had had an early supper one evening, and she was in the kitchen washing up, while David worked in his study. Cat was asleep upstairs; she must have been around twelve or so.

It was one of those still-light spring evenings, where the birds sing softly, the black earth is alive with promise, and the cool air is sweet. *Rhapsody in Blue* was playing on the radio. Martha loved Gershwin, and she was banging a wooden spoon on the sink in time to the piano, staring at nothing really in the soapy water, when suddenly she saw it, in front of her eyes.

She and David. They were walking down the lane together, like the first time. David was wearing the hat Violet had given him, all those years ago; light was falling between the trees. They went toward it gladly: it seemed to be sunshine. But the light fell on her like a cloak, and suddenly changed. She stared up at the sky, but saw only a gray, heavy nothing, and she realized she didn't know where the light was coming from, and so she started to shout, to call for help. The lane, the trees, the hedgerow, David: they all disappeared, and she saw only gray around her, like a plane plummeting through clouds. She could hear him calling her; she could hear her own screams, could feel herself desperately running toward something; but nothing seemed to work, to change, and she was racing into the mist, into nothing. . . .

Martha had started running then, through the house, to the study. She'd flung the door open, and it was only then she realized she was soaking wet: dishwater all over her top, her hair, her cheeks. She was crying, shaking from head to toe.

"My love, what on earth's wrong?" said David, standing up.

"I . . ." Martha began, and then she felt stupid. *I have just seen how I'm going to die. I'm going to leave you.* She couldn't stop shaking now, and there was a sharp metallic taste in her mouth. She put her hands on her cheeks. "I saw something awful while I was washing up. It sounds crazy. How . . . you and me."

The music floated in from the kitchen, but otherwise the house was still. David walked around the desk and took her in his arms. "Darling. Washing up can be dangerous, can't it? Goose walk over your grave?" He held her tightly, and she rested her head on his shoulder, as she always did. She loved him then, more than ever, if it were possible. He understood, he knew.

"Something like that. I can't explain it. It was terrifying."

His hands, holding her close to him, patted her back softly. "Must have been."

"I don't want to leave you. I don't want to be without you. Ever."

"You won't," he said, and there was laughter in his voice. "Silly girl. I'm in the study drawing, and in twenty years' time I'll still be in the study drawing."

But Martha couldn't laugh. "Promise?"

"Promise. You and me, remember? Just us."

From the radio in the kitchen there came the clashing final bars, a drumroll, and then applause, and it broke the tension. They laughed.

"I feel silly," Martha said, but the strength of that deadening terror was still with her, and she felt sick.

David pulled his battered old hat off its hook. "I'm finished anyway. Let's go and sit outside and have a drink, darling," he said. "First outside of the year. No more ghosts tonight."

Later that evening, he had suddenly said to her, as they sat on the steps by the French windows, "I'd die if you left me, you know that, don't you?"

"David. Don't be dramatic." She felt completely herself again, remote, amused, in control. How unlike her that earlier scene had been. How silly. He was the romantic one who cried at films, who had wept when the last of Cat's baby teeth came out and that was their final night of doing the tooth fairy, drawing chalk flowers and stars on the floor by the child's bed. He was the one who had brought them all here, who had brought Florence into the family, who had fought tooth and nail for his own life. She was the pragmatist who said the dog had to be put down, who wrestled with wiring.

A life without each other was too far away to think about; they had conquered everything when they were young, and so they were careless about the future. It held no fear for them. She dismissed the premonition from her mind, for many years. Neither of them ever considered the possibility that their time together might end. They never thought about it: the truth was, Martha knew he would never leave her.

David

June 1968

MARTHA STOOD IN the hallway, mouth pursed into a worried bud, watching David as he put on his hat and picked up his battered old portfolio, which contained what he hoped was his best work yet.

"If he says no," she said, "you'll—well, you have to at least ask him if there's anything else you can do for him. Cartoons, or some other kind of work. You have to come back with something, David. He's known you for years; he can't throw you off entirely."

"For goodness' sake, someone like Horace Sayers doesn't deal in favors, Martha. And neither do I." His voice was raised. "This meeting, it's very important. Let me handle it, please, will you?"

"You're the one who wanted us to move here." Her voice was sharp, the Cockney she'd left behind sneaking away with her consonants, as it always did when she was cross. David had a tighter grip on it. He never let his past show through.

"We both wanted to come back here, Martha."

"Dear God, David!" It was the same old argument they'd been having for months. "You're the one who said it'll be fine. And there's damp in the dining room, we've got rats everywhere, I hate this paint, nothing keeps in this heat and we can't afford a refrigerator, David. Daisy needs new shoes, for God's sake. She crams her toes into the only ones she's got, she's walking like a cripple! All because of you and your bloody rewriting-history complex." Martha was close to him now, her green eyes glowing with fury. She pushed her hair out of her face. "I gave up doing my job for this, David."

He knew she was as good as he was. They both knew it. Somehow, this made him angrier. "Daisy's a damned liar and she'll say anything to get you on her side."

"Fine. Do whatever you want." Martha had turned and walked back into the kitchen, slamming the green baize door on her way.

He should have kept his mouth shut. Martha wouldn't hear a word against Daisy. He stood there in the empty hall looking around him, wondering whether it was all worth it; but he told himself it had to be, he had to make it all right, otherwise something else would have won. He wasn't sure what. As he fiddled one final time with his tie, he felt a wet nose nudging the fold of his knee, and he turned and crouched on the ground.

"You like it here, don't you, old fellow?" he said to Wilbur, who looked at him with dark, solemn eyes, his lopsided pink tongue hanging crazily out of his mouth.

Wilbur gave a small, soft, yelping bark. As if to say, *You're all right with me.* David fondled his soft, warm ears, touching his cheek to his muzzle.

A voice beside him said quietly, "Dad?" David jumped. Daisy was standing next to him; he never seemed to hear her approach. "Dad, did you look at the drawings? Of Wilbur?"

"Oh. Darling, I didn't, I'm sorry." He stood, picking up the portfolio. Her small face got its pinched, dead-eyed look. "Oh."

"I'll look tonight." He wished she'd leave; he wanted to look in the mirror, talk himself up a little. Daisy threw him off balance. In abstract he wanted to draw her closer to him, and yet in practice he frequently found himself wishing he could keep her at arm's length. "What did you draw him doing, then?"

She curled a twine of straggling hair round one thin finger. "Look, they're here." She took a sheet of paper carefully out of a book of wildflowers on the sideboard. "Look at this one. He's bouncing up and down so hard like he did the other day to catch the piece of meat that he hits his head on my hand and falls over. Then in the other one he's waiting for me to come back from school and making that strange noise that he makes. And in the other one he's chasing his own tail. And he's saying, 'It's like a merry-go-round, but I'll just catch this tail and then I'll get off.'" Her eyes shone as David laughed and glanced at the drawing she held tightly in her hand. She was a funny little thing. He found himself dropping a kiss on her head. "Do you like it?"

"Love it, darling. His nose looks very wet. I'll look at the rest of them later. Be nice to Florence."

Her voice took on that wheedling, surprised tone. "Daddy! Of course I will be, I always am nice to Florence, it's just—"

He patted her shoulder, and said good-bye. "I'll miss my train."

As he strode up the driveway he saw, as through fresh eyes, the gate hanging off its hinge, no post to attach it to. Wood pigeons cooed lazily in the trees above. David turned to look at the view of the valley sliding away from him, and breathed in once again. He knew where he'd come from to get here. Anything was better than that.

"Come in, come in, old chap, sit down. Drink? June, get Mr. Winter here a drink—what—G and T? Whiskey?"

"Oh—whiskey, please."

"Wonderful, wonderful. Got that, dear? Right. David, jolly good to see you. How's that beautiful wife of yours?"

"She's very well. Says to say we must get you down to Winterfold sometime."

"I'd love that." Horace Sayers slouched and slid his arms across the table, fingers touching. "How is that house of yours? Pretty amazing place, I hear?"

"We're very happy with it."

"You, in the deepest English countryside. It's really rather amusing. How long's it been now?" Horace pointed one long finger precisely into his ear and wiggled it about in an explorative fashion.

"About a year now." David put the portfolio on the table, fingers itching to open it. He didn't want to make small talk. He especially didn't want to discuss the house.

"Making the place your own, I hope."

David found he was sweating. It was a close, oppressive day, thick cloud hanging heavy over London, trapping in the heat. The boardroom of *Modern Man* magazine was dank and reeked of stale cigarette smoke: a typical Soho office. "Can't wait to see what you've got for me, old chap,"

Horace said, lighting another cigarette and pushing his drink out of the way. "Truth is, we're up against it for next week's issue. Could be your lucky day."

Delicately, David slid the sheets of construction paper out. He had labored all day and night for months on this project, and it sounded pompous if one said it aloud, but put simply, it was the climax of everything he wanted to achieve as an artist. He'd ignored Martha, swatted away the children, walked unseeing around this crumbling, malfunctioning white elephant he'd taken on while winter rain dripped through the old roof and rodents gamboled in the kitchen.

Meanwhile, deadlines for his existing commissions came and went. The weekly cartoon for the *News Chronicle*, the illustrations for *Punch*, the funny little details he was supposed to sketch for the theater column in the *Daily News*—he'd let them all down, these past weeks, chasing some ghost. He had known for some time he had to exorcise whatever it was that hung over him, even more so now he'd moved into Winterfold, and it had seemed to him that this was the only way he knew how.

"I'll show you . . . I'm rather excited about them myself." He cleared his throat. "Right, here we go."

"Jolly good." Horace rubbed his hands together.

But his thin smile grew rigid as David spread the sketches over the table. "As you know, I began this series when I was"—he swallowed, his voice high and formal—"younger. It came about through my experiences in the war. I have always wanted to return to this subject, to explore the impact of the last twenty years on the bomb sites of London, and the people who still live there. So I went back to the East End, talked to the residents, drew the new landscapes that are springing up there alongside the craters that still haven't been filled in."

"Right." Horace wasn't really listening. He was scanning the drawings, fingers drumming the table. "Let me have a look. . . . Oh, I see. Pretty grim, David."

"Yes, it was."

Images started flashing through David's mind: falling masonry like rocks raining down from the sky, houses ripped apart as if they were made of paper, bodies in the streets, rubble everywhere; and the sounds—screaming, whistling bombs, crying, agonized pleas for help, children hysterical with fear; the smell of shit, of piss, of terror and sand and fire.

Suddenly he was back there, curled up into the small shell shape his mother had told him to make, time and time again, crouching on the floor beside him in the kitchen. "Like this, little one. He doesn't mean to hurt me. If you hide, though, he can't see you and he can't hurt you. So make yourself small. Like this."

He couldn't stop these memories. They came like a stabbing pain in the heart, and he couldn't stop them, couldn't acknowledge them, would simply have to go on as he had always done when this happened—

"David?" The laconic voice recalled him to the present. "I say, David!"

"Sorry." David covered his mouth, trying to hide his panicky, labored breathing. "Miles away."

Horace was giving him a curious look. "Right. Listen, are you in town this evening? I'm rather keen on going to a club in Pimlico I think you'd like—it's got a—"

"No," said David, louder than he had meant. "I really just came up to show you these. I have to be back tonight. Work and . . . other business." He hoped he sounded vague. As though the real reason he had to be home wasn't just because he hated being away from Martha, whether she was speaking to him or not. But that was the truth. He was only happy when he was with Martha, was only able to work when he could hear her low, clear voice singing around the house. She was his home.

"Well, what a shame." Horace glanced again over the pen-and-ink drawings. He scratched his chin, jangling the glass of melting ice in his other hand, and muttered something under his breath: David heard the word "domesticated."

"Listen," Horace said after a moment. "It's certainly an impressive collection, old bean. I'll give you that. You're rather . . . brave. I'd have thought you'd have learned your lesson with the dying industries lot you shoved my way last year."

David stared at the sheets of paper spread out over the table. "This isn't some Sunday Hyde Park artist's stuff, Horace—this is my life's work. What happened there, it's all been forgotten. We build new things and make new homes and it all gets bulldozed over, and we mustn't forget, that's all." He could hear himself, how desperate he sounded, and he tried to modulate his voice. "You know, I'd rather hoped you could see your way to something rather like that prisoner of war series you did with Ronnie Searle."

"Ah, but he's—he's got the whole package. Wonderful chap. Anyway, it isn't what people want these days, David." Horace swilled the liquid in his glass around languorously. "It's a hip, crazy world out there, everything's changing, old order gone, all of that, and—"

"Exactly," said David. "I want to—"

A flash of anger lit up Horace Sayers's face. "Do let me finish, old thing, will you? I'll be frank. We can offer you work, but it's got to be light entertainment, you savvy? We want to make people laugh. Give them a break from their dire little lives."

David couldn't bear to look at the sketches, spread out in front of them. Instead, he saw the overdue electricity bill . . . Martha's face that morning . . . the gate that hung off the hinge. He saw his own ridiculous folly, how trying to pull himself out of the past had led them to this house; how stupid he was, wanting something he couldn't afford and didn't deserve. "I got the wrong end of the stick, I'm afraid. Not clear what you were looking for in my mind, and that's my fault." He was talking, saying anything to hold Horace's attention, his nimble mind jumping over the conversational rubble to get to safety, away from the demons that pursued him.

He knew, without stopping to think, that this was the moment everything hinged on. "How about dogs? They off the table too?"

"What do you mean?"

"We have a dog called Wilbur." His mind was racing; he tried to sound calm, as if this was part of the plan. "Wonderful chap. Mongrel. Very affectionate, bit stupid, but wise in his way. You see?" He raised his chin, meeting Horace's eyes, smiling gently as though they were both in on a joke he hadn't even thought of yet. "My elder daughter, Daisy, got him for Christmas a few years ago, but he's all of ours, really. Now, Daisy's very naughty and Wilbur gets her out of scrapes. But they're also rather sweet together. The other afternoon, for instance. I came into the kitchen. Hot day, I rather fancy a bottle of beer. I catch him chasing his

241

tail, round and round. . . ." He twirled his finger in the air, and Horace nodded. David knew he had him then.

"Daisy was watching him, nodding solemnly, and I thought he was talking to her, saying something like, 'It's like a merry-go-round, old girl. I'll just catch this tail and then I'll get off.'" Horace laughed. "And he appears at the other side of the table like a jumping bean at supper, bouncing in the air in case there's some spare food. He's jolly funny. Here," David said, his heart beating hard, "let me show you. Do you have any . . ." He looked around for paper, but there was none in the empty boardroom. "Never mind." He turned over one of the sketches, pulled his pen out of his pocket, and swiftly drew the picture Daisy had shown him that morning of Wilbur whirling round in a circle, and he added Daisy, brows drawn together, arms crossed, glowering at him in confusion.

"Something like this. A little girl and her dog. You call it *The Adventures of Daisy and Wilbur*. Have a page every week. How Wilbur helps the family and hinders at the same time. Hmm?" He rapidly traced his pen across the page again. Now that he knew what he had to do, he was in control. "Wilbur's waiting at the end of the lane for Daisy to come back from school." He laughed. "He does it every day. It's sweet. But he doesn't recognize her, keeps running up to the wrong people and licking them, and they often . . . let's say they don't welcome the overtures. The young mother with the pram, she screams and says, 'Leave my Susan alone!' Then there's the vicar. Wilbur likes chewing his waistcoat. And the barmaid at the Oak Tree, well. You can imagine what Wilbur goes for there, I'm sorry to say."

Horace gave a snickering giggle. "It sounds idyllic. You're a clever chap, David. I like it. I think we've got something there. Will your daughter mind?"

"Daisy? She's six. Don't worry." David wanted to clear the other drawings up now, to stow them away, safe and sound. "She'll love it. So—should I get something off to you in the next couple of days? I have a deadline, but I can easily work with you to—"

"We want to get this rolling as soon as possible, you know," said Horace. "Come into the office with me and let's discuss the terms and all of that."

"And these?" David gestured to the sketches as he swept them into his portfolio folder. "Any interest in seeing these again?"

"Oh, gosh no. This way, please. June, would you fetch me another drink? David—another for you? Marvelous. Yes, I think this could be the start of something rather special."

AFTERWARD, HE WALKED out of the building with a contract and a cigarette, and he thought he would go straight to Paddington, but he didn't.
He headed out of Soho and through Bloomsbury, up the leafy, wide
climb of Rosebery Avenue toward the Angel.

He didn't know why after all these years, couldn't have explained it.
He just kept on walking, getting closer and closer. He thought he was
fine, to begin with. Merely an interested party revisiting an old place; but
his stomach started to cramp and he winced when he saw the Clerken-
well fire station. How often after Mum died he'd stood there waiting for
news, rather than go back home, as if they might suddenly tell him she
wasn't dead and it was all a mistake, if he waited long enough. He'd hear
the bells ringing and see them racing out at full pelt. By the end of the
war he'd got so used to it he'd know already, just by the sounds of houses
collapsing, where it was, whether their place was in danger.

The flashbacks started again as he crawled up and over the City Road,
up to the backstreets near Chapel Market. Rubble like rain, the sounds
of the baby screaming, the bewildered faces of the tiny kids who'd huddle
together, moving in a pack toward the shelter of the Angel tube station.
And his stomach started knotting up again. No food, the whiskey Horace had given him curdling the milky coffee he'd had for breakfast. Bile
rose in his gullet, and his throat thickened as if it had swollen shut. He
kept on walking, past the Lyons, past the old Peacock Inn.

"You all right, love?" an old woman with a headscarf asked him, peering into his face as he held on to some railings, trying not to retch.

As he walked down Chapel Market, past where the mission used
to be, where his mother'd go to have her face dressed after his father

244

had kicked her or hit her with the pan or held a coal to her face or . . . whatever else he did, the images in his mind's eye grew stronger and he couldn't stop the sweating, the agony of his stomach cramping. The sounds in his ears. And he was back there again, running toward the hell of his home life, that freezing clear night, January 1945.

He'd seen his dad at the pub and knew he was drunk already, but he didn't know where else to go. It was always the same: should he go home when the siren sounded, to make sure his mother and the baby were safe? Because it was always there, the fear that his dad really would get him this time. So he'd run along the street with the sirens sounding, caught up in the rush inside to be ready, and then, getting to the front door, creep in, hearing the sobbing, juddering screams as his father slammed his mother into whatever it was he was hitting her with that night. Tom Doolan wasn't scared of the fucking Germans. He wasn't fucking scared of anyone, not like that little drip of shit she said was his son.

The first time the bombs had fallen, David was ten. He got used to the Blitz, got used to the shelters and the drama and the sobbing. He learned how to climb over rubble and pretend he wasn't scared. But in 1945, when everyone thought the war was coming to an end, it started up again. V-2s. David didn't understand at first. Because D-Day had happened, we'd invaded France, wasn't it all over? But January, February, March, these new, infinitely more terrifying bombs hit London, and you never heard them until it was too late and they smashed into you. And this time he really was scared.

His mum was so tired these days. The new baby took up all her time. She'd come out of the blue, a tiny little thing, and when David looked at her he felt no connection. He was fourteen, nearly fifteen. This mewling scrap of red skin and bone, she was nothing to do with him, was she? He was angry with his mum for having her, for being so sad, for letting his dad do this to her. Hadn't she learned how not to have any more babies?

The night she was killed they heard V-2s over toward Shoreditch and the City. You heard them when they weren't for you, which didn't make it any less frightening. It just meant you might not hear the next one, and then it'd be too late. He'd run home from playing outside the Spanish Prisoners, the pub down the road from their house. There was a man there selling oranges if you gave him a fiddle, and one of David's friends had pulled him off, but David didn't want an orange that much. He'd hung around outside the pub, watching to see if his father was coming home, what temper he'd be in. He liked to do that, to warn his mother. He had to try to look after her. He'd always done it.

When he ran home and into the house, upstairs was having another row about something and his mother was playing her beloved piano—to block out the noise, he thought. Calm as you like, smooth hair coiled up around her long, slim neck, and the little baby beside her, asleep in a drawer. Her tiny legs were waving. He thought she might be cold. Her blanket had fallen off.

"Ma," he'd said. "Didn't you hear the sirens?"

"No, I was singing, to cheer her up," she said, turning round and smiling. "Hello, my lovely boy. I suppose we'd best get off to the station, then."

"It's too late, Ma," he'd said, half-angry, half-proud of her, playing her painted, dusty piano while the city exploded around her. "No time. And, Ma, he's coming back. He's in a bad way."

He remembered her face then. "Oh, Davy."

They hid under the piano, because he was sure by now there wasn't time to get to the shelter, and David didn't know if they were hiding from the bombs or from his father. His mother's calm breathing, her hands smoothing his hair back from his head: he could still remember the feel of the tags and cuts on her red-raw fingers decades later. How small she always seemed, curled next to him.

They were quiet as mice for ten awful minutes. The baby didn't make a sound. And just when the silence had stretched to an unbearable break-ing point, the baby woke up and started crying; and just like that, there was a crashing sound, an explosion, a crunching, elemental force like the earth was cracking open. The piano buckled above them from the weight of the floor above collapsing, and David felt his mother's warm, heavy body fall on top of him and the baby, as the house crumpled down around them all. It seemed to go on for ages, louder than anything. A great blow of something fell onto them, the baby was screaming, his back felt as though knives were stabbing him, and his mother was crushing him, hard, the weight of something above her like a battering ram.

Everything was white. David didn't remember crawling into a tiny shape, as small as he could possibly make himself go, just like his mother had always said. But he must have done. He stayed there until he was sure there weren't more bombs coming, until he saw the sky, out of the corner of his eye, turn from black to gray. It occurred to him he couldn't usually see the sky from his home, and something was different.

It must have been a long time. He stank of his own urine and he didn't think he could move. He could hear voices, calling, and he crawled slowly out from underneath his mother, blinking away the sharp dust in his eyes. One of her arms, and the side of her, had been ripped away. The ribs, like ribbons of flesh. David looked at her face and then looked away again, and was sick on the ground.

"Someone in there? Is that Emily's place?"

He'd forgotten about the baby till a little sound from beside his mother's body made him look over. There it was, this tiny little thing. Her mother had taken her out of the drawer. She must have had her on her lap, and the baby'd rolled away onto the floor beside her mother. Her legs were still waving in the air. She was thick with dust. He pulled the blanket over her, wrapping it tightly round her, then picked her up carefully, clutching her to him, like girls with dolls he'd seen playing on the bomb sites. His legs almost buckled but he walked toward the voices. He couldn't work out where the door was, which way round he was.

"There's a kid in there. Oi, son! You all right? You hear me?"

"It's Emily's kid. Where's Tom Doolan?" he heard someone else say. "Maybe he's under all that rubble."

There was a hole at the edge of something. He saw it and knew it had been the front door. He crawled through it, still clutching his sister. The light was bright; his eyes stung with the dust.

"It's all right, Cassie," he said to the tiny bundle, which barely seemed alive to him, or even human. "It's just you and me now. But we're going to be all right."

HE HADN'T BEEN back there since—he knew well enough when. It was five years ago, and he wondered if she still worked round the corner. Perhaps that was what had pushed him up the hill. The hope of seeing her again.

Stumbling slightly, flashing lights in the corners of his field of vision blurring everything, David found himself standing outside the Spanish Prisoners, and without knowing what else to do, he went in. Before and during the war it had been a dark place, but not like this. Then at least you had a community, even if the community was poor and desperate and afraid. His mother had played piano there, and he'd sometimes sit next to her on the long, worn wooden bench and sing the old songs with her. Everyone went in there, even if when they came out they were apt to be drunk and sometimes violent. It was just where you went.

Now it was dirty, unloved, dusty. Full of memories. An old thin man behind the bar, bent almost double. Flies buzzing around the curling sandwiches next to the tills. Ashtrays full to overflowing. A few mean-faced old-timers, gazing into empty drinks. Only men. He wondered if one of them was his father. He'd no idea if he was alive or dead somewhere, under a railway arch, chucked in the river after a fight. Or waiting, just biding his time to come back and get his son, the bogeyman of his nightmares.

His stomach started cramping unbearably now, and David went to the lavatory outside in the backyard. He emptied his liquid bowels, shaking and staring into space in the narrow, cramped privy, grateful that no one could hear him. Then, standing up at the bar, he ordered himself a gin this time, and drank it whole, wondering what he should do, if he was brave enough to hang around, see if he could find her, just see her for a few seconds, make sure she was all right. Aunt Jem had said she was living here now, working a stone's throw away. That was why he'd come back, wasn't it? Even though half of him didn't even know if he should walk along the market, in case he bumped into her. He was sure she didn't want to see him.

That silly cartoon again . . . he sketched out another picture of Wilbur in his book, tearing out the page, marooning it on the dirty old wood. He stared at the dog, his head spinning. What had he agreed to, back in that office? And why on earth had he come here?

He finished his drink and walked slowly down Chapel Market, picking up an apple on the way, hoping that might make him feel better; and as he bit into the sharply sweet juice his sense of self, the story he believed about himself, returned a little. He'd got out; he'd got his sister out. He'd gone to the Slade, got his degree. He'd met Martha, and that had saved him, he was sure. She was his angel, his great love, his muse, his friend; he did everything for her, for her first, and then the children. He sometimes wondered what would have happened to him had he not gone out and met her that day.

Somehow he'd managed to escape his father, and the life that had nearly sucked him in. But that didn't mean he forgot. He couldn't forget, much as he wished he could.

In another minute he was going past Cassie's work. A framer's, now that was funny too, when you thought about it, him an artist. The shops were mostly hidden from view by the market stalls in front, and the framer's had an old chap selling a pile of shoes right outside it, so David couldn't see in. He stopped behind a fishmonger's stall and peered over, to see if he could spot her bright hair through the window. She wasn't there, and it was a good thing. What would he say to her, anyway?

"Davy! *Davy*, is that you?"

He froze.

Instantly, David knew it had been a mistake to look for her. *Stay calm, act like nothing's happening.* He began walking casually away.

"Davy!" The voice bubbled in and out of the crowds. "Davy! It's him, I know it is. . . ." There was a muffled sound. "Let me through! Oh, please stop! It's me, Cassie!"

David wished he had the guts to just walk on. But he couldn't; there was something in her tone that drove right through him.

"Hello, Cassie," he said. He wheeled round so swiftly that she almost bumped into him.

"It is you! I bloody knew it was." Cassie hit him on the arm. "You bloody deaf or something? I was yelling all the way back down the market."

He glanced at her, and his heart started thumping in his chest. He wished he could feel nothing, wished she seemed more like a stranger, but she didn't. She was smiling at him awkwardly, tall as ever, slim and gangly. Still so young, how old was she? Twenty-four? He thought of the last time he'd seen her, terrified, tired, her pale face determined.

"How you doing, Cass?" he said.

"All right," she said, and then she shrugged, and he knew she was regretting calling out to him. She crossed her arms, her bobbed hair shaking as she said, "Terry's got some work up the reclamation yard off the Essex Road. We're living back here now. Funny how things work out, ain't it? How . . . how are you, Davy?"

"I'm not too bad." He almost couldn't bear to meet her gaze. His little sister, who sucked her thumb so hard there was a red welt on the joint, who had thick black lashes and funny little scrunched-up toes, who screamed like a rat in a trap if you put a barrette in her hair. His sister, who looked so much like his mother. "It's been a long time, hasn't it?"

"Bloody right. I saw you in the paper, one of them exhibitions. 'Hark at him!' I said to Terry. 'Who the hell does he think he is!'"

"What do you mean?" He shrugged. "It's my work, isn't it? Can't help that."

"You had a flowery sodding necktie on, you big jessie."

"It's what I wear to . . ." He trailed off. It sounded so stupid. She laughed.

"I'm only having a go at you, Davy! I'm your sister, ain't I? I can do that? I'm the only family you got." That wasn't true anymore, though. She realized it as she was speaking; he saw it. "How's everyone? Your lot?"

"They're all good." He could feel his heart pounding in his chest, painful.

"How is she, Davy? My little girl?"

He realized this was why he was so scared. He was terrified she'd want her back again.

"She's really well. She's ever so bright, Cass. Into her books, she loves history. I read to her every night."

"You tell her where she comes from?" She shifted, moving away from him, and he thought she might suddenly run off again.

He shook his head. "No. Never. Like you wanted."

Then Cassie gripped his wrist, her thin face pale in the afternoon sun. "You don't ever tell anyone. You promised me, all right? I know I was a mistake. Dad hated me. I know what it's like. I couldn't have another mistake round here. She's better off with you."

"You can come and visit her whenever you want, Cass." He wished he could share just a tiny piece of the joy her daughter, *his* daughter, brought him. "She's wonderful. We come up to London together, she and I, we visit a gallery, have lunch, and she always—"

"Don't talk to me about her," Cassie said, and she lowered her head, looked away, curling her face into an expression of agony. "I don't want to know. I want to start over, see? Me and Terry, I'm sure we'll have our own kids, sometime soon. That little one, she was a mistake, I was too young." Her face darkened. "That piano poof, eh? All that time Aunt Jem thought it'd be nice for me to learn like Ma, and all the time he was just waiting to get into my knickers."

It was Aunt Jem who'd called him. From a phone box, outside the Tube station. He'd picked up, thank goodness. "Cassie's in trouble." Just like that, after—how long had it been? Ten years? And he'd known right away who it was, what the problem was, known exactly what they wanted.

She was nearly nineteen. It was her piano teacher. Like her mother, she'd always loved the piano. Sentimental Jem had given her lessons every year as a birthday present. A moony-eyed, thin-faced, hungry boy in London with no money, come down from Edinburgh to study music, passionately in love with her, he said. Angus was his name. He wanted to marry Cassie; Cassie, out of her mind with fear and shame, had said no. She was seeing Terry already. And she couldn't bear the idea that she'd be the girl at secretarial college who'd have to leave because she got knocked up. She'd got the measure of Angus too, got him to agree to pay for the backstreet abortion, and Aunt Jem, full of surprises, had known just the woman. But Angus had done a bunk the day before, never turned up with the money. Aunt Jem didn't have it, and then Cassie started saying she'd run away. Have it, then ditch it. That's when Jem called her nephew. "I don't know what to do," she'd said, her voice breaking. "I think she might hurt herself. Or the baby. Can't you—come and see her?"

That summer was the last time he'd been back here, several visits culminating in the final time, when he came to collect his new daughter. For though things were changing on the King's Road and elsewhere, in working-class Walthamstow where Cassie lived with Aunt Jem, a nineteen-year-old unmarried mother would have found herself alone and friendless fairly soon. Terry wouldn't stick around, Cassie was sure of that. She'd lose her place at the secretarial college.

They told everyone Cassie was spending the summer in Ireland, helping a sick aunt. In fact, she came back to the old neighborhood, to Penton Street with Aunt Jem, took a room by the market, had the baby at the University College hospital down the road.

When Cassie handed the ten-day-old baby girl over to David, he took her gently, cradling the soft wrinkled head in one hand.

"Now, listen," Cassie told him. "I don't want to see her again." She was very calm. "I don't want nothing to do with it. I want to go on and forget all about it."

He remembered her face when she said it. Only people who'd had a childhood like theirs would understand the need to start again, put the past entirely behind them. He'd done the same thing, after all, hadn't he?

"Of course," he'd said, and he'd leaned over and kissed her forehead. "Don't worry, Cass. Don't worry anymore."

He thought about that now, and Florence growing every day at home, and the leaks and the money pouring down the Winterfold drains.

"I'm not sorry I did it," she said. "Maybe I should be, but I'm not."

And David said the first heartfelt thing he'd said all day. "I'm glad you did it too, Cassie. I love her more than—I love her more than if she was my own."

She gave no sign that this pleased her, but he knew it did. "What'd you call her in the end?"

"We named her Florence. We call her Flo most of the time."

"Flo." She said it a few times. "It's nice. She like me?"

"Yes, she is," he said. "Really like you. She's very clever."

"Oh, sod off."

"Her language is better than yours, anyway." She laughed. "She's very gangly, but very charming."

"That's her dad, the weirdo."

"I think it's us too. Mum." They moved out of the way to let two shuffling old ladies pass.

"I was right, wasn't I? To give her to you? Tell me I was right?"

"I think you were right." He wished he didn't feel so sick, so apprehensive, being back here. He'd throw his arms round her, squeeze her tight. "I know you were right, Cassie. Don't you want to come and see her one day?" He thought of Florence, kneeling on her bed that morning, trying to make a flower out of paper, tongue sticking out in concentration. "She's lovely."

Cassie closed her eyes briefly and gave a bitter little smile. "No, Davy love. I don't want to ever see her again, all right? Please don't ask me again. You said you weren't ever coming back. What are you doing?"

"I don't know," David said.

His father hadn't seen the point of Cassie, but her being born meant he didn't bother David's mother for a while, and that was a good thing. He kicked David around instead. Balanced him on the mantelpiece once, so he sat there, legs dangling, the coals from the fire burning his bare feet, while his father ate supper and laughed; and when his mother came home and scooped him back onto the floor, he hit her across the face. That time he broke her nose.

So every time he thought of his mother, something would remind him, lead him back to something else. David couldn't see that the memories were important, that he shouldn't bury them deep in his heart, that he might do himself more injury that way. He could only see how much they hurt him and his sister, and the damage they could do to Florence. He was sure Daisy knew the truth, he didn't know how. And he sometimes felt Martha didn't understand Florence the way he did.

He shivered. Cassie put her hand on his arm. "Listen, Davy. I'd best be off. They'll be wondering where I went. I only said I was going to the post office. You get back home to Molly and those kids."

"Martha."

"All right, then." She tossed her hair, and he knew she knew what

Martha was called. It was just bravado, what they did to get by, the Doolans of Muriel Street. "Good to see you, Davy. Honest."

It occurred to him she was called Bourne now; that was Terry's name. And he'd changed his name to Winter. Aunt Jem was dead, a heart attack last year. In a generation, there'd be nothing left of their old family, or their father's name. Just their children, being brought up in the same house. David took out his little sketchbook, scribbled down his address, tore out the page and pressed it into her cold fingers. "Here. In case you ever need me."

Cassie shook her head, her mouth clamped shut, her gray eyes swimming with tears. "Don't ask me again," she said after a minute. She looked down at the paper, then shoved it into her pocket. A gesture just like Florence's, full of confidence and strangely awkward. "Got to get back to work now. Good seeing you again, big brother."

"You too." He kissed her cheek. "Terry treating you well?"

She waggled her head. "So-so. He's all right. I'm all right. Hoping to have our kids next year. That's what Terry wants. Suppose I do too. Anyway, bye, then." She raised her hand like a signal, and then she was gone.

As he walked through the crowded backstreets, the old roads he knew so well, past the site of the old mission hall and Grimaldi's churchyard and the old fishmongers, Cally Road toward King's Cross, he knew he wouldn't tell Martha he'd seen Cassie. And afterward, on the train going back to Winterfold, David flicked through the bomb-site drawings again, his eyes taking in every last detail, as if there might be some salvation in it. He knew he'd put them away when he got home, maybe never look at them again. Perhaps it was right they stayed in the past. Perhaps Cassie was right. For the remainder of the journey he practiced drawing Wilbur, as the coal-black steam threw smuts against the carriage windows, taking him farther and farther away from hell and back to his own home.

When he came into the kitchen that evening, teatime was over and the children were outside. He could hear them chanting, some strange game. Martha was slicing up onions for supper. He stood in the doorway watching her, her slim fingers sliding the moon shapes into the red pot. She wiped her eyes on her forearm at one point, her hair falling in front of her face; then she looked up and blinked, laughing to herself, and saw him.

"Hello there," she said, and he knew he loved her more than anything and anyone in the whole world.

"Hello," he said, coming toward her. "I'm sorry for this morning. I'm sorry for everything. I didn't sell the drawings, but I've had an idea. A wonderful idea." He gripped her shoulders and kissed her. "Everything's going to be great."

She stepped back, holding the knife, still smiling. "Careful, I'm armed. Well, that's good news. What's got into you?"

"Just as I say." He threw his hat onto the table. "Everything bad is in the past. Everything good is in the future."

Martha stroked his cheekbone, tracing the line of his eye sockets. "You look exhausted."

The onion scent on her fingers made his eyes water. He kissed her again and she leaned back in his arms, her back curving away, arms outstretched; then she flung herself around him again and hugged him.

"Oh, I'm sorry," she whispered in his ear, head lying on his shoulder. "I hate arguing with you. I love you, darling."

"Em, Em . . ." He breathed in the scent of her, closed his eyes. "It's in the past. I'm getting us a drink. I love you."

When he'd made them both strong, lime-scented gin and tonics, Martha threw the thyme from their garden into the pot with the chicken, and they went outside and sat on the lawn, watching the children chase the dancing dragonflies, their rainbow wings catching the summer light. Martha sat back in her chair, humming, occasionally calling out to one of them. David gulped his drink down like a dying man. He knew he had seen his past today, in all its forms. And now he had to remake the future.

Martha

March 2013

Bill, Daisy, Florence.

In the weeks after David died, Martha realized that she did not see things clearly anymore. She had lost all sense of what was normal and what wasn't. She could see the fear in people's eyes if she walked into the village, when she went to the shop or to church. The horror of grief. She felt marked, like a leper. They wanted to shy away from her because of what she had done, and what had happened in her house that day.

She had to change several aspects of her day-to-day life. At first some were difficult, but it was much better this way.

She didn't go into the study. There was time to go through his papers, his sketches, the documents of their family. Not yet.

The night it happened, she had found Florence in there, and something about her face, her searching eyes, was like a warning signal. There was too much in the study; it was all him. She couldn't be going in there, and neither could anyone else. Martha saw that quite clearly.

"I need to use the study," she told Florence. "Papers in there I need to find."

"I was just looking for something." Florence's eyes were red raw. Her fingers flapped uselessly; she had beautiful hands. She swallowed. "Ma . . ." Then she started crying. Martha stared at her daughter's sunken, heart-shaped face and knew she couldn't tell her anything. She stroked her lightly on the arm.

"Just give me a couple of minutes in here, please, darling. The police need some information."

The next day, Florence left. Left the house less than twenty-four hours after he'd died. Something about a manuscript on loan in London only for one more day. It was a lie, of course.

"If I don't go now . . . I can't explain." She'd rushed forward and briefly embraced her mother; and just as Martha inhaled that familiar Florence smell of coffee, something spicy, her soft hair brushing Martha's cheek, Florence gave a soft cry that seemed to stick in her throat.

"I don't know what else to say to you," she'd mumbled; Martha wasn't sure, afterward, exactly what it was she'd said. For how could she know? How could her baby girl, the one she didn't choose but had been handed on a plate, the one she hadn't loved to begin with, not at all, how could she know? Was it a memory, the truth of the years rolling back like a stone to reveal the emptiness at the beginning, the huge lie at the heart of it all?

When you were little, you loved to chew my finger. Your long, white, slim little fingers gripping mine, your tiny hard pink gums, your mouth sucking my knuckle, your huge blue eyes as clear as a summer sky. The solid small heft of you in my arms. You in your place with us. And I loved you, even though you weren't mine.

And then she was gone, like that.

She came back for the funeral, that awful, cold, icy day when everyone except Martha cried, and the earth was frozen so stiff that the men took twice as long to dig the plot, and the ice seemed sewn into the mud, glittering underfoot, as the family gathered around the open grave and watched the coffin lowered in. Martha saw him there, saw the earth she was handed scattering onto the wooden lid, saw the faces of her family— Bill's eyes hazy with grief, Florence's red with weeping, hands in front of her mouth, Lucy's hunched shoulders and flushed cheeks, mouth turned down like a clown's, Cat biting her woolen-glove-clad finger.

Martha didn't cry. Not then.

Since the funeral, Florence, like Daisy, had vanished. She was fighting this court case. She was always busy: *I have to meet my barrister tomorrow. I have a paper to finish.* She'd say she was coming back and then she didn't. *I'm staying with Jim in London. I'll call you.* She never did. *The trial's in May.*

And in December or January, May seemed so far in the future as to be ridiculous. He would have come back by then; this was all like the episode in the kitchen, when she had felt herself slipping away. He had gone and would come back. It seemed logical to her.

Bill, Daisy, Florence.

This is what Martha kept remembering: how it was when they returned from the hospital, nearly five years ago. A hot summer's day, the hills beyond the house golden and lazy with late-afternoon heat. David was limping, his knee still bandaged. She'd helped him from the car, and then walked with him through to the garden.

"I need to show you something."

His arm was heavy around her neck as she helped him along the rocky path toward the daisy bank. When they reached the scar of the freshly milled brown earth, he stared down at it.

"What's been going on?" he said in a strange voice, and she knew he understood.

"Daisy," she began. "Darling . . . she's gone."

His hand gripped the metal crutch the hospital had given him. It pressed into the wet soil. "Oh, Daisy," he said. He scrunched his face up and looked at her. His eyes were dark. "What happened, Em?"

"She . . . did it herself." She couldn't say "killed herself," it was so brutal. "She . . . I buried her."

He gazed at the crumbling earth, at the crushed daisies around the long rectangular grave. He didn't speak for a long time, but eventually he said, "Don't you want to tell someone, Em?"

All Daisy had asked for was to be buried here, to not be bothered anymore. And Martha had felt she had to give her that. She could have rung the police, yes, of course. But since it had happened, she'd realized that she didn't care about other people. She never had. She cared about the fact that her daughter, who hadn't ever felt at home in this place, had wanted to stay here at last.

Don't you want to tell someone, Em?

"I thought I wouldn't," she said. "I thought I'd just let everyone think she's gone away again."

"Yes," he said gently.

"I . . . I think she's happy here now. Do you . . . ?" And Martha faltered, the fatigue and sadness swamping her. She sobbed, stumbled against him, so that he supported her for a moment. "Does that make any sense to you?"

"Yes. Yes, of course."

They'd dug Daisy up. Three policemen and forensics and a pathologist, a big white tent around the daisy bank and the light of huge arc lamps flooding the side of the house, the earth churned into new banks of brown mud. She'd sat at the window, watching them, with her usual cup of tea and gingerbread, trying to tell herself they couldn't hurt her, no one could anymore. She stood up and drew the curtains that looked out onto the daisy bank and the garden from the dining room. She kept them drawn from that moment on. She left the garden well alone.

Bill, Daisy, Florence.

He'd been eighty-two. Not young. By the New Year, Martha couldn't bear to see anyone other than close family or strangers, because someone would say again, "It was a good run, eighty-two," and the fear that she would turn on them in rage and lose control grew to possess her.

He didn't tell me he was ill. I could have helped him and he didn't tell me. I saw how he suffered. I watched him die.

So she stopped going into the village. Karen did her shopping, and then when Karen moved in with Joe in the New Year, Bill did it, Bill and Lucy.

Karen was there that day they took Daisy away, two or three weeks after the birthday lunch. She sat with Martha in the dining room. She had her laptop with her and pretended to be working, but occasionally she'd look up and ask Martha a question, get up to make some more tea, fetch a book.

There was something restful about Karen, something calm and logical about her in those days after David went, when Christmas was approaching and everything was supposed to carry on as normal. Martha was glad of her company.

But come the New Year Karen had left Bill, moved in with Joe. David, Daisy, Florence, Cat, now this little one, another grandchild, gone. Bill had known his father was ill. She knew it, she didn't know how. To see him and think of the skinny, muddy, serious, joyful little boy he'd been, nearly, but not quite, brought her down. It would if she thought about Bill then. The little boy who'd thrown himself into her arms, who'd run along the lane with her, jumping up with questions like a kangaroo, who'd left for medical school and said in the doorway, an awkward, acned eighteen-year-old, "Thanks for a great life so far, Ma, really wanted to just say that," then got into the car with David, waved once, and driven off.

Bill, Daisy, Florence.

Through the long, cold nights of late winter, Martha lay awake, staring at the blue-black ceiling, listening to the silence outside. Though it was never silent, not really: the owls, the dreadful sound of night murder in hedgerows, a lone dog barking somewhere, and always a blackbird, throughout it all, in the tree outside.

One night she was lying, eyes fixed on the ceiling as though a movie reel were playing there, when she suddenly turned to look at David's side of the bed. It had been cleared, but the book he had been reading still lay there. *The Day of the Jackal*. The tatty green woven bookmark that Cat had made at Brownie camp when she was nine marked his place: only halfway through.

Suddenly Martha saw grief, like the sky, covering everything, all over her, around her, impossible to penetrate. That feeling again, the one she'd had before. The gray mist seemed to fill up the room; it slid along the floor, up the bed, over her, covering her like water.

He's never coming back.

He is. Don't think about it.

He's never coming back, Martha. You threw the earth on the coffin. You cleared out his cupboard. He's dead. David's dead.

She fought it, literally, wrestling with the bedclothes, scrambling out of the room, pulling the door shut behind her. Memories, like a vortex. David in only a pair of pants, painting the kitchen. Lying on the grass with Bill by his side, listening to the cricket game on the radio. His sweet, hopeful face, staring at her as they lay in bed. The long, sad day they brought Florence back from Cassie's maternity ward, and his suddenly joyous expression at their hotel as he peered at the small bundle, clasped tight in Martha's arms. His screams at night, when the bad dreams came and he'd moan and sob so loudly, sometimes wetting himself, sometimes curling up in a ball so tight she had to wake him to free him.

He needed her, wherever he was. She wasn't there and he needed her. Who would hug him and comfort him; who would be there wherever he was to smooth his hair, to hold his hand and whisper those words; who would help him draw, help him cook, help him make a house, a home, a family together? He was alone. He had never been without her and she needed him, now more than ever. Just to see him once more, to tell him once more, one more evening together . . . Tears poured down Martha's cheeks. She retched, her throat swelling up so much with the power of grief that she thought, then and there, she was losing consciousness. She leaned against the wall, panting, sobbing, gasping for breath. But there was no one to hear her in the empty house. No one.

Eventually her breathing returned to normal. She put her hand on her throat, wishing this thickness, this lump would go away. She leaned in and listened through the bedroom door. As if she were trying to hear something.

All was quiet again.

"He's somewhere round here," Martha muttered to herself. She clicked her tongue.

In the darkness, she smiled to herself. She understood now. She thought she wouldn't say anything to anyone about it, but she knew she was right.

She just had to put a few plans in place, then, and she would see him again, when things were ready. She didn't go back to her room at night-time. She started sleeping in Cat's room, hugging the old patchwork cushion with Cat's name spelled out in blue, and which smelled faintly of Cat, close to her. She avoided Lucy's calls, because Lucy wanted to come over to look after her, to boss her around and pry and get into things, to find out things. She mustn't let her do that.

She couldn't go into the village, so she went into Bath to do her shopping. She would walk through the supermarket, pushing a cart, thinking about what he would like for supper, and sometimes see another person like her. Eyes blank. Face smooth, unlined, frozen. And Martha would think: *I know why they're like that. They are waiting for someone too. I hope they come back soon.*

She stopped cleaning the house, opening the post, answering the phone. She read and reread her old gardening books. She learned the name of every plant, its soil, its situation, its family. Memorizing them so that, if someone started talking about him and how sad it was, or what she should do, or how plans should be put in place, she could just nod and smile and not listen, recite different varieties of forget-me-nots in her head to shut out the words so she couldn't hear what they were telling her. Because if she couldn't hear them, she couldn't let them in. Since the first day, the day she'd met him and he'd worn that silly hat on his head, since the two of them walked away from the past and into their future, he had always been nearby.

Karen

"Easy now," said Dawn, as Karen heaved her shopping bag over her shoulder. "Let me get the door for you. Where's that Joe, then?"

"He's up on the Levels, meeting some meat guys," said Karen. "Thanks, Dawn. I'm fine now."

Dawn stared at Karen's vast, domed stomach, hidden by her coat. "Look at you. That's a big baby in there, isn't it? Sure it ain't twins?" She roared with laughter.

Karen smiled and hitched her bag up again, unlocking the front door. "See you later."

"You're sure you're all right up here?" Dawn persisted, peering inside at the nondescript carpeted hallway and the stairs that led up to Joe's flat. Trying to collect information about the adulterous love nest, Karen knew, because no matter how many times she said, "We're not together. I'm just staying with Joe for a bit," no one believed her. That wasn't how the story went, was it?

"Oh, yes. Till I work out what I'm doing next. It's very kind of Joe to have me."

"Hmmph," Dawn said. "You must be lonely, what with Joe and Sheila and everything that's going on at the pub these days."

"I don't mind. He deserves it. They both do."

"It's mad, though, isn't it?" Dawn folded her arms and leaned against the door.

"Yes, it's great. Please, Dawn—I hope you don't mind if I just take that other bag and . . ." Karen began, trying not to snap. Her feet ached more each moment she stood on them, and she felt if she didn't sit down soon she might just have to slump onto the stairs, wait for Joe to finish work so he could haul her up to his flat in a sack.

"All right, Karen?" Sheila appeared from the pub. "I'll help you upstairs with them bags, shall I? Bye, then, Dawn, good to see you. Len's all right?"

"Oh, he's fine these days," Dawn said. "Ever since the varicose veins got done, he's a new man. All thanks to Dr. . . . ." She trailed off. "Well, bye, then."

"She's a nice girl, but she needs more to do with her time, now Bill's fixed Len's legs." Sheila huffed upstairs and into the tiny kitchen, dropping the bags on the counter, as Karen followed behind. "Only thing keeping her going before that, running around after him. Now, shall I put the kettle on? You look done in."

Karen sat down slowly and eased her swollen feet up onto the coffee table. "That'd be great."

"How long you got to go now?"

"I'm due end of May. I wish it was over, Sheila. Those celebrities they interview in *Hello!* or whatever who go on about how they've never felt better—what are they on about? And I've still got two months to go."

"Those magazines conspire against women to keep them in their place. It's the patriarchy's finest work," Sheila said grimly, and Karen looked at her in surprise. "Oh, the last bit's the worst," she added in a normal voice. "Everyone knows that. You got all your baby gear ready?"

The same questions, twenty times a day. *How long have you got to go? Have you got everything ready? Is it a boy or a girl? How are you feeling? You look well!* Karen knew from her fellow mothers-to-be in the parenting course they were doing that there were just as many questions she wasn't being asked. Whether they were going to stay in their current home or move somewhere with more space, for example. No one in Winter Stoke asked Karen that.

"I've bought some things but I don't want to go overboard till it's here. I'm superstitious. Joe had some journalist down from London last week—she swears by IKEA. He's obsessed with it now, keeps trying to buy stuff online, only there's so much you have to go in the stores to buy. That's how they make their money, isn't it?"

"Those bloody wineglasses. Ten pounds for twelve, they do them, and those patterned cardboard storage boxes." Sheila leaned on the counter, laughing. "Every time I go in there I promise it's just to get a desk for the office or whatever, and every time I come out with a pile of those patterned cardboard boxes and a lorry-load of glasses and they smash on the way home and I never use those cardboard boxes, never."

"Well, maybe you should go mad and treat yourself, Sheila." Karen tried to reach her foot, but her bump prevented her. "Take Joe. He's desperate to go. I can't face IKEA, walking round like a beached whale in flats. No way."

"You look beautiful," Sheila said. She poured from the teapot. "Honestly, you do. Suits you, being a bit more . . ." She stopped. "Well, never mind."

"Now you've got me worried." Karen smiled. She hadn't ever really cared about her appearance. She knew she was attractive—it was part of her pragmatic nature that she accepted it as fact—and often it was boring, men coming on to you because you were short and had big boobs. It was one of the things she'd liked about Bill, that he hadn't minded much about her clothes or nails or hair, or that she was seventeen years younger than he. He'd liked *her*.

It was Joe she'd tarted herself up for, almost as if she knew she had to play the part of the scarlet woman to make sense of what she was doing—and the irony was, he didn't like it. They'd only slept together four or five times, but they'd met a few more than that. In summer, going into September . . . before he'd found out she wasn't just Karen Bromidge, the lonely girl two years older than he, who was new to the area and from the north and sexy as hell and lots of fun, whom he could talk to about his son, and the weirdness of the village, and starting over again, and then have sex with—intense, heated, silent sweaty sex that matched the wet, humid summer. He didn't know her married name was Karen Winter, and that she lived down the road with the doctor who'd sewn up his finger. She was married, and Joe—Joe was a damn prude, she was starting to think. He'd ditched her faster than a rubbish truck at full speed, and he'd been so angry with her, so bloody furious!

"You should have told me, Karen," he'd said gently, but his voice was cold. It was early October and chilly in his small flat, where they'd had their secret summer. But summer was definitely over now. "It changes everything."

"What's the difference? You weren't into me," she'd yelled, not caring who heard them, how mad she sounded. She'd have been pregnant then, two or three weeks, how weird to think of it now. "You didn't want to go out with me. I know you didn't. I'd have thought you'd have been glad, no strings attached, what's wrong with you?"

"What's wrong with *you*?" he'd said angrily. "Karen, you can't just go around lying to people like that. I really liked you. I'd—if I'd known, then . . ."

It had been hard enough to get him to sleep with her, she'd thought. Then she found that if she just kept playing the part of the bad girl, she'd start to believe it, and somehow she'd be okay. But it hadn't worked out like that. She'd engineered this whole sorry mess, and there was nothing to do but make the best of it.

The memory of it made her shiver. She took a biscuit from the tin and dunked it in the tea Sheila handed her. "This is lovely. Thanks, Sheila."

Since Karen had moved in with Joe, just after Christmas, Sheila had been nothing but kind to her. It couldn't have been easy, her star chef suddenly lumbered with a hormonal, homeless, pregnant ex, four weeks after that review in the *Daily News*.

It was funny, when she thought about it. How Lucy had babbled on for weeks about this guy at work, how he was old and sad and keen on her, how he kept saying he'd review the Oak Tree, and Karen just hadn't believed her. She was too worried about Lucy's obvious crush on Joe to see any further than that.

Karen sometimes wondered if Lucy knew how profoundly she had changed everything, really. The review had run the week after David's funeral, Saturday, December 1. A copy of it had been framed, and hung above the bar.

. . . In the cooking of Joe Thorne, the young, gentle chef who spent two years under Jean Michel Folland at Le Jardin in Leeds, we have the very best of British cuisine today. The apparent simplicity of the names of dishes belies the extreme complexity with which they are created. Pressed ham hock, salmon roulade with beetroot relish, goat-cheese ravioli—they all sound straightforward, and they are, for this is no snob's menu, designed to dazzle and intimidate. Rather it is a menu for a neighborhood restaurant, which happens to be situated in a pub, one that is as old as the

Civil War, in an idyllic little slice of Somerset just outside Bath. The food is locally sourced—in an unpretentious and sympathetically realistic way, none of your foraging for borage nonsense here. The execution is perfect. The atmosphere—under the eagle eye of landlady Sheila Cowper—is welcoming, laid-back, and yet with just a touch of magic: witness the rose hips on the table and the complimentary damson vodka offered to me after my meal. I booked another table for the following week when I left. I cannot recommend this wonderful place highly enough.

It had happened fast. Bookings started coming in that day for dinners and Christmas parties. Tables of six, eight, ten. Then weekend lunches, then requests for birthday parties, private room rental, the works. By New Year's Eve the restaurant had been booked out for two weeks, and though Sheila and Joe both fully expected the slump in January, it never came. There were mutterings from some of the villagers about cars blocking the high street and not being able to move for Londoners up at the bar now, and there'd been some defections to the Green Man, but as Joe told Karen, he was sure he'd win them back. If necessary, they'd buy the field behind Tom and Clover's, turn it into a vegetable patch and a car park. Maybe institute a locals-only night, where you had to have a council tax bill with you to claim your table and all you could eat for £40 for two, including wine.

He was full of plans. So was Sheila. Karen went along with them, smiling at their enthusiasm, even as the endless winter passed and the days grew wetter and longer, and her body grew bigger and began to drag her down. She had no idea what the future might hold. She was too terrified to ask herself the question, so she avoided it from anyone else.

She had left Bill after Christmas. Since his father died he was a robot, a man who put on his overcoat every morning, went to his office, solved his patients' problems, and in the evening came home and either went up to the house to be with his mother or sat in an armchair listening to old episodes of *Hancock's Half Hour* and staring into space, square fingers drumming on the arms of the chair. She tried to help: she ran errands for Martha, she fielded calls, answered letters. But Lucy wasn't talking to her, Florence had vanished off the face of the earth, and Cat was back in Paris. Karen was worried about Martha, more than merely concerned she wasn't coping. There was something strange about her, about the language she used. Karen didn't believe some of the things she said, didn't think she was quite well.

She tried to talk to Bill, to ask him what he thought, what he wanted for tea, what he wanted to watch on TV, but every time he'd just say, "I don't know, Karen. You do what you want."

On New Year's Eve he sat in front of the television, gin and tonic in hand, a plump quarter of lime trapped under the ice cubes. He always had lime, not lemon, just like Martha and David. It was a Winter thing; there was always a pile of jewellike limes in a brown glazed bowl on the table at Winterfold, even in the depths of winter. Karen stood behind him, twisting her fingers together over and over.

"Bill. Bill?"

He'd turned round, and she saw the tears in his eyes, the glazed expression. He hadn't really been watching anything.

"Yes." He'd cleared his throat and stood up, with the sofa between them.

"I think I should move out," she'd said. "I just wondered what you think about it." There was a pause and, because she was terrified of his answer, she rushed ahead and said, "I think we need some time apart. So you can work out what you feel about all of this. You've got so much to deal with at the moment."

He'd shaken his head. "No, it's not that, Karen." He'd moved the empty glass onto the shelf, carefully. She loved how precise he was with everything, how neat and modest his movements were, how he inhabited his space so comfortably, how being with him was to feel safe and secure and . . .

Karen had put her hands in front of her eyes so he couldn't see her tears.

He'd said gently, "I think you should move out because you have to work out what you want. I can't make you happy, that's clear. I loved you. If you want to go, I think it's best you go. We got it wrong, didn't we?" He'd looked up, his eyes puckering together, his mouth creased into an awkward smile. "It was always going to be a risk, wasn't it? Suppose it was worth it. . . ." And then he'd come round the sofa and squeezed her arm. "Do you have somewhere to go?"

She'd gritted her teeth so he wouldn't see how ill-prepared she was. She hadn't booked a hotel, rung a friend—she had no friends here now, anyway. "Oh, yeah. I thought I'd . . . I'll . . . Yes, I'm staying with a friend," she lied.

"Really?" Bill picked up his keys. "Well, then," he said quietly. "I'll leave you alone to get your stuff together. I'll go and see Ma."

He'd stood a couple of meters from her and they'd nodded, trying to keep the conversation alive. The distance between them . . . Then Bill had pulled on his coat.

"We'll talk soon, then. Let me know . . . how you are."

And he went out, leaving her alone in the little house. Karen packed her bags, tears falling on the duvet cover. She could see every stepping-stone on the path that had taken her to this point, every wrong turn, every mistake. She was completely alone, and there were no fireworks that signified the end of her relationship with Bill. He'd made her chicken Kiev sandwiches. Suddenly that was all she could think about.

Joe met her at the end of the street and helped her with her bags. He didn't ask any questions, but that first night, he gave up his bed for her.

"I'll sleep in Jamie's room. It's absolutely fine."

They were very formal with each other. "Thank you," she'd said, looking at his short, curly hair, the dark hairs on his arms, his strong hands gripping her bag. Trying to remember how it felt to be naked with him, to feel him inside her. She couldn't; she couldn't remember it at all. "I won't be here long. I'll start looking for somewhere."

He'd hung in the doorway. "Please, Karen. Stay as long as you want. I know it must be difficult for you. It's my responsibility too." Then he cleared his throat. "Isn't it?"

"I suppose it must be," she'd said. "All the evidence would suggest it is."

Joe had swallowed, and for a split second he looked terrified. But it was so fleeting she might have missed it. He'd hugged the towel he was holding to his chest. "I love kids, Karen, you know that. I won't let you down. I'll be there, I promise."

Four months ago. Karen heard the thundering footsteps on the stairs, and her heart lifted. "There he is," Sheila said, smiling. "He'll make it all all right, just you see if he doesn't."

269

"You've already done that, Sheila," Karen said, raising her mug as Joe came in.

"Sheila! We got Brian to commit to becoming our supplier, and we'll sell his meat through the pub." Joe vaulted over the back of the sofa, landing next to Karen, who was jolted into the air, spilling her tea.

"Oh!" Karen mopped at her dripping lap.

He cupped his hand under her mug. "I'm so sorry, Karen. How are you?"

"I was tired, but that's woken me up." She smiled at him. "Let me get you a cup of tea."

"I'll get it," he said, standing up again. "I can't stay long."

"I thought you weren't working tonight?" She tried to keep the disappointment out of her voice. After all, they were merely flatmates, and he was absolutely adamant he was going to do right by her—they'd talked seriously about her buying the dilapidated cottage two doors down, Karen pulling up Excel spreadsheets on her laptop and tapping figures into her computer, going through the motions of some plan that, frankly, alternately depressed her and terrified her. All so that when the baby was born he could come and help most days, and even stay over there instead when Jamie was down—the cottage was bigger, it had a garden, and Jamie and this new little thing, his half brother or sister, would have room to grow.

When they sat on the sofa to watch TV on the rare evenings Joe spent in, there was at least two feet between them. They couldn't ever agree on what to watch anyway. She liked documentaries about people with bodily disorders. He liked US TV series. He thought she was prurient for recording programs about men with engorged testicles or conjoined twins; she thought he was bloodthirsty for enjoying the spectacle of a fantasy king murdering a prostitute and someone being made to wear his own severed hand round his neck. She knew all this, but she couldn't say it, couldn't joke about it, the way she used to tease Bill about his love of Ealing comedies.

"I am working, I'm so sorry," Joe said, peering through the hatch from the kitchen. "But I'm going to quickly make you some bubble and squeak on a tray. I brought most of the ingredients up with me. Sheila"—he threw her a balled-up wad of paper—"here's the receipts for the fishmonger. He says we're his best customer now. Can you do me a favor? Start running Karen a bath?"

Sheila unfolded the receipts and put them into her pocket, watching Joe affectionately. "Hot baths and tea on a tray? Ooh, you're a lucky woman, Karen."

Karen watched Joe's head moving back and forth in the kitchen, and she felt the baby move, shifting and sliding around inside her. All she could think of was that bubble and squeak was Bill's favorite meal, the one he'd cook singing along to his northern soul albums in his tuneless, awkward bass.

"I must be, mustn't I," she said.

Cat

CAT HAD SOLD the red Lanvin shoes on eBay eventually, for one hundred euros. She had taken out a credit card too, and with that paid for the Eurostar for her and Luke to go back to Winterfold in early April to see her grandmother. They arrived very late on Friday, and the plan was to leave before lunch on Sunday.

Staring out of the train at the still-freezing English spring, she told herself that coming back was the right thing to do, though Gran had told her not to. Everything had changed, that day in November. So there was no point in fearing what might come, as she had always done: it had already happened. No point in hanging on to memories. No point in fearing a debt when the people who needed you needed you now.

That first night back she lay next to Luke on one of the high twin beds in Lucy's room and wondered if she'd been right. Martha was sleeping in Cat's room. Something about damp in her own room. Cat didn't believe her. She'd said she had to go somewhere the next morning, to get some milk. When Cat asked her where, Martha had said, "Bristol." Cat had laughed, thinking it was one of her grandmother's impenetrable jokes, but she had been quite serious.

Everywhere she looked, the house seemed to be covered up, like shrouds over the dead. Curtains drawn. Dust on surfaces. Doors shut, locked. Shawls and blankets she'd never seen before covering chairs and sofas, and when Cat asked why, Martha said simply: "They're dangerous. They can't be touched."

"Of course," Cat said carefully, trying not to show Luke how much this scared her. It was because they were the pieces of furniture Southpaw had sat in, the things in the house he had used most frequently. His chair in the kitchen, a heavy oak thing with arms and carved feet: Martha said it had woodworm and might have to be thrown away.

On Saturday morning, they sat in silence, Luke pushing cereal around his bowl, Cat eating some toast, Martha quite still, staring at nothing, humming very slightly. It was a cruelly cold day. A gray sky, no sign of spring.

"I have to go in a minute. The traffic into Bristol will be poor." Martha stood up.

"Bristol?" Cat had forgotten momentarily. She rubbed her eyes. "No, Gran. Don't be . . ." She trailed off.

Her grandmother's tone was even. As though Cat were being hysterical. "I need some milk, and I don't get it from the shop anymore. Problems with supply."

"Gran—you really don't have to go into Bristol, honestly. I'll walk into the village in a little bit, get some milk, some things for you."

"No, thank you." She collected the plates, though Cat and Luke hadn't finished.

Luke climbed onto David's chair, pulling an old green shawl to the floor. He rocked it back and forward, against the table.

"Luke, stop it," Cat said.

Martha, at the sink, turned. "Don't do that," she said, but Luke ignored her. The old chair creaked as he teetered backward, his full weight on it.

Cat said, "Luke. Stop it now."

"I want to sit in it," said Luke. "I miss him. I miss Southpaw."

Martha crossed the kitchen. Her expression remained unchanged. With one firm movement she grabbed Luke's skinny arm and yanked him out of the chair. As if he were a rag doll. She staggered a little, catching the weight of him against her, and his legs flailed wildly in the air; then she let go, and Luke fell to the floor.

"I said, don't do that."

Luke lay crying on the floor, looking at his great-grandmother with a bewildered expression. Cat helped him up with one hand.

"Darling, she asked you to stop." She hugged him close to her. "I'm sorry, Gran. He was cooped up in the train all yesterday, and now—"

"I don't care." Martha was facing away from them; she turned and draped the shawl over the chair again. "Perhaps you'd better go out now, then."

Cat, who was used to being in control of everything, felt helpless. She couldn't remember being at Winterfold and wanting to escape. She didn't know how to talk to her grandmother. Lucy, with whom she spoke regularly on the phone now, had warned her, but Cat realized she hadn't really grasped it.

They walked down the lane, Luke happy again, running in zigzags, Cat holding the list Martha had given her. It gave her a shock to see Gran's strong, elegant, sloping handwriting again.

> *Milk*
> *3 limes*
> *3 potatoes*
> *Bombay Sapphire gin. From the pub. Not from the post office.*
> *They only sell Gordon's gin.*

Pushing the scrap of paper into her pocket, Cat ran to catch up with Luke. She didn't want to go into the pub. She didn't want to see Joe. *I mean,* she'd tell herself when he came into her mind on those dark winter nights in Paris, lying in the chilly, tiny *chambre de bonne* in the Quai de Béthune, *it's almost comical—the first man I allow myself to like, the first man I kiss in years, about whom I think:* For once, you might actually be a good guy, a nice man. . . . *ha.*

Compared to what had happened after that, she supposed her encounter with Joe was the light relief of the weekend. She was no judge of men, that was clear, and she thought she had probably had a lucky escape. Olivier, Joe—silver-tongued and black-hearted, both of them. And when she thought about his lips on hers, their bodies meeting in the chill damp, the way he'd pretended to understand, worming his way in, when Karen, his pregnant girlfriend, her *aunt*, was lying low at home less than a mile away . . . Cat, arriving at the village shop, shook her head, surprised at the power the thought of him still had, five months afterward, to make her this angry. She'd have to lie to Gran. Tell her the pub was all out of Bombay Sapphire.

• • •

After they'd done their shopping at the post office, Cat waved good-bye to Susan and chivvied Luke along the high street toward the playground. It occurred to her that by now, for all she knew, the Oak Tree was so famous there'd be hordes of people outside, food bloggers and critics and liggers waiting for Lily Allen or whoever it was who was supposed to love it there, and she was possessed by a curiosity to see how different it was now. On the pretext of looking at the new cul-de-sac of ugly executive houses that were being built right on the fields, she walked them briskly to the end of the high street; and as they passed, she glanced hurriedly in the windows of the Oak Tree. But it was late morning and the lights were still off, the stools and chairs on tables. No other signs of life. She glanced up at the rooms above the pub. Karen was living there with him now, she knew.

As they turned back and crossed the waterlogged village green toward the playground, Cat felt more cheerful. As if she'd exorcised some silly teenage crush, and now that it was over she could admit she'd liked him. She'd enjoyed kissing him. Joe Thorne was cute—he was handsome, funny, shy, he loved *Game of Thrones*, and he'd told her about *The Gruffalo*. So it turned out he was bad news. So what? He was just someone she'd kissed after a long day and too much wine. It was done now. She'd been living the life of a nun on an island the last few years. She needed more experiences like Joe.

"Mum, swing me?" Luke said, leaping up at her side, his face flushed with cold, his huge eyes imploring.

"Sure." One of the many little pinpricks you felt about being a single parent was that there weren't two of you to swing your child along on either side. So instead Cat did her special thing, which was to loop her arms under Luke's shoulders and spin him around and around on the boggy grass till they were both dizzy and stumbling. She did it three or four times, then pretended to stop. "Okay, all done."

"But that was hardly any spin! No! Again! More spin!" Luke laughed, jumping up and down, and she laughed back, the happiness at being alone with him in this huge expanse of green, away from the dark dusty house, the feeling of fresh country air in her lungs, in his little lungs too, making her almost drunk with sensation.

"Okay. One more."

"Okay! Okay! Okayokayokayokayokay!!" Luke shouted, bouncing up and down.

"Spin!" Cat shouted, staggering around in a crazy circle, as Luke's shrieks of ecstatic excitement grew louder and louder, and the more they both laughed, the unsteadier she became, going faster and faster. Suddenly one of her wellingtons squelched, suctioned in by mud and water, and she began to topple. She slid to the ground, Luke on top of her.

"Oh, no," she said. "I'm covered in mud."

"Joe Thorne!" Luke screamed. "Mummy, it's Joe, he hit me with the car!" He scrambled to his feet and pointed, as if seeing a miracle. "Mummy! He's got a boy with him. A BOY!"

Luke broke out of Cat's grasp and ran toward the two figures on the other side of the cricket field, his little legs drumming on the ground.

"Luke!" she shouted. "Come back."

When she caught up with him, she was panting hard. "Hello," she said, not looking at Joe. "Luke, you don't *ever* run off like that, do you hear me?"

"I wanted to see Joe, Mummy, don't be strange." Luke was jumping up and down, almost beside himself to see not only Joe but a big boy as well. "Don't you want to see him? Who are you? Who is this? Is his jacket blue or green? I can't tell."

Joe pushed the little boy forward. "This is Jamie. He's five, Luke. Luke's three, Jamie. He likes *The Gruffalo* too."

Jamie nodded shyly. He had thick, curly blond hair, which hung like a messy halo around his head. His skin was dark caramel, his eyes a warm gray.

"Hello, Jamie, I'm Cat."

"Hullo." Jamie had a deep voice. "Does he like Moshi Monsters?"

"I love them! I really do love them!" Luke bounced up and down as though he was on an invisible pogo stick, and Joe put his hand on his arm, laughing.

"All right, Luke. Eh, you silly lad, it's good to see you."

At the warmth in his voice, Cat involuntarily smiled at him, and their eyes met. He was exactly how she remembered him. Bit thinner. Stubble on his firm chin, his thick hair curly. Disappointment shot through her, taking her by surprise.

Joe's eyes were fixed on her, his gaze steady. "I didn't know you were back."

"Just for the weekend," Cat said.

"I wondered . . ." He cleared his throat. "I've been wondering how you were getting on."

"I hate Madame Poulain. I used to like her. Joe, can we watch *Ratatouille* again?"

"He's talking to me, Luke."

"I live in France, Jamie, do you? Can you speak French?"

Stoic, silent Jamie looked up at his dad with something like alarm.

"What's with him, Dad?" he said quietly, and Cat covered her mouth, trying not to laugh.

Joe bent down, resting his hand lightly on the back of his son's head. "Listen, Jamie, why don't you show Luke the swing? He won't have seen it. It's new, isn't it?"

"Yes," Jamie said, his serious eyes meeting his father's. "Are we still having lunch soon, Dad?"

"Course," Joe said. "Can you pick some bay leaves off the tree over there, too? That'd be great. You know what they look like, don't you?" He lifted Jamie up, then pretended to drop him, and Jamie gave a shriek of laughter and ran toward the playground, Luke following him, one red jacket, one blue, maybe green.

They stood together watching them go. Joe cleared his throat. "I won't ask how you all are. It must still be very hard."

Cat shoved her hands in her pockets. "We're okay." The waves that hit her during the day at the market stall or staring out of the window of Madame Poulain's sitting room, tears pouring down her cheeks, Luke saying, "Come here, Mummy! Maman! Why are you crying?" Flashes of her grandfather's sweater he used to wear to keep warm in his study, navy wool, eaten by moths to a cobweb. His smiling, shining eyes, his darling hands, so swollen and painful. And her mother—she hadn't even been able to think about her mother properly yet. Not at all. As for Gran, and the family and all of it—there wasn't a place to start, a place to begin, a thread that would lead them out of the maze. Cat turned her head so he wouldn't see the tears in her eyes. "That's not true. We're not okay, really."

He nodded, and he didn't try to hug her, as Susan Talbot had done, or grip her hands with tears in his eyes, like Clover, or shake his head pityingly. He just said, "I'm so sorry, Cat."

"Me too."

"How's Mrs. Winter?"

"She's not great. I don't know. Sometimes I'm not sure she really understands what's happened."

"What do you mean?"

Cat found she couldn't explain it. "I think she is . . . I think she thinks he's coming back." She spoke softly. "Gran's always right. She's always had a plan. I don't know what to do."

"I don't think you can do anything," he said. "Just be there for her."

"I'm not, though, am I?" She thought it was a peculiarly insensitive thing to say. "I'm in Paris." She tried to keep her voice steady. "I can't do anything for her."

"I'm sorry. It's—it's none of my business."

"Too right," Cat said, and he stiffened, and she instantly regretted it; she hadn't meant to get into it, not now, it was so childish. One of the things that felled her constantly since Southpaw's death, since Daisy's body had been found: the struggle to think of anything else, anything that was normal. She had this idea that she should only be concentrating on them, grieving for them, and not on small, silly things, like how much she hated the way Madame Poulain's lipstick bled out of her lips, thin red veins reaching up to her wet nose. How endless the winter seemed that year in the stall, and how useless her thermal socks were. How her rage at Olivier gathered new strength every day, so that she wished she could find him, grip his neck like he used to grip hers, watch the veins bulge in his face and see the fear in his eyes. *You nearly finished me off. But I have our son, I will find a way out, and you can't do that to me anymore.* How angry she was with Joe, the memory of them that night, talking together on the porch, the dripping rain surrounding them like a curtain. She shuffled. "Look, forget it. Sorry."

"What—what happened with us, Cat—" Joe turned to her. "I don't do that kind of thing normally."

"Normally! What does that mean?"

He closed his eyes and shrugged. "I shouldn't have. It was wrong."

"You knew she was pregnant when we kissed."

"Yes."

"Exactly." He opened his mouth but she cut him off. "How's Karen doing?"

"She's doing well. She's tired, quite heavy. Still a way to go, but already she's slowing down. She finds it hard."

"Right."

"She's living with me."

"Yes, I know."

Cat thought of Lucy's voice, when she'd rung her to break the news.

"She just moved in with him, upped sticks and walked out, right after New Year! The brass neck! Apparently they're thinking of renovating Barb Fletcher's old cottage together."

More than ever, Cat had been glad no one else knew she'd kissed him. "No. The one with the old hearth and the massive garden? It's got an outside loo, right?"

"Well, Joe can afford it. He'll be rolling in it soon. I can't believe I got him that restaurant review. I cannot believe it."

"He deserves it, though," she'd said, trying to be fair. "He's really good."

"Well, yes." Lucy had said. "But I still can't believe the way he's behaved. To think I fancied him! Oh, my God. All that time he was shagging Karen. All that time . . ."

All that time.

Standing there in the wide open air with him, everything out in front of them, Cat knew it was time to leave. "I'd better get back to Gran," she said.

"I'm sorry, Cat. Really sorry. I wish it hadn't happened like that."

Cat leaned forward; he'd spoken so quietly she wasn't sure she'd heard right at first. Luke was running around Jamie in a circle with a couple of bay leaves stuffed in his hands, shouting out pieces of information he thought Jamie would want to know: "I'm a fish in the play at school. . . . I had a beef burger with Gabriel. . . . We are reading a book about cars."

"Right, thank you." She sounded like a prim schoolmarm.

He looked down at the bag of supplies he'd been carrying, then up at her. "Screw it. Can I just say one thing?"

"What?"

"Cat, listen. I keep thinking . . ."

Often, afterward, she wondered how he'd meant to finish that sentence, but he just stopped. No yelling children, no interruptions, no random acts of God, as in a rom-com. He just stopped and said, "You know, I think it's time we went."

"What's in your bag?" she asked him suddenly.

"Oh." He peered into the blue plastic. "We've been foraging. On our walk. Dock leaves, wild arugula, some rosemary . . . and some roots. We're going to try a few things back at the pub."

"You know where the wild garlic grows? Up over the hill, past Iford? Miles of the stuff. Not long now. And there's Bath asparagus everywhere in the hedgerows in May too."

"I didn't know that. Any of it. Thank you."

"Yes. I used to pick it, with—never mind. Luke! Come on! We need to get home."

"Home?" Luke stood still, looking stricken. "You said we were here for the weekend."

"I mean to Gran's," she corrected herself. "We need to walk back and see Gran and make lunch."

"Okay!" Luke shouted.

"See you, then," she said to Joe, wanting to part on a friendly note. "Good luck with everything."

Joe nodded. "You too. Thanks." Jamie ran over to him and buried his head in his dad's stomach. Joe pulled him toward him, and covered him with his coat.

Jamie stayed perfectly still for a few seconds, then opened the coat, looked up at his father, and shouted, "Boo, Dad!"

As Joe threw his head back and laughed, Cat realized she'd never really seen him grin before. Properly, like his face was made for it. He picked his son up and gave him a big kiss, then turned, to see Cat and Luke still standing there, watching like children waiting to be picked up at school.

Cat set off down the field toward the north exit. She walked briskly, a harsh spring wind on her cheeks. Luke scrambled to keep up with her. "We see Joe later?" he kept asking.

"No," Cat told him. "We're going back home. Tomorrow."

Back home.

• • •

The train the following day was crowded. Luke had to sit on her knee for most of the way, squashed up against a Moroccan lady who gave him pita bread and pieces of apricot. Cat thought about her grandmother. How being with her was almost worse than leaving her, because it was clear they couldn't help her, no one could, and she didn't know what would happen.

They'd all, all of them, mocked Lucy gently over the years for being so sentimental about Winterfold: the awards ceremonies at Christmas, her lists of favorite things about the holidays that she had pinned up on her walls. But they were no better, any of them, were they? Lucy was the most straightforward member of the family. She told the truth, at least, always had.

They went into the Tunnel, the sudden dark rushing past them, and Luke settled his head against the window, watching the single lamps that lit up their route. Cat made her plans. She would keep ringing up Lucy and Gran, and writing and e-mailing, even if Gran didn't want to hear from anyone. She'd go back to Winterfold twice a year at least, even if Gran didn't want to see anyone. And she would remember Southpaw, and try to remember her mother's life, and the mistakes she, Cat, had made before and mustn't make again. She told herself summer would come soon, and then things would be different.

But in the following weeks Cat was almost glad when it became cold again and the rain started. She had the excuse she wanted to feel as miserable as she liked.

Martha

Natalie, the lawyer, was a dark-eyed, brisk sort of person, Karen's friend. She reminded Martha of Karen, in fact.

"We have good news," Natalie said, spreading out the paperwork on the dining table. "So, to explain briefly—"

"Could I open the curtains before you start?" Bill stood up. "It's rather close in here."

"It's fine," Martha said. "Leave it."

"It's very dark, Ma."

"Bill, she said leave it. If she wants it like that, she can have it like that." Florence drummed her fingers on the table.

Natalie looked at Martha, unsure how to react, and Bill came back to his seat, jaw set. The sun was shining brilliantly outside, the first splash of spring. It flooded through the curtains into the lamplit room. Birds sang in the eaves of the house.

Martha knew what the daisy bank should look like by now, on a day like this. But after nearly six months she had still done nothing about re-sowing the grass and daisies. She thought she would leave it for when he came back. They could do it together, perhaps, remember Daisy together. She liked to think up little things like that for them to do. When he was here.

"Ma!"

Martha realized someone was talking to her. "Yes?" she said. "Sorry, Natalie. Go on."

"We've been lucky," Natalie said. She took a sip of water. "We've got the court date through. I think in other counties or under different circumstances we'd be looking at a trial or at least some kind of arrest, but here I'm pretty sure you'll merely be summoned to the magistrates' court and given a conditional discharge."

"That doesn't sound very mere to me," said Bill, looking carefully at his mother.

Florence sounded incredulous. "Nothing else? After what . . . happened?"

"No." Natalie looked from mother to daughter. "You sound surprised, Florence. Is there a reason for that?"

"No. None at all." Florence crossed her arms.

Martha didn't know what to say to Florence. Her eyelids were still red, as though she had eczema. She'd had it when she was little; so had Bill. Not Daisy. David had eczema when he was worried or overworked. She had bought him special cream from the old pharmacist in Bath, the one that Jane Austen had used. It had always worked. She wondered if there was any left, and made a note to check upstairs. He'd need some more soon.

"There'll be a small fine and, Mrs. Winter, you'll probably have to pay the court costs too, but that's all." Martha nodded, staring into space, thoughts swirling in confusion around in her mind. She heard Bill muttering something to Natalie, who turned to him and said, "Foul play can't be proven either way, and there's no case to answer. Plus we have enough evidence that suicide was the likely cause of death to satisfy the police. More importantly, we have testimony from several witnesses— which I'm sure you'd back up—that Mrs. Winter was under a great deal of psychological stress in the weeks leading up to her elder daughter's death, and much of that was due to the behavior of her daughter. The balance of her mind was disturbed."

"*Daisy's* mind was disturbed," Florence said, kicking her legs out under the table. "She was crazy."

"No, Florence." Martha rapped her fist smartly on the polished wood. "She wasn't."

Natalie cleared her throat. "With respect, it's Mrs. Winter's state of mind that is relevant here. And we are able to suggest that it played an important part with regard to her uncharacteristic behavior."

Bill's arms were crossed. He leaned forward, trying to move things along. "So—that's it?" Karen was a friend of Natalie's; it occurred to Martha that perhaps she should have asked someone else. This business with Karen, and all of that. But Bill was being so strange lately, bossing everyone around, butting in where he wasn't wanted, acting as though he owned the place. The trouble with Bill was that he'd always been convinced he was a disappointment. That he wasn't enough like David. And it made his mother want to laugh. No one could be like David, absolutely no one in the heavens above or on the earth beneath, or whatever it was the bit from the church service always said.

"That's what?" Florence said sharply.

Bill glanced at his sister. "I suppose—this whole business. It's over?"

"You really think that's it?" Florence laughed. She leaned forward and tapped on the table close to Natalie. "Natalie, is that really all there is to discuss? Nothing else you want to bring up?"

"Florence, whatever axe you have to grind—" Bill said sharply, and Florence whipped round, glaring at him.

"Shut up," she said fiercely. "Just—just shut the hell up, Bill. You have no idea what you're talking about."

"I do actually, I'm the one who—"

Florence hissed, as though it were just the two of them, "I said shut up. For God's sake, Bill, you pathetic little man. You don't even know, do you?" She turned to her mother. "He doesn't know, does he?"

Martha didn't know how to reply to this. This poem she kept thinking of, they had been made to learn it at school and that was a long time ago, a very long time. It was in her mind all the time now. The first line made her think of the way up to the house.

Does the road wind up-hill all the way?

But she couldn't remember the rest of it. She stared at Bill and Florence, who looked back at her, and it was as if they were all three of them strangers, meeting in this room for the first time. *They hate each other, don't they?* she found herself thinking. *This pulled-in, tight-lipped man; this unhinged, wild woman—they're supposed to be my children. Supposed to be: isn't that funny?*

She stood up. Her hips ached; her knees clicked. She felt old lately. Old and fragile, made of bones, not flesh. She nodded at Natalie.

"Thank you so much, my dear. Will you stay for lunch?"

Natalie was tucking the papers into her plastic folder, and she didn't meet her eyes. "That's very kind of you, but no. I have to get back. I'll be in touch when I've spoken to the CPS again."

"The CPS?"

"Crown Prosecution Service." Natalie picked up her coat.

"Oh, of course." Martha twisted her fingers together. She said flatly, "A biscuit? Some more tea?"

Natalie shook her head. "You're always so hospitable, Mrs. Winter. I wish I could, but I won't, thank you again. As I say, I'll be in touch." She looked at her watch. "I am hopeful we'll have a satisfactory conclusion soon."

"What about the body?" Florence said. Martha jumped; her voice was loud. "What happens with that?"

Natalie looked quizzical. "Daisy's, you mean?"

"Of course. Unless there's someone else in the garden we don't know about."

Bill thumped his palm on the table. "For goodness' sake, Flo, why on earth are you being such a b-b-bitch today?"

The stuttering word fell into the heavy atmosphere of the room, and Florence, for the first time that day, looked taken aback, vulnerable. "I—suppose I wish we'd all been honest with each other." She turned to Martha. "I'll ask you again. Is there anything else you want to say to me? Anything?"

"Like what?" Martha said, shaking her head in bemusement. She knew that, whatever idea Florence had got into her head, she had to act the part. This, this was the real secret she couldn't ever give away, because she knew by now if she did, then something would alter forever. David was adamant about it, and he would be very cross. Florence must never find out. The door of the study would remain locked. She just had to stick to their story. "What is it, my darling?"

Florence glared at her, and then her expression softened, and she said sadly, "Nothing. It doesn't matter."

The younger Florence had delighted Martha, because in so many ways she was not her creation; she was like an exotic creature come to stay in the house, to be cared for, looked after. And in all other ways she was a mini-David, with her lanky limbs, her big smile, her sweetness, her earnestness. She knew the names of Persian queens and obscure butterflies, of symphonies on the radio and the different types of Greek columns. And here she was now, a stranger.

Martha's mind, starved of sleep, of emotion, was blank. She couldn't seem to see things clearly anymore. The thought she kept hold of was: *I have to carry on like this.*

Florence rolled the edges of her folder over and over again, eyes fixed to the table. Martha wondered why she had a folder—what was in it?—and suddenly, without warning, Florence pushed her chair out and stood up.

"I have to go now," she said. "I'm needed in London. I don't know when I'll be back here. If that's all. Natalie, will you need me again?"

"No." Natalie clasped her files to her body, obviously uncomfortable. "That's all. Thank you all."

"I have to fetch something upstairs before I go," Florence said loudly. "Something I want. I won't be long. I'll say my good-byes now."

"Are you going into the bathroom?" Martha asked, perfectly politely. "What?"

"The bathroom. Can you check in the cabinet and see if there's another tube of your father's eczema cream? I might buy some more if not."

Florence shook her head. "I don't know what's wrong with you, Ma. Honestly I don't. Thank you, Natalie. Good-bye, Bill."

Bill didn't even look up as Florence stalked out of the room. Less than a minute later they heard her feet on the upstairs corridor, heard her rummaging around in the bathroom, opening cabinet doors, shutting them again.

"What the hell is she looking for?" Bill muttered. "I'm so sorry," he said, turning to Natalie. "She's—upset. We all are. I shouldn't have been so unkind to her, but she . . . oh, never mind." He sat down again, his hands covering his face.

"Of course," Natalie replied awkwardly, as Florence thundered downstairs. Martha waited in silence. Surely she would come in, tell her? But the door slammed shut without another word. A minute later the car roared off down the drive.

A hazy, fuzzy sort of buzzing sounded in Martha's head. As though the edges of some soundproofing were coming unstuck and the sound was leaking out of them. She clasped her hands over her ears, trying to shut it out.

"Right, then," Natalie said after a brief pause. "Florence asked about the body. I'll be in touch with the coroner's office. We will have to apply for a burial order and permission for your daughter's reburial or—or cremation, whichever you choose."

The buzzing grew louder. If they all knew about Daisy, then it had happened. He was gone, and she would never hear him chuckling over the TV, or listen to his soft, kind voice talking to someone on the phone, or look up from a book to see his soft brown eyes resting on her, late in the evening when the two of them sat up alone in the cozy drawing room. She would never turn to him as evening fell and smile and say, "Another day, David darling."

She would never take his still-warm pen in her hand and do his work for him, never have him lean on her, never ever walk into a room and know he was there waiting for her. Never hold him close in her arms at night when the dreams seized him and he screamed and cried aloud in his sleep, calling out hoarsely, waking up sobbing, sweating so much his pajamas were soaked, when only she could tell him it was all right. Her boy, her man, her darling husband.

The sound was really loud now. Like the wasps in Florence's room. Martha could feel a ball pushing against her throat, pain welling up in her heart. She imagined the curtains weren't closed, and pictured the garden. She counted the blossoms that would be on the trees behind Natalie's head.

"Ah—they may say no—given the circumstances. But once we have cleared that up and you've completed the procedure, that'll be that."

"That'll be what?" Bill asked.

"Well, she'll be reburied or the ashes interred, and the case will be closed," Natalie said, moving toward the door as if she felt the poison in the air of this house, didn't want to stay here another minute. "You can all get on with your lives."

Bill and Martha looked around the empty table, then at each other, and nodded. "Fine," said Bill. Martha watched him, wishing she could see. But suddenly all she could see was blackness. She sat still, hoping it would pass.

Lucy

"The India Club. The Strand. It's just before Waterloo Bridge. After the Courtauld."

Lucy listened to the message again, and stared around her, bewildered. Buses and taxis shot past at an alarming speed, and pedestrians crossing from the Strand to Lancaster Place pushed past her, buffeting her. The first days of warm weather had foxed her, as they seemed to every year—she was in a navy wool-mix long-sleeved dress, and it clung to her back, now slick with sweat. "I can't bloody see it," she muttered, standing back and staring up at the shops in front of her. "Arrgh," she said, letting out a low groan. "Oh, Florence."

"Florence?" An amiable-looking middle-aged man standing in a doorway stepped forward. "Are you—I'm sorry to interrupt. Must seem a bit odd. You're Lucy, aren't you? I'm Jim Buxton. I—I know your aunt."

He held out his hand, and Lucy shook it uncertainly. "Good day," she said crisply, thinking if she sounded like a heroine from a BBC war drama she might somehow deter this strange man from mugging or murdering her, if that was indeed his intent. "I'm looking for the India Club. I'm supposed to be meeting—"

"I've just left her here. It's upstairs," Jim said with a smile. He pushed his phone into his pocket, and opened a scuffed black door. "I'll show you."

Two floors up, Lucy found Florence in the small restaurant, which had murky yellow walls and was almost empty. She was seated at a large table, papers strewn everywhere, scribbling furiously, an uneaten dosa at her side.

"Hi, Aunt Flo," Lucy said loudly. She wasn't sure if Florence would hear her or not.

"Florence," Jim called. "It's your niece. I found her on the street." He said tentatively, "It's . . . Lucy."

Florence looked up then, pushed her glasses up her nose, and broke into a smile. "Hello, darling." She enveloped Lucy in a big, messy hug. Pieces of paper flew to the floor. "So you know Jim?" she said, slightly confused, scrambling to pick them up.

"No, Florence," said Jim patiently. "I bumped into her outside." He pulled at the arm of his glasses, slightly like Eric Morecambe, and then hugged the Daunt Books cloth bag he was carrying closer to his chest. "I forgot to ask. Are you in for supper?"

"No, Thomas wants me for a conference call with the lawyers."

"Well, Jesus wants me for a sunbeam."

"Bully for you," said Florence, shoveling papadum into her mouth. Jim slung the bag over his shoulder.

"I'll leave you some casserole out, that suit?"

"That'd be marvelous. I left the *LRB* review on the kitchen table, by the way. Do look. Utterly wrong about Gombrich, but it's a good piece."

Lucy, not understanding a word of this conversation, sat down, glancing longingly at the dosa.

"Is Amna back tonight, by the way?"

"No, she's not," Jim said. Something in his tone made Lucy glance up, curious. "She's gone till May, I'm sure I told you that, didn't I?"

"The lawyers need to talk to her." Florence slid the menu over. "Pick something, Lucy, it's all wonderful."

"What do they want to talk to her about?" Jim asked.

"Oh, it's rubbish. Peter's lot are saying you and I are having an affair. That you're not a credible expert witness. Et cetera." Florence rolled her eyes. "Bloody idiot. I think it makes him sound pretty desperate, I must say."

Jim pulled at his tufty gray hair. "I see. Florence—maybe we should discuss this all later."

"Of course," Florence said heartily. "I am living with you, it must look rather odd. But we need to be clear on the matter. I hoped Amna could clarify or provide some kind of statement. . . ." She shuffled through some papers. "It's here somewhere. Ah. Now, I'd forgotten about this passage." She pulled out a cracked Biro and started writing furiously.

"Good-bye. Nope, she can't hear me." Jim smiled at Lucy. He put his hand on Florence's shoulder gently, then turned to Lucy. "Good-bye. It's very nice to meet you. Very nice to meet any of Florence's family, in fact. I was starting to think she was a water-baby or something. Have the pakora, it's jolly good."

"Oh—" Lucy began, but he'd gone. Florence waved vaguely at his back and carried on, her huge, looping handwriting covering the paper.

"Just a moment." She scribbled one more line, and put down her pen. "Sorry, Lucy. Thank you for coming."

"My pleasure. It's so good to see—" Lucy began tentatively.

Florence interrupted. "I wanted to ask you something."

Lucy glanced at her aunt curiously. Florence wasn't the kind of aunt who took you to the ballet, or to tea at Fortnum's. She was the kind of aunt who'd spend hours playing battles or making up stupid songs with you. But she didn't generally confide, or expect you to confide in her.

There was something else, too. Something that, since that awful day, had been pushed to the back of Lucy's mind. The evening Southpaw died. Bursting into his study to fetch her for supper, Lucy had found Florence sitting in Southpaw's chair, a glass of wine next to her and a postcard of a painting in her hand.

She was sobbing her heart out. When Lucy moved in the doorway and Florence saw her, she wiped her nose and gave a great, huge, galloping sigh.

"It's true," she'd said, staring right through Lucy, her swollen eyes glazed, and she'd pushed away a piece of paper lying on the blotter, crumpling it up. "Oh, no." Her face collapsed again. "Oh, no. It's really true."

Lucy had reached to her across the desk. "Oh, Flo. What's true?"

"Nothing." She'd wiped her nose. "Absolutely nothing. I'm coming now," she'd said, folding the postcard and putting it into one of her capacious pockets, but she didn't move, didn't move at all, until Gran went in and got her out.

Now she said carefully, "What's up, then?"

"Why don't you order," her aunt said. "Then I'll tell you."

When Lucy's pakora arrived—and it was delicious—she ate in silence for a few moments. She was ravenous. Lately, all she seemed to want to do was eat.

"You're in Hackney, aren't you?" Florence said. "Not that far from Jim and Amna."

"Of course."

"Jim's a clever fellow. Very astute. Known him since Oxford, we rub along nicely together."

"He seems lovely." Lucy looked at her watch.

"You should come over one evening. It's a great place. Stuffed with books. Jim is—"

"Flo, what's this about?" Lucy interrupted. "I don't want to be rude. It's just I have to be back by two." Her aunt looked startled, and Lucy said hurriedly, "Work's horrible at the moment. I can't be away too long."

Florence picked at the uneaten dosa. "Oh. Why's it horrible?"

"I'm not right for it. And my boss is gunning for me." *Especially now Southpaw's dead*, she wanted to say, but couldn't. The article about Daisy was of course not possible now. There was no talk of promotion, and last week Lara had left to join *Vogue* and Deborah had looked at Lucy and said, "Not to be brutal, but it'd be a waste of your time. I don't want to sound negative, though, Lucy. I'm just being honest. Okay?"

Lucy told Florence this.

"Oh dear. What would you like to do instead?"

The question caught Lucy unawares. It hadn't occurred to her that she could do something else. She squirmed on her chair. "Oh. Well, I'd like to be a writer."

Florence didn't laugh, or look amazed, or cough in embarrassment. She said, "Good idea. Pleased to hear it. You can help me out, you know." Lucy looked blank, and Florence waved her hands. "Luce, it's a good idea. You can write. Remember those funny stories you used to tell Cat? What are you doing about it?"

"Oh. Nothing." Lucy laughed self-consciously. "Well . . . I write down bits and bobs." Lately she had taken to writing at all hours, on her laptop, late at night. About Dad, and Karen, about Gran and Southpaw. "I had an idea, about us—it's . . ." She clamped her suddenly sweating armpits into her sides, before remembering that Flo simply didn't care about things like that, and relaxed. "Don't ask me yet. I don't think I'm quite there."

"No time like the present," Florence said grimly. "What do you want to write?"

"Stories," Lucy said vaguely. Now that it was out there, now she'd said to someone, *I want to be a writer*, she wished she could pick up the string of words floating on the air between them and cram them back in like a jack out of its box. She shrugged and said brightly, "I'll get round to it, one day. So—um, how long have you been in London, then?"

"Oh, over a month," Florence said abruptly. "Had to go home—to Winterfold for the night last week. But I'm staying with Jim till June, I think. Have you heard about this court case I'm involved with?"

"Of course."

"It opens next week," said Florence. "I'm suing Peter for a share of the royalties of his book and a coauthor credit."

"Golly. Is he the TV bloke? Didn't you once—"

Florence interrupted. "Oh, yes. I've been a total idiot. And I didn't want it to get this far." She gave a grim smile. "I'm a bit afraid about what they'll drag out, actually." She laughed nervously, and pushed her glasses up her nose. "Embarrassing stuff."

"Like what?"

Florence said quietly, "Oh, Luce. I'm a solitary person. I've spent a lot of time in my own head, all these years. You get used to it in there. It's rather nice."

"I know what you mean."

"You do, don't you? One gets these ideas about things. . . . Anyway, I made a fool of myself over him." Florence swallowed. "When I think about it for any length of time, I feel quite sick. And I feel quite al—alone." She stumbled over the word.

"You're not alone." Lucy put her hand over her aunt's, then pulled it away.

"I am. Believe me. Now that Pa's gone and the rest of it—" She bit her lip, and put her hands in front of her face.

"You don't have to go through with it," Lucy said. "You could always pull out, couldn't you?"

A change came over Florence's face. She sat up straight and put her hands together. Her expression was determined, her chin stuck out. "All I have is my reputation, Lucy. Middle-aged men are seen as being in the prime of life. Middle-aged women are dispensable, my darling girl. Just wait, you'll see." She paused, and Lucy thought she was trying to convince herself as much as anyone else. "Look. I wanted to ask your help."

"What do you need my help for?"

"Can you write an article? For your paper? A little bit of, I suppose one would call it persuasive PR on my side, would do me a world of good." Florence leaned forward, brushing her hair in some chutney. "I don't—want to look ridiculous. A nice piece about how respected I am—your—your paper would do that, wouldn't they?"

"Oh." Lucy put her fork down and dabbed her mouth with a napkin, buying some time. She caught Florence's hair in her hand, brushing a blob of chutney off.

"Um. I'm your niece, Flo. That would look a bit ridiculous. 'Why Florence Winter Is Great,' by Lucy Winter (No Relation). They'd buy something on our family history—they wanted to do a piece on Daisy and Southpaw, but I couldn't bring myself to, and then—everything else happened."

"Well, can't you now? With me in it?"

Lucy stared at her aunt rather helplessly. "Well, no. You can't just write articles about your relatives without some sort of angle. That's why I wouldn't do it before."

"What sort of angle did they want?"

"Oh, Southpaw's sad early life, Daisy the missing daughter . . . et cetera. But it was too hard, and now, obviously, I'm not going to do it."

Florence reached over and took a piece of Lucy's chicken. "What if I could give you something else?"

Lucy looked at her aunt's hands. They were shaking.

"What?" Lucy said, not really believing her.

Florence whispered, "I—well. *Come on, Flo, come on,*" she added under her breath. "Look, Lucy. I'm—I'm not your aunt."

"You're not—what?"

Florence's heart-shaped face was gray with misery. "Oh dear."

"Flo—what do you mean?"

"I'm adopted. That's what I mean."

Something stuck in the back of Lucy's mouth. She coughed. "*Adopted?* Oh, no, you can't be."

"I am, I'm afraid." Florence gave a twisted smile. "Daisy told me, when I was younger. I didn't believe her, I thought it was one of her little games, but at the same time you never knew with Daisy." She swallowed. "In fact, she was right. It's true. I . . ." She stopped, and looked down at the congealing food on her plate. "I found my birth certificate. The night Southpaw died."

"I saw you—" Lucy began.

"Yes. I was looking for Daisy's passport, the police wanted it, your grandmother said it was there and I went to look for it. I was going through this old folder of his drawings, of Pa's . . . Pa's East End drawings, and there it was. Just tucked in there, thin as tissue. I almost threw it away."

"Oh, my goodness. Flo . . ."

"I've—I've always known, really. Known I wasn't like them. It's just, finding out like that was rather a shock." Her eyes brimmed with tears. She pushed her glasses furiously up her nose. "Anyway! I thought you could help me. Write an article, it doesn't matter if you say you're my niece or not. I just want some coverage that doesn't make me sound like a crackpot. It's become rather important to me now, winning this court case. I have to have some reputation afterward, don't I?"

"Florence," Lucy said, "please, wait a minute. Does Dad know? Who knows? Do you know who . . . who your mum was?"

She shook her head furiously. "Some eighteen-year-old girl. No idea of the father. Somewhere in London. I wrote her name down. Cassie something, Irish name." She pressed her long hands over her face, and her shoulders shook. "I've always known my mother didn't love me the way she loved the rest of you. I couldn't work out why." Her voice was muffled. "You can blow the whole thing right open, if you wish."

"Oh, Flo, I couldn't do that." Lucy reached over the table. "Gran loves you, of course she does! She's always going on about you to us, how amazing you are, how there's nothing you can't do."

Florence sat back, and said very softly, "Look, it's true, Lucy. I used to think I was happy. Used to think that it didn't matter I didn't fit in, that I had my dad to talk to, and that our home was a safe place, and now I see that was all a lie."

"It was a safe place. It still is."

"It's not. We've all gone our own ways, and why? Ask yourself that. Look, I just thought you might want to help me. If you can have a word with someone on the newspaper, get them to write an article if you won't . . ." Florence stood up, stuffing sheets of writing and newspaper cuttings into a battered red folder as Lucy sat back in her chair, her head spinning. She felt dizzy. "Does that make sense? Did you hear what I said?"

"Yes, I heard you, Flo. I just don't know what to say."

"You don't believe me."

"I do. Oh, Flo, I wish you'd talk to Gran about it."

"I've tried to, but she's like a brick wall." Florence's mouth creased into an awful rictus smile, and she gave a great heaving sob. "Lucy, I've tried. If Pa were around, maybe, but—I can't get through to her. I've realized that it's easier not to try, at the moment."

Lucy squeezed her eyes shut. "She needs you." Her heart ached for Flo, for Gran. "Oh, Flo, you know you're still one of—"

"Don't say it. Don't say 'one of us,' Lucy, I swear, I'll—just don't say that." Florence put the folder under her arm and cleared her throat. "So you won't help me."

"Write an article saying you were adopted? Just to get you some good PR? Absolutely not, Flo—come on, can't you see it's a terrible idea? You're just—you're just terribly upset, you're not thinking."

It was all wrong, talking to your aunt like this. Florence's mouth was pursed, her expression pinched. Lucy frowned. *How can we not be related? She's just like Dad.* Her mind was still whirring; the idea of these various shards of family china that lay shattered on the floor was overwhelming, and she felt she was the only one of them who wanted to start to put the pieces back together.

"I've had enough of this," Florence said. "I told myself, you see, it actually makes everything easier, now I can get on with my life. Without all of you." She pulled some money out of her coat pocket, scattering receipts and coins on the floor, and threw a couple of notes onto the table. "Bye, Lucy."

"Flo—don't go."

Florence strode out of the restaurant, knocking a chair across the floor. Lucy sat still, not knowing what to do. A waiter came over apologetically and gave her the bill, then started cleaning up the mess Florence had made.

I've got this all wrong, Lucy kept thinking. *This idea I had of this perfect family that Gran fed me over the years, it was obviously not true. Because these terrible things have happened to us all and we can't seem to help each other. We fold like a pack of cards.*

The waiter brought her change, and as it clunked into the bowl beside her, Lucy stared out the window at the pale blue sky, the faint roar of London buzzing outside. She wished someone would pick her up, pull her out of the city, put her in her bright, warm room at Winterfold, with the sound of Martha singing below and Southpaw chatting about something, the radio on, dog barking . . . people talking . . . But that world was gone forever, and Florence was right. Lucy picked up her change and lumbered slowly down the stairs, out into the warmth of the London spring sunshine.

David

June 1947

THE PREVIOUS DAY he had been drawing in Limehouse, where he'd watched four children wrestling over a doll. China face, pink blush dots on her cheeks. Nose smashed off, cracked inside her head so she rattled as they tugged at her and wrestled in the cobbled street.

"Givithere, you little sod, it's *mine*."

"Won't, so fuck off."

"I'm gon' tell your mum how you're speaking to me, Jim."

"Don't care."

The doll was from a bombed-out house at the end of a short road, a Victorian terrace. They had gone in and excavated—not much, though. No one had survived, he knew that much from the Public Record Office. He'd tried to forget their names. Who knew what was still there? That doll had belonged to someone. A little girl had received it, maybe last Christmas, never thinking it would belong to someone else soon.

David hadn't been able to bear it then. He'd made drawings he'd never show anyone. He'd seen things, noticed details too many had overlooked. Like there were bits of people still, everywhere. He'd found a finger once, in a cave of rubble, right by where the children were playing. An old person's finger, he thought, knobbled at the joint, the skin wrinkled.

Now he and his dad and Cassie were waiting, like so many others, for the housing that was supposed to come after the war. They were building along the City Road and behind the market, and then, David supposed, then they'd have their new family home. What a joke. The idea that they were family.

Aunt Jem and Uncle Sid had moved out to Walthamstow. Aunt Jem came for her tea sometimes, to see little Cassie, she said. Make sure she was being looked after properly. But she never stayed more than an hour; other than that, they never came back to Islington. Too many bad memories. They'd seen Angel bombed, seen the looting, the way people changed. Uncle Sid had a cousin thrown in jail for stealing lead after a raid. They said it was too hard, coming back. But David knew it was also because they didn't want to see Tom Doolan. They sent Cassie little presents, knitted cardigans, a ribbon for her hair, that kind of thing, but they didn't send David anything. He was nearly seventeen now. He'd be all right, he was going to that posh art school near them in Bloomsbury, wasn't he? Mr. Wilson, the art teacher at school, had written to the art institute, and they'd asked to see Davy and his work, and offered him a full scholarship. Aunt Jem was alternately proud and bewildered at the idea of a nephew who didn't do anything . . . just drew. "Emily'd be so proud of you if she knew," she'd said. "You'd have made her so happy, love."

The hottest Saturday so far in the year, she came for her tea. They didn't have anything to give her beyond tea from day-old tea leaves, briny and bitter, and she brought some shortbread a neighbor had given in exchange for some curtains she'd made. David and his aunt sat on the floor either side of the old chest that served as a table in the first room of the flat, while Cassie crouched next to them playing with the doll she always had by her side. Her mother had made it for her, the winter before she died, a patchwork girl carefully sewn from the tiniest scraps of discarded material.

Though a bright blue sky could be seen at the far corner of the small window, the flat was dark. It never really grew light no matter how much sun there was outside. Bluebottles buzzed loudly, crashing at the windows, hovering above the little tea party.

Aunt Jem was uneasy, rushing through the meal, starting at every sound on the street. "You get paid to go to them classes, sit there and draw?" she asked, dotting her fingers with shortbread crumbs from the floor, licking them off, as if nervous of leaving a trace behind.

"Don't get paid, do I? I got a scholarship that covers tuition and all that. Everything else I got to pay for. They say sundry expenses. That means shoes and that." David looked hopefully at his aunt. "I need a job, Aunt Jem." Uncle Sid's other brother, Clive (not the one that was in prison), had a fishmonger's off the Cally Road. Before the war David's mother used to take him there, let him pick a piece of fish for tea, when times were good. Clive'd give him a bucket of eels to play with. David thought it was the best thing ever, sticking his hand in a bucket of shiny, slippery, snakelike creatures the color of tar. "Is Clive looking for anyone, you know?"

Jem shook her head. "No, love, he ain't, and if you want my advice you won't ask him."

"Why?"

"Just the way it is, love," she'd said, and she'd leaned forward and stroked his cheek.

"Aunt Jem?" Cassie looked up at her aunt. "Can I come and stay with you?" She fingered her aunt's shawl.

Jem laughed, and glanced at the door again. "Me? Oh . . . we'll see. That'd be nice." She said it in the vague way that adults had of saying no without you noticing.

"But I don't like it here anymore."

"Why not, little Cass?" Jem said, feigning surprise, and David wanted to slap his aunt's face or punch her on the arm. *You know why. We live with our dad and he's a monster.*

"Dad's horrible," Cass said quietly, looking around. "Smacked me on the head for noise."

Jem's eyes filled with tears. "Oh, love, no."

"He hits Davy and he shouts."

"Just—hitting?" Jem leaned forward, took her young niece's wrists. "He don't . . . try anything else on, does he?"

But Cassie looked at her blankly. "What's it?"

She'd say that all the time to David. *What's it?* Like there was all these things she didn't understand. He hated the fact that they were bad things and he didn't know how to explain them, like Dad smacking them, or the flies everywhere, or the old man who'd died in the street outside that last freezing winter, or the women you saw crying to themselves as they walked through the market. *What's it?*

"It's fine," David said, cutting across them. "No, he don't. Don't put disgusting ideas like that in her head. Don't ask her things like that." He stood up. "You'd better be off if you're to catch your train, Jem. Thanks a lot for coming. It's been a real tonic."

His aunt scrambled to her feet and pulled on her hat, then gripped his shoulders. "Oh, Davy." He stepped away from her. "I don't like to leave you."

He hated her guilt; it was fake. She didn't mean any of it. "Thanks again, Aunt Jem."

"I ain't done right by you. Neither of you. It's just Sid's so funny about it. He don't like me having anything to do with . . . with your father. He thinks I'm well out of it now we've left the Angel. I wish I could . . . If I think about Emily—oh dear." The tears came to her eyes again. "The state he'd leave her in sometimes." She gave a big sniff. "God, I wish things was different. You don't think he'd . . . proper hurt you, either of you?"

He was going to say it, tell her what she wanted to hear: *Yeah, course. We're fine, me and Cassie! Don't you worry about . . .*

But something stopped him. The stifling heat, the buzzing flies, Cassie's bruised face. How quiet she was these days. "Not sure anymore," he said flatly. "He's . . . he's drinking all the time. He don't care if it's day or night. He hit Cassie so hard she couldn't hear the rest of the day. Still can't sometimes. I . . . I don't know."

"What you mean, you don't know?" Jem said, clicking her tongue against the roof of her mouth, cold fear in her eyes.

David said, staring at the floor, "He knocked out two of her baby teeth. It's not . . . it's not right, Jem."

"Oh, God. Oh, no," Jem muttered.

Every old street had a dad like that. Since the war, every house had someone affected by what had happened. A daughter killed in a raid. A son missing somewhere in Burma or France. A father in the slammer for bashing his kids. A mother on trial for stealing from a bombed-out house. The war had changed everyone. You walked past a dead dog on the street and you kept on walking now. Perhaps they'd get back to like it had been . . . only David couldn't remember life before the war. More and more he couldn't remember his mother, only the feeling of her hair as she sat next to him at the piano and the sound of her voice when she'd sing to him at night. She'd loved Gilbert and Sullivan.

Ah, pray make no mistake,
We are not shy;
We're very wide awake,
The moon and I.

He was trying not to think about his mother, trying not to remember what she'd been like, when there came the sound of shouting in the street, and someone swearing, a woman calling.

"Damn you, damn you to hell, Tommy Doolan! You—"

"He's back," Cassie whispered, sitting up ramrod straight on the floor, her eyes like saucers. "He's comin' back now."

And Aunt Jem swallowed and breathed in. She muttered something to herself; David heard his mother's name. Then Jem's nostrils flared, and she stood up. "Listen to me, Davy, you hear? You get out of here."

"What do you mean?"

"Clear out." She put her hands on his neck, held his head steady. "I can't take you both. I'm sorry, I can't. You understand?"

He didn't understand, but he nodded. Now that she had made up her mind, Jem seemed more resolute.

She said quickly, "Sid won't go for it. Lord knows how I'll get Cassie past him, but I'll do it. He'll have to like it, he'll come round to her. But if I turn up with both of you, he'll kick me out, sure as eggs are eggs. Oh, Emmy, darling. I'm sorry." She glanced up, gave a little sob, and patted Cassie on the shoulder. "Come on, Cassie, sweetheart. We're going."

Cassie stared up at her. "What's it?"

"I'm taking you home. To my home. Only we got to move quickly and be quiet. I don't want your dad hearing us." She crouched down on the ground. "Fancy coming to live with your aunt and uncle?"

Cassie looked at him. "What about Davy?"

"I'll be fine," he said. "I'm going to college, aren't I? I'm not going to be here much longer."

Tom Doolan had stopped in the street to argue with someone. David could see him, swinging on some railings, his punching arm flailing, like a sheet in the wind. *I'm going to get that if someone else doesn't,* he thought.

Cassie crossed her arms and turned to her aunt. Her gray eyes were steady. "Want to stay here with Davy."

"No, Cassie, love," Jem said weakly. "You gotta get out of here. It's time to leave, all right?"

"Cassie," David interrupted, "I'm off to college soon. I got plans. I don't need you, you got that?"

She stared at him and put her hands in her pockets, a sign she meant business. "I don't want to go." Her lip trembled. "I want to stay here with you, 'cos you said we're together, you and me, you said you and me 'gainst everyone else. You said it."

He'd say that to her all the time: when the bombs fell, when the looters came, when Dad rolled back late and they hid in the passage where David's bed was, when they didn't have enough food, when they were scared and cold and lonely. He said it all the time.

David shut his eyes tightly. He told himself it'd be easier just looking after himself, so he'd believe it. Repeated it in his head a few times. Then he gripped her wrist.

"Listen, Cassie. I don't want you around no more. I'm sick of you. Best you piss off and live with Aunt Jem. They'll look after you."

Her small hands caught his ragged shirt, and her thin face was blank with confusion. "But you said we was our family, Davy."

"Well, I didn't mean it. It's okay, so off you go." He stretched one arm nonchalantly and touched the soft curls that bobbed around her head. Just one more time. *We were our family.*

She stared at him, her small face pinched with misery, then turned away. "Let's go, Aunt Jem."

"How'll we get out?" Jem said softly, urgency in her voice. "He'll be here any minute."

David flung open the door, avoiding his sister's gaze. He didn't think he could bear even to catch a glance of her. "Come with me."

"Clothes for nighttime?" Cassie said. She looked around the sparse, mildewed room that had been their home these past two years.

"No time, sweetheart," Jem said. "We'll get you new things. It's all right."

Cassie bent down. "I take Flo," she said, and picking up her patchwork rag doll, she hugged it tight to her small body.

"Yes, take Flo." David scuttled along the corridor and banged on the last door. "Joan?" He hammered frantically. "Joan, let me in, he's back again."

An old lady, hair tied up in rags, neat silk scarf snug over her head, opened the door cautiously. "Oh, look at you, little one," she exclaimed, pinching Cassie's cheek. "It's all right. Come in with me till he gets over it. He don't mean it. He's just angry. Oh, hello, Jem. What you want?"

"Let them in, Joan." Footsteps sounded on the staircase behind them. "Show Jem the fire escape. Bye, then." He squeezed Jem's arm. "It's the right thing, Aunt Jem, you know it is."

His aunt pushed Cassie through the door, but she lingered on the threshold for a moment. "You're a good boy, Davy. Come and see us, all right?"

His sister's face appeared under Joan's armpit. "Davy?" Tears ran down her cheeks. "Want Davy."

David tried to keep calm. He swallowed. He could hear his father, boots tramping loudly on the cracked old boards. Swearing. "Where's that little streak of shit, that fucking boy? Why the hell don't he come when I tells him to? Some git trunna swindle his dad and he don't even fucking give a toss. He don't even wan hear it, I'm going to—I swear. . . ."

David crouched down. "Listen to me, Cassie," he hissed. "You gotta go with Jem. You can come back here when you're older, when Dad's not here. But you'll have a better life away from him. All right? If you ever need me, you just come back here, and you ask for me at the pub or down the market, someone'll find me. I promise. I'll always be there if you need me."

He gripped her thin shoulders. "You understand that? Promise?" She nodded. "But that's for when you're older," he said, and swallowed. "Anyway. You'd better fuck off now, I ain't got time."

The serious gray eyes fixed on him for a clear second, and he felt like his heart was being cut right in two. Then she nodded again. "Yes." And she turned and disappeared, Flo clutched under her arm. The smell of Joan's armpit flowered under David's nose. He stood up.

"Bye, then," he said. Aunt Jem kissed his cheek, squeezing his arm so hard it hurt.

"Bye, Davy. I'll come and see you soon. Get out of there soon as you can, eh? Work hard, be good, all right?" The words caught in her throat. She turned, and then she shut the door in his face as the footsteps grew louder, and David turned round to face his father.

• • •

Tom Doolan was feared before the war, but things were different then. He'd fought in the Great War, after all. Got some shrapnel in his knee and it gave him pain. So he'd been a hero once, albeit with a violent streak. There were worse men than he—at least he had a job and a wife and some outside respect, even if he did knock his wife to the floor with the vase she'd bought at the Sainsbury's grocers, or punch his boy in the face after one too many, and even if David heard screams and sobbing late at night when he should have been sleeping. At least there was a home, a roof.

Now Tom Doolan was a wreck. He'd always been a drunk—now he was drunk all the time. David was properly afraid of him, the three of them in the tiny one-bedroom apartment the council had found for them off the Essex Road. Sometimes he'd wake up and see his father watching him, or Cassie while she slept, in the corner of the room, rolling imaginary tobacco between his fingers, his black eyes glittering. Last week he'd woken Cassie up, dragged her by her thin arms and banged her head against the wall until she screamed, and that was why she couldn't hear properly still. All for saying she was hungry that afternoon when there was no tea.

Course she was hungry. He didn't work and he did nothing to provide. They lived on handouts from neighbors and Aunt Jem, and what the welfare could give them, and they were lucky to have this flat, David knew—thousands of families didn't, were instead crammed into other people's houses. David wished they were living with someone else, though, because then Dad wouldn't be able to use his children as punching bags.

It was when their father called Cassie "Emily," not once but a couple of times, that David realized the danger was real. If the bomb hadn't killed their mother, he was sure their father would have done soon afterward. He'd murder one of them, David knew it.

"What are you doing, skulking round like a sneaking little thief?"

His father grabbed his arm and yanked David against the wall, dragging him back along the corridor to their flat. A tearing, hot pain in his shoulder made David scream. His father threw him in through the open door, then slammed it shut behind them. He looked around, and David looked up at him.

He was blond and tall; before the war people had said he looked like a matinée idol. Now he was flabby and red-faced, his teeth nearly all gone, his wide mouth permanently set in an ugly grimace, and his bloodshot eyes always open, darting around, looking for trouble.

"Where's Emily?"

"Cassie, Dad." David crawled backward and then pulled himself up. His shoulder and neck felt as though they were on fire. The first thought that crossed his mind was, *At least it's not the arm I paint with.* "Not Emily. Cassie. Your daughter."

Tom Doolan took one step toward him and punched him hard in the face. David staggered back as his father kept walking, pushing him up against the wall.

"She's gone. She ain't coming back," David said. "I got her out of here. The police took her away, and they said if you came looking for her, they'd have you arrested."

And he spat in his father's face. "They're going to put her with a family that wants her and can look after her, like she deserves. She don't deserve a father like you. *Hitler* don't deserve a father like you." He pushed him away, his heart thumping so loud in his chest he thought it might explode. *I'm for it now,* he thought. *Bye, world.*

"You little shit," Tom Doolan said, and he grabbed his son by the neck, pushed him over toward the range in the corner, and held him down against the hot iron; and as David yelled and called for help, his father banged and banged his head on the surface, his fingers a vise around his neck where Jem's had been, firm and loving, only minutes before.

"No one leaves me. No one walks out on me, you hear? You get that, you fucking pansy?"

David struggled, writhing like mad, flailing out his arms and legs, kicking at his father, and when the grip tightened and he couldn't speak, he stared into Tommy Doolan's face, his red eyes, and he spat at him again, and kept on kicking. He could not articulate any particular thought, but a deep, primeval sense told him to keep fighting until his father killed him; and even though he couldn't see anymore, couldn't think straight, with every last drop of strength he had he just kept on writhing, kicking, lashing out, doing everything he could, until at last his father simply let go and David sank to the floor, heavy as a chain. His father gave him a sharp, hard kick in the stomach, then dropped into the armchair.

"I'll kill you one day soon," he said. "You won't get away with it. You hear me?"

David stayed still, just kept on breathing, and he focused on Cassie and Jem, the door shutting on them, where they'd be now. On the bus together, heading out northeast. Cassie'd get home with Aunt Jem, to that nice new house David always dreamed they had. He'd never been there, but he liked to picture it. Tiles on the path to the front door; stained glass in the window. A knocker in the shape of an owl—he'd seen that on one of those smart houses down the road; he liked it. Maybe even some honeysuckle, growing up the wall. Uncle Sid would open the door. He wouldn't be cross, or look suspicious with that weaselly stare, like *What are those brats doing here?* which was his normal expression when he saw Emily's kids. He'd say, with a smile, "Well, hello, Cassie! What you doing up this way, sunshine?"

"She's coming to live with us," Jem would say. "Come in, sweetheart, let's get you something to eat."

And they'd go in, hang their coats on the hooks, and go into the kitchen, which would have one of those tables with panels that slid out, to make room for visitors, like David. Maybe he'd spend Christmas with them. He'd drawn a picture of a Christmas meal he'd seen the previous year through a window over on Thornhill Square, the house that had the owl door knocker on it. David liked owls. He liked drawing them from pictures in books.

He'd stood looking up into their front room, clutching the railings so tightly his palms were covered in rusted dust afterward. Paper chains in bright colors hung from the ceiling, and there on a chair was a little girl singing "Noel, Noel" over and over to herself. She was bouncing up and down on her chair with excitement, at the whole thing, the whole day, and David knew exactly how she must feel. That was what was strange. He knew how lovely it would be to be that girl.

As he stared in, a man appeared carrying a glistening brown Christmas pudding, electric blue flames shimmering round it, and the people at the table all clapped. None of them noticed him, face at the window.

Jem and Sid would have a Christmas pudding. And there'd be a lovely parlor with proper sofas and chairs to sit and read in all day long. A proper wireless—Cassie loved the radio.

All this for his sister, safe now in someone else's house. David closed his eyes, playing dead and waiting for his father to fall asleep. Then he could go out again and draw some more. And hopefully not get killed, today at least.

Lucy

May 2013

"Have some gingerbread." Martha slid the plate toward Lucy, who took a piece, peering down as she always used to at the scene that opened up each time someone removed a biscuit. As she popped a square of gingerbread in her mouth, she squinted to make out the familiar image of three Chinese men crossing a tiny ornate bridge. Lucy sighed loudly. Martha's gingerbread was like nothing in this world: crumbly, spicy, thick with juicy, sweet flavor. This batch was stale, but it was still delicious.

"Hungry, Luce?" her father said, a faint smile on his face.

"Mmm," she replied, saying what she thought her grandmother would want to hear. "Lovely. It's the best, Gran."

Martha nodded. "Glad to hear it." She gazed out of the window, fiddling with a piece of wire tag fastening.

The paraphernalia of the house, once charming, now threatened to overwhelm it. Bowls full of old pre-euro coinage, scraps of paper, leftover Christmas cracker toys, and wooden clothes pegs spilled onto the dresser. A mug with a broken handle sat forlornly on the table in front of them, covered in a light film of gray dust.

Summer hours had started again at work, and though Lucy had left early, the weekend traffic meant she hadn't arrived until teatime. It was dark and drizzling when she arrived, rain spread out like a cloak covering the valley. Gran had said she was busy with something upstairs when Lucy arrived, and left her in the sitting room, unsure whether to touch anything, move the scarves away, clean up. She wished she were staying with Dad. She kept pushing herself at Gran, and Gran didn't seem to notice whether she was there or not. Lucy didn't know what to do. She couldn't seem to fix on anything at the moment: work was making her miserable. She was eating too much, not sleeping; she was either at the *Daily News* and hating it, or at home dreading the next day. She worried about everything, kept making stupid mistakes, couldn't seem to get anything right: change for a coffee, matching socks, remembering to charge her phone. She felt as though she was starting to lose experience, as though everything she'd learned was slipping away, and that she was slipping away too.

Lucy put the gingerbread down on the plate and stared sadly around the dark, messy room. Martha followed her gaze.

"As you can see, I'm not quite up to speed with everything. I haven't had a chance to get your room ready. Cat slept in there. I didn't realize you'd want to stay here. I thought you'd be at your father's."

"I can do it, it's fine. I only wanted to see how you are." Lucy knew her voice was too loud. "It's wonderful news that they're not prosecuting."

"Yes," Martha said blankly. "It's simply *wonderful*, isn't it?"

Lucy folded her arms uncomfortably. "Sorry, I didn't mean it like that."

Bill tapped the table. "Well, Ma, as I was saying to Lucy, at least we're all set."

Martha poured some more tea. "All set for what?"

Bill's fingers drummed a steady, almost jaunty rhythm. "Just that—good news there's nothing further to be done. You—you could have gone to prison, you know."

"Yes, I know that."

"We can talk about what you want to do now. About Daisy." Martha didn't seem to be listening. "Her funeral. They say we can rebury her now. Not here, but we should think . . . think about what you want to do. Ma?"

Martha folded her arms. She gave a brief smile. "I suppose so."

Lucy watched her father, patiently wrestling with Gran. "It's awfully dark in here, Ma. Mind if I turn the lights on?" Bill got up, flicking the switch. "Oh."

"They've blown." Martha poured herself some more tea. "One by one. I keep meaning to fix them, and somehow . . . I never get round to it." She shrugged. "I've got this one here." She flicked on an old bedside lamp she'd plugged in next to the Aga. "It's fine."

"I'll pop to the hall and get some bulbs—"

"I said it's fine." Her voice was sharp. "You know, Bill, I've been think-ing. I'll probably sell Winterfold this summer anyway. Move out of here."

Lucy looked up, and Bill twisted round in his chair awkwardly.

"Are you sure, Ma?" he said. "Isn't that a bit soon?"

"Soon? What, leave it a year and I'll be ready to move on then?" She laughed. "Listen, we can't be sentimental about this house. Not any-more."

Lucy swallowed, something hurting her throat. "I think that's a good idea at some point, but, Gran—"

"At what point?" Martha said, accusatory, swiveling round to face her granddaughter. "I ask you, at what point?" She stared at Lucy as if she wanted an answer, and Lucy, tired, sad, didn't know what to say. She simply shrugged.

"Well, let's discuss it later. I can get an estate agent in to value it, if that's what you'd like," her father said. "Maybe it's a good idea. Just let me know what you want to do."

"I will," said Martha, and Lucy saw the panic flitting across her face.

Her father changed the subject. "You know, I think Flo's case must be over by next week. I read something about it in the paper today. I don't think it's going that well for her."

"Oh, really?" Martha gave a weary smile. "I don't know. She's said nothing to me."

"I think she didn't want to bother you," Bill said.

"Right. When do you suppose we'll know?"

"When she calls, I guess. She's so funny about mobiles. She's staying with Jim and his wife in Islington, but I don't have his number."

"Islington," Martha repeated blankly. "I see. I didn't know she was there. That's funny, isn't it?"

Lucy didn't understand what she meant. "He's nice, Jim," she said. "Met him the other day at lunch with her. He—"

"You had lunch with Flo?" Martha said, amazed.

"Yes, she asked me."

"Why?"

Oh, she found out the night Southpaw died that she's adopted, and I suppose she wanted to talk to someone about it, as no one seems to have mentioned it to her before. "Um. Well, she wanted me to do a puff piece. I wouldn't. I said I didn't think the *Daily News* would go for it."

Lucy shrugged. "She's pretty . . . worried about everything at the moment."

Martha began collecting the tea things smartly. "Florence has always been in her own world. It's hard to get her to listen."

"Gran, she needs your—" Lucy began, and then stopped. It wasn't for her to tell Gran that Florence knew. She didn't even know for certain it was true, anyway—these days, she was barely certain of what was real and what wasn't.

"Don't make me feel guilty. I'm too hard on her, I know it." Martha shook her head; it was as though she was talking to herself. "I can't help it."

Lucy twisted her skirt around her finger. She looked at her dad, but he said nothing. Outside, rain dripped into a bucket by the back door.

Suddenly her grandmother said, "We've gone wrong, you see. I've done it all wrong. I thought when all this was out in the open, it'd be better. He wanted a family home. A place we could all be safe, a unit. And we tried so hard, but it went wrong somewhere."

"No, you didn't, Ma." "All families have problems." Bill and Lucy spoke simultaneously.

"You would say that. You're the only ones left." There was spite in her voice, something Lucy had never heard before. "His wife ran off." She jabbed a finger at Bill. "Both of his wives, in fact. Florence has run off. Daisy ran off. I raised her daughter and then she ran off."

"Not both of my wives. Clare didn't run off," Bill said lightly, trying to make a joke of it. "We both decided it was for the best. And Karen . . . she hasn't run off. She's just moved out. We agreed she should."

Dad, Lucy wanted to cry, *stand up for yourself!*

Her grandmother turned to him, her green eyes glinting. "Oh, Bill, you live in a dream world. You didn't even notice your wife was having an affair under your nose for the best part of six months."

Her father got up and took some plates over to the sink. "Actually, I did know. I knew all along."

"What?"

"Susan Talbot. She told me. Saw them kissing once." His face twisted. "But I'd already worked it out. I'm not stupid. I know her so well, you see. I've always known her, since . . . anyway, I—I thought she'd come to her senses. I thought we worked because of what we didn't say to each other, not the other way round."

"What an odd way to conduct a marriage," Martha said. She blinked, too hard.

"So it would seem." Lucy's father sat down and swiftly drained his tea. "Okay, well, I'll be off, then." He stood up, moved toward the door, then looked back at his daughter. "Luce—I'll see you tomorrow. You'll pop in for a coffee or something?"

"Absolutely." She wished she were going with him now, throwing her arm round his thin shoulders, bringing some noise and life back into the cottage. Suddenly she really didn't want to be alone with Gran. "Let us know if you hear from Florence, won't you?" she asked. "Tell her we all hope she's okay."

"Yes," said Martha. "Do let us know. . . ." She reached out her hand as her son passed by, and he bent down so she could kiss his cheek, and then she whispered into his hair, "Oh, Bill, my love. I'm sorry. It's bad at the moment."

He hugged her, squeezing his eyes shut. "It's all right, Ma."

She clutched his wrist and stared up at him. "Bill."

"Ma?"

Her green eyes were clouded. She wasn't focusing on him but on something behind his head. "It's beginning. It's here. I can't shake it. I keep putting it away and it keeps coming back." She turned away. "No. No."

"Ma, it's fine," Bill said calmly. He put a hand on her shoulder. "That's good."

"I don't think you understand."

"Of course I do." Bill bent down to look his mother straight in the eyes. "You're in denial, Ma. It's normal."

"I'm not," Martha said, very softly. "I just . . . I hate him sometimes."

He crouched in front of her as though she were a young child, and tucked a piece of hair behind her ear. "Look, Ma—can I give you some advice?"

"Of course."

"Don't force it. Any of it. Stop trying to control it."

She looked straight at him. "I want to stop it all," she said. "I want to be able to put it away."

"But you can't, Ma. Okay?"

Lucy watched in agony. "Ma," Bill said softly, "he's gone. He's not coming back."

To Lucy's horror, her grandmother's face buckled, her mouth slumping into a slack hole, her jaw thrust out. "He said he would. Just for a while. He lied to me." Her voice shook. "I wish I'd known. I'd have helped him, I'd have made him feel better—"

"No." Bill's voice was steely. "Ma, I knew, and I couldn't help him and I'm a doctor. There is absolutely nothing you could have done. Please, please believe me. He lasted a lot longer than I thought he would. He'd been so ill for so long, you have to understand. He lived to see Luke, didn't he? And Cat again. He had the exhibition coming up. He'd have wanted us to be proud of it, to celebrate it. And he knew you were okay, and that you'd be okay. You have to remember all of this." He put his hand on his mother's cheek and she nodded, the rictus smile of her face ghastly. "Yes? Do you believe me?"

She stared at him. "I don't know."

They walked to the hall and stood on the threshold, the three of them glancing at each other, until Martha broke the silence. "Well, good-bye," she said, and turned and went into the study, shutting the door behind her.

"Are you okay on your own?" Lucy said as they walked down the drive together. "Are you sure you don't want me to come back with you?"

The rain had stopped, and heavy drops fell through the newly green trees onto their heads. "Absolutely not, but thank you," her father said, brushing the glistening blobs away from his jacket with precise fingers. "I'll see you in the morning."

"Yes, Dad," she said. She wished she could ask him what came next, what they should all do—but his bowed shoulders and heavy, sad eyes told her he couldn't help. "You should be more like that, you know."

"More like what?"

"More direct. Action-taking, Dad—you're really good at it."

He gave a helpless laugh. "I'm afraid I'm not, Lucy."

"Yes, you are, you just think you're not. She needs you to tell her the truth."

He laughed. "I've never really understood the truth. Proves my point, all of this." He hugged her. "Good-bye, Luce. You're so grown-up lately. I barely recognize you."

She stared curiously into his face. "Dad, I'm still the same."

"Nothing's the same, Lucy," he said. "The sooner Ma gets used to that idea, the better."

Walking back up the drive, Lucy stared up at the house. The wooden gables were gray in the dusk and moss coated the window casements. Weeds had sprung up on the gravel driveway. As if confirming the gloom of Lucy's mood, it started to rain again, heavy, like mist. She rubbed her eyes. It was as though the house was disappearing in front of her, and she wished she could click on the carousel and move the image, replace it with . . . her tenth birthday party, when the house became a pirate ship and Cat gave her her old Benetton T-shirt. Or the time Florence was so enraged by some critic's interpretation of her reading of some old painting that she threw the book through the study window out onto the lawn, hitting Dad on the head, and Southpaw, Cat, and Lucy laughed so much that lemonade came out of Cat's nose. Or the time she kissed her French exchange student, Xavier, in the woods full of wild garlic, the taste of his salty, plump lips, the smell of garlic and fresh earth. Any memory but this one, the present day.

Opening the study door carefully, she found Martha sitting behind Southpaw's desk and, as ever, the sight jarred. She was holding an itemized phone bill, and on the side was a scribbled drawing of Wilbur, scampering along the margin.

Lucy let out an *"Oh!"* at the sight. She'd avoided Wilbur as much as possible, because to look at him made her cry. But now, as she watched, Martha ripped the paper in two, slowly, one end to the other, all the time her eyes fixed on her granddaughter.

"Don't do that," Lucy said furiously.

"You don't understand," Martha said. "I drew that one. It's my Wilbur. I can't ever draw him again. Now he's gone, Wilbur's gone too."

Lucy slammed her hand on the desk. "Wilbur's not yours to draw. What are you talking about? What the hell's *wrong* with you?"

Martha looked up in shock, her green eyes wary. "What's wrong with me? Nothing. You're all wrong, not me." She laughed. "God, I really am going mad, aren't I?"

"Gran, what is it we're all wrong about?" Lucy asked, folding her arms.

"This idea of us all, in this place." Her grandmother tore the paper up into smaller and smaller pieces. "It was all a lie. I thought I'd make it better by telling everyone about Daisy, and I didn't."

"No," Lucy said suddenly. "It's not true. We were strong enough. We are."

Martha gave her an almost sweet smile. "Oh, Lucy, no, we weren't. Look around you."

"That's you, that's you thinking like that because everything seems so grim and sad, and I can understand why," Lucy began, twisting her fingers together. "No one's happy all the time. I'm not Pollyanna. I know everything wasn't perfect, but, Gran, it wasn't a lie. We *were* happy. I used to love coming here more than anything else. I loved growing up here, being with Cat . . . being your granddaughter." She swallowed. "Seeing you and Southpaw all the time, and making coffee and reading books with Florence and all of that. It happened, Gran, it's not made-up."

Her grandmother shook her head. "Wake up, Lucy. It's not a fairy story. Name me one person who's still standing after this and—oh, I can't do this. Go away. Leave me alone, for God's sake."

Lucy put her hands on her hips. She was trembling. "No. I won't."

Suddenly Martha shouted at her, her voice hoarse with anger.

"Go *away*." She pointed at the door. "God, Lucy, you have no idea. You've never woken up wondering if this is the day you'll be kicked to death by your father, like Southpaw, or been put on a train, sent away from your family for four years, like I was, so that by the time you go back to them you're so different no one knows you anymore. You float around saying you want to write and saying you love it here and how wonderful this family thing is and—you're wrong." Her voice softened. "I know you idealize it here, I can see you must because of the divorce and your parents, but—but you're wrong."

Lucy willed herself not to cry. She nodded. "Okay."

"I'm sorry," Martha began, but Lucy backed away, out into the hall, away from her.

She ran upstairs to her old room and shut the door. It was above the sitting room, and the other side of the L shape from Gran and Southpaw's room, so often Cat would creep in here late at night and get into bed with Lucy, so they could chat and laugh until the golden moon shone high like midnight sun through the thin floral curtains. The tall twin single beds were covered in the same worn, woolly coverlets, like shrouds. This was the room where Lucy had had her first period; it was where she'd written her first short story, "The Girl Who Ate the Moon." Where she'd painted her hair with nail varnish and had to cut it off

315

into a disastrous side fringe. She'd shown Cat her breasts and vice versa; though there was three and a half years between them, Lucy blossomed early, Cat late. The long window with its wooden casement was lined with her favorite books from childhood: *The Bell Family, Lanterns Across the Snow, The Box of Delights.* The Christmas after her parents split up, she had spent the whole holiday here, lying on her bed, reading. No one bothered her, tried to make her "join in." She felt sorry for families who were always having to join in. You just did your own thing here, and sometimes that involved everyone, sometimes just you. Martha made her Scotch eggs, just for her, and she and Cat went into Bath on the bus by themselves and watched *The Fellowship of the Ring.* And then there was that Christmas when . . .

Lucy stared out of the window at nothing, clutching her notebook, wondering about Martha, about Florence, about all of them. Then she sat on the bed and crossed her legs. It was very quiet; the only sound was the ticking of the old clock in the hall. She took out a pen from the bedside table and, calmly and clearly, she began to write.

YOU SAY WE weren't a happy family, Gran. But I remember the Christmas I was nine. Our car broke down on the way to Winterfold, on the A road just outside Bristol, and Mum stormed off and went into a pub, and we called Southpaw and he came and picked us up, only Mum was kind of pissed by then, so she wouldn't leave the pub, and she and Dad stayed there drinking and I went back with Southpaw, snuggled up in the back of the car in the big car blanket (the orange one Joan Talbot knitted with the patch of purple in the middle because of her bad eyes).

I remember really clearly how great it was to leave them both in that pub. Because, you know, it wasn't a terrible secret that their marriage was disintegrating. It was obvious to me. I worked it out much earlier than they did. I just wanted <u>them</u> to work out they weren't right together. Just wanted them to get on with it and stop trying to pretend we were a happy family. We <u>really</u> weren't—you forget, Gran, I've lived in an unhappy family before; it's obvious. And it's awful being the only child in between these two people who are lying to you because they think it's for the best.

So I think of that Christmas a lot because, really, it was the first time I realized that children are often right, but no one listens to them. Southpaw whistled all the way as he drove us home, incredibly slowly, because the roads were slippery with that two-day-old packed-down ice, and by the time we got nearer to Winterfold it was dark, we thought because it was night, but in fact it was because snow was coming. We sang "Jingle Bells" and "Blue Christmas" and "Let It Snow" from Southpaw's Rat Pack tape in the car, and Southpaw did his Dean Martin impression, which was absolutely, as ever, terrible, and we wished you were in the car singing too, because you always knew all the words, and you loved singing. It's funny. You love singing, so does Dad, so does Southpaw. And Florence. You all sing, all the time.

You heard the car drawing up as we arrived, and you were standing in the doorway, and I remember this Christmas best of all because of that moment. You had your Christmas apron on, the one covered with berries, and you'd covered the door with holly and ivy, glossy green leaves that shone in the porch light. And it had started to snow by then, like someone had unzipped the clouds, and it was just pouring out like feathers from a pillow. We jumped out and ran toward you, and I can still smell it as we came close, that delicious, woody, piney smell, wood smoke, spice, Christmas trees, earth, snow, cold, all mixed up together as I hugged you.

And you said, "I'm so glad the travelers have returned." Returned, like we were supposed to be here.

That day the snow fell, and we watched out of the window as it settled freshly over the valley like a drift of white on the gray trees. When it was dark, Mum and Dad appeared, and you always knew how to make Mum more cheerful. You gave her some chamomile tea and asked about her patients and we had your gingerbread, and we decorated the Christmas tree. Cat and I were in charge of the decoration scheme, only you and Southpaw kept moving things around and putting strange things on the tree when we weren't looking, and we all got hysterical with laughter. Like the packet of tissues, or one of Cat's socks, or your reading glasses, or whatever. That night, Cat and I worked out a play to "She's Electric" by Oasis, which was so stupid we knew we couldn't show it to anyone. Cat said she wouldn't do plays anymore, which was fair enough, but I was pretty upset about it, until we watched Romancing the Stone *on the new TV and video player until about 3 in the morning. I loved* Romancing the Stone, *because Kathleen Turner's a writer, and really square, until all these wonderful adventures happen to her and her hair gets better, as does her blusher and the cut of her silk shirts.*

The next day it was Christmas Eve, and the snow was inches thick. We made a snowman using one of the buckets we'd got on holiday in Dorset for his head, so he had a strangely machinelike yet sandy appearance. Our faces were red and our knees and hands were soaking with melted snow. We turned him into a proper robot. An old plug for his mouth, some fuses for his eyes, a wire coat hanger as a kind of metallic carapace indicator, and rusting tiny seedling pots on his hands, all to make him look as mechanical as possible. He was five feet tall! As tall as I was then.

We got the Christmas cake ready to eat, and I made Welsh rarebit with Flo (who always, always burns toast, even to this day) and you filled the old brown teapot to the top, as by then not only had Florence arrived but also Gilbert Prundy had popped in to fetch the extra heater from the shed. (I remember him really well, the old vicar with his embroidered waistcoats, and his signet ring with the weird masonic symbol on it. We were convinced it opened the door to another dimension like in an Indiana Jones film.) In the kitchen, you dropped a plate, one of the willow-pattern blue platters, shattered it to bits, and as we swept it up together you said, "Easy come, easy go," and shrugged, and I thought then, That's the way I want to live. It struck me then, That's a different way to see the world. *I was always a worrier, always concerned about something in the back of my mind. And you made me see then that everything was perfect as it was, in that moment. Because we were happy there, sweeping up the pieces, you singing Dean Martin songs, and Southpaw joining in from his study. So that's what I remember, when I try to think about all of us. That Christmas. And it's not the beautiful house or the lovely table arrangements or the food you'd probably spent days preparing. It was all of us, the fact that we were together. Singing. Southpaw's voice, warbling and terrible. Like Dad's is now, Flo's too. Isn't it funny that she sounds just like them, Gran? Cat's voice, very low. Your voice is beautiful. It used to remind me of a clarinet. We always sing, and I think that's so funny.*

I am crying as I write this now. I can still see the sandy robot snowman. The fire, and the tree, and the warmth of all of us together. The sense of breathing out and letting everything go, because we were safe, together, with the door closed and the windows shut against the rest of the world. It is always there, even though he's gone. It won't go away.

Martha

THEY STOOD AT the bottom of the stairs, facing each other. Martha's hands shook as she read the thin piece of paper. After a few minutes she put it down on the hall table, and went into the sitting room, not looking at Lucy. She stood by the French windows, gazing out over the lawn, the sky above. She felt her breath, coming, going, in out, in out, shoulder blades rising and falling. She was here.

It was very quiet. She knew she had to say something.

"I don't remember it like that," she said eventually.

"Right," said Lucy. "How do you remember it, then? Because, Gran, I was happy. It's not some fantasy in my mind. I knew my parents weren't getting on. I knew so many things in the world were terrible. But when I came here, I was happy."

Martha looked at her granddaughter. Lucy's heart-shaped face was flushed pink. "I remember it being . . . I suppose I remember . . ." She stopped. "I don't know. Maybe I've got this all wrong. I remember Daisy, wishing Daisy was there. For all of us, but for Cat most of all."

"She was never there, though—how could Cat miss her?" Lucy scratched at her neck, up which a rich red blush was creeping. "We didn't like it when she was there—it was tense, and a bit strange. You'd all be on tenterhooks. And her breath always smelled."

Martha flinched in surprise. "What?"

Lucy blinked, mortified. "I shouldn't have said that."

"Her breath smelled?"

"Yes. Like she'd eaten . . . something rotten. I hated it. Didn't like hugging her and all that."

"Did Cat think that too?"

Lucy nodded slowly, not meeting her eye. "Oh . . . yes, Gran. She wished she'd go away. It wasn't nice when she was there."

"Because of . . . the breath?"

"No, because she was fake. She made me uneasy. She was too nice to Cat, you know what I mean?" Lucy watched her grandmother. "No, you don't. Just—over the top. And she was horrible to Florence. You'd see it, these tiny little ways. Snide remarks and things like that, and Flo just took it. . . . You know what she's like, just gets on with it, she's miles away. . . ."

Martha's stomach clenched at the memory of a seven-year-old Florence, coming up the drive with her reddish plaits covered in mud, her too-long school skirt torn, sucking her thumb and crying, then saying phlegmatically, "Oh, I think I fell over." The wasps that nearly killed her, the stuck door. When Hadley had bitten her, way before he went mad, but Florence couldn't say how or where. Her books, pages ripped out, which she just taped in and carried on reading. Martha knew all that, yet she knew Daisy had needed someone to defend her, and—

Florence. She looked at her watch, then outside, as if Flo might suddenly be arriving, though she knew she wasn't. She desperately wanted to see her then, hold her fierce, angular daughter in her arms, tell her the truth, tell her how sorry she was, how silly she had been. She rubbed her eyes, tired.

"We liked it when it was just us, people popping round, everything normal," Lucy was saying. "Southpaw doing silly drawings. You singing. You helping us do plays. Helping us make weird drinks."

Martha stared at her granddaughter's face. Lucy, sweet Lucy, her honesty, her openness. Lucy, who had told her the truth because she had never learned to lie. Lucy, who loved this house and everything about what Martha had created, despite the secrets and untruths that Martha felt had, for decades now, spun Winterfold up into a web, skeins of silken spider thread covering everything over.

So something I did worked. Lucy believed it all. One person alone couldn't bring that down, one person against the rest of them. She hated to think of Daisy as the enemy; she wasn't. But Martha suddenly knew she had shielded her for too long, carried her. Maybe . . .

Her heart started to beat faster. A strange, metallic taste swept her mouth. It was frightening simply to consider that one might think differently about this. Try a new way of thinking.

Yet she had to. She blinked and shut her eyes, forcing herself to think about what Lucy had said.

"Apple . . . what was it called, your favorite drink?" she asked eventually. "We used to have to make it every time you came over."

"Yes." Lucy nodded. "I liked Apple Mingo and Cat liked—"

"Banana Bomba," Martha said. She could feel her chest opening out again, as if some invisible weight that had been sitting on her breastbone had been lifted away. All this love that she had to give, buried so deep. *Cat, oh, Cat, my sweet, sweet girl, what did I do, why have I let you go like this?* "Banana Bomba was my favorite."

"No, Apple Mingo was the best, only Cat wouldn't ever tell us what was in it," Lucy said seriously. "Wow, I still think she put maple syrup in it. Which is bloody cheating because we weren't supposed to use sugar. And some—oh!"

Lucy jumped as Martha stepped forward and brushed her granddaughter's hair away from her forehead. "Sweet Lucy." Martha cupped her chin, staring at her flushed cheeks, her beautiful hazel eyes, the round, sweet face. "Thank you."

"For what?" Lucy laughed. "Are you all right, Gran?"

Martha hugged her. "Apple Mingo." Then she squeezed her tightly, till Lucy gave a muffled yelp.

"You're strong, Gran, blimey." She pulled herself away. "What do you mean? Do you believe me now?"

"Yes, I do," Martha began, then corrected herself. "Only—yes, I do. But listen, Lucy. No one's happy all the time. We weren't living in this golden kind of cage of lovely memories. It's important you remember that, too."

Lucy gave a rueful smile. "Well, of course I do, Gran. I said that to you, remember? You keep forgetting I had Mum and Dad's divorce when I was thirteen. That was pretty awful, even if we were all glad it happened. Hell, I remember Dad's wedding to Karen. That certainly wasn't some lovely memory I'm writing up as a keepsake."

"I like Karen."

Lucy raised her eyebrows as if to say something, then relented. "Actually, you know what? The sad thing is, I did too."

"She's not dead," Martha said, and they were both silent for a moment in the gloom of the room.

"I'll never stop missing Southpaw," Lucy said after a while. "But I've been thinking about it a lot." She threaded her fingers through her grandmother's and took her hand in both of hers. "I say to myself, *It's dreadful you're gone, but we're so so glad you were even here. That we knew you and you were in our lives.* I'm sad, but I can't help being glad I knew him for so long. That's what I think."

Martha put her head on Lucy's shoulder. "Yes," she said quietly, thinking about all the stories Lucy didn't know, how her grandfather had suffered to get to here, and how much happiness he'd brought people, how strong his spirit was. How he had saved Cassie, taken Florence; how they had found each other . . . But that was all for another day, she knew. "Yes, you're right." Then she gave a big, deep sigh, and nodded. It had happened, and she saw it now; and it would be hard, but she could see the way out, the way she had to start again.

She said, "All right, then. It changes. Everything changes here."

"What do you mean?"

"I mean, enough of this. I'm in charge now. Let's put the kettle on and work out what we do now. What I do now." She said quietly, "I have to do everything differently now."

She went to the huge cupboard in the hall and took out some light bulbs. "A light bulb moment," she said, and Lucy, who was in the kitchen, called through, "What?"

"Nothing, nothing."

As the kettle boiled, Martha pulled a green scarf off Southpaw's sturdy old chair, and Lucy climbed up onto it, standing on tiptoe to fix the bulbs in. But halfway through the chair gave an ominous creaking crack, and buckled to one side. The first creak was enough warning for Lucy, who jumped off just as it collapsed to the ground. She landed heavily on the tiled floor, rubbing her bottom, and looked up, her face already burning red with mortification, at Martha.

"Southpaw's chair. Oh, Gran. I'm so sorry. I'll get it mended."

Martha merely stared at the chair. "Goodness! Are you okay?"

"I'm fine," said Lucy. "But I know he loved it and—"

Crouching, Martha ran her hands over the smooth, warm wood, pricking the pads of her fingers on the cracked, broken back legs, one of which had simply buckled. "It had a lot of wear and tear," she said, patting her granddaughter's leg. "Please, don't worry. It's my fault."

Lucy tried to laugh. "I'm sorry your lard-arse granddaughter broke one of your chairs."

"It was very old. I think we should go into Bath and get a new one tomorrow, hmm? We can burn this old friend," said Martha, pushing the carcass of the chair to one side and standing up again. Then she helped Lucy off the floor, gripping her arm in her strong hands. "Easy come, easy go, darling. Now. Let's see about booking some tickets."

PART FOUR

The End and the Beginning

I think that just now we are not wanted there. I think it will be best for us to go quickly and quietly away.

—E. Nesbit, *The Railway Children*

Florence

IT WAS STRANGE, coming out of the Royal Courts of Justice. The building was so near to the Courtauld, in the one bit of London she knew really well. The sun had broken through the purple-gray rain clouds of the morning and, as Florence made her way through the great hall of the Victorian Gothic building, buffeted by swarming men and women in black, she found she had to squint as she emerged onto the pavement. A huge din greeted her, a mass of yet more people calling out, shouting. She felt completely bewildered. She still wasn't even sure she'd heard the judge right.

Outside, crowds and TV cameras thronged the pavement, and she stopped still in shock. Protesters were waving placards. Florence peered at one of the signs; did they all hate her that much? FRACK OFF, one of them read. She remembered brushing her teeth this morning at Jim's, frowning at herself in the mirror while listening to the *Today* program: yes, of course. Some judgment was expected today at the Court of Appeal on a fracking company's right to drill in Sussex.

One of the signs of paranoia is the belief people are out to get you. Not today. Florence gave a shaky laugh, walking with relief into the furious crowd, almost touched at the strength of their belief, the passion on their faces. She had been like that once, and it wasn't real, she knew it now. It was fake, a comfort, something for her to cling to alone at night, like the cloth bunny she'd had when she was small—and now she'd taken it away, exposed herself, everything about her own sad, strange life . . . and she didn't know what on earth she'd do.

Florence shook her head, trying to stay calm, and looking wildly around for an escape.

"This is not a matter of 'passing off' or of academic judgment for the court to decide upon. . . . This is a matter of deception and of income fraudulently obtained on the basis of character assumption. You led the general public to believe you were an art historian who not only wrote and presented his own television documentary series, but also produced a tie-in book to accompany this series for which you received a not inconsiderable advance of £50,000 from Roberts Miller Press. You have heard from the managing director of that company. Ms. Hopkin says she believed, as did the public, that you were the author of this book, which was so well researched and written as to attract not merely favorable reviews in the academic world but also word-of-mouth success, thanks to an endorsement from a television book club, and so on. And as a result of that belief, you received a further £100,000 for a new book, not to mention substantial royalty payments on your first book. Professor Connolly, this case brought against you by Professor Winter is one of credibility. She is possibly the foremost expert in her subject in the world, and your cynical attempt to exploit that, your arrogance, and your sheer deceit are frankly breathtaking. I find her credible, and you to be liable for the costs of this case. The plaintiff's complaint is upheld."

She wasn't crazy; she hadn't misheard, had she? She had won. She had done it, this weird, unlike-her thing. Hadn't she?

Florence had stood in the narrow wooden pew after the judgment, not sure what to do next. Her barrister, a florid young man called Dominic, had patted her on the shoulder and disappeared. She'd seen Jim earlier, but he was teaching that afternoon and hadn't been able to come. Lucy wouldn't be there, of course, or Bill, or Ma; she'd deliberately pushed them all away.

Before all this had happened, she'd always thought she was close to her brother. She and Bill weren't usually in daily contact, but they'd talk occasionally, amusing, low-key chats when he'd tell her about the village and what she was missing, ask about her job, that sort of thing. Bill was dry, and funny, and kind. He was *very* kind. He was calm too, always putting things in perspective. He *had* been calm, rather. Now he seemed to be pitted against her, on Ma's side. But against Ma too, somehow. . . . And there was no one she could talk to about the night Pa died. And that was . . . well, that was fine, because she was on her own now. So best get used to it.

Yes, get used to it. So much to get used to. Florence blinked and closed her eyes, longing for a moment of quietness in the bright, loud street. When she opened her eyes, she saw a rather strange man with a notebook standing nearby. In an effort to ignore him, she fiddled with her new gray suit jacket, which she'd bought the day before the trial began. "You have to wear something vaguely businesslike, Flo," Jim had said, laughing at her discomfort. "You can't show up in tie-dye skirts with mirrors on, or that dress with the pockets. Even I think so." This was indeed strong stuff coming from Jim, who was usually in creased cheesecloth from March to September, so Florence had gone to a charity shop on Upper Street and come home with this. She'd been very pleased with it.

Today, though, Florence wasn't quite sure whether she'd bought a man's or woman's suit jacket. It had been on the women's rack, but it looked really awful, as if she were a tycoon in some program like *Dallas*.

She undid the button again, and began to look along the street for the bus that'd take her home to Jim's house, when a voice called: "Happy now, then?"

Her heart leaping, Florence turned round. "Oh. Peter," she said. "I thought you were—never mind. Yes, I am. Thank you." The *Thank you* sounded more jubilant than she intended.

Peter Connolly stood a few meters away on the edge of the crowd. His jowls were gray-black, as they always were by midafternoon, dark with stubble. He really was very hairy. Hair in his ears, in his nose—it was actually not at all pleasant, when you thought about it.

He nodded a farewell greeting to his lawyer and came toward her slowly, and when he reached her he said, "Well, you've proved your point, I suppose. You really are a bitter, dried-up old coot, aren't you?"

"It's over now, Peter. Come on."

He was spitting, he was so angry. "Living in your sad little apartment with your sad little mementos, waiting like a spider in her web to trap me." He shoved his hands in his pockets, made a gormless face, and loped round in a circle in exaggerated imitation of her, as the anti-fracking protestors looked on curiously, and one or two of them, recognizing him, nudged each other.

"Peter." Talitha Leafe appeared and put one pale hand on the crumpled arm of his blue linen suit, the kind he always wore on television.

Florence knew that one: he'd had it on the day she'd seen him eating in Da Camillo with a couple of students, and she'd pretended to walk past and popped in to say hi, and they'd had to ask her to stay, of course. . . .

"No," she whispered to herself. "Not anymore."

"God," he said, his large face looming over her. "I—I—you have no idea how much I *wish* I'd never laid a finger on you."

Talitha said quietly, her lips curling in cold rage: "Peter, for God's sake, shut up! The press are everywhere."

"*Is* everywhere," Florence muttered under her breath. She was amused to see the slightly untidy-looking chap with the notebook ambling up to them.

He stopped in front of the awkward group and said mildly, "Hello, I'm from the *Guardian*. Any comment on the court's ruling today?"

"Um, well . . ." Florence could feel perspiration forming under the jacket, between her shoulder blades. She had no idea what the right thing to say was. "I'm delighted."

Peter shook his head and said under his breath, "You'll regret this, you know that, don't you? I mean, it's the end for you, one way or another. You've burned your boats. George isn't going to want—"

Someone called his name, and his expression changed, the whole cast of his face. He turned round and said in his most mellifluous voice: "I say, hello! Kit! Hello there, Jen!"

"Hello, Peter," said the first woman in a neutral voice. Florence suddenly recognized her: she was the producer of his TV series.

"Yes! Thank you for coming. Wondered if you'd be here, if you'd come—thanks for your support, Kit—"

Kit said, "We had to come. We were subpoenaed, Peter."

Peter spoke loudly. "I need to come in for some dubbing, I know, for the last section outside Santa Croce." Florence thought for the first time how like the snobbish English vicar in *A Room with a View* he was, how that had been part of his charm for them—and her too. And it was an affectation, of course. The real Peter was simply a mediocre person.

As the two women walked away, nodding farewell politely, the older one stopped suddenly and whispered something to the younger one, then ran back toward Florence, avoiding Peter's gaze.

"Here," she said. She thrust a small card into Florence's hand. It dug into her palm and Florence looked down at it in surprise. "Take my card.

We'd love to talk to you about a project we have in mind—now's not the right time, I know. But you'd be fantastic. I'm Kit. I'm the commissioning editor. Give me a call because—well, yeah. You really were terrific in there. I was really proud . . . anyway." She avoided Peter's incredulous, shell-shocked expression and dashed off down the road to where Jen was waiting.

Peter and Talitha stalked off in the opposite direction without another word, Talitha's heels clicking angrily like tap shoes on the pavement. Florence was left holding the card in the middle of the street, feeling dizzier than ever. The noise from the fracking protestors grew louder. She didn't want to be on TV, did she? What would happen with Peter's next TV series? With his new book deal, his villa near Siena, the flat in Bloomsbury, his lecturing role on the *Queen Mary*? She had ruined it all for him, and for what?

"So," said the *Guardian* journalist. She'd forgotten he was still there. "What's next for you? I mean, do you think this kind of case is reflective of the current state of academia, of television commissioning policy?"

"Oh," Florence said, "I don't know. I just had to do it. I had to tell the truth. Everything out in the open." She could feel her throat constricting.

"Right." He scribbled furiously on his pad. "Of course. Right . . ." He scanned the pad with his pen. "And is this correct, you're David Winter's daughter, right?"

Florence found, to her horror, that she couldn't speak. Her eyes filled with tears, her fingers clutched at her handbag strap. She opened her mouth.

No, actually. No, I'm not.

"You must miss him," the journalist went on. "He was very well loved, wasn't he? It's not long since he died, is it?"

How could he ask her questions like this? She stared at him blankly, not sure what she was about to do, and then someone took her arm gently.

"Come on, Flo." She looked up to find Jim standing in front of her, puffing hard, out of breath. "Let's go and get a drink."

"Oh, Jim." She wanted to throw her arms around him, and remembered just in time the journalist, still watching them.

Jim leaned against a wall, wheezing. "I'm so unfit. I only just made it. They wouldn't let me miss the lecture. It's all anyone's talking about in the common room, I can tell you." He turned to the journalist. "Good-bye, then," he said in his firm but awkwardly shy way, and took her arm. "Shall we go back to the Courtauld?" he asked, shepherding her across the street. "There's a bit of a hero's welcome there for you, if you fancy it?"

"Oh, no, absolutely not, I'm sorry. I want some peace and quiet."

"Right. Want me to leave you, then?"

"No, please don't." She clutched his hand so ferociously that he laughed.

"All right, of course. Come on, we'll go to the pub."

In Ye Olde Cheshire Cheese, a tiny, warrenlike pub off Fleet Street, Florence found a table deep in the vaulted cellars, while Jim went to the bar. She sat waiting for him, blinking hard, clutching her handbag on her lap and wishing everything weren't so loud in her head, the clamor of too many voices all shouting to be heard.

Jim appeared and handed her a stiff gin and tonic. "Congratulations!" he said, clinking her glass. "How do you feel?"

Florence gulped down her drink. "Relieved, I suppose," she said. "Glad it's over."

Jim watched her. "Are you going to call your mother? Your family?"

"Oh. Maybe later." She shook her head. "They won't care. I haven't told them much about it. Anything, really."

"Come on, Flo. They'll be over the moon. We all are."

Florence couldn't tell him what she wanted to, what she'd told Lucy. She couldn't bear to say it again. *They're not my family. I don't belong to anyone.* She just shrugged.

Jim said softly, "Flo, the way those lawyers tried to bring you down in there was horrible. You could sue Peter for defamation."

Florence felt her eyes twitching, with tiredness, with mortification at the memory of what they'd said. She rubbed them. She couldn't really bear to think about the last four days of the trial, how Peter's barrister had, in his opening statement, exposed in five short minutes the sad, pathetic nature of her outer life. "My suing days are over." Florence downed the rest of her drink. She didn't feel triumphant. Just reckless, and quite mad. "Maybe I shouldn't have done it. I wish everything hadn't come out like this."

"Come on, Flo!" Jim looked appalled. "You can't say that."

"It's mortifying." She looked almost with surprise at her empty glass. "They made me look so—so pathetic. I haven't had that since . . ."

Since Daisy.

"Let me remind you, Flo," Jim said, "that when you took this on, you were very clear to me. You wanted to prove your point. You wanted to show them they couldn't push you around."

"Yes. Yes . . . I suppose so. I can't remember why now." She brushed her forehead with her hand, bewildered. "Peter—he and George, they were trying to get rid of me. And I'm better than both of them. I didn't know what else to do."

"But you know you could have moved back here."

"And do what?" She looked up uneasily as the door swung open.

"Flo, you've just won a plagiarism case that says you wrote the biggest-selling book in recent memory on the Renaissance. Students come from all around the world to the Courtauld just to hear you lecture. You know that admissions to your course rose by nearly sixty percent after you joined us?" She shook her head. "You've written three other books. You're—you're about to be in demand. Get used to it. Stop thinking you're not part of the rest of society."

"Sure. Okay." Florence picked at the worn trim of the stool. "Sure. It's just . . ."

Jim said gently, "Just what?"

She glanced up, and caught his kind gray eyes staring at her. She thought how well she knew him, how lucky she was that, in all this, she still had a friend, one friend.

The fact that she'd kept in a special bag a tissue Peter Connolly had left at her apartment. The lists she'd kept of things they'd done, found in one of the manuscripts he still had. The stories, repeated over and over to colleagues, the notes she'd written him . . . The mug he'd used that she never washed. A piece of pink paper stuck to the fridge, a flyer advertising a joint lecture at the college: *Professor Connolly and Professor Winter.* Seeing their names printed together had continued to give her a thrill long after the paper grew faded and crinkled in the sun.

Florence had always told everyone that she didn't care what they thought of her. She had told Daisy she didn't care about the notes left on the bed, the wasps' nest, the constant pinches and bruises her sister gave her that no one ever seemed to notice. Only once had she cracked and told Ma, creeping into the kitchen while Daisy was out with Wilbur, silent tears running down her grubby face. And Ma had kissed her and said, "Oh, Flo. You have to learn to get on with other people, birdie, instead of telling tales. Like I say. Fight back."

And Florence was left with her mouth open, her tongue dry, wanting to speak but too frightened. *I think she might kill me if I fight back.*

It had always been easier and safer to retreat into her own mind. And who was there who could help her, who would listen? She had burned her boats with everyone, really, except Jim. As she smiled awkwardly into his kind face, she knew she couldn't talk to Jim about it. She liked him too much. She could feel the doors sliding shut, feel herself pulling the trapdoor in, retreating. The fact was she'd been living in her own world for so long she wasn't sure if she could ever live anywhere else again.

Jim interrupted her thoughts. "What will you do now?"

Clearing her throat, Florence tried to sound businesslike. "I think I might go back to Florence next week. Get on with some work. A new paper for the *I Tatti Studies* Harvard journal on the relationship between Lorenzo de Medici and Gozzoli and how the latter controlled Lorenzo's public image, you know, not only the frescoes but—" She saw that Jim was staring at her with a slightly glazed expression, and she stopped. "Anyway, I need to work. Most of the summer, I suppose."

"What about the TV people?"

"Oh, they were just being nice, don't you think?"

"They're not charity workers. You should call them."

"Listen, Jim," she said, wanting to change the subject, "thank you. Thank you for everything the last few months. I don't know what I'd have done without you. Gone mad, probably. Thanks for having me to stay too. It's great that Amna doesn't mind me clogging up the house."

He laughed. "I don't think she'd be bothered one way or the other."

"When's she back?" Jim had said something about Istanbul for a conference, but conferences didn't last a month. Florence had been so wrapped up in herself lately, it only occurred to her now that this was unusual.

"Oh. Well, she's back. Back a couple of weeks ago, in fact. It went well." Jim nodded, then looked into his glass.

"Is she?" Florence didn't understand. "Oh. Where is she, then?" She wondered if Amna had been eating breakfast with them every day, chatting about history or academic gossip in the evenings while making pasta in the kitchen, and she simply hadn't noticed in her self-obsession.

"Florence, we've split up."

"Who?"

"Good grief, concentrate. Me! I mean, me and Amna."

She shook her head, blindsided. "I didn't know that."

"You didn't ask."

"You should have said." She felt embarrassed. "I wouldn't have stayed if—"

He laughed. "What, like a Victorian maiden? You don't think it's appropriate for us to be in the house alone without Amna as a chaperone?"

"Don't laugh at me," she muttered, flushing.

"I'm not, sorry." His nice old face grew serious, and he said, "I never saw her. She was away three weeks out of four. The house is too big for one person waiting for the other person to come home. And—well, no big surprise, but there's someone else."

"Oh. Oh, my goodness." Florence impulsively put her hand on his, which was wrapped round his glass. "I had no idea, Jim. I'm so sorry. I feel I've been no friend to you while it's been going on and you've been . . ." She could feel herself wanting to cry again, and dug her hand into her thigh. *For God's sake, stop feeling sorry for yourself. Wait till you get home. You can indulge it then. You can do what you want with your life then.*

And a seed took root in her thoughts then, a seed that sprouted and grew rapidly and that was, she realized then, really the only solution to all of this. But she didn't say anything to Jim, who was watching her intently.

"I'm fine about it," he said. "It's been over for years, really, and now I can get on with life. Leave it behind me." He cleared his throat. "Do you understand what I mean?"

They stared at each other. "Yes," she said. "Perhaps I do."

"Everything's changed," Jim said, and he shifted a little closer to her; but Florence's knees knocked against the stool that was between them, and she flung it away impatiently so it rolled on the floor. As Jim picked it up and set it right again, she watched him and knew that she wasn't in any state for this, not now, probably not ever.

Dear Jim. With a monumental effort she plastered a smile on her face and said, "Let's change the subject. I want to know what you thought about Talitha Leafe. I heard from someone at the academy that she asked David Starkey out before she went for Peter. She's apparently a well-known TV historian stalker. Have you come across her before?"

Jim was silent for a moment, and then gave one of his delighted chuckling laughs and shifted his weight on the stool, and she was glad to have made him smile, to leave everything else behind, to be gossiping and talking about someone else for once. When she got back to Florence, that's when she'd take the next step, the final one. Not today.

Cat

SINCE THEY HAD come back, all Luke could do was ask when they'd be seeing Southpaw again. When they would be going back to England. He still cried when Cat left him at crèche, though nearly five months had passed. He was four and naughty now, when during the supposedly terrible twos and threes he had been sweet-natured and gentle. She had braced herself and contacted Olivier to ask if they could come and visit him in Marseilles. Now that she was stronger, perhaps it was time to loosen the reins a bit, let Luke get to know his father, though her every fiber screamed that this was not what she wanted for him.

But Olivier had completely vanished. She'd e-mailed him several times, even called him, though she dreaded speaking to him. All to no avail. Cat even went back to Bar Georges and asked Didier if he'd heard from him. Didier thought he'd left Marseilles and gone to live in La Réunion. A new girlfriend who owned a jazz club on the island, in Saint-Denis, had offered Olivier a regular gig, Didier said. He had given Cat a café cortado on the house while Cat stood at the bar, shaking with rage and then relief. Pure, sweet, relief, at the idea that Olivier might just not be her problem anymore, that the guilt she felt and the worry that he might, like a bogey monster of her childhood nightmares, appear from under the bed and snatch her son away had gone, that that might all be over.

So now it really was just her and Luke, and he was more difficult every day. He seemed to have grown nearly a foot since Christmas. He was too big for the small, intricate apartment. He was rude, and so badly behaved that Madame Poulain now refused to look after him when Cat went to the doctor about her swollen toe. She had stubbed it on a treach-erous cobblestone, dodging a group of Italian schoolchildren by Notre-Dame, two weeks ago, and it had grown huge and turned an angry red, like a cartoonish injury in an Asterix book. She couldn't sleep, and every time she moved in bed, pain shot through her like a bolt of fire. It was waking Luke up too.

"I'm not taking care of that child. He is *méchant*, a horror. He is a bad child. He draws disgusting animals."

"I know—I apologize. . . ." The dragon in green pen on the bathroom wall still hadn't come off, despite Cat scrubbing it twice a day for the past week.

"And he sticks his fingers in his eyes and calls me rude names."

Cat, clasping her hands in the doorway, had paused. "What does he call you?"

Madame Poulain had shaken her fist. "A troglodyte. He says"—she had cleared her throat—"that his great-grandfather taught it to him. Disgusting that he does this, puts lies in the mouth of your dear dead *grand-père*."

Cat's shoulders had started to shake, almost involuntarily. It kept hap-pening to her, this feeling when she didn't know whether she was about to laugh or burst into tears. "I'm so sorry," she had managed to say. "So sorry. Please, if you could just—"

But Madame Poulain had refused, and Cat had had to drag Luke out with her, screaming and crying, "No! Stop trying to snatch me!" across the bridge toward the boulevard Saint-Germain and the doctor.

This afternoon, two days later, it was still pouring with rain. As Cat hobbled along uncertainly, one bandaged toe now encased in a cartoon-like plastic boot, she slipped on the cobblestones again, and nearly knocked over a smartly dressed old man. She clutched him by the shoul-ders. "*Excusez-moi, Monsieur.*"

He turned to her. "It's quite all right," he said, in a voice so like South-paw's it made her heart stop. "Don't apologize. It's treacherous out here."

She went on her way, trying not to cry, though as it rained harder and harder she gave in to it. How did he know she was English? That she didn't belong here, more so than ever?

• • •

340

"Luke, please will you clear away your pens and help me set the table?"

"I can't, not yet," Luke answered. "I have to finish . . . this . . . Gruffalo . . . very carefully. It's very impotent."

"Important. No, you can finish it later. After supper."

"He is a monster," said Madame Poulain into her vermouth.

"That's right," Cat said absently. The rain dripped through the tiny crack in the steamed-up kitchen window. The stench of drains and rubbish from the tiny galley kitchen hung in her nostrils. Her broken toe ached more than ever—she was sure now that going to the doctor had been a mistake. They'd strapped it so tightly to her second toe that now all of her foot, rather than just the big toe, throbbed with pain.

Suddenly Madame Poulain screeched at Luke. "Put these things away. Away! It is my house, my rules, you dirty, naughty boy."

"Madame Poulain—" Cat said wearily.

"No!" shouted Luke. He picked up the felt-tip pens, like candy-colored plastic sticks, and threw them, all of them, at Madame Poulain. "I hate you! I hate you! I hate being here! You are horrible, you keep us here like a witch, you should let Maman go! I hate you! I hope that you turn into a bird and fly away into an electricity pylon and *zzzzzzzap*! You get fried and you die and it's really horrible!"

As Cat watched, frozen in horror, Luke picked up the nearest pen, a bright acid green, and ran over to the white wall. Her phone rang, buzzing loudly on the table beside her and jerking her into action. She ran over to him and scooped him up from behind, swinging him around away from the wall.

"Luke! No! You don't, you *don't do that!*" She plucked the pen out of his hand and slapped his wrist—she felt it was a pathetic action, and he gave her a strange, almost humorous look, and that half-sob, half-laugh wave of emotion swept over her again. She swallowed it down. Her phone rang again and she knocked it off the table in fury.

"Take the child upstairs and leave him there. And then . . ." Madame Poulain hesitated, and Cat saw that she didn't know what to do next, and neither did she, Cat. They had no formal arrangement, no ties that bound them together. They were not family.

As Cat stood there panting, holding a screaming Luke, her phone rang again, on the floor. She released him too suddenly, and he jumped onto her foot, stamping on her strapped-up toe. Cat screamed too, a great big howl of pain, and Luke looked up at her, his dark eyes huge. She stroked his hair. "Sorry. It's my toe. I'm—I'm fine."

Madame Poulain did not move, so Cat very slowly hobbled over to the dining table, reached down, and picked the phone off the floor. She put her arm around Luke's shoulders. "Please, Luke. Say sorry." Ignoring the searing pain in her foot, she answered. "*Allô?*"

"Is someone being murdered in there?" came a clear voice. "It sounds like it."

"Who's—who is this?" Cat said slowly. "Is that you?"

"It is, darling."

"Gran?" Cat whispered into the phone. "What are you doing here?"

"I'm downstairs," said Martha.

"*Where?*" Cat swallowed.

"I'm downstairs. Waiting outside. You said I should come and visit. Well, I'm here. Is now a good time? I heard the most awful sounds. Even with the rain."

"Now . . . now's a very good time," said Cat, laughing. She didn't know what else to do. "I'll buzz you up."

She looked around the crowded, bright apartment, like an antiques shop. At Madame Poulain's cold, furious face. At Luke, scared and cross, arms folded, looking at the floor. "No. Stay there. I'll come down. I don't want you to come up here."

"What, darling? You cut out for a second."

"Wait a moment." It seemed clearer and clearer by the second, like the sun coming out.

"When will you be back?" Madame Poulain said icily. "I need more vermouth, and some ice. Who is that, Cat? Who's downstairs?"

"My grandmother," Cat said. She pulled Luke onto her lap. "Luke, let's put on your shoes." She looked up at the thin, lined face. "I don't know when I'll be back, Madame Poulain. Don't wait for me. I'm going to call Henri. He'll come over and help you. Luke, put on your coat, please."

Madame Poulain's eyes seemed to grow entirely round, her eyeballs bulging from her sunken skull. "Don't you dare to say that. You said you would clean the bathroom this evening. I need it done tonight and before my wash."

Cat opened the drawer of the bureau and slid two passports into her jeans pocket. She didn't know why, just that the card file of her mind was flipping over and over, the thoughts that constantly raced through her head of what needed to be done, what she had to take here or there, what she could afford, what she owned, all neatly, precisely itemized; and she realized then that all she needed was Luke. And the means to get Luke away from here, away from this overheated glass menagerie, away from the shadow of Luke's father, who hadn't even been in touch since their return, away from this strange, beautiful little island living that was, day by day, slowly torturing them both to death.

Her heart was thumping so loudly in her chest she thought it might burst. "Good-bye," she said, buttoning Luke's coat up. "Thank you." She pulled on her old mac and grabbed her handbag, opened the door, and, hobbling down the steps as fast as she could, calling to Luke to follow her, eventually reached the bottom of the stairs.

She flung open the front door. There, in a great yellow mackintosh with a hood, stood Martha, her green eyes ringed with dull brown circles. She was smiling.

Cat said nothing, just flung her arms around her, sobbing into her squeaky yellow chest. Martha pulled Luke into her embrace and the three of them stood on the narrow little pavement, clutching hold of each other.

"Gran!" Luke shouted, breaking the grip first, and leaping up into his great-grandmother's arms, so that she staggered back and nearly stumbled. "Gran, you're here! You are here!"

Cat caught her grandmother, felt how thin she was. She hugged her again, tears flowing along with the rain down her face, and she realized then what it was, this feeling of half sadness, half happiness that stalked her all the time lately. It was love.

"Let's go and get some hot chocolate," she said, steering her grandmother away from the apartment. "I think we could all do with it."

Martha took Luke's hand. "Of course. Do you—need an umbrella? What about your fearsome-sounding landlady? Does she need to know where you've gone?"

"I'll call her in a while and tell her we'll be back later," Cat said. Up above she could see the thinnest seam of silver in the sky. She breathed in, and then she said, "But we might not. We might just never go back there again." She gripped Luke's other hand. "What do you think about that?"

She was asking Luke, really, not entirely serious, half-acknowledging that it was clear now that their situation had to change, but Martha said, "I think that's a very good idea."

Cat glanced at her. "I was joking really," she said.

"I know, but—do you have to go back? No. I mean, pack up and get your things, of course, or I could do that, or, you know what?" Martha squeezed Cat's hand and crouched down next to her grandson. "I could go back to the flat now, get your passports, and we could all go home tonight. Back to Winterfold."

Cat's hand was shaking as she took out the passports. "I've got them here."

"Why?" Her grandmother laughed.

"I really don't know. Just that—I heard your voice." She started crying. "And I thought we need to be able to not go back there. I'm always trying to think of a way out. All the time." She hiccuped. "I've got used to it."

"What else do you need?" Martha said quietly.

Cat looked at her son. "Nothing else," she said. "But we couldn't do that—so rude to Madame Poulain, and . . ." She trailed off. The idea of walking away from here—it was intoxicating, like drinking champagne. Knowing this bit was over, these years of living this thin, sad, lonely life. She felt almost light-headed. And then she looked at Luke's face.

"Look, my darling girl, it seems fairly simple," Martha said. "I need you, Cat. You need me. Luke needs more than this."

Cat hesitated, then said, "Yes. We do. Yes."

They hugged again, squashing against a wall to let a chic elderly lady walk past with her little dog. She stared at them from under her umbrella: Cat's hair swinging in wet black strings around her smiling face, Luke jumping up and down, and Martha, her hands over her eyes, trying not to cry. Her small, Gallic shrug said it all: *Crazy English people.*

Cat picked up Luke and hugged him tight, and she put her arm round her grandmother as they walked along the road.

"Why are you here, Gran?" she said. "I mean, what made you come?"

"Something Lucy said," Martha replied. "I'm not sure I can explain, not yet. Not till I've finished it all."

The rain thrummed on the pavements and the swollen gray-blue

Seine churned below them, the golden spires of Notre-Dame black in the afternoon gloom. "You don't have to explain."

"I do. To you, and to Florence, you see. I've got things all wrong." Cat tried to speak, but Martha said, "I have to put it right. I was always trying to be in control, you know. I was wrong to try to protect you from the truth all those years. You and Florence."

Luke was fiddling with the toggles on his raincoat, twisting them round and round so they spun out in a corkscrew, the tension released. Cat watched him. "What's it got to do with Florence?"

"I'm going to see her after you, if she'll let me. She's won her court case. I'll tell you then." She shivered. "This really is appalling weather. Where's that hot chocolate place, then?"

"Yes, appalling," Luke agreed cheerfully. "Appalling weather!"

"It's just around the corner," Cat said. She shook her head, water flying everywhere. "Do you—I should go back and get some of Luke's things afterward, shouldn't I?"

"Of course you should, and I'll come with you. You don't need to run away like a thief in the night, you know, Cat. And I would like to see where you spent all this time. I'd like to meet Madame Poulain. Then we will leave, and I promise you won't ever have to go back there." Martha nodded to herself. "Right. That's . . . that's done." She gave a little shiver. "And it was easy! Wasn't it?" She looked down. "Would you like to go home after that, to Winterfold, Luke? Would you like to come and live with me for a bit?"

"Thank you, baby Jesus and the Holy Mother," Luke said solemnly, putting his hands together in prayer and looking up at the sky. "At least you did listen to me about that, for once." He pushed open the door of the crowded, cozy café and stood looking at his mother and great-grandmother as they gripped each other's arms, caught somewhere again between laughter and tears.

Florence

Her sandals slapped loudly on the cold marble as Florence heaved her suitcase up the stairs, sweating silently in the late afternoon heat. She had been away from Italy for nearly two months, and summer had arrived in her absence.

As she unlocked the door, a cloud of stale warmth hit her. A pile of post lay scattered on the floor, the printed names on the envelopes leaping out at her: Oxford University, Harvard, BBC, Yale University Press. She was in demand, as they'd all predicted.

Everywhere else a light film of dust sat on the surfaces, on the little wooden table she ate at, on the tumblers by the French windows. Florence dropped her bag on the floor and opened the door to the balcony. A faint breeze blew softly into the apartment. She ran her hands through her hair, looking out over the rooftops, trying to feel glad to be home. But being back here was curiously mortifying, after the things that had come out about her life in this place over the last couple of months.

The flight had been delayed. She was dirty and sticky and tired, that kind of dazed weariness you get from traveling. She made herself a coffee and began to unpack, and as she did the phone rang. She ignored it. Her mobile rang next, as she sorted out her clothes, put in a load of washing, slotted her books back onto the shelves in her study. The landline rang again. She put the papers from the case into a box file and shut the lid firmly. She didn't ever want to see them again. Sometimes, when she thought about what had come out in that courtroom, she thought she'd sink to the ground, pass out. With the momentum of the case carrying her along, it had been bearable; but in the intervening week the memories—the notes, the mug, the strange behavior, the witness state-ments—had burrowed into her brain. They haunted her so that it was all she could think about now. Florence had gone to court to stand up for herself, and she'd made herself a laughingstock in the process. Before, she'd been merely mildly risible.

And that was what they wanted, all these people who kept calling and writing to her. They wanted a slice of her notoriety, not her mind, and it wouldn't stop. The hammering in her head about not knowing who she was, what she should be doing: it wouldn't stop.

"All my own work," she said, as she sat down with her coffee to go through two months' worth of post. Three letters from publishers who wanted to "have a chat" with her about her next project. Two TV com-panies aside from the BBC who wanted to meet her. Endless letters of support or abuse from strangers who didn't know her, and she didn't know how they'd found her address. She read them with a weary kind of acceptance: they either wanted to tell her she was great, or that she ought to be ashamed of herself. One of them even said, "It's women like you who are responsible for the mess we're in today."

Florence thought about writing him a letter back. A really beautifully crafted, exquisite riposte that would put him in his place so firmly he'd never write another cruel letter to another person again.

But she told herself there was no point.

And then she found his letter. Postcard, really. The Sassetta Saint Francis, taming the wolf of Gubbio. A very small, doglike wolf with his paw in Saint Francis's hand, and a plethora of severed limbs and savaged bodies lying behind him. It was, she knew, one of Jim's favorite paintings.

Dear Flo,

A little card to welcome you back and to say

> *I HOPE YOU BREAK AS MANY OF*
> *YOUR MUGS AS YOU DID MINE*

and also

> *COME BACK SOON*

because I'm writing this and you've just left and well—damn it, why not just write it down? I miss you. I really miss you, Flo.

Jim x

She pressed the card to her heart, feeling her pulse racing. Darling, kind, sweet Jim. But as she did, she remembered doing exactly the same with Peter's communications, such as they were. She'd overlaid each one with some ridiculous symbolism. In this very room, she had done it.

As if she'd conjured his spirit, as she put Jim's card down she caught sight of Peter's handwriting, black, spidery, and difficult, on a small white envelope.

Florence's hands shook as she opened it. She glanced anxiously around, as though she wished someone else might appear, a friendly ghost to battle the demon, alive with her in the apartment.

Dear Florence,

I shouldn't be writing this letter, I'm sure. Am sure it'll get me into more trouble. I just want to make one thing clear:

I really regret everything I did.

Really regret it.

I regret ruining my career because of you and your second-rate mind. You think you're an expert, but you don't expose yourself to anyone else. How you swung that Courtauld job is a mystery to me, and to George. You are not an expert in your field. You are the worst an academic can be: you're trenchant and ignorant.

Having sex with you and seeing you déshabillé is one of the great regrets of my life. Again, it has cost me a lot, and it wasn't worth it.

I'm writing for two reasons: I will ask you for the final time now that this case is over, please leave me and Talitha alone. I think you are a very strange, sad woman with many problems, the greatest of which from my point of view is that you have no concept of real life. I am very sorry I met you, sorrier still that we live in such close proximity. Secondly, in the light of this unfortunate case, and speaking as a member of the same institute as you, even though it be beyond my jurisdiction as your manager, I strongly advise you to seek psychiatric help.

> *With many regrets,*
> *Peter Connolly*

Florence put the letter down as though it were very heavy. She frowned, thinking about her last night with Jim at his home in Islington. How she'd looked up from grating the Parmesan while they were making pasta one last time, found his gaze resting on her. His kind gray eyes, his sweet face, long, lean, and still handsome, even though he had a few years on him now.

She wished she'd reached over, taken his hand, kissed him. Just once.

She wished he were here. So simple—she could see it now that she was back—but it was almost certainly too late. Florence flapped Peter's letter between her fingers, wondering if she ought to keep it.

Then she saw the bottle of pills again on the wedding chest, and it suddenly seemed as though it would be so easy to do it now. It was simply a gentle idea, but it grew, like a breath growing into a gust, then a storm, the butterfly effect.

It would be very easy to go now. No one would really miss me. Not really—Pa's dead.

There was a list that she kept running through in her head. *The way I feel, all the time. The court case. Getting up tomorrow and going on. Home. How awful I was to Lucy, to Bill, to Ma . . . Pa is dead. Pa is dead, he's dead, and I don't know who I am.*

It was the truth; she didn't. The knowledge of this had been forcing its way to the front of her mind for ages now. Before David's death, really. When the invitation to the party had arrived, nearly a year ago now. Maybe even longer ago than that—all her life, perhaps. Florence saw that it had all been building toward this moment, this reckoning, this first night back at home. She bit her tongue so hard she tasted blood. *Don't think about Pa.* If she thought about Pa properly, she'd cry, and if she started crying, she'd never do it.

She didn't know how long she stayed there. It was quiet up on the top floor of the old palace. As the evening came and the sun started to slide over the roofs, Florence sat still, not really thinking. The phone rang again; she ignored it. Moths crashed into the glass of the French windows; ambulances raced by. She felt frozen to the spot, only her clicking tongue reminding her she was still breathing.

Eventually, when it was quite dark, Florence stood up and went over to the chest. She heard her feet clacking on the floor, thought how strange it was. Sound, sensation, taste. How hard would it be to stop them, to take them away from herself?

She picked up the bottle and shook a handful of the pills out onto her palm, stared at them. A church bell rang out over toward the river, a loud arrhythmic clanging. She remembered, suddenly, the story of Lorenzo de Medici's doctor, who was so upset after the prince died that he jumped into a well. She smiled, thinking perhaps that was a good way to go. Brave, if nothing else.

The phone rang again. Florence reached down and pulled the cord out of the wall. She stood staring with surprise at the flex in her hand, the hole where the plaster had crumbled.

"Now," she said, brushing away a tear.

She looked at the bottle in her hand properly for the first time. She read the label. And then Florence looked again, and laughed and laughed.

Joe

IT ALL STARTED because Joe wanted to collect some nettles. To make nettle soup. It was a beautiful May day and he was going mad, cooped up here. He wanted to feel the stretch of his legs and the blue sky above him. Back home he'd be up on the moors first thing on a day like this, feeling the turf underneath him, the sound of his mother's voice still ringing in his ears: "You be back here before lunch, Joe Thorne, or I'll come fetch thee and then tha'll be sorry!"

"I'm just going up to the woods. I won't be more than an hour." He hesitated, scrunching the plastic bags together in his hands. "Do you want to come with me? It's a beautiful day."

Karen looked up from the sofa where she was reading a magazine, eating some crisps. "Joe, do I look like I want to come with you?"

"I don't know. I thought perhaps you'd like a walk."

She gave a short, sharp bark of laughter. "I'd love a walk, but since going more than a hundred meters makes me feel I've run a marathon, I'll pass, thanks."

"Right. Sorry."

This only seemed to irritate her more. "I'm not saying it's your fault. I'm saying I just don't want to go. Don't take it personally."

"Of course not." He grinned at her.

But that wasn't true. There were still three weeks till her due date, and a kind of sullen acceptance hung over the room. Lately, whenever they were together Joe had the sense Karen was angry with him, and he didn't know what to do about it. It wasn't like he could tease her into acquiescence, or give her a hug, or massage her feet. They were strangers, he knew it now, living in a tiny flat, bound by four or five nights together.

Sheila had tried to ask him about it a few weeks ago. "But this—you two. Everything okay? You all right about it?"

"Of course I am. I'm responsible for that baby." Joe wanted to tell her to mind her own business.

"No, she is," Sheila had said sharply. "I know you finished it when you found out she was married. I know the truth, my love. So do you. You had no idea who she was when you started it. It might not even be yours, Joe."

He shrugged. Joe couldn't tell her that the only part of it that made sense was the fact that he knew he had to do the right thing. She was having his baby. A person to hold in his arms, to look after, to help into the world. He was going to do it right this time. This baby would have a proper dad—they'd see him every day, he'd make it the best packed lunches in the whole country, he'd live next door, so close he could hear if they woke in the night. Maybe it wasn't the most conventional way to bring a child into the world, but they'd make it work.

She shifted on the sofa, not looking at him. Joe saw her purplish, bloated ankles, the yellowing rings under her eyes, saw her hand shift under her back to knead the aching muscles that supported her huge belly. Sympathy flooded through him. He couldn't screw this up, not again.

He put his hand tentatively on her shoulder.

"Go on, Karen. It'll do you good to get out of the house."

"I'm just worried about bumping into . . . anyone."

She didn't want to meet Bill, or any of the others, for that matter. That lot.

"I know. But it's going to happen at some point. I'm here, aren't I? Come on, Karen, love. I'll walk slowly. It'll help. And I'll run you a bath when we get back and make you your tea. You'll sleep much better and you'll wake up feeling much better. I promise."

"Oh, Joe. Thank you." Karen's eyes filled with tears. "I don't deserve you, I really don't. . . ." She gave a big, juddering sigh. "Sorry."

"Don't start that up again," Joe said lightly. He came round the sofa. "Listen. I know it's not ideal, but we're going to make this work, aren't we?"

"Dead right we are." She swung her legs off the sofa. "Okay, I'd love to come for a walk with you. Let's go."

It was the first really warm weekend of the year. As they went slowly up the high street, the faint smell of blossom and barbecue hung in the air. He sniffed, and she laughed.

"Two nicest smells in the world," she said. "I could murder a hamburger right now."

"I'll make you one later."

Karen hesitated. "That'd be lovely. Thanks, Joe."

He kept trying to make her things, to feed her up, to give her what she wanted so she'd be happy and he wouldn't have to listen to her stifling her sobs in the bathroom at night, radio turned up, water draining. But his first macaroni and cheese had truffle oil in it, which made her sick. His passion fruit cheesecake was too "passion-fruity," she'd said. "I just like it plain. Sorry, love." He made her pizza, but she didn't like peppers and thought it was too thin. They'd at least laughed about it then.

He touched her arm softly. "Hey, I know you don't like talking about it, but what else do we have to get, do you think?"

"It's okay. I'm on it now. I've even done a spreadsheet." They both smiled. "I think we just need a few more onesies and then we're set. Mum's got some stuff back in Formby—she'll bring it down after it's born." She looked up at him. "By the way, it is okay if she stays for a while? I mean, the pair of us have no idea what we're doing, have we?"

"Well, with Jamie—" he began, then stopped. "But, yeah, it was probably all completely different."

She shook her head. "Of course. I always forget you know all this already. Sorry."

"I don't mean that, no, it's great if your mum wants to come down."

Karen stopped in the middle of the street by the war memorial. She stood up on tiptoe and kissed him on the cheek. "Oh, Joe. You know, you're a good man. A lovely, good man."

Her bump was in the way, and they laughed as he twisted around and pecked her cheek back. "You too. A lovely, good woman. You're going to be a great mum."

She smiled, and sank down on the bench by the memorial. "My back's killing me, Joe. I might just stay here for a bit."

"Joe Thorne!" someone called, and Joe and Karen froze, as if caught in the act of doing something wrong. A little boy was racing toward them. "Joe Thorne, hello! Hello!"

Joe squinted. "Luke?"

Luke's hair was long, and crazy from running in the wind. He stood in front of them both, panting. "Hi! Hi, Karen," he said, looking at Karen. "You have a baby in your tummy."

His inflection was slightly French, and it sounded like a question. "Yes," Karen said. "It's going to come out in a few weeks—" She stopped as she saw Joe's face, and followed his gaze as it traced the two figures who'd appeared around the bend down the hill.

Martha was carrying a string shopping bag containing an open carton of eggs, smeared with muck and straw, and she was telling a story, her hands animated. Beside her walked Cat. She held a bunch of wildflowers, frothing Queen Anne's lace, yellow cowslips, bright red campion. She was covered in goosegrass, stuck to her blue sweater, in her hair, on her jeans. Martha reached the punch line, knocking her fists together, and Cat threw her head back with a loud, throaty laugh.

Joe stared, transfixed, as the two women caught sight of them and halted by the bench.

"Hello, Joe," Martha said politely. "Karen, my dear. How are you? You look well."

She had such a graceful way about her, a kind of calmness. He'd seen her in the village lately, face knitted all wrong, mouth pursed, eyes tight with anger, glazed as if she wasn't there. Now she looked—looser. As if someone had released the strings that had kept her tight, like a puppet.

"I'm fine, thanks," Karen said politely. "Not long now . . ." She trailed off awkwardly.

"Yes," said Joe staunchly. He could hardly tear his eyes away from Cat, though he knew he had to; it must be obvious to everyone else, mustn't it? This juddering, wild sensation of coming alive at seeing her again. When they'd met at the playground she'd been so pale, so thin, so sad. A bare tree in winter. He'd pushed her firmly from his mind since. How he wanted to fold her into his arms, feed her, take her for long, hearty walks that put the pink back into her cheeks.

He was ashamed of himself, then and now, for thinking like that. With a huge effort, he shut his eyes briefly, turning to Karen. "We're very excited," he said, nodding at her.

"That's wonderful," Martha said. Her tone was entirely neutral, though she smiled at Karen in a friendly way.

"I heard Florence won her case," Karen said, resting her hands on her bump. "That's great. She coming down soon?"

Martha's calm expression clouded momentarily. "I—I don't know. Her friend Jim says she flew back to Italy yesterday. I need to get hold of her. I keep trying her and she doesn't answer." She smiled. "But, yes, she won, and we need to get her back here."

"He sounded like a right berk, that bloke."

"Yes, indeed, I think he was," she said, smiling. "She was awfully brave, wasn't she? It's just like Florence."

"Florence! Florence!" Luke chanted, then stopped and looked at Karen. "When are you having the baby?"

"In about three weeks," said Karen. "Supposedly."

"Where's Bill?"

Biting her lip, Cat stepped forward. "You look great, Karen." She kissed her on the cheek and said frankly, "Look, I'm sorry I haven't been over yet. I've felt a bit awkward and wasn't sure what the deal was, and whether you'd want to see any of us."

Karen swallowed. "Oh—Cat. Thanks. Of course I—it's . . ." She looked nervously at Martha. "It's difficult, and I can appreciate that—I'm so . . ." Her hand flew to her throat and then she said, "I didn't know you were back."

"Been back more than a fortnight now," Cat said. "We've decided to move in with Gran, haven't we, Luke?"

Luke smiled. "Yes. We live here now! I don't ever have to see François again. He has smelly feet and he bites people. He bit me, and he bit Josef."

"Well, but that's not why we left."

"Why did you leave?" Karen asked. "Quite sudden, wasn't it?"

Cat grimaced. "When you know you can do something, you have to go for it." She shrugged, and then smiled again. "Sounds mad, I know. I sound like a hippie when I start trying to explain it."

"No, it makes sense," Karen said slowly. Joe looked at her curiously: Karen was the least likely hippie in the whole world. "What are you going to do, then? For a job, I mean."

"No idea." Cat made a face. "I have to find something soon, though.

I want to open a nursery garden eventually. Herbs and greens for eating, lavender and roses for oils, that kind of thing. A café, soft play area." She smiled. "Anyway, it's a pipe dream, but one day. Gran and I have talked about doing it at Winterfold maybe. I just need to find some work first."

Martha said, "I keep telling you, you don't need to work for a while, Cat. Take a few months, relax, decide what you want to do."

But Cat replied firmly, "I've always worked. I can't leech off you forever. I couldn't just sit around not doing anything. For Luke's sake. I have to plan."

He heard himself say, "There's a job going at the pub, if you've waitress experience."

"Yes, absolutely." She looked amazed. "You serious?"

"We're pretty busy. Yeah. Are you sure? What about the gardening, market stall thing?"

"All in good time. I want to get Luke settled in at school, work out what we do, before I plunge in. Why, do you want advice on a kitchen garden? You should do it, that's my advice." She put her head on one side, looking at him. "Joe, this job sounds perfect. Thank you. Should I ring—"

"Yeah, ring Sheila," Joe said, too loudly. "But I would like your advice on a kitchen garden too. That's our next—"

But he stopped, unable to say more. It was true, but it sounded too neat.

"Look, I'm not going to make it much farther," said Karen. She stood up, leaning on Joe. "Why don't you two go and find Sheila and talk about it, and I'll go back and have a nap? How's that sound?"

"I can take Luke back, if you like," said Martha.

Luke jumped up, grabbing Joe's other hand. "Joe, we slept in the woods last weekend. Mum and I built a tent."

"It was awful," Cat said. "I didn't sleep a wink. I'd forgotten how sad the owls sound. And there were all these rustling things around us. And bats. Everywhere." Her lips parted in a big, easy smile. "I love being in the garden more than anything in the world, but I'm not cut out for camping in the woods. Never was. Poor Luke."

Joe said, "Hey, Luke—I love camping. I'd go with you." Karen looked up at him, and he felt himself blushing. *No. You have a son. They don't need you. Karen needs you.* "I mean—sometime. I'd love to."

"Next weekend? How about next weekend?"

Cat bent down. "Luke, Joe's going to be very busy because he's having a baby soon. Maybe later this summer he'll take you, or when Jamie's down. Remember Jamie? You could all go together."

Luke nodded. He smiled at Joe. Joe wanted to cry then, to hug Luke close to him, just to feel his slim frame and inhale his small-boy smell, to have one small moment when he might just believe it was Jamie he was hugging, Jamie who was here with him. He swallowed, looked up and met Cat's eyes. She was staring at him, squinting in the sunshine, a flush on her cheeks, but she glanced away immediately, pulling another string bag from her pocket.

"We were going to pick some elderflower for cordial, but it's too early. Stupid of us—I've forgotten my country ways. Well"—she glanced at Martha—"if you're sure, Gran."

"Very sure," said Martha. "I'll try Florence again. See you later. Good luck!"

"I think it's going to work out very well," Sheila said. She threw a tea towel over her shoulder. "I'm so glad you came in, Cat. Honestly. I never knew you had waitress experience."

"I've done it all," said Cat, sitting down at the table by the bar. "Thanks for this." She took a gulp of the large glass of white wine Sheila had given her. "There's something truly wicked about drinking for no reason in the afternoon."

"There's a reason," said Joe. "No more Sheila trying to waitress, which is an extremely painful process to watch, I can tell you."

"Leave it, Joe Thorne. Just you try it," Sheila said. Cat laughed loudly, and Sheila smiled at her. "It's lovely to have you back, my dear. I'll leave you two. Let me know when you want to talk about the kitchen garden, Cat. I'd love to think some more about it." She walked off almost abruptly, leaving Joe standing beside the table.

Cat gestured. "Aren't you going to join me? I can't sit here drinking alone." He glanced at his watch. "Oh. You've probably got loads to do before dinner service." She shuffled along the bench. "I'll leave you to it."

"No—no." Joe put his hand on the table. "I'm good for a while.

Please, don't go." He poured himself a glass from the fridge behind the bar and sat down opposite her. "Cheers," he said. "To new beginnings."

"In more ways than one," she said, clinking his glass. "Good luck with . . . with baby Joe or Karen."

She tucked her hair behind her ear and then held the glass by the stem, looking into the yellowy-green liquid. It was very quiet in the bar, warm sun streaming as far as the floorboards behind them but not making it all the way to their table, next to the kitchen. He let his gaze rest on her for a moment. Her thin fingers, short stubby nails, the faint lines around her eyes. She had a few freckles on her nose, he'd never noticed them. He didn't really know her. At all. He cleared his throat.

"We're excited. Both of us."

"I thought you were an item, you and Karen," she said frankly. "Gran says you're not."

"Oh. Well—no. She's living with me."

"Of course."

"And I'm helping her with the baby."

"Yes."

Joe said steadily, "We're in it together. We'll probably buy the cottage down the road and knock through so I'm next door but I'm there all the time. You know . . . I can pick him or her up from school when she's working late, that sort of thing."

"That sounds like a very good plan," said Cat. She nodded, then smiled. "You know—oh, I shouldn't say it."

"Go on," Joe said, intrigued.

She drank some more wine. "This is going straight to my head. Last time I drank a bit too much, I ended up kissing you."

"Well—I liked it," he said. "For what it's worth."

"I did too." Their eyes met over the wine and they both smiled. "I just wanted to say . . . I'm sorry I was so rude to you. I thought you were a bit of a sleazebag. And maybe you're not."

He shrugged. "I've let so many people down. It's not great."

"How so? Who?"

Joe shook his head. He didn't want to get into it. "Never mind."

He wished he could be the man who said what he was feeling. He looked at her, imagining saying the words: *I'm sorry I dicked you around. I was a total idiot. Karen's gorgeous and funny and we had fun and we really were a comfort to each other, before I found out she was married. I like her. But I like you even more. I like everything about you, your smile, the way you think, the way you frown because you're afraid of all these things. How you are with Luke, with Jamie. How brave you are.*

He wouldn't ever say it, though. He liked making things, but he wasn't good at explaining things. He rubbed his chin and, looking straight at her, said, "I'm not that kind of person. But there's no reason on earth you should believe me, I know that. And with Karen . . ."

Cat leaned across the table. She said, "Don't take this the wrong way, but I have to do this," and she kissed him.

Cat

SHE'D FORGOTTEN HOW good he tasted, how lovely the feel of his mouth on hers was, the connection like memory foam, leaning into him again in exactly the right way.

Across the table, he kissed her back, pushing into her, a strange soft sound in his throat, and then just as suddenly pulled away from her. "What the hell did you do that for?" he said, startled.

Cat shrugged at him, and twisted her hair up into a ponytail. "Listen. I just wanted to . . . to wipe the slate clean. That injured-pride thing. I've been rude to you. You were stupid to kiss me, but I've kissed you too. We're not kids."

"We're not kids? So what the hell, Cat—anyone could have walked in, Karen—"

She interrupted. "We've both been through some rough times, okay?" She could feel her heart thumping high in her chest, in her throat almost. *Just say it, just get through it.* "I like you, you like me, the timing isn't right, that's all there is to it." She nodded and sat back against the settle. "Okay?"

"Okay?" He started laughing softly, then almost helplessly. "Cat, you're bloody crazy. That's an insane way to neutralize a situation, can't you see that?"

She shrugged again. "I have been crazy. I'm not now. Clean slate, like I say."

He was watching her, still laughing. She said, "With everything else that happened, it just feels like years ago. I don't want you thinking of me as some victim. Or you feeling bad about what happened with us, carrying this guilt about so we have to shuffle around each other and it's

360

awkward every day at work. *Oh, she's damaged goods. Oh, he's a terrible person.* Treading on eggshells."

"Well, that's for me to decide." He was still looking shell-shocked, and Cat's stomach lurched. "Like I say, if someone had come in—"

"No one cares about your own life as much as you do," Cat said frankly. "Most important thing I've learned, over the last few years. It's really just you." She leaned across the table again. "You know the thing about men and women? You know what's completely crap about relationships?"

"What?" he said cautiously.

"People start playing roles. All that's bullshit. You and Karen should just do what you want."

"What do you mean?"

"Before I started going out with Olivier, I was this confident person. I knew how to put up a shelf, how to argue with a gendarme, how to order steak right. And then because of him, because of the way I felt when I was with him . . . how worthless he made me feel . . . I changed. I wasn't that person but I became that person, and he treated me like shit, so everyone else did too. I became shy, pathetic, afraid of everything. Just content to let it happen to me. Anyway . . . all I mean is . . . I wasn't like that to start with. And that's what relationships are about. Good ones, I mean. You have to be flexible. It's not about someone being in charge and someone following, or someone being the star and someone the applause. Gran and Southpaw, they were everything, the whole package. He was better at some things, she was better at other things, but they were both in charge." Cat smeared the wineglass with her fingers, frowning into it. "They led from the front, they were a partnership, because they knew what mattered to them, they knew what was important, and they worked everything else around that. Sometimes he was the star, sometimes she was." She knew he was watching her, but she was too embarrassed now to stop and look at him. "I've always thought it, that's when bad stuff creeps in, when you start having roles and suddenly you can't break them." She nodded, and stood up. "That's all I wanted to say. It's about being flexible. Rolling with the punches. Good times and bad. When I think about Olivier, I don't think there was a day with him I was ever actually myself."

"That's the same as me and Jemma," Joe said. "We were pretty mismatched. I'd been the spotty fat kid a year before, I wasn't in her league. I couldn't believe she went for me."

"But you weren't with her because she was some stunning model. You liked her too."

"I did, but it was more I thought I could look after her. Prove I wasn't a bastard like my dad. Save her from these sleazy blokes who'd treat her badly." She watched him work his cheek, rough with stubble, with his fingers.

"And where is she now?"

He leaned on the bar, facing her. "Oh, living with *Ian Sinclair*."

"Who's Ian Sinclair?"

"He's got everything, hasn't he? He's a lawyer, got a nice pad in York, drives a big Subaru, buys her everything she wants, Jamie's going to private school . . . all of that." Joe said, "Her mum's got her own flat now too; he's bought that for her. He's a wizard."

"Well, aren't you happy for her? For Jamie?"

"Yes, of course I am," he said impatiently. "Of course."

"And don't you stop to think that if she hadn't been with you and had Jamie, she might have ended up somewhere worse? She might have gone off with one of those blokes, and who knows what might have happened to her?"

"Jemma's pretty tough," Joe said.

Cat said, "I was pretty tough too, when I met Olivier." Her mouth was dry. "You know, women often don't have choices. They get sucked into things. My mum left when I was a few weeks old." She touched his hand to try to make him understand. "I don't know how she did it, it must have hurt her, but I never thought about her, only me. She felt she didn't have any other option, and that's awful. We live in a sexist world. We make girls think they'll be rewarded for being decorative, and then they think it's fine when they get treated like crap."

"Your grandmother never did that to you."

"Of course she didn't. But I grew up without a mum and a dad." Cat's voice was soft. "And it meant I really wanted people to like me, all my life. I wanted my mum to come back and say she loved me and she was going to look after me, and she never did. I think that makes you into someone who's a bit desperate for approval, that's all." Tears clouded her vision; she blinked them back. Daisy still had the power to overwhelm

362

her, but she knew that power was fading. "Look, Joe, all I'm saying is, you might have saved Jemma from something worse. You came in and loved her, and you gave her Jamie. You had a son. And Karen . . . she and my uncle were always an odd fit. She was using you a bit, I think? You know?"

"I used her, too," Joe said. "It's been strange, living down here. Without Jamie." He brushed something off his forehead; she saw the spasm of emotion crossing his face. "I was so lonely. I mean, I was up for it. You can imagine, Karen's pretty determined when she sets her mind to something."

Cat didn't want to hear about how great Karen was in bed. She didn't want to think about anyone touching Joe, wrapping her arms round him, having him all to herself. She wanted to stay like this, in this deserted warm room, sun setting, the two of them leaning on the bar in their own perfectly sane world.

Already the spell was fading, though. She drained her drink. "Well, Karen's lucky. Lucky you're such a good guy, Joe. You really are. I'm sure it's going to work out really well." She pushed the glass to one side. "Shake on it?"

She was appalled at what a big lie it was. She wanted him to shrug off his responsibilities, right here, right now. Say, *I want you, Cat. I want you now. I'm leaving Karen to do it by herself, she'll be fine. It's right with you, I know it, you know it too. I'm going to lock the pub door and pull down the blinds and make love to you on the floor, and it's going to be the best sex you've ever had, Catherine Winter. Hair-messing, earthshaking sex, and then we'll move in with Jamie and Luke and make even more babies and grow plants and cook and love each other every day, in our own place.*

She smiled a little to herself, then held out her hand. He shook it vigorously. "Thanks so much, Cat," he said. His smile was ironic. "It's good to have a friend. I mean it. Thanks for . . . for understanding."

"Of course," she said, nodding.

She walked back up to Winterfold feeling flushed with shame and attraction. The shadows were lengthening across the newly green fields. The evening was coming, and the warm breeze soothed her. Dog roses bloomed in the hedgerows, and stalks of Bath asparagus waved softly. She picked a small bunch to take in to work the next day. She imagined Joe's face, the pleasure it would give him to see it, and she smiled. She knew they weren't going to be together. It was fine, she understood why. After everything else that had happened, just to have him in her life as a friend was more than she'd counted on. It was getting better, every day.

Luke and Martha were having tea outside as she walked up the drive. Luke was kicking a ball over to his grandmother, who was alternately deadheading flowers, drinking from her mug, and pacing up and down. When she heard Cat she turned.

"Darling. So great you're back. Luke, run inside and fetch your mum a mug for tea. And some more cake."

Luke ran off, and Martha came toward Cat. "How did it go?"

"It was fine," said Cat. "It was . . . good."

Martha watched her shrewdly. "He's nice."

"He's very nice," said Cat robustly. "Isn't it great?" She noticed her grandmother's expression was drawn. "Everything all right?"

Martha shook her head. "I can't get hold of Florence. Neither can Jim," she said. Her lips were thin. "She's not answering her mobile and the number at her flat has been disconnected. No one's heard from her."

Florence

THE DAY AFTER her return home, Florence slept as though she had been knocked unconscious, and when she was woken by the sound of a car horn and someone shouting in the street below, she felt muzzy. Hungover, as if her head were filled with wet sand. She looked around, her bleary eyes taking in the lines of her tiny, nunlike bedroom.

Then she saw the small scratched bottle, full to the neck with tiny little white pills. Remembered the previous night, the inscription on the label.

Martha Winter
Magnesium tablets
Two a day when constipation occurs
Use before 09/12/12
DO NOT EXCEED THE STATED DOSAGE

The poster of a Masaccio exhibition on the opposite wall had faded over the years so that the figures looked like greenish-yellow ghouls.

A pile of typewritten pages splayed across the cold stone floor; the transcript of the judge's ruling. Florence rolled onto her side, blinking. *"She is possibly the foremost expert in her subject in the world, and your cynical attempt to exploit that, your arrogance, and your sheer deceit are frankly breathtaking."*

Florence rolled back and sat up slowly, staring cheerfully at the ghouls opposite. "Good morning," she said, trying to sound happier than she felt. "I'm talking to you," she said to the figure of Adam. "Yes, you. How rude. Fine, ignore me then." She sat on the edge of the bed, wiggling her toes and stretching, then got up and made some coffee.

Peter's letter lay, along with the rest of the post, on the wedding chest. It had curled up in the night, as if trying to fold itself back into an oblong. Florence gathered up the post, the letters, the periodicals, the invitations, the prying, all of it except Jim's postcard. She threw the whole pile into the rubbish bin.

"If you could see me now, Professor Connolly," she said aloud as she waited for the coffeemaker to bubble, smelling the old, familiar, comforting scents of her home. She glanced at her desk, almost delirious with the thought of losing herself in some work again. "Yes, I talk to myself. Yes, I'm crazy. And I don't bloody care."

She didn't have wireless Internet in her flat, so Florence had no way of knowing who'd been trying to contact her, which she rather enjoyed, but she knew she had to check her landline and her mobile, which had both rung consistently since she'd arrived back. Her mobile seemed to be crammed with missed calls, but the only thing she noticed, with a leaping heart, was a text from Jim. Florence took a deep breath, and read it.

Did you get home okay? Rather lonely here without you.

She was feeling so brave that she replied, tapping laboriously with many mistakes and much cursing.

Absolutely. Long dark night of soul but it's over. Thank you for your lovely postcard. I miss you too, Jim. Can I come over and stay soon? Will bring new mugs to break.

After she'd sent this message, she became terrified of what she'd done and threw the phone onto the sofa, where it slid down behind the cushions. She couldn't bear to hunt around for it, already certain she'd made a terrible *faux pas*. She felt like a teenager.

The demons of the night before seemed far away now, but she knew enough to know they might come back, and this tempered her cheerfulness, for she did feel surprisingly cheerful, considering. Would she laugh at this one day? How she tried to kill herself with her father's sleeping pills, but accidentally snatched her mother's constipation prescription instead? She thought it was maybe symbolic of something: she knew Daisy had killed herself with pills purloined from that same cabinet, but Daisy had taken the right pills, and heroin too. In short, Daisy had known how to kill herself.

And now Florence, who had felt for the longest time as though the last few months were leading up to that night, that moment alone with these pills and the decision to end her life, was faced with the question of what came next.

She let her mind drift. Either she changed something, went forward in a different way, or she continued upon the same path and accepted that, at some point, she would go around in a circle, come to this bend in the road again. Florence had trained her brain over the years. She had nourished it, exercised it, treated it with respect. She had to listen to it now, to feel there was some point to the very clear conviction she'd had that last night was the night everything changed. Coming back gave her some clarity of thought. She tried to pin it down, but perhaps the whole couldn't be seen yet, and she accepted that too.

"It was the right thing to do," she said aloud, as she picked up the pages of the transcript and filed them away. "It was the right thing to do," she said, as she pinned up Jim's postcard. "It was the right thing to do," she said, as she took a deep breath and reached for the landline to call her mother, before remembering she'd pulled the phone cord away from the wall.

She tried to plug the socket back in, but it wouldn't work. So she hunted around down the back of the sofa, and pulled her mobile out from deep inside the frame. In addition to Jim's text, there were two voicemails from Martha. Florence knelt on the sofa, the frame creaking underneath her, and listened intently to the last one.

"Listen, Flo—please call me? I don't know where you are. *Are* you back in Italy? Your phone doesn't seem to work. Darling, please call me. I'm— Cat's here. She's back. I need to talk to you. I need to tell you something and we need to talk. I want to see you. Call me back, sweetheart."

Florence looked at the postcard on the wall. She took a deep breath.

She felt as if she were staring out of a plane, parachute on her back. She said softly to herself: "Yes."

She made another coffee and rang her mother.

"Hello?"

"Hello? Who's that?"

"It's me, Ma. Flo."

"Florence!" Martha's voice was joyous with relief. "Oh, my goodness, darling, how are you? I've been . . . I've been trying to get hold of you. I was getting rather worried."

"Worried?"

"Oh, I had a . . . a silly feeling." Her mother laughed. "It's silly."

Florence said slowly, "Oh. I'm back now. Got in last night."

"Ah. How are you?"

"I'm good." Florence looked at the bottle of pills and smiled to herself. "I'm really well. How—how are you?"

"Yes. I'm really well too. Flo—"

She interrupted, suddenly terrified of what came next. "Ma, I was just ringing to say I forgot something when I was last over. My old notes on Filippo Lippi, I need them for an article I'm supposed to be writing."

"Well, tell me where they are and I can post them for you."

"They're in Dad's—the study. With all my other papers, on the shelf below the encyclopedias. It's a cloth folder, kind of red and black."

She could hear her mother walking through the house. "Fine, well, then. I see it. So you want me to send them to you?"

"Yes, please, Ma."

"Grand."

There was a pause. Small, expectant pause.

"And—I wanted to say something too."

"You do? Oh—well, I—okay. You go first."

Florence blundered on. "I'm sorry about how I was when I was over. The court case and everything else. It made me rather lose the plot for a while. I've been very unhappy. Very selfish. I wasn't . . . Anyway, I am sorry."

"You're sorry?" Her mother laughed. Florence stiffened. She wondered if she should just put the phone down, but then Martha's voice softened. "You're not the one who should be sorry."

"Oh."

"Darling Flo, this is ridiculous. . . . When are you coming back? I really would like to see you. Talk to you properly. Just us two."

With one finger, Florence slowly pushed the pill bottle across the kitchen countertop. "I'm not sure—I've just got back here. I can't leave for a while, there's various things. . . . Probably August?"

"Right." Martha's voice sank.

"Ma, do you need me to come back?"

"No. Yes."

"What's going on? Are you okay?"

"I'm absolutely fine. I need to tell you something." Martha gave a small sigh. "It's about you, Flo, darling. Something you need to know."

Florence stepped out of the sunny kitchen into the darkness of the large sitting room, her heart beating like a drum. She put her hand on the bureau to steady herself, glad that she was alone and no one could see her face. She had been waiting for this moment for most of her life, since she was nine in fact, and now that it was here she didn't want it to happen.

"I know," she said.

"You know what?" Martha's voice was close to the receiver.

"I've always known. Ma." The word fell heavily out of her mouth. "I know I'm not your child. I know my mother left me on the street and you adopted me from some orphanage. Daisy told me, Ma. After Wilbur died and she got really nasty. She used to whisper it in my ear at night."

There was silence but for one small sob.

"Ma?" she said tentatively, after a long pause.

Eventually her mother said, "Oh. It's not even ten in the morning."

"What?"

"I'm sorry. I don't know what to say. That's . . . that's awful, sweetheart. Is that really what she told you?"

"Well, yeah, Ma. You never believed me when I'd tell you about her, so—so I stopped after a while."

"Oh, Daisy." Martha's voice was low. "Florence, sweetheart . . . you're not from some orphanage. You're Pa's niece. His sister was your mother—she, she was only nineteen."

Below her, a car trundled too fast down the narrow street; someone cursed, a dog barked, backing out of its way. Florence stood very still.

Eventually she said: "I—I'm Pa's—I am his . . . his niece?"

"His niece. You were always part of him, oh darling, yes, of course."

"His sister?" Florence turned around slowly, kept turning. "She was my—my mother?"

"Times were different then; she was engaged to someone else. She—we agreed—we wanted to take you. You became ours."

Florence had stopped revolving. She stood with her hand over her face, eyes covered, as though terrified of what she might see. "Why didn't you tell me?"

Martha's voice was hoarse. "Cassie begged us not to tell anyone. Your father promised her. They had an awful childhood, and—I can't explain it all now. Oh, Daisy. What did you do?" Martha gave a sob. "Daisy lied, darling. I don't know how she found out, but she must have heard us talking—you know what she was like."

"I do, Ma," Florence said.

"Well, she was wrong, it's not true. You're not Daddy's daughter, you're his niece, but—oh, you were the one he really loved. 'My angel.' That's what he used to call you."

"Who was—the father?" She didn't want to say "my father."

"I don't know. A music teacher. Older than her. He did a bunk, but I'm sure we can find out, I don't want you to—oh dear! Oh, goodness." And Martha started to laugh, a weak, silvery rattle. "This is all wrong. Get you and Cat back, that's what I wanted to do. I wanted to do this face-to-face, not for you to find out like this." She took a deep breath. "Telling you over the phone. It's just not right."

"I knew all along, Ma."

"And you knew all along." Martha was breathing hard. "I'm sorry. I think I'm going mad."

"Where is she?" Florence said, trying not to sound as scared as she felt.

"Who?"

"My—my real mother."

"Your—Cassie. Cassie, of course. I—oh, love. I don't know. We hadn't seen her for years."

"Really?"

"Yes." Martha drew a deep breath. "I wish—I've just started going through the study, all your father's papers. There must be something there. Last thing I heard, she was in Walthamstow."

"When was that?"

There was a pause. "Twenty years ago."

Florence bowed her head. "Didn't Pa ever—"

"I called her number, darling. She doesn't live there anymore. I . . . but we'll see, okay? We'll find her. Cassie Doolan. But she was married, and I don't know her husband's name. I'm sure she'd have changed her name. But, darling, she didn't want to stay in touch. She was quite adamant about that to your father."

"Really?"

"Yes. I'm so sorry. But we'll start looking for her. We will find her."

"Ma, I need to think about it all. Take it all in."

"Of course, darling."

The sound of nothing, crackling over the phone line. Florence imagined the cables running under the sea, through the land, carrying this weight of silence between them, and still she didn't know what came next, and then Martha cleared her throat.

"Right. That's enough time. Flo, darling, can I come and see you? I'll be there by teatime. Would that work?"

She picked at the worn wicker chair. "Ma—I think you're getting confused. I'm in Florence. I'll come and see you soon. I will, I promise."

The voice down the line was amused. "I know where you are, darling. I haven't lost my marbles. I want to come and see you."

"What? Come today? Ma, you can't just jump on a plane and . . ." Florence trailed off. Why couldn't she?

"I've been looking at flights with Cat. They had availability this morning—there's a flight in a little while leaving from Bristol. I wanted to sit opposite you, tell you all this in a sound and sane way. Look you in the eye, my darling."

"But that doesn't mean you have to . . ." Florence looked around. Her mother, here? "It's so far."

Martha broke in. "No, it's not. I'll see you later. Yes. I'll be with you for a drink this evening. Gin and tonic. Make sure—"

"Of course, Ma. Lime. Of course, who do you think I am?" Florence smiled, her throat tight.

"I know who you are, my darling. Right, then." Martha sounded crisp, efficient, as if this was completely normal. "I have your address, and I'll get Bill to call you with my flight details. I'm perfectly capable of getting a cab from the airport. You have that drink ready. Good-bye, my sweet girl. I'll see you soon." And with that, the phone went dead, leaving Florence staring, openmouthed, into her receiver.

Karen

May 2013

THE PAIN STARTED in the morning, right after she booked the taxi. But she'd had these pains before, the midwife had said it was false labor. So she carried on packing. It didn't take long—she knew what she needed. The list said nighties, but who wore those these days? She had her Juicy tracksuits, three pairs, loads of tees, Uggs, flip-flops, breast pads, nursing bras, and that was basically it. Some knickers. Her iPad loaded with seasons two and three of *Modern Family*. And some onesies, nappies, T-shirts, a very, very small hat, and some socks that made her want to cry when she looked at them, they were so tiny. All the rest of that beautiful new gear for the baby, it could be sent on to her mum's, or Joe could keep it, if he needed it. Whenever that might be.

Karen wasn't a stubborn woman, she was just determined. She was used to knowing what she wanted in life and going for it. Men got rewarded for being bold; women didn't. She knew that, and sometimes it meant she had to step back and restrategize. But on this day of all days, things had to go exactly the way she wanted.

Joe had left early that morning, thinking everything was normal.

"Bye, Karen. See you later," he'd said, halfway out of the kitchen, mind already on the restaurant and the day ahead. Then he'd turned and faced her. "You all right? Yeah?"

"I'm grand." She'd looked at him. "Thanks, Joe. Thanks a lot."

"Okay." He'd smiled, sort of uncertain, like he didn't know what that meant. "Call me if you need anything, won't you?"

She'd waited till she heard the door slam, then pulled the little suitcase out from under the bed and, moving slowly as a hippo, packed the last of her meager possessions. She left out *Project Management for Dummies,* then put it back in. It had been a present from Bill. Sort of a joke, really, because he knew how much she loved business books. How much she loved planning, getting it right. Three pages of that and she'd be calm again. "Like a hit from a bong," he'd say.

"Part IV: Steering the Ship: Managing Your Project to Success." She'd been planning for a while, really, ever since they'd met Cat in the lane that day. Did they know it, each of them? They must. Something had happened with them, something before that. He'd run into her kid; it was hardly a rosy start, was it?

She'd asked him about Cat that evening, and Joe had said, "Yeah, she's great, isn't she? Really glad she came back."

Karen knew when people were hiding their feelings. She wasn't stupid. And Joe wasn't. She was stumped. She bumped into Cat the following week on the green.

"Joe? He's brilliant. I'm so glad it's all working out," Cat had said happily, and Karen had scanned her expression, searching for cracks in her demeanor, but she could see none.

Suddenly she had felt sick, like she'd throw up there and then. She'd blinked and lurched forward, and Cat had caught her, and Karen had to excuse herself. "I'm tired. Blood sugar low. I think I'd better get home." Moving slowly back to the flat above the pub, she chewed her nails. Now, now she knew this was all wrong, this brotherly living arrangement with Joe—all wrong. She knew what she wanted, but it was too late.

How could she leave Joe when he'd done so much for her, when he was so excited about this baby? When it was almost certainly his kid? Karen knew she was cornered. She had no idea what to do, and the one thing she knew was that you didn't start making major life alterations with a tiny baby on board. Unless you were Daisy, and she was no role model. Time was running out. Then the next week, in the pub, Karen saw something magical. She saw a tea towel being thrown.

She was sitting in a window seat in the snug, having a blackcurrant and soda, and wondering whether this would be the highlight of her post-baby social life, when a tea towel sailed through the air toward her. She turned and saw, as though in slow motion, Joe's hands raised as he threw it, Cat catching it and hugging it to her, eyes shining, that wide mouth with its huge smile.

"You're a rubbish thrower, Joe Thorne," she said. "I can see why you got kicked off the cricket team. Jamie's better than that."

"You have the coordination of a day-old lamb, Cat Winter. Your legs wobble. And your arms look like a faulty windmill." Cat's mouth dropped open in outrage. "It's true. You're a crap fielder. Now, get back to work."

It wasn't even so much that they were flirting. She really didn't think anything was going on between them—it was just that they were completely happy, totally absorbed in each other's company.

Two days later she'd walked into the post office to see them there together at the counter, picking out seeds from a catalogue. Their heads were bent over the pictures as they talked intently about this variety of thyme versus was there room for sorrel—*Who eats sorrel?* she'd thought. What the hell even *was* sorrel?

Feeling like Miss Marple cracking the village mystery, Karen had cleared her throat, and they'd turned to apologize for being in the way, and seen her.

"Hello!" Cat had said, beaming. "Wow, that caftan is great. Wish I'd been that stylish when I was pregnant."

"Oh, hello, Karen, love." Joe had come over to her. "Everything all right?"

"Fine, fine, I just saw you two in here and thought I'd come in. . . ." She'd nodded coldly at Susan. Susan shifted behind the counter awkwardly.

Suddenly Karen wanted to be on the sofa under a blanket, crying her eyes out. She'd told herself it was the hormones. She felt completely surplus to requirements. "I'll be off, then. I don't want to stand around too long."

"See you later," Joe had said. "I'll—get you what you want for tea, yes? Cat, I'd like to try some of those verbena plants. It may be the wrong time to get them, though."

"I think they can be the first thing we put in the greenhouse, if we ever get round to building it." She laughed. "I'm sure it'll collapse at the first gust of autumnal wind. Susan, do you think Len would help us? He built that greenhouse up at Stoke Hall, didn't he?"

"Oh, he did, a girt big one. They're ever so pleased with it."

"Well, maybe that's it." Cat leaned on the counter. "I might go over and ask him later. Then you can grow squash and suchlike to your heart's content, Joe." She turned to Karen. "And the baby can eat all homegrown food. It'll be wonderful. A girt big greenhouse!"

Oh, God, homegrown squash. I hate squash. And I'm not going to be one of those mums who spends her time puréeing foods. That's what supermarkets are for, aren't they, convenience?

But she smiled at Cat, unable to resist her infectious, happy enthusiasm. "Grow some bacon sandwiches, Cat, my love, and I'll help you dig them up."

"Deal." Cat nodded, as Joe tapped her on the arm.

"The verbena, Cat. What about it? I'd like to try flavoring something like a lamb stew with it. Very delicately, see if it takes."

She shrugged, smiling at him, and Karen felt a bit sick again.

"Yes, you're right. Let's do it."

"Okay." He scribbled on the form.

He didn't even look at Cat when he was talking to her, the way he carefully, solicitously, nervously stared at Karen when asking her how she was or what she wanted, as if she were a Chinese firework with indecipherable instructions that might suddenly explode. Karen left the silly little village shop, the flimsy door banging behind her, the jaunty bell drilling into her tired head.

Karen didn't know lots of things. She didn't know if Joe knew he was in love with Cat. Or if Cat knew either. She didn't know, if she went back home, where she'd end up having this baby—she assumed she'd have to go up to the hospital at Southport. She didn't know what she'd do afterward, or how she'd care for the baby on her own. She didn't know if Bill would ever want to speak to her again, and whether it was worth trying. She was pretty certain the answer to that was no. She wanted him to fight for her. He wanted to let her go. She didn't know why, and she didn't know how to ask him anymore. Even as the days seemed longer and longer, and she thought of more and more things she wanted to say to him.

I thought we couldn't have kids.

I thought you didn't love me anymore.

I'm so, so sorry about your dad, I loved him too.

She was certain of two things: one, she wasn't in love with Joe, nor he with her, and it wasn't fair anymore. He'd been good to her, and it was time she grew up and took responsibility.

Two, she had to get out of here and set them both free, because he was never going to do it. If she didn't go now when there was just one of her, she'd be trapped here until they made other plans, sitting upstairs above the pub with a screaming baby night after night listening to the noise of happiness, of life going on below her. It was time to leave.

The pain got worse as Karen rang the cab company again.

"Could you tell the driver I'll need a hand with the bag? And—"

She gave a strangled cry and bent over the bed, breathing hard and trying to moan into the pillow, sweat running down her forehead into her hair.

"Ma'am? Are you all right, ma'am?"

"Yes. I'm pre—*aaah.*"

Karen rested the phone on the duvet. She took a deep breath, trying to calm herself. This couldn't be it; there was no other sign, nothing. It had come on so suddenly, and she wasn't due for another two weeks, no matter what they'd said at the scan about her due date being earlier than she reckoned. She knew the last time she and Joe had slept together, of course she did. It was false labor, she'd had it for days now. She looked at her watch.

"Ma'am? The cabdriver is just outside now."

It was do or die. She had a few minutes to get downstairs in case it started again, and she wanted to be in plenty of time for her train. Karen gritted her teeth. "Thank you," she said, and she put the phone down.

In the center of the coffee table she carefully placed the note she'd written. She'd spent days composing it in her head, setting down carefully and concisely the reason for her departure; and then, at the last minute, writing it out this morning, had suddenly scrawled at the bottom:

> *PS I think you're in love with Cat. I don't know if you realize it, but you ought to do something about it. She's in love with you too. I want you to be happy, Joe. You're a good man. X*

She eventually got herself downstairs, and as she appeared in the bright sunshine the cabdriver stared at her. Karen realized she must look a sight. Her hair was tied up on top of her head, her shapeless brown maxi-dress looked like potato sacking, and she was bright red, sweating, mascara running down her cheeks. But she straightened herself up and smiled at him. "Thanks. We're going to Bristol Parkway. I need to catch a twelve p.m. train." And she buried her head in her handbag, leaning over the seat to check she'd got everything, buying herself a few seconds' time to stop panting.

"I don't know, ma'am," the taxi driver said doubtfully. "I don't know if you should be traveling. I heard you screaming upstairs—are you, uh, in some kind of trouble?"

Karen faced him, hoping that one day, when this was all a long way in the past, she'd be able to look back and laugh at that moment. *In some kind of trouble.* "I'm fine," she said firmly, shielding her eyes from the sun. "I just need—" She stopped. "I just need you to take me to the station."

"Are you going to have the baby?"

"At some point, love," she said in her sharpest voice. "That's why I don't want to stand around chatting. Okay? My bag's upstairs, could you be very kind and fetch it for me?"

He disappeared upstairs and reappeared with her suitcase, but it was all done with a bad grace. Heaving it into the car, and staring at her again, he said, "Look, I need to call the office again. 'Cause I don't think we're insured—health and safety. . . ." he said vaguely.

Karen closed her eyes, trying to stay calm, trying not to burst into tears. "Listen. I booked you and asked you to take me on a job. Are you going to do it or not?"

"I'll take you," said a cool, quiet voice behind her, and Karen froze, as though caught in the act. "I'll take you, Karen," and she turned round, and there was Bill.

Slowly, Karen stood up straight.

"Hello," he said.

"Bill. Hi."

He patted the back of his neck awkwardly. "How are you?"

Karen swallowed. "I'm—not too good. This idiot won't take me to the station."

"How strange." He was eating an apple, and he wrapped it up carefully in a paper napkin—it was a very Bill gesture, and the calm familiarity made her head spin. "Where do you want to go?"

"Bristol Parkway," she said, trying not to sound panicked. "I just want to go home."

She hadn't seen him for weeks. He'd kept himself to himself, and she'd heard he'd been away too, to join his mother visiting Florence in Italy, the trip he was always trying to get her to take. He was tanned, and smiling slightly. Karen stared at him as if he were a long, cold drink, something icy and sweet.

The cabdriver had got off the phone with his head office. He jammed his hands awkwardly on his hips. "Listen, love. I can't take you. Insurance won't cover it. Sorry."

"Hey . . ." Karen looked wildly around her at the quiet high street, baking in the late morning heat. "But I need to go now!"

Bill said again, "I'll take you."

"Don't joke with me," she said, almost crying. She pulled her suitcase out of the back so swiftly that Bill didn't have time to get it, and she nearly hit him with it as he leaped forward to try to take its bulk. The car engine revved and she stepped back, exhausted.

"Screw you! You jerk!" she shouted at the taxi driver as he sped away, tires screeching. He beeped his horn, aggressively and long, as he passed out of the village and up the hill, and Karen turned to Bill. "Look," she said brokenly, "I'm going home to Mum. I have to get there soon. Otherwise . . ." She paused, wincing.

"Otherwise you're going to have the baby in the street," Bill said.

"It's not that," Karen said. "It's not coming just yet."

"I wouldn't be too sure of that," he said.

"How the hell do you know?"

"Well . . . I'm a doctor. I do know some things, Karen." His arm tightened gently on hers. "Look, come ho—come back to New Cottages."

"No, Bill!" she said, raising her voice. "I'm not coming back with you! I'm not!"

An old man, passing slowly on the other side of the narrow street, looked over curiously, then stared straight ahead.

"I'm not trying to kidnap you. I just mean so that you can sit down, have some ice. I'll check you over and we'll see what to do next. Okay?"

He held out his arm. Karen stared at the pub, at the long, narrow stairs leading up to the flat. Maybe she should go back up there, plonk herself down on the sofa for the rest of the day, and wait for Joe to finish work this evening, then act like none of this had happened.

She couldn't. No matter how mad it seemed, now that she had decided upon this course of action, she had to keep moving. "I'm leaving Joe," she said, taking Bill's arm, and they set off, Bill pulling her suitcase. "I know this isn't the best way to have this conversation, but it's not going to work out, us living together like that."

She didn't know what he'd say to this, and she supposed he had the right to say anything, but he stopped and said mildly, "Well, good that you realized it now, I suppose. What does he think?"

Karen ignored this. "I think it's best if I go back to Mum's. Then see what's what."

"Right," Bill said. "That seems sane."

"Don't make fun of me," she said quietly. A tear rolled down her cheek.

Bill stopped pulling her case. He stood in front of her on the narrow pavement and wiped the trembling tear away with one finger and said softly, "I'd never do that, Karen. I'm sure you've made the right decision. You always were good at rational thinking. Most of the time. Keep walking."

She remembered why she'd liked him so much at the start—he'd never been threatened by her, where so many men were. That she could work out the tip on a bill faster, could drive better, drink more, strategize better. That first year they'd been dating, he'd bought her *The 7 Habits of Highly Effective People* and read it out to her on holiday in the Seychelles while she sunbathed with the dedication of a pro.

And she remembered too how much they had both loved her tanned, glowing body, slick with cream, and the hot, lazy afternoons with cool wind blowing in through the room as they made love for hours, each as surprised as the other by how close, how good it felt to be together, how right it was. His kind, steady gaze on her, his huge smile that broke over him after they'd finished, his boyishness. He really was a little boy in so many ways, pretending to be old and grown-up, but really wanting approval, wanting to make people feel better.

He'd asked her to marry him in Bristol, at the top of the Cabot Tower, overlooking the whole of the city. And afterward they'd walked down past a playground, and he'd sat on a swing while she'd fastened her shoe, and she'd seen him there, clutching the cold chains of the swing, feet scuffing the ground, watching her with this look in his eyes, so happy and smiling and warm, swaying gently back and forward. So hopeful. So glad.

Karen blushed, pushing the thoughts away. "So, how have you been, Bill?" she said as they progressed slowly up the street, Bill carrying her small case.

"I'm well, thanks. Been busy."

"How was Italy? You were there, weren't you?" She leaned on him, grateful for the strength of his right arm.

"Yes, four days. It was great, actually. Didn't do very much, just pottered around. Flo's flat is wonderful."

"Is she glad about the court case?" Karen asked.

"Oh, she's much more pleased than she lets on. Some TV producers want to make a pilot with her. Don't you think she'd be wonderful on TV?" Bill smiled. "I can see her, waving her arms around in front of some painting, can't you?"

One foot in front of the other, slowly and surely. Already Karen felt calmer. "Yes," she said. "She'd be absolutely great." She added, "Good for Florence. I'm so happy for her."

"Me—me too. We've just worked out Skype, you know. It's great. She's coming back for a visit in August, and Ma's already worked up about it."

"Is she? Why?"

Bill hesitated. "Long story. Daisy . . . you know. Dad . . . all of it." He looked at her, and a sweetly sad look came into his eyes. "Some other time." She didn't have the right to hear any more about his family, about Winterfold, she knew. "I think Flo pretends to like being alone, but she doesn't, not really." He stopped. "I don't think anyone does."

They were silent for a few minutes. As they passed the church, Bill cleared his throat delicately.

"So, does Joe know you've left him?"

"No."

"Shouldn't you tell him?"

"I've left him a note."

They were back at their old home. "I'm sure you're right, Karen. But I don't know why you have to leave today, this very minute." Bill opened the door and she went in, grateful for the front room that had always seemed so poky and was now welcomingly cool and fresh.

She heaved herself onto the sofa. "I have to get to Mum's before the baby's born. Otherwise I'd have been there—been trapped there, above that pub. I wouldn't have been able to get away."

Bill stood in front of her, chewing a finger, and he said quietly, "Of course you would. Do you really think that?"

"Yes," she said sharply. "Look, Bill, thank you, but can you just get me a glass of water and the keys and we'll go? Oh. *Oh* . . ."

She turned on the sofa, sliding herself slowly onto the ground until she was on all fours, eyes squinting, trying to focus on the shelves, counting anything she could in an effort not to scream at the splitting pain that seemed to twist her in two. She didn't care where Bill was, whether he was watching her. It seemed to last for an age, and when it was over, she sat back on the sofa again, light-headed, clammy, legs sticking out in front of her like a child's.

Bill put a glass of water in front of her on the cool glass table.

"Karen, will you let me examine you?"

"What?" She blinked. "No! No way."

He grinned. "Why do I keep having to remind you that I'm a doctor, Karen? You were always complaining about me working too hard, you'd think you'd remember why I wasn't around."

"I don't care. You're not—" She stifled a moan of pain.

"Oh, my love." He looked at her with concern. "I really do think you're in labor, you know. I've seen plenty of contractions in my time. That was a contraction. Has your water broken?"

She shook her head miserably. "No. It's all fine. I just need you to—" But her voice cracked into a whisper.

He crouched down in front of her. "I'll take you there."

"To Mum's?"

"No. To the hospital. Here in Bath. The RUH. And after that, I'll drive you to your mum's. Promise. If that's what you want, I'll pack up your stuff, I'll collect you and the baby and drive you over. It's two hours, three hours. Please, don't keep worrying about that."

"Why would you do that?"

"You're my wife, Karen," he said, and there was a catch in his voice.

"You mean because this is your kid according to the law." Karen buried her head in her hands.

Bill shrugged. "No, because we're not divorced yet and I promised to love and protect you. That's why." Karen looked up, and thought she'd never realized before how much he looked like his father. "I still love you. Don't worry, it's not a big deal, I'll get over it at some point. But I want to look after you because you need some help and you're—you're having a baby. It's a wonderful thing, whatever the circumstances." He picked up his car keys. "Will you trust me?"

"Why are you doing this?" She wiped the clammy nape of her neck.

"Because . . . well, what I just said."

"Oh."

"And because I—I didn't do enough when we were together. I was too . . . too stiff. Not enough like my dad, you know." He rolled up his sleeves. "But don't let's think about that now. You've got enough on your plate."

"That's nice of you, Bill." She wanted to tell him how sorry she was. How she'd got them all wrong, called them snobs, and she was the snob. How much she wished she could be a part of it all again, only—she shook her head, waiting for the next wave of pain.

"Come on, then," he said.

"Just give me a minute. Let me sit still for just a moment."

He smiled and sat down next to her. "You know," he said conversationally, "I've been thinking of moving back to Bristol anyway. I always liked it there."

"I like Bristol too. . . ."

She thought afterward she'd heard a soft, high *pop*, but she must have been mistaken. But suddenly there was water everywhere, gushing onto the floor, coming out of her like a torrent. She rubbed her tired eyes, tried to stand up. "Look—oh! Oh, no, I'm so sorry. Oh, God. I've peed all over the sofa. Oh, my God! Oh, my flaming God!"

Bill looked down. "No. But now your water has broken. I told you you were in labor. Let's go."

She sat still for a moment. "The sofa's ruined! I loved this sofa!"

"I hated it," he said.

Karen glanced away from her stomach. "What? We bought it at the leather workshop sale! You said you loved that color."

"It's slippery, and it doesn't fit in here. Nothing really fits in here." Bill put his jacket on and jangled his keys in his pocket. "Come on, then," he said calmly. "I'm making no promises, but I'd say you'll be a mum by teatime."

"Bill . . ." Karen looked down at the mess of her water, the immaculate sofa and floor awash in sticky gloop. "Thanks."

She wanted to say more, wanted to tell him how he'd broken her heart, slowly driven her away, how she'd loved him so much. But of course she couldn't, not right now. "I—I never meant to hurt you," she said, and then she smiled. "You know? That's crap. I did want to hurt you. I wanted you to notice me."

He was bending over to pick up her bag, and at that he straightened up, his expression tight. He said in a small voice, "I always noticed you."

"You didn't, Bill. I'm sorry. I'm so sorry, but you nearly sent me mad. You did!" She was laughing, through her tears.

"Oh." Bill swallowed. He closed his eyes briefly, as if in pain, and nodded. "I expect I did. I got used to doing my own thing when I was growing up, as Lucy keeps pointing out to me. I had to. I've changed, anyway. Hope so."

She put her hand on his arm. "Bill. I shouldn't have said it, now's not the time, let's—"

"It's the perfect time." His sad, sweet face broke into a smile. "Karen, come on, stand up—otherwise I'll carry you to the hospital myself and very likely you'll have to give birth in a hedge. I won't leave you. Let's worry about the rest of it all later. Deal?"

"Deal," Karen said. They nodded, smiling at one another, and then Bill heaved her to her feet and slung her bag over his shoulder, and they left the house, shutting the door on the ruined sofa, the immaculate front room, and the plastic gerberas, the home that had never quite worked for them.

Cat

July 2013

"I THINK A surprise party's a terrible idea," said Cat, finishing her coffee. "Isn't it a bit much, having a party that says basically 'We love you even though it turns out you're adopted and you don't know where your mother or your father is'?"

"No!" said Lucy, outraged. "Cat, where's your sense of soul?" She leaned across the kitchen table and pulled the butter dish toward her. "Listen, it'll be great." She began vigorously buttering her toast. "A welcome-home party, you know? A big banner and everything. For you and Luke, too. Dad can come, with Bella and Karen. Everyone together."

"What would it say? WELCOME HOME, EVERYONE?" Cat said, trying not to laugh at Lucy's enthusiasm. "AGAIN?"

"Exactly." Lucy looked at her. "Oh, you're taking the piss."

"I'm just not sure . . . does Florence want a big banner saying, 'Hi, you're adopted'? What about Karen?"

"Hmm," said Lucy. "Karen doesn't notice anything these days other than Bella."

Cat knew from Facebook that two-month-old Bella Winter (she had Bill's name, and Bill was certainly featured prominently in all the photos) was a gorgeous little thing, although according to Lucy she didn't sleep and was already showing signs of taking after her mother, in that she was extremely determined and spent a lot of time glowering at you, when her eyes were open.

"I bet your dad doesn't mind."

"He doesn't, actually. You know Dad. But"—Lucy lowered her voice—"they're doing a paternity test."

"Really?"

"He said he has to know if she's his or not. I don't think he'll mind if she's not his. I mean . . ." They looked at each other. "Ugh, well, let's not get into the merits of my father's . . . reproductive stuff versus Joe Thorne's. It doesn't bear thinking about. Oh! Completely ick. Let's move on. So I thought a nice welcome-back party for Florence and at the same time we can all say hi Bella, et cetera." Cat put her head on one side. Lucy said, "Well, I like it. Maybe we make it a christening party instead. I'm going to suggest it to Gran when she gets back from London."

"How long's she there for?"

Lucy shrugged. "She said two days. She has to approve the exhibition, she said. I don't believe her, though."

"What do you mean?"

"Don't know. Sure it's nothing serious. She's so different now."

"Yes, she is," said Cat. "Even from before, when Southpaw was alive. It's strange, isn't it? I can't think of the word."

"So . . ." Lucy buttered her toast, and gazed out of the window. "So light-hearted. That's what it is. Poor Gran." They were both silent, and then she said, "Look how lovely it is outside. I think it was a great idea of mine, having a staycation here."

"Brilliant," Cat said. "Oh, Luce, it's lovely to see you again."

She dipped the last of her bread into her coffee, to hide the tears that sprang to her eyes. Everything made her cry these days, these last few months. As if she was making up for the years of control. She cried at the news, at a dead bunny rabbit by the road. She cried when the teacher at Luke's new nursery said he was a "sweet, kind boy."

"Me too, Cat. Do you miss anything about Paris?" Lucy said thoughtfully, chewing her toast.

"Proper croissants. And Petit Marseillais shower gel. That's it." She hesitated. "Not really. I do miss it, I suppose. I miss—something in the air. The feeling of walking through the streets first thing in the morning, there's something about it that's magical; you could sense it, even on the worst days."

Lucy said, "Well, we should go back there someday. I'd love to go to Paris properly. You could show me the sights."

Even though she was younger, Lucy always knew what to do, always had since they were little. There was such comfort in that. "That'd be a great idea, actually. I don't want Luke to forget that part of his life." She hesitated, her mouth suddenly dry. "I want him to remember he's half-French, even if he never sees Olivier again." It was the first time she'd said his name in a long time, and it surprised her, how little weight it carried. She was strong now.

She glanced into the window and smiled. The two cousins sat opposite each other, in the same position as they had done all their lives: Lucy hunched over her food, feet on the bar of the chair, licking the crumbs off her fingertips; Cat in the worn blue chair she always sat in, her elbows spread-eagled on the table, fingers pressing into her cheeks, watching her cousin, younger, brighter, irrepressibly more alive than she.

"Do you know," she said suddenly, "Luke asked me what my favorite song was yesterday, because Zach's favorite song is "Firework" by Katy Perry, and everything Zach does is apparently perfect. And I didn't know what to say. I had to go upstairs and look through an old box of CDs to remember what music I used to like. It's as though . . . oh, I blame myself, but he really did strip me down to nothing, Olivier."

"Why on earth do you blame yourself?" Lucy demanded. "It was an abusive relationship, Cat. Don't smile and shake your head. It was. How on earth can you blame yourself?"

Cat felt a red flush rising up her neck, and she crossed her arms and gave a twisted smile that she hoped didn't look as bitter as she felt. "You always do, Luce, no matter what everyone tells you. You just do." There was a gentle breeze at the window, honeysuckle and roses, and she stood up. "I have to go to work. Are you sure you don't mind picking Luke up from Zach's?"

"Absolutely not," said Lucy. "I'm going to go back to bed for a while. Read the paper. Stretch out and think about what I'm going to do with the rest of my week."

"Find another job?"

"I don't think anyone'd have me, to be honest," Lucy said.

"Write a best-selling novel about our family?" Cat saw the look that flashed across her cousin's eyes. "Oh! Oh, I'm so right. What a guess! You are. You're going to write a novel. Can I have a good name?"

"Don't be ridiculous." Lucy took her plate over to the sink grumpily. "I'm not, and even if I were to, I certainly wouldn't tell anyone about it." She dropped the cutlery into the dishwasher with a clatter.

"Okay," said Cat, disbelieving. "Well, good for you. Can I be called Jacquetta? I've always wanted to be called Jacquetta."

"Look, for the last time, stop going on about it." Lucy was bent over the dishwasher. "I'm not going to. Anyway, I've got enough on at the moment, what with Dad and Karen. I've said I'll help out with Bella when they're back from her mum's." She rolled her eyes. "Wherever they end up. And I said I'd help Gran field everything for Southpaw's exhibition. It's moved to October now, and already people are asking me about it. Then find a new job that I don't hate."

"You know, no one likes their job when they're starting out. Or loads of people don't. I think you're too hard on yourself."

"Believe me, I'm not." Lucy poured herself some more coffee and stood in the doorway. "Honestly. Don't worry about me. I just have to figure it out. I know what it is, I just need to wait a bit. Like Liesl in *The Sound of Music*. I know I want to be a writer, but I'm not sure how I'll do it yet. Some people are born knowing what they want to do, like Dad being a doctor. Or Southpaw being an artist."

"Southpaw told me once that he absolutely hated his job at first. He wanted to be a serious artist, and he kept getting asked to do these cartoons to go with theater reviews of John Gielgud in *Richard II* or pictures of ladies waiting at the vet with their sick parrots. And he wanted to tell the story of where he grew up, and no one was interested. And then he came up with Wilbur, out of the blue."

"Well, he owned him already, he was his dog," Lucy said.

"Yes, but he had the idea to make him into a cartoon, I suppose. All I mean is, he got a bit sick of Wilbur over the years. I remember him in tears when his arthritis was bad, saying he couldn't do it anymore. But he kept on, didn't he? He loved it because he knew how much other people loved it. He was a real people-pleaser, Southpaw."

Lucy opened her mouth to say something.

"What?" said Cat.

"Doesn't matter," said Lucy. "It was about Wilbur. I think he had a trick to get by toward the end. If that helps. Anyway, what's your point?"

"Oh. Well . . ." Cat felt as though there had been an eddy in the conversation that she'd missed, and she wondered if she had gone too far, teasing Lucy. "I just mean we don't all have our dream jobs. Someone to love and someone to love you and enough to eat and enough to drink, isn't that how the saying goes? That's all you can hope for, that's more than most people."

"Okay, thanks, coz," said Lucy solemnly, and she nodded. "Deep."

"Very deep," said Cat. She slung her bag across her body. "See you later, coz."

Cat loved the walk to work. Down the winding lane from Winterfold to the village, the hedgerows heavy with summer green, wood pigeons cooing in the midday haze. She cut through the field at the bottom, swinging her long legs over the stile, glancing at the blackberry bushes fringing the road. The fruits were still tight and green, but a few showed a hint of pinkish-purple. Joe had said they'd go out to pick blackberries in a few weeks, for crumbles, jam, coulis. He was supposed to be coming up to Winterfold next week to look at the apples—Martha had told him he could have as many as he wanted when they were ripe. Not for a month or two now, but soon. Autumn was coming. Not now, but it was coming. Nearly a year since Gran had sent out the invites. A whole year, and everything had changed.

Much as she loved working at the pub, she knew she needed a project, something that gave her a future here. Apart from anything else, she didn't want to live off her grandmother forever. Lovely as it was at Winterfold, it wasn't her home, though to wake up in that old room every morning, to come down to breakfast and look out over the hills and touch the warm wood, to watch Luke run himself ragged with whoever was around in the garden, was a dream she never wanted to wake up from. But she wanted her life to feel real again, for the first time in years. She wanted a stake of her own, because she knew she and Luke belonged here, in these comforting green hills.

Her mother's ashes had been scattered here too. Perhaps a scintilla of her was in the air she breathed. In her, in Luke, on the leaves of the apple trees, in the daisy bank, settling over the house. Daisy had been cremated a week after the magistrates' court had fined Martha and released her. They had scattered the ashes in the garden. Cat had been home a week when the ceremony, if it could be called that, had taken place. She'd been weeding the vegetable patch when Martha had stood at the kitchen door and called out, "I think we should do it now." So Cat had gone up to her room, her mother's room it had been too, and changed out of her jeans into a dress. Silly, but she felt she ought to. Some kind of observance for Daisy, who'd chosen this way out, but who'd never had a proper good-bye. And when she came downstairs again, Natalie the lawyer, Kathy the vicar, and Bill were all in the garden too.

"I asked them," her grandmother had said. "I thought it would be right."

They stood quietly, and Bill smiled at Cat and squeezed her arm as she passed him, and she was suddenly very afraid of the whole thing. Because Gran asked her to, Cat took the first handful, fumbling fingers feeling the cold metal and then the gray powder, throwing it gingerly out into the breeze. So little ash for a whole person.

She'd handed the urn to Martha, and seen her grandmother's unreadable expression. Grim, her mouth clamped shut in a straight line. She stayed still, not moving, and Cat didn't know what to do; but Bill had reached forward, taken the urn, and said quietly, "Good-bye, Daisy. Rest well now."

He shook the contents of the urn into his palms, and then ran forward. They were facing the orchard, down toward the valley. Bill threw his arms up in the air, and the afternoon sun picked up the motes of ash as, like a swarm of bees or wasps, it glided, almost golden, airborne for a few seconds, then sank into nothing.

Now there was nothing to show Daisy had ever been here. It made Cat sad, in a way, and in another way she finally understood the truth, which was that Daisy hadn't really ever existed properly in this place anyway. She hadn't ever really been Cat's mother, or Bill's sister, or Gran's daughter. Had she ever been herself somewhere else, or not? And still it terrified Cat, though she couldn't say this to anyone. Was she like her mother? Was there something, something stopping her? She thought often of how successfully she had convinced Joe that she was over him. How easy it was to push him away, suppress her feelings. Because it was easy to keep yourself covered up, and very, very hard to peel down to that layer, the one that smarted in the sun, shrank from touch.

Cat leaped over the final stile and crossed the lane toward the pub. It was quiet when she entered, no one in the bar except for the radio, playing

"Call Me Maybe." She could hear Sheila, out in the garden at the back, singing along. Cat followed the noise.

Sheila was on the tiny pub terrace, bending over and snipping rosemary off a tiny plant, slipping the sprigs into her apron pocket, all the while miming a *call me* motion with her hand as a substitute phone. "Hello, my love. We're short-staffed again. John's off again. Says it's his varicose veins, but I don't believe it. He's twenty-eight, he don't have varicose veins. He heard it off Dawn complaining about hers, I bet you. He's hungover. The little tinker." She suddenly yelled out, " 'Call me maybe!' " There was a long pause, the music playing in the background; then she bellowed again, " 'Call me maybe!' I don't know the words," she said as Cat watched her, laughing.

"You know *some* of the words," Cat said.

"Oh, what a song. What a song. Better than 'Blurred Lines,' all that nasty talk in the rap." She tunelessly hummed the chorus, making it into complete gobbledygook. "What can I do you for, my dear?"

Cat looked round for Joe, but he wasn't in the kitchen, and she peered into the bar, but couldn't see him there either. She took the scissors out of Sheila's hands, playing for time. "You shouldn't be doing that with your back. What else do you need?"

"Very kind of you, my dear. What did I do before you came along? We need some thyme. Parsley, big bunch of it. And some tarragon."

"Oh." Cat started cutting. She looked up at the fence. "Hey, Sheila, I was thinking something."

"Oh, dance here," Sheila said. "I love this bit. She's got a great way about her with a song, hasn't she? I love dancing."

"Me too," Cat said, beaming. "Me too!"

They danced round the garden a bit, clapping their hands and singing, laughing together, and eventually Sheila leaned against the windowsill and turned the radio down. "Ooh, my sides. You have brightened this place up, Cat, you really have."

"Oh, right." Cat shrugged, trying not to show how much this pleased her, and pulled her cardigan off. "I wanted to ask you, Sheila. I've talked about this with Joe, but it was a while ago now. Have you ever thought of extending the garden? Making a vegetable patch down the back, putting some tables out under an awning?"

"Well, we were going to, this summer. But it got away from us, what with one thing and another. Now I'm off to Weston tomorrow, and he's ever so cross with me. Doesn't understand why I want a holiday." Sheila crossed her arms. "Ooh, the way he is at the moment, it's work, work, work. He wants everything yesterday, that's his trouble. Well, he'll have to wait."

"Joe's lucky to have you."

Sheila chuckled. "My dear, I'm lucky to have him. Bless his heart. For all his moods, and he's a right pain at the moment, isn't he?"

"How do you mean?" Cat kept her voice level.

"Oh, Cat, you know. He's like a bear with a sore head lately."

"Karen?"

"Of course. He's devastated. Never known him like this."

Cat moved on to the tarragon bush. "I just—I thought maybe he'd be glad. I never knew—right, that's . . ." She knew Sheila was watching her curiously, and she swallowed, trying to sound normal, any earlier jollity all gone. "It must be very hard for him." As she handed Sheila a bunch of herbs, she was alarmed to feel her cheeks flaming red. She changed the subject. "What about the herb garden, kitchen garden, then? Should we choose a time when you're free to talk it over properly?"

Sheila nodded, watching her. "Good idea." She leaned against the window ledge and banged on the window, which Cat now saw was open. "He's back. Hey, Joe! Get out here! Cat's telling us how we ought to do the garden. You should have a chat with her. I'm sure she's right."

A few seconds later Joe appeared in the doorway. "Hello, Cat." He nodded at her.

"Hi," she said. Any easy communication they'd had earlier in the summer was gone since Karen had left, and the past fortnight he'd barely spoken at all. The one time Cat had stopped him and ventured to ask how he was, in the dark passageway out to the garden, Joe had stopped, fists clenched, and stared at her. "Fine, thank you for asking. Why?"

"Oh. No reason. Just—been a while since we talked."

"Yes. I'm in the middle of something, Cat, I'm sorry. Best get on." Then he'd pushed open the door to the gents', leaving her standing in the passageway feeling like an unwelcome smell.

Now he stood in front of them, his arms crossed. "Sheila, the portobellos weren't in the veg box this morning. Can you call the suppliers and find out what's happened to them? Otherwise we've only got two main courses today."

"I'll murder them, I will. That's the third time this month." Sheila heaved herself off the window ledge. "Cat, you come and find me later," she called. "Joe, get her to tell you her idea. It's a good one, it is. Stop this from happening again."

The two of them were left standing on the shaded patio, where the sun hadn't yet arrived. "Excuse me, will you? I need to check the soup," Joe said, and he turned back inside.

Cat followed him into the cluttered white kitchen. She watched a buzzing fly, dangerously close to the ultraviolet insect killer, high up on the wall. "It's quiet today for once," she said, wishing she was better at small talk.

"It's July. I've got two people away and a reviewer and a party of ten in for lunch. You'll be busy, I should think." He said it with almost grim satisfaction. "So, what's up, then?"

Cat looked around for a place to stand. She felt in the way, and she didn't want to talk to him if he was going to be like this. She'd thought he wasn't the type to be moody, the kind who liked watching others squirm because he dictated the atmosphere—she was wrong, though. How could he be acting like this?

"Joe—it's about the garden—but it doesn't matter today."

"Not today?"

"No. Another time."

His tired eyes narrowed to a flinty stare. "Have you been talking to Lucy?"

"Lucy? Yes, why?" Cat said, surprised.

"You Winters. You stick together, don't you? I should have remembered." He looked at her angrily, something like disgust on his face, as if she were a grub on a fresh green lettuce.

"What's Lucy got to do with it?"

"You know perfectly well, Cat. You waltz in here making a racket dancing round the garden with Sheila, trying to get her into your little gang too. 'Hi, I'm one of them, everyone loves us, we're better than the rest of them.'"

Cat felt as if he'd slapped her. "What the hell does that mean?" she demanded. "You've got totally the wrong idea about us. We're not glued together like some clan."

"'Clan.' Very posh." His expression was ugly.

"Oh, shut up," Cat said, fury suddenly uncoiling inside her. "It's all in your head, whatever it is. These past few weeks, the way you blow hot and cold. Stop going on like you've got some chip on your shoulder about—"

"Chip on my shoulder?" he shouted, and she stepped back, astonished. "That's funny, Cat. I could almost laugh at that." He looked away and covered his eyes with his arm, then looked back. "You should all be glad to kiss my boots—that baby'll grow up and one day she'll wish it had been the other way. That I was her dad. But I'm not, am I? She's stuck with you lot. What a life." He turned his back on her, and began grinding garlic cloves with the head of a wooden spoon.

"Oh, Joe." Cat cleared her throat. "Is it little Bella?" She bit her lip. "Joe? Did they get the tests back?"

He didn't answer, just carried on pounding the garlic, pulling the skins off and smashing the cloves to pulp. Cat watched his curved back slump. Her eyes stung. She could hear his breathing.

"She's Bill's, isn't she? Joe, I'm so sorry."

She couldn't see his face. "Why are you sorry? I've not met her, I don't know her."

"I thought it'd be nice for you if she was—" That sounded completely wrong. "I—I just wanted you to be happy." The atmosphere was excruciating. She wiped her hand across her brow. "Look, I shouldn't have asked. I'm sorry."

"No." Joe put the spoon down, back still to her. "I'm the one who's sorry. I'm sorry for yelling like that." He stared out the window. "I shouldn't have taken it out on you, you . . . Never mind."

"You really wanted her to be yours, didn't you?"

He shrugged. "Maybe."

Cat reached forward and gave him a tiny pat on the back, then stepped back. He hung his head, hand up to his eyes.

"It's silly things. Seeing Luke . . . every time I see him around, I think of Jamie. And I think, *Oh well, Jamie's met Luke, they played together, so at least when I'm looking at your son there's a connection to mine even if he's—he's two hundred miles away.* 'Cause I miss him that much. Does that sound mad?"

When Daisy came home when Cat was eight, for a week, Cat had memorized everything she'd touched in the house. The William Morris print book. The orange casserole dish. The phone. The chair on the right of Southpaw's in the kitchen, painted blue many years ago, worn at the edges. She still sat in that chair out of habit, every time. That was why. It occurred to her only now that that was why. "I know what you mean, Joe."

"I thought it'd be different with this one. And there it is, I'm not even her dad." He turned round and gave her a small smile. "I only found out this morning. Came in the post. Old-fashioned . . . and I wasn't expecting it. Just a bit of a shock . . ." He trailed off, his head hanging. She thought he might be crying and moved toward him, patting his arm softly.

"It must be really hard."

This time he didn't stop her. He said quietly, "I went to work one day and I said bye to her before I left, and she looked at me and said, 'Thanks, Joe.' And I thought it was weird. 'Thanks, Joe.' I get back and she's gone. Nothing left of her."

"Do you want to see her? See Bella, anyway? I'm sure she'll be back. You never know, this thing with Bill . . ."

But he gave her a strange look. "They'll be all right together. I knew it all along. Always."

"Really?" Cat said.

"She needs an older man, Karen does. She needs someone who's a different pace from her. He can look after Bella and she can take on the world."

"I never really understood them, to be honest," Cat said. "I like her, I love him, he's my uncle. I just don't get them together."

"Don't you? I do. More than she did, I think. Look, I have to get on, Cat. Sorry again. I really didn't mean to bite your head off."

Cat nodded. "Honestly, Joe, it's fine." She dared to reach out and pat his arm, wondering if maybe he'd start yelling again, but he didn't. "I wish it didn't make you so sad. Look—if you need to chat to anyone, okay?"

"Okay," he said. "Thanks. You're a good friend."

She wished there was something else she could do: wrench that baby away from Bill and give her to Joe, for just a couple of hours, so he could at least see her, say hello. Cat shut the kitchen door quietly behind her and went out into the pub.

"Cat, can you fold the napkins?" Sheila said from behind the bar. She pointed at a basket of gleaming snowy linen.

"Sure. Need to hurry now, I suppose."

She was talking to herself really, not to Sheila. Though it was still a beautiful day, she shivered in the cool of the bar. Trying to ignore the old voice that shouted, that tried to panic her, bring her down again. The voice that said she was like her mother, that Luke was in danger, that relationships were trouble, that life was better small and cozy, not loud and scary and exhilarating like the roller coaster at the fairground they'd been to last week on the Bristol Downs. She hummed "Call Me Maybe" as she folded the napkins. She had almost learned to ignore the voice. Almost.

"Did you talk to him, then?" Sheila asked. "Joe?"

"Now's not a good time," Cat said, pressing down on the pile and feeling the cold smoothness of the linen beneath her skin.

Martha

August 2013

THAT MORNING, HER eyes flew open, and she realized she had barely been asleep. She had been thinking, dreaming again. It was happening a lot lately.

As she lay in bed staring at the beams on the ceiling, Martha's dream came back to her. The disastrous summer party: was it 1978 or '79? Such a long time since she'd thought about it, and there it was, a fully formed memory, like a settled snow globe.

It had been a terrible summer. It rained for weeks. The lawn was a bog, so bad that Hadley (their dog after Wilbur, a tough act to follow), who was of a nervous disposition, sank into it whenever he went outside for a run around and had to be unplugged like a suction cup. The iron-with-plastic-carapace DIY gazebo did not exist then, and so Martha, helped but mostly hindered by David, constructed her usual awning out of a shaky combination of bamboo sticks, two iron poles, and plastic sheeting, which was folded away neatly each year and shaken out onto the lawn in August once again, rampant with spiders that scuttled across the neat grass. The action of taking the awning out, spreading it across the grass—it was summer for her, just like Studland Bay, and David's hat, which he wore every day the sun shone.

That year, despite the ceaseless rain, Martha and David had put up the awning, decorated the tables, organized the food, and waited for evening. Secretly, she hoped some of the guests might cry off—but no, they tramped up the drive in wellies, in long floral floating dresses, in caftans and jeans, in suits and ties. Martha watched them crowding under the awning with a kind of bemused despair. There they all stayed for the rest of the evening, staring out at the drizzling, misty garden, which she'd worked so hard in all summer, so that it would look perfect for this one night. The *High Society* album was playing on the gramophone in the sitting room, the window ajar so that Louis Armstrong and Bing Crosby floated out across the garden. The women sank farther into the grass, all except sixteen-year-old Florence, who took immense pride in pointing out to everyone that she was wearing flip-flops. Bill, on holiday from medical school, all Adam's apple and legs, dutifully handed round drinks, chatting politely, asking after people's holidays, people's children, people's health. Daisy was, as ever, nowhere to be seen. She'd been out all day. Shopping, she said. She was off to polytechnic in Kingston in the autumn, to study sociology. But her plans didn't seem quite real; with Daisy, they never did.

Usually Martha loved parties: the ideas, the little touches, the food. The bringing together of people, the delicate social tasks often required. Not tonight. She just wanted it to be over. To be inside, dry and warm. To stop having to keep an eye on Hadley, who was more hyperactive than ever, circling and wheeling around the tent, shaking wet grass and mud all over the guests. The party wasn't working; everyone was cold and formal and annoyed—with her, maybe. She wished she were tucked up in bed with a hot toddy and even a hot-water bottle, David next to her, the pair of them chuckling over the worst parts of the evening.

She could still see it now: the moment when Hadley, out of nowhere, suddenly stopped chasing his tail around on the lawn and turned, snarled at the assembled crowd, and dashed into the awning, catching a dancing piece of twine with him, crashing into the outermost pole. He made for Gerald Lang, who lived up at Stoke Hall and whom the Winters loathed: Bill said he was a cheat; Florence said he was a sex pest who'd put his hand down her top at the church fête. Now Gerald was flung to the ground as Hadley went for him.

The tent began collapsing around them and the guests fled, scream-ing. Martha could see Hadley's yellow teeth tearing into Gerald's thigh. Patricia, Gerald's formidable new wife, tried to pull the dog off him, but something had flipped inside Hadley's always slightly confused brain and it was almost impossible to detach him.

Bill, clamping his hand around Hadley's muzzle and his knees around the snarling dog's trunk, eventually managed, with one hard yank, to jerk Hadley away. The guests looked on in the rain, some screaming.

Daisy came running onto the lawn. "I've called an ambulance," she said. Then she stopped, and smiled down at Gerald. "Hope he's ripped your cock off, you disgusting man."

"Daisy!" Martha said, as David came forward with a lead and took Hadley by the collar, and locked him up in a shed at the back of the orchard.

The next day when the vet told them Hadley had been destroyed— "He has to be, I'm afraid. No saying he won't do it again, now he's done it once"—Daisy was furious. She said Martha must be mad, must be making it up, and they had a terrible, blistering, white-hot row, and Daisy went to London the day after, to stay with some school friends. She returned for a week before poly started, but only to pack. It was never really her home again.

But they didn't know that, just then. Didn't know Hadley would have to die, that Daisy would leave and not really come back, that Gerald and his new wife would never have any children and the rumor would always be that Gerald, who was to be avoided at drinks parties, as the polite parlance had it, wasn't the man he used to be. It became something of a terrible, black joke between David and Martha, a couple's private jest, which, if anyone else were to hear it, would sound utterly appalling.

After the ambulance had taken Gerald Lang away, Martha sought a moment's sanctuary in the kitchen, where she leaned on the sink, head spinning. Then she opened the kitchen door and found her son, vomiting into a bucket.

"Bit green still," he said, wiping his mouth, looking wholly ashamed. "It wasn't pretty, I'm afraid. Poor Gerald."

"You were wonderful, Bill." She gripped his shoulders. "You're so grown-up! I can't believe it. You are, aren't you! You're going to be a wonderful doctor. So brave." She kissed his hand, unbelievably proud of him. Gilbert Prundy, their old vicar, had appeared in the kitchen doorway.

"The hero of the hour. William Winter. I say, well done, old chap. Well bloody done."

The strange thing about that night was: the party went on. In fact, it went on rather late. Gilbert Prundy fetched his Oscar Peterson albums from the vicarage, and he and David sang along and danced. Kim Kowalski, the new owner of the cottage down the hill, played his guitar. They stayed outside among the ruins of the party, the torn awning muddied on the floor, useless, the old trestle table buckled and broken. The moon didn't come out that night, but after enough wine and enough Pimm's, no one really cared. The rain grew heavy at around midnight, so the guests moved inside and the party went on until dawn. And Martha, relaxed for the first time ever, enjoyed herself. Because it had been pretty much the worst party you could have, and yet they were all still there, when even the rabbits, which scampered constantly across the lawn in summer, stayed out of the rain.

She thought about that party constantly as she prepared the lunch, the first proper entertaining she'd done since David died. Poor Hadley. What was it that had set him off that day? They had constantly wondered afterward. Was it something they'd done? Eventually David had just said, "Put it down to flipped-switch syndrome." But he hadn't drawn Wilbur for about a month afterward.

She said out loud, "What did you draw during that month instead? I can't remember."

The lunch was all ready: cold cuts, pie, salads, and burgers. She moved around the kitchen, touching her familiar things, feeling very calm. *What's the worst that could happen? You've arranged it now.*

She thought about Florence and Jim, somewhere on the motorway. Lucy, singing in the shower upstairs. About Luke and Cat, down by the river. Karen and Bill, out for an early morning walk with Bella, having driven over last night from their newly rented flat in Bristol. And she thought about Bella, her newest granddaughter, whom David would never meet.

More time. All she wanted was a little more time. Not much: one more week, one more day, even just one more hour with him. That was all. Just a little more time, to sit in the kitchen as she sat now, her hands wrapped around the same old mug, gazing out of the window, to know that he was in the house too. Upstairs, shaving, singing. In his office, laughing at something. Calling out into the hallway, "Any chance of some tea, Em?"

His voice. She could hear it so clearly it might have been real. Not in her head, this once. She breathed, feeling the tight ball of pain that, ever since he died, seemed to sit above her lungs. It made her breathless, it made her cry, it made her throat swell with sadness. It was always there.

Any chance of some tea, Em?

What would happen if, for just one minute, she believed he was here, in front of her? Really believed it? Martha relaxed and closed her eyes, letting the sun warm her face.

The room was still, noises off, as if her ears were stopped up with wax. She sat, waiting. She felt something cold brush over her and found she couldn't open her eyes, didn't want to.

Then she knew he was here. That he was waiting for her, that he was here.

Martha froze. Very slowly, she opened her eyes, and he was in front of her, in the doorway. Without his stick.

"Any chance of a cup of tea, Em?"

"Yes," she said, and she smiled at him, and it was as though nothing had happened. As though he'd always been there, waiting to walk in through the door. "It's a bit thrutchy. It's been in the pot awhile."

"Fine by me." David sat down in his chair. "What's happened to this? It feels different."

"Lucy stood on it and it broke." Martha poured him some tea, unable to tear her eyes away from him. The crease in his shirt, it was real. His eyes, his chin, his chest. He really was here again, really was. She missed the mug, and tea splashed onto the table. "I fixed it."

"Of course you did," David said, and he slid the Rochester Castle tea towel over to her, his eyes crinkling, his wide smile. He was there, he was in front of her. Somehow she kept looking at him, and he didn't disappear. Somehow she kept on talking.

She said, "It's amazing what wood glue and some tape will do."

"Not amazing. You can fix anything, darling," he said, and they both drank their tea, together in the warm kitchen, nothing remarkable about it at all, really.

Suddenly Martha didn't know what to say, and the ball of grief seemed wedged so high in her throat she thought she might choke.

"I miss you, David," she said eventually, tears in her eyes.

"I know you do, Em." He couldn't smile now.

"I did it all wrong, all of it. I shouldn't have had that party."

"No, darling. They had to know. We had to tell the truth."

"But I lost you."

"I would have gone anyway." He seemed to be altering before her eyes. Was his hair less gray, more brown, was he younger every time she looked at him? "Em, I was dying. Nothing you could have done to change it. You do understand that, don't you? You had to tell them the truth about Daisy. I had to die. Those are the facts. They had to happen in their own time."

In their own time. For the first time, she believed it. "Yes."

The table was too wide, she couldn't reach over and touch him. She hesitated.

"Good," he said.

"I hate it here without you."

"I know. But before that . . ." David said. "Before that . . . we loved it. We loved it here. We were happy. We *are* happy."

Martha wiped her eyes. She cleared her throat and said, "Is it right, what I'm doing today? Is it the right thing to do?"

"Of course it is," he said.

"I don't know anymore. I don't seem to be able to fix on anything these days. They think I'm much better, but I'm not. I—we—we—" She broke off with a sob, her head bowed, rubbing at her chest.

And he said, "I'm here, you know that. I'm with you always. I won't ever go away." He stretched his hands out to her, across the table. The hands. She stared down at them. They were strong and supple, almost as good as new.

Martha tried to touch his fingers, to stretch toward him, but he didn't move.

"I can't reach you." Tears were blinding her eyes. "David, I can't—" She stood up, stumbling, and when she looked up he was gone.

There was a knock, a tiny knocking at the back door, and she started, looking around. *I was here. He was here.*

"Martha?" The door creaked open. "Ma?"

Karen came in, carrying her tiny daughter, Bill behind her.

"Everything all right?" Karen said, staring at Martha. "You look as— you're very pale."

Martha looked around wildly. He was still here, wasn't he? Behind the door, perhaps just next door.

"I—did you see someone?"

Bill looked at his mother. "Who?"

"I . . . nothing." Martha shook her head. "Nothing." She kissed her daughter-in-law's cheek and stroked her granddaughter's dark hair. As though it was normal, everything, all of it, the same; as though he wasn't there with her, but then she saw that of course he was. She looked behind them, and thought perhaps she glimpsed him there, by the doors that led to the dining room. Perhaps it was only the wind from the open casement, blowing in fresh air from outside.

She looked down at the table, and saw the mug of tea she'd given him. It was only half-full now.

"Is it all ready, then?"

"What?"

"Florence's lunch?"

"She's not here, not yet. Everything else is ready." She blinked, trying to concentrate. "Bill, I was thinking about that summer party today."

"The one when Florence got drunk on gin and sang 'Luck Be a Lady' out of the bathroom window?"

"No. The terrible one."

"Oh, my goodness. I must say . . ." Bill rubbed his eyes. ". . . that was a great party."

Martha said, "Not for Gerald, of course."

He looked contrite. "Course. Poor Gerald. I always forget about him."

"What happened?" Karen said.

"Well," Bill began, and then he stopped. "It was a long time ago. Past history."

The kitchen door slammed, with a force so great they all jumped. Martha whirled round, but there was nothing there. Bella woke and started crying, and Karen said, "I might give her a feed if she's awake. Bill, have you got my . . ."

They disappeared into the hallway, consulting in low voices.

And then someone said, "Well, I didn't expect to sleep so late. What on earth was that bang?"

A figure in the doorway, so like David that Martha started again, and her hands felt instantly clammy.

Their faces were the same shape, their eyes were the same. But she was younger, her face less lined, her skin smooth. She was slightly portly—*stately* was perhaps a better word. Reserved, a little shy maybe: when she'd arrived last night, Martha had struggled to talk to her. She hadn't seen her for nearly fifty years, and they acutely felt the absence of David and his easy conversation. She was elegant, her silver-and-gold hair twisted neatly up into an old-fashioned chignon. Like her brother, she had remade herself.

"Cassie," said Martha. She came forward. "Did you sleep well?"

"I did, and I've been up for a while. I had a bath, had a nice read of some of David's old Wilburs." She advanced into the kitchen. Martha took her hands and held them.

"I'm so glad you came. Thank you."

"Well. He wanted me to. He wanted me to come up before he died. I . . . I'm so sorry. I wish I had."

"He hadn't told me he'd even met up with you. . . ." Martha tightened her grip on Cassie's hands. "I didn't go into the study for months, you see. I didn't see your letter."

She had been up to London three times, looking for her. She had been to the Public Record Office in Kew, sat poring over parish registers and censuses, and could find nothing. She had even been to the Angel, walked around the streets David knew so well, looking for a woman who looked like him, like Florence. But there was nothing, and she had begun to despair.

It was only three days ago when, looking for something the gallery wanted for David's Muriel Street exhibition, she had finally opened the little drawer of his desk and seen it lying there. On top of old erasers, pencils worn to stubs, blotting paper, and ink cartridges. David opened that drawer each morning to get his materials out; he must have seen it every day after it arrived before his death. But now that he was dead, no one else, much less her, had thought to look in it.

Dear Davy,

I'm sorry I haven't been in touch since our drink. It was nice to see you, it really was.

I have been thinking about what you said. About family, and how we're the only ones left who remember. I'd like to come up and see you all sometime. See Florence. I'd like to meet her. Could I come to your posh house and drink tea like a lady one day? I'll be on my best behavior. How does that sound?

My phone number's on the back.

Maybe it's a bad idea. Not sure. Just thought I'd ask.

Love, Cassie
Your sister x

"I heard he died," Cassie had said when Martha immediately rang her, shaking, "but I didn't know how to ring you. I didn't know if it'd be what anyone wanted."

Florence was due home on the Saturday. She was coming here, and she was bringing Jim—who had been with her in Italy for most of the summer—ostensibly just for the night (Florence had given some excuse about how Jim needed to go to the Holburne Museum in Bath to check out a Joseph Wright of Derby portrait, but even she hadn't sounded wholly convincing about it), but it was really a much bigger event than that. Bill was bringing Bella and Karen home. Lucy and Cat and Luke would be there.

So they would all be there. It was supposed to happen. Martha kept thinking of the wasted couple of months she'd spent looking for Cassie. She thought of how, the night of David's death, Florence, unbeknown to her, had found her own birth certificate. She'd asked Florence to leave the study, and if she'd only left her in there a while longer, she might have opened the drawer, found Cassie's note.

But what if she had done? Wasn't David right? It had to happen in its own time. She, Martha, had to be ready to change things, to alter their family's script.

Cassie said: "I'd have written right away if I'd have known."

"I know, and we should have found you sooner. It's my fault."

Cassie shook her head. "It's all fine. Oh, look, Martha, I'm kind of nervous about all this," she said frankly. She sat down in David's chair. "It's so fast. Not sure, what if she freaks out? It's a big shock to land on someone."

"I know." Martha's mouth was dry. "I know. But it has to happen. She wants to meet you, I promise you. She knows I'm looking for you, that I couldn't find you anywhere."

"We liked being able to blend into a crowd, me and Davy," Cassie said. "Think we got that off our mum. We had to. Well, I'm glad. It's going to happen, it had to sometime, didn't it?"

"Yes. It did." Martha stared at her sister-in-law in David's chair, and something settled within her. She felt quiet, for the first time in a long while.

"I don't know what I'll say to her." Cassie was fiddling with her buttons, slim white fingers fluttering. "I'm not a mum, I don't know how to be a mum."

Martha took her hand. "You are a mum," she said.

The sound of car wheels on gravel. The sound of Bella crying, of Lucy clattering down the stairs, noise and chaos. Cassie sat still, clasping her hands together.

"Yes."

Martha left her alone in the kitchen, hurrying through to see the front door open.

"Flo! Jim!" Lucy was advancing toward the pair at the front of the house, with Bella in her arms. "Look, my new sister! Your new niece, Flo, look at her! Isn't she gorgeous? Look at her schmoochy cheeks." She kissed the black-haired, black-eyed Bella, who stared at her aunt, then Jim, unimpressed. "Well, come in!" Lucy said, a little too loudly.

"Thanks," said Florence, hugging Karen and Bill. "Bill," she said, gripping his elbows. "Wonderful to see you, dear brother. This, this is Jim."

With one finger pressed into his back, she propelled Jim forward, and Jim, swallowing, held out a hand. "Bill. Good to meet you. Hello, Martha." He gave her a kiss, and Martha, who had been with him in Italy at the same time, smiled and threw her arms around him.

"It's awfully good you're here," she whispered. "It really is." Then she turned to Florence. "Hello, my darling."

"Ma." Florence kissed her cheek. "Hello. Look, I brought you that almond cake you like." She thrust a large waxy packet awkwardly into Martha's hands. "Right."

There was a sort of silence. Lucy said, "You should come inside."

"Yes, please," Jim said in his mild tones, and they all laughed nervously.

Lucy led the way. "Everyone's here. And Gran's got a surprise for you, Florence."

How do you do it? How do you do the next part?

You simply took a deep breath and kept on going.

She put her arm through Florence's. Lucy opened the sitting room door. Martha saw them through the crack in the open door, Bill lying with his head on Karen's shoulder, Karen with her feet up on the footstool, looking exhausted. She smiled as Lucy came in, reaching her arms out for her daughter. Lucy laughed quietly at something and closed the door. "She just . . ."

Her voice was a low murmur as the door shut.

"Jim," Martha said calmly, "Flo needs to go into the kitchen first."

"Why?" Florence was looking through the open door toward the table, the figure sitting sedately, head turned toward them. "Who's in there?" she said. She froze. "Ma? Who . . . ?"

She looked at Martha, and Martha blinked and nodded. She wanted to say something, to beg her not to love this new mother more. She wanted to run in there now, ahead of Florence, pave the way. Call out to Cassie: *Be kind to her, tell her how wonderful she is! Ask her about her new book. Don't make her feel awkward or stupid. Don't tease her, she mustn't be teased. She loves the sunshine. She loves coffee, like her father. Like David. Please don't take her away from me. Please don't hurt her.*

Florence looked back and lightly touched her mother's cheek. "Oh, Ma," she said. "That's quite a coup. Well done." She handed Jim the car keys. In the kitchen, framed by the door, they saw Cassie stand up stiffly as Florence walked toward her.

"Hello, Florence, my dear," she said simply. "I'm . . . I'm Cassie."

Florence stood very still. As though she were hesitating.

"Hello, Cassie," she said eventually, her hand on the door, in a small voice.

Martha wished she could hold her hand, push her forward, but she knew she couldn't. This was, maybe, the last thing she could do for her. For any of them.

"It's lovely to meet you," Florence said. She turned back and smiled at Martha. Then she closed the door, and there was silence in the dark hall, only the sound of Lucy's voice and Karen's soft laugh, and then nothing else, really.

Jim and Martha were left facing each other. He put his hand on Martha's. "Shall we go for a walk? Would you show me the garden, Martha?" he said. "I'd love to see it."

"I'd love to show it to you," Martha said. She tucked her arm through his, and on the way out the door, picked up her garden pliers. The wisteria was too wild, and the honeysuckle would strangle everything one day. There was always something to do, there always would be. They walked outside into the sunshine, down the lawn toward the daisy bank, away from the house and the people inside. Just for a little while.

"Good-bye, my love," she whispered, and she looked up at the sky. "Thank you. Good-bye."

Cat

AT THE BOTTOM of the hill but before the village was the edge of the wood, and a web of streams that had flowed down from the hills around and converged on this shallow spot overhung with trees, babbling loudly and full of tiny, clear fish. It swept into one stream around the side of Winter Stoke and ran beside the green.

Cat sat on the bank, dangling her feet in the water, trousers rolled up, wearing a piece of paper folded into the shape of a hat on her head. In one hand she held a wooden spoon, and in the other a plastic trumpet.

"Where are you?" a voice called from the other side of the river, and Luke's face, black with burned-cork marks, popped up between the reeds.

"I'm here," said Cat.

"You stay there. I am still building my boat. If you try to escape, my men will beat you and kill you with sticks," said Luke, and he disappeared again.

"Oh, no," said Cat. "Well, I'm going to escape anyway. I've got special powers. I've turned into a monster and I'm going to cross the river and come and eat you."

"No!" Luke shouted. "You can't eat me."

"Oh, yes I can!" Cat yelled, advancing slowly across the stream. "I'm going to—oh, darling, I'm sorry," she said, as Luke's face crumpled into terrified tears. She splashed across the rest of the stream toward him and took him in her arms.

"I don't like monsters, Mum."

"Me neither. But they're not real, are they?"

"Well, sometimes they are. Zach says when you die you go to hell, and a monster eats you every night, and then the same bit grows back again in the day. His mum is a vicar. She told him."

"Right." Cat kissed the top of his head. "Well, Zach's telling you porkies. That's not true."

He shivered against her. "I'm still scared."

"Oh, Luke, I really am sorry," Cat said, hugging him close again.

"Let's go back home."

She hesitated. "We can't. Not just yet. Gran's visitor wants to meet Florence, and I said we'd go and play while they talk." She didn't know how to explain the real reason. "Now," she said, "have I shown you this?" She took some string out of her pocket. "Real pirates, they stab their fish in the water. Trainee pirates, they catch their fish like this."

"Where in the world?"

"Oh, all around the world. The Amazon, mainly." Cat fixed the bread she'd brought on the string and tied it to a stick. "That's yours."

"When can we go back?" Luke said, staring at the stick in concentration as he lowered the string carefully into the water.

"Later. After we've caught a fish."

"Jamie doesn't eat fish. We won't give him any fish."

"Jamie? Right." Cat wasn't really listening.

"Jamie's dad likes fish. He likes eating fish. He told me there are small fish you can eat all of them, including their heads." Luke nudged Cat. "Mum! Why don't you listen to me? Why are you always thinking about something?"

"I'm a busy pirate," Cat said.

"What are you thinking about?"

"Never mind. Oh, look. There they are."

She could hear their feet, crunching on the dry leaves and twigs of the undergrowth.

"Hey there," called Joe, advancing toward them. "Hi. Hi, Luke. How's your frog?"

"What frog?" Cat said, surprised.

"I got a frog in a box," Luke said. "When we camped, me and Jamie and Joe." He waved at Jamie. "How's your frog?"

"Dead." Jamie fished around in his satchel as Joe sat down and opened the coolbag. "Dad made some sandwiches. Do you want sandwiches?"

Luke looked at Cat. "Do pirates eat sandwiches? Do they?"

"Yes, they do," called Joe. "Big pirates eat them with bones and eye-balls." Luke's eyes grew huge, and he added hurriedly, "But that's just in films. Not really."

"Okay, Joe," said Luke happily.

"You're a pirate too, Luke," Joe told him. "You can't be scared of other pirates. That's like . . . like one of your toes being scared of the other toes." He sat down next to Cat.

"What's up?" he said.

"Nothing, why?"

"You look like you haven't slept," he said.

"I know we're friends again," she said, "but a word of advice: don't go around saying that to people." He said nothing, but she saw him glance again at her out of the corner of his eye. Cat took the sandwich he offered and took a huge bite, savoring the fluffy sourdough, the crunch of the crust. "That's so good. What is it?"

"Leftover beef slices from yesterday, bit of mayo, some watercress from down the way. You like it?"

"I've said it before, Joe. You make the best bread alive."

"It's my pleasure," he said. "Honestly. You and Luke are my best bread customers."

The boys were advancing farther into the wood, shouting with joy. Luke looked back at Cat, waving, his eyes alive with excitement. "See you later. If I don't come back . . . please don't be sad, Mum, okay?"

"Sure," Cat said. "Okay. Roger. Jolly Roger."

Joe and Cat sat in silence, Cat swinging her legs in the water again. Even in the cool of the trees it was hot still. Two dragonflies danced above the stream. She watched them, the dappled light catching their wings.

"Thanks for meeting up. There's a thing up at the house and I wanted to clear out for a bit."

"Right," said Joe. "Family gathering?"

She looked at him. "All of them, yep." She swallowed a bit more sandwich. "Karen's there, with Bill. And Bella."

"Of course," he said mildly.

"Just in case you—you know."

"I heard he's looking to buy into a practice in Bristol, then," Joe said.

"Yes."

"It's a shame."

"Oh, Joe."

"I mean, he's a great doctor, we'll miss him round here." He ate some sandwich. "There's not enough pepper on this, Cat. I'm sorry."

She ignored him. "You're very circumspect about it. About Bella."

"I'm happy for them, that's why." He wrinkled up his nose. "I'd love to meet her someday. The little one."

They were both silent for a few moments, and Cat remembered yet again with gratitude how easy it was to be with him. He understood.

"It's Florence," she said eventually. "She's meeting her mother. Her real mother. Florence is Southpaw's niece, they adopted her. His sister couldn't look after her, they had a very difficult childhood, and he wanted to help her—something like that. Southpaw was always so cagey about his past."

"Why?"

"I've seen the pictures he drew, the ones going into that exhibition. It was awful," she said sadly. "Anyway, she's here now. I thought I'd take Luke out. Enjoy the sunshine." She took a deep breath.

He smiled at her. "Cat, is that why you didn't want to be up there this morning? Because of your mother?"

She reached for an apple. "Maybe."

"Why?"

"Mothers and daughters. Still makes me sad." To her horror, Cat's eyes filled with tears.

Joe immediately pulled her toward him, stretching his arm around her. "Oh, Cat. Hey. Don't cry."

She leaned against him. "Sorry. I didn't mean to."

He patted her back. "You poor girl. It's still hard, is it? I'm so sorry." Cat nodded. She turned into him, and he wrapped both his arms around her. "You cry if you want," he said, his voice muffled by her hair.

She held on to him, thanking her lucky stars she had a friend like him, that they had found their way through. "All those years," Cat said, drawing back and wiping her nose on her hand. "I spent so many years thinking one day we'd get close, that she'd come and find me, take me home, you know." She sat up, sniffing, and pushed her hair out of her face. "I'm so sorry, Joe. I just always had this idea of her, even after I knew she was always going to let me down. But I think a part of her might have wanted me . . . might have missed me. Oh, goodness. This is the eight-year-old in me. Forgive me."

He leaned toward her and touched her cheek. "Nothing to forgive, Cat. Never, ever."

She stared at him. At the sprinkling of freckles on his nose, his blue eyes. He held her gaze.

"Gran told me this morning it's been a year since she wrote the invitations to her party," she said eventually.

"I heard the food at that party was amazing."

"I heard the chef was a liability, he nearly mowed down her great-grandson and slept with her daughter-in-law."

"*But* his miniature toad-in-the-hole canapés were sensational."

"It's been good, hasn't it?" she said after a while. She spread her arms wide. "All of—this. This year."

"Oh. Yes, of course."

They smiled at each other. She could stare into his eyes, see nothing hidden there at all except honesty, truth, kindness. Herself, and him, and all of them. And she was terrified suddenly, as if a bubbling river had risen up and was about to sweep them away. She couldn't do it.

She just couldn't. She touched his hand gently, and stood up. "I have to go. Would you mind watching Luke for an hour or so?"

Joe got up and looked at her in confusion. "Where are you going?"

"I have to go back to the house."

"Why?"

"Just need to," she said. She had to go. "Is that all right?"

"We have to collect Jamie's hat from Winterfold, so I'll drop him off in a while. I think it'd be good to say hello to everyone, anyway."

Everything was straightforward about him. No silly, petty games, no overthinking. He was as clear as the water in the stream.

"Sure, good idea," Cat said. She tried not to look like she was backing away from him. She wished there were dust, something she could kick up, anything to create an obscuring cloud that would enable her to get out, run away. "Thanks. Bye."

She ran out of the wood, yanking at her top as though it were covered with brambles that would pull her back in; and as she ran back up the hill, she swallowed back tears, already disgusted with herself.

At the top of the lane was a gentle curve, and as she turned into it, Cat started. There was a figure on the bench, holding a baby, her long hair falling over her face, both of them apparently sleeping. Cat slowed down, her head still spinning. The sun shone on the woman's hair, and Cat found herself thinking again of her mother's ashes, scattered over the garden, still flying somewhere in the breeze around the hills. She stopped and shook her head, smiling at herself. It was Karen, and Bella. She paused a few yards away, not knowing what to do. Her legs twitched; she felt quite mad, as if she ought to just keep on running, past the house, up the hill.

The inscription on the bench was: "Seek rest, weary traveler."

Bella was in Karen's arms, her body almost entirely wrapped up in an old shawl of Martha's. Her chest went up and down. Cat had forgotten how quickly babies breathed, how alarming it had seemed to her at first. She watched her, suddenly transfixed. The tiny fingers of one hand waved involuntarily suddenly, like a magician's flourish, and Cat laughed softly.

"Hello," said Karen, suddenly raising her head and opening her eyes. Cat had thought yesterday, when they'd arrived, how different she looked, especially without her makeup. Much younger. "I'm getting good at catnapping. Sorry. Just went for a little post-feed stroll and sat in the sunshine and fell asleep. I bet you thought we were tramps."

"You both looked very peaceful," Cat said, smiling. She sat down next to her, trying not to fidget.

"Thought it might be good to clear out for a while." Karen pushed her hair away from her face. "The sound of a baby crying isn't necessarily the most appropriate . . . erm . . . vibe they want right now, do you know what I mean?"

"Totally agree," said Cat. "You're very wise."

"Where's Luke, then?"

"He's with Joe and Jamie. They're just down by the river, actually. They're so happy down there." Cat hesitated, and shifted on her seat. "He'd love to see you and Bella, I know he would."

"Really? I never heard back from him. I've e-mailed. And called."

"He was pretty upset. You know Joe, he loves kids. Loves a family."

She laughed, already feeling exasperated with herself for running off like that. "That's why I've given him mine."

Karen stared at her; then her face cleared. "Great. That's so great, Cat! I really hoped he'd go for it. I didn't realize. You two, at last! That's fantastic."

"Oh," said Cat hurriedly, "no, Karen. I meant—not that. I meant I've given him . . . No, he's just looking after Luke. For an hour or so."

Karen shifted the sleeping Bella under her arm. "Oh."

"There's nothing going on with me and Joe," Cat said, mortified. "It's not—we're friends. We're really good friends. Actually. It's great." She nodded. "Great." The sun flickered in her eyes.

Karen stared at her, and then she laughed. "Bollocks!"

"What?"

"I said that's bollocks. Cat, he's in love with you."

Bella slowly opened her eyes, glaring sleepily at her mother.

"Joe," said Cat, as though Karen just hadn't understood her.

"Yes, Cat. I know who you mean. Joe Thorne. Six one, blue eyes, black hair. Got a scar on his finger, loves *Game of Thrones*, makes nice bread." She spoke slowly, as if Cat were a bit deaf. "He is in love with you."

Cat stroked Bella's hair, her heart thumping. "He's not, honestly. We don't have that kind of relationship. Once . . . you know. We sort of once . . . anyway . . ."

"Cat, it's obvious. I've watched the two of you together. I'd see the way he looked at you. That's why I left. Wasn't fair on him, on you. On me, on Bill." She gave a funny smile, then took Bella and clipped on the baby's sling. "Look, Cat, none of my business, but I think you need to stop looking to the past. Forget about what's happened. I think we all need to."

"Yes," said Cat, looking at her. She stood up. "Yes." She looked down the drive, toward the old house. She could hear laughter through the open windows and peered forward, to see what she could make out. Blurred figures, distorted by the leaded diamond panes of glass. She couldn't see who it was, who was there.

She could go back to the house now. Walk in, say hello to the reunited Cassie and Florence. Be part of that family, the niece, the granddaughter, the cousin; and then Joe would bring Luke back and say hello to everyone and it would be fine, of course it would be, and then he would leave, and she'd see him the next day and the next day. . . .

But she didn't want to be part of that family, not in that way. She wanted her own family. She wanted her own life. She wanted him. She wanted them, together. She wanted his baby inside her, his food, his life; she wanted to make him feel so safe and secure he never got that look of desolate loneliness that puckered his brow; she wanted him to have a home that Jamie felt was as much his as anyone's.

I want our life. Our family. Our home.

What if it was too late?

"Karen, tell them I'll be back later, will you? I have to—I have to collect Luke."

"Yes," Karen said, and she nodded. "Of course."

"I'm—fine," Cat told her, unnecessarily. "I need to go now."

It might be too late already.

She knew what she needed to do now, but what if it *was* too late, what if in one of the infinitesimal ways that the earth moves and millions of tiny changes happen, the world had altered and the path they were on could now never be reversed? What if she had missed her chance? She ran, feet thudding so hard on the bone-dry road her body juddered in time, one foot in front of the other, each stride longer than the last, longer, faster than she had ever run before.

Cat turned off through the woods, taking the shortcuts, the old paths she knew so well. She jumped across the stream and kept on running, as though someone were chasing her.

She saw him at the edge of the wood, at the bottom of the lane. Right by the bridge that crossed over into the village.

"Hey!" he shouted. She could see Jamie and Luke in Zach's front garden, swinging on a rope hanging from a tree. Joe gestured back toward them with his thumb. "Luke's there! He's okay."

"Joe!" she yelled back, almost terrified he might vanish, disappear into thin air before her eyes. She saw his boots on the ground, the sandwiches sticking out of his pocket, the sticks poking out of the bucket he was carrying. His eyes, so warm when he looked at her, and he was smiling; he smiled all the time now. He came forward to meet her at the foot of the hill.

"What's the hurry?" he said, clutching her arms to make her halt as she ran toward him, almost unable to stop. "Hey! Are you okay?"

She looked around, panting, unable to speak. The boys were paying no attention. A car wound round the corner, and they stood to one side.

Cat took Joe's hand. She stood close to him. Her finger stroked his palm. She smiled into his eyes.

"I had to come back," she said, her breath short, her cheeks flushed, mouth dry. "I had to tell you, before it was too late."

"Cat," he said, his voice low. He knew, she could tell. She had to say it.

And she was still so scared, fear and adrenaline pumping through her body. She was terrified, in fact, because this was life, falling in love, loving your children, fearing the worst, wanting the best. She had been away from it for so long. She had kept Luke away from it, too.

"I have to say it," she said. He put his hand up to her cheek, his fingers stroking her face, palm to skin. They were inches apart. "Let me say it."

They stayed there, fixed together, smiling at each other.

One of the boys called out from the garden, but they ignored him.

"It's like home, with you," Cat said. "Just like home. For the first time. Ever."

He nodded. "I know," he said.

"I don't want us to be friends," Cat said urgently. "Please, can we not be friends?"

His face clouded over, and then he relaxed. "Yes."

"I want you," she said, and she leaned toward him, across that final gap that separated them, and she kissed him, feeling how warm he was, how solid, how well she knew him, then broke away. "I've been so scared, of stupid things," she said.

"No, they were real. And you're not stupid." He pulled her closer, cupping her face. "Cat, I've been in love with you since November, you know. I didn't know what to do about it. I tried to pretend it wasn't really real."

"Me too," she said. The release of emotion, of tension, of the buildup of years and years of running away from this, and here she was, and she was holding him, kissing him, and he loved her, though she didn't believe he could love her nearly as much as she loved him. "We can't do this now," she told him eventually. "Not out here, can we?"

"We can if it's for the rest of our lives," Joe said, and he untangled their fingers, put his hands gently on her cheeks again, and kissed her.

The sky above them was clear, no clouds, nothing, the woods beyond dark green, the last burst of summer. She knew the house would be there behind them, if she turned. Over toward the vicarage garden the boys carried on playing, oblivious, and she kissed him again, laughing. It was just them, the two of them.

EPILOGUE

August 1948

THAT MORNING WHEN he woke, the stench of shit and something else, something rotting, hung in the stale air. He realized a noise outside had woken him and kneeled up to open the window. There was his father, slowly descending the steps. He stopped and looked up as if he knew he was being watched. David hid behind the moth-eaten green curtain, praying he wouldn't see him, praying it wouldn't move.

After his father had disappeared around the corner, David sat up and looked around him. The bare room with two mattresses, a chest that the local church had provided, a jug filled with water, a bowl. Flies gathered around the bowl, and he saw that his father had, once again, used it as a chamber pot. When he was drunk, he couldn't be bothered to go outside to the privy.

As he was pulling his filthy trousers on, David caught sight of a childish scribble of green pencil on the wallpaper, and remembered the last time he'd seen Cassie. It was the previous summer, three months after she'd gone to live with Jem. He'd caught a train out to Leigh-on-Sea and gone to the beach with them. Cassie was three, as she kept telling him, a lovely little thing, bouncing curly hair, a wide smile, just like his mum. In three months she'd already changed. She still knew who he was, but Jem was her favorite person now. It killed him, just a little bit, to see her curling into Jem's lap, running to her when a tiny crab got in her bucket, shouting information at her at the top of her voice. But that was the choice he'd made, and he knew it was the right one.

"She's the spit of Emily, isn't she, love?" Aunt Jem stretched out on the sand, pulling her cotton dress demurely over her shins.

David had nodded. He couldn't yet talk about his mother. He'd stared at his little sister determinedly hacking at some seaweed, laughing with some children, and felt more alone than he'd ever been. He knew it wouldn't do any good to see more of her. It'd just hurt him. He knew she couldn't ever come back to London with him. Time would move on and he had to as well. The Blitz had taught thousands of London children that. Things got broken, destroyed. You lost your friends, your parents, your siblings. But you got on with it. You played in the ruins, you got a new house, maybe a new baby brother or sister, maybe not. That had been a year ago. Jem sent a postcard now and then to keep in touch, but that was it and that was how he'd wanted it, wasn't it? His plan had worked. He just had to keep on reminding himself: Cassie was all right. She was out of there.

Suddenly David felt a lightness steal over him. He looked out the window again, to make sure his father wasn't coming back; then he scrambled into a shirt and grabbed his sketchbook, his photo of his mother, the locket she'd been wearing the night she was killed, and he checked under the brick for his father's cash, and took it, all of it. He didn't write a note. His father couldn't read. And he didn't want to leave any trace. He might come and find him.

He wasn't really sure where he was going; he just wanted to go away, somewhere unlike here, unlike this little patch of London that was all he really knew. At first he got on a bus thinking he'd head toward Buckingham Palace, but he fell asleep and ended up at Paddington Station and they turfed him out. He thought about walking down to Hyde Park, but that wasn't far enough. He told himself that now he'd started, he had to keep going. It was still early, not even nine thirty. He didn't want to go home.

And then suddenly it occurred to him that he didn't ever have to go back, if he didn't want to. He had his scholarship, he had a room near the school from September. That was two weeks away now. The same teacher who'd sent his stuff off to the Slade, Mr. Wilson, he'd given him a spare room in his house, down toward the Cally Road, and the rent was subsidized by the council. He had the money he'd stolen from his father, and he'd the promise of a couple of weeks' work from Billy from school's dad down at Covent Garden, moving veg around. He didn't ever have to go back, did he? Did he?

The knowledge wasn't frightening. It was the most glorious feeling he'd felt for a long time. He could sleep in hedgerows. He could draw wherever he wanted. He could even get the boat train from Victoria, go to France!

But no, he wasn't going to do that, not just yet. But he was going to go away from here, today.

A loud, piercing whistle shrieked right beside him, and David jumped. He turned to see the train behind, its engine puffing gentle balls of steam into the smoggy station.

"Where's it going?" he said.

The guard jerked his head. "West," he said gnomically.

West. Well, he had to go somewhere, didn't he? This wonderful feeling of freedom was still with him, and he didn't want to think about it, just enjoy it. David climbed onto the train with the vague idea he might go to Bath, see the bombsites there and do some more drawings to add to his collection. Maybe he'd have some lunch at a pub in the country. Maybe he'd do all sorts of things. The day, and indeed time, stretched out ahead of him, splendid, never-ending, like the perfect blue sky.

He sat on the train watching the buildings stream past, the rows of houses with bombed-out gaps, the men at work rebuilding the city. The empty warehouses, the vanished streets. All those stories in their spaces, of loss and sadness and sometimes hope and happiness. He didn't feel jingoistic; he didn't feel pride in his country. He only felt numbness, a quiet sense of gladness that he and Cassie had survived. When he disembarked at Bath Spa Station he looked around him, wondering what the noise was, a little engine bolt clanging against something, an organ? And then he realized it was birds singing, so beautifully it made tears spring to his eyes. You didn't heard birdsong these days in London.

David stood outside the iron-girdered ticket hall, looking this way and that, at the empty square of land where buildings had once stood. He crossed through a tunnel, over a road, not really caring where he was going. And he walked.

He walked and walked, up a hill lined with gracious villas and leafy gardens, until he could see countryside sweeping away from him. And he carried on walking. At the top of the highest hill the land leveled out, and he stopped for a drink at a quiet pub, the Cross Keys. The landlady gave him some bread and cheese and told him, in a broad accent he'd hardly heard before, that he was in the most beautiful part of the world. He'd forgotten his hat, so before he continued he rolled up his trouser legs and put his handkerchief, tied in knots, on his scorched head, bid her farewell, and set off again.

He could see the Georgian town curved like a gold and cream sea-shell, tucked into the wide valley below. Perfect puffs of cloud now drifted above him, but otherwise the sky was still a deep, kind blue. So David kept walking, as the road swooped down again into another fold of land, until he came to a river, and fields, and long-distant woodland. He looked at the watch Mr. Wilson had given him when he got into the Slade—he had been walking for nearly two hours, and it occurred to him only now that he would have to walk back to the station, unless he didn't go back at all, just stayed here in this beautiful place. Who would miss him? He was a half person, that was what you became if no one else cared whether you came home at night. Living in the shadows of other people's lives.

So he lay down on the grass that had only just emerged from the shadow cast by the dark woods and was deliciously cool and damp. And he chewed a ripe stalk of wheat, staring up above him at the sky, at nothing whatsoever at all.

When he got up to walk again, the hill above him was steep this time, the going arduous, and he began to regret the absence of a hat more and more. But he fell into an easy rhythm. His limbs were strong, his heart was light; and, when he found two apples the landlady must have sneaked into the bottom of his knapsack, he ate one, grateful, smiling. After walking uphill again for half an hour he reached the crest of the val-ley, turning toward the north again, and then he saw it. A dark driveway, framed by heavy oaks, and a bench in front.

"Seek rest, weary traveler."

He sat down on the bench, panting, and ate the second apple, staring out at the view. The still, heavy trees. The curling road, leading to the river. Homes dotted here and there in the plush landscape, a line of white rising up from some. Swallows swooping wildly about his head, darting in and out of hedgerows. The scent of wild roses and wood smoke.

When he'd finished, he wandered down the drive, ready to run if need be—his months of clambering around the ruined capital had given him a quick eye and a fleet foot, as well as a sense of danger.

There was a house behind a circular driveway. Low, quiet, tucked against the hill. Toffee-colored stone and leaded windows on the first floor, soaring giant wooden clapboard gables on the second, a moss-tiled roof. Purple flowers scrambling along the golden exterior, the windows glinting in the late afternoon sun. A riot of pink, red, yellow flowers—Jem would know their names—hugging either side of the house, and behind to the right side he could see rows of vegetables. Like Peter Rabbit, then, he thought he might die if he didn't taste one of the lettuces, cool and green in the black earth. He could hear laughter, shouts of glee inside the house.

David did not know why, but he kept on walking toward the front door. He lifted the knocker. It was a great big owl. It made him smile; he knocked, hard.

A lady answered, gray hair dressed in a bun, a lace-covered blouse, a stiff back, and a battered straw hat. She stared at him inquiringly.

"May I help you?" Her hazel eyes were huge, flecked with blue and brown.

"Ma'am, I apologize for disturbing you," said David. "I've walked all day and I'm afraid I'm extremely thirsty. Could I trouble you for some water?"

She opened the door wide. "Of course. That hill does tire one out, I know. I'm Violet Heron." She held out her hand and he shook it, a little stunned. "Please, come in."

He followed her into the hall. Someone was screaming with pleasure, and he looked to his left to see two children wrestling on the floor, one a young girl in a torn pinafore, the other a boy whose shorts were covered in some kind of black creosote-like substance.

"Is that Em?" one of them yelled. "Where is she? She said she'd come and play with us!"

"Ignore my embarrassing grandchildren. I do apologize," said the lady, but she didn't look embarrassed.

"Where is Em, do you know, Grandmother?" the girl asked.

"She's upstairs, reading. She said she'd be down soon. Don't be so loud." She turned to David. "One of our old evacuees from London has been visiting us."

She opened a door, which led into the kitchen. A red-faced woman stood tackling something in a brown earthenware bowl. "Dorcas," said Mrs. Heron, "this young man wants some water."

Dorcas heaved a mound of glistening, rubbery dough onto the marble surface and pushed her hands down on it. She glanced him over appraisingly. "From the looks of him, he'll be needing a lot more than water. You want some bread and stew?"

David nodded mutely. He stared out the kitchen window at the valley. He'd never been anywhere so beautiful in his life.

"They say on a clear night, when the bombs were coming down over Bath, you could hear the bells over at Wells Cathedral in the opposite direction, in the silence." Mrs. Heron shrugged. "I don't believe it, but it's comforting to think it, somehow." She watched him for a moment, then stood up again. "Dorcas, bring the tray out onto the terrace, would you?" She gestured to David. "Follow me."

As they opened the door, the afternoon sun hit them in the eyes, and Violet put her hat on. She gestured to a stone terrace, beyond which the garden ran riot, turning into woods. "Sit down."

David sat. The sun seemed to be bleaching his bones, and a great feeling of peace stole over him. Time seemed to stand still. The only noise was the hum of bees, birds singing in the woods ahead, and occasionally, the screams of children echoing inside the house. It was like being in a dream. He still didn't really know why he was here. He couldn't explain why he'd walked down that drive.

"Their father went missing at Monte Cassino," Mrs. Heron said suddenly. "They still believe he's coming back."

David sat up. "I am so sorry. Where—where's their mother?"

Mrs. Heron looked across the valley. She said flatly, "She died in London. One of the last bombing raids."

David wanted to say, *Mine too*, but the words wouldn't come. Dorcas appeared with a tray of bread, cold stew, and water, and he thanked her, resisting the urge to gulp it all down. The stew was thin and more like soup—meat was scarce still—but to David it was the most delicious meal he'd ever had. He felt as though he'd been away from London for months. With every step out of the train station, he had walked away from the war, from the sound of his father's threats, his sister's howls, his mother's dying scream.

Mrs. Heron crossed her hands neatly in her lap while he ate, and when he had finished she said, "So what do you do?"

"Nothing, at the moment," said David. "But I'm going to art school next month. The Slade," he added proudly.

"Goodness, you look older than that. Where are your people from?"

"Islington." David didn't elaborate.

"I grew up in Bloomsbury, very near the Slade," she said. "I miss the shops. And the buildings."

He gave her a big smile. "How can you miss anything, in a place like this?"

"Oh, you miss some things." She smiled at him. "But you're probably right. I don't, really."

"How long have you been here?"

"Fifty years. As long as the house."

David scooped up the last of the stew with his bread. "You . . . you built this?"

"My husband built it for me. Winterfold was my wedding present. He died ten years ago. I'm glad he didn't live through the war, it would have broken him. He'd fought in the Great War and . . ." She trailed off and looked away, and David saw that the beautiful hazel eyes were brimming with tears. "Everything must go on."

He changed the subject. "Winterfold? That's the name of the house?"

"Yes. The village is Winter Stoke, and we are here in the fold of the hill. It's a fine name, I think."

His mother's maiden name had been Winter. He sat up. "It is a fine name."

"What's your name, my dear?" Mrs. Heron said kindly.

"It's David," he said, and his youth betrayed him. "David Winter."

Her mouth twitched. "Is it, now."

David's father had fought in the Great War, too. He'd come back with a hand that didn't quite work, screaming nightmares, and an iron strength he deployed nearly every day in some way. He could have told Violet Heron that. He could have given her his name, been a real person, one whom she could trace if she'd wanted to. His father's son. His father who, the previous week, had beaten his new girlfriend, Sally from the butcher's, so hard she'd been put in the hospital. His father who, when he found David's cloth-backed folder crammed full of drawings of London

427

children, of bombed-out houses, of rubble and decay and hope and ex-perience, had kneed him against the wall, forced his arm across David's neck, and pinned him down while he ripped every piece of paper into precise, inch-wide ribbons that fell on the floor into nests of color.

"Yes. My name's David Winter," he said. "For my mother. It was her maiden name." He stuck his chin out and tipped his head back, because he didn't want to cry. "Don't believe me if you don't want to."

She nodded, her eyes kind. "Of course I believe you."

He regretted it now, and felt young, stupid. He'd told this woman too much, and he shouldn't have come here. David fished his handkerchief, still in knots, out of his pocket. He was suddenly uneasy.

"Thank you for your kindness. I should probably leave now. I have a long journey back." He wanted to go right away. He felt embarrassed, as if coming here had released something within him, felt that he shouldn't have knocked on the door, should merely have stared at the outside and turned back down the hill. They walked around to the front of the house in silence. "Well, thank you again," he said. "Good-bye."

Violet Heron paused for a moment, as if wanting to say something, and then she took off her hat, gave it to him. "Take it. For the walk. It was my husband's. I have my own and I'd like you to have it. It'll fit you."

It was battered, frayed around the edges, the straw soft to the touch and pliable. "That's very kind of you. It's more than I deserve. I—" He stopped, unable to speak. "I mean it."

Then a voice called out, "Mrs. Heron! I'm going now. I have to make that train."

And a girl appeared, flying limbs, cramming a hat on her sleek head. She was his age, or maybe a year younger. "Thank you so much, it's been absolutely lovely—oh." She stopped, and stared at him. "Sorry. I didn't know I was interrupting."

Her voice was husky; South London, he thought. Mrs. Heron turned to her. "You're not interrupting, my dear. The children were looking for you. I hope they didn't spoil your work."

"It's fine. I have everything I need, I think. Thank you so much. Hello. Who are you?"

She held out her hand to him, and he took it, gazing at her.

"I'm David Winter," he said, and it sounded perfectly, totally right and normal when he said it. "That is my name."

What an idiot, why did I say that then?

She looked at him as though he were a simpleton. "Right, then."

"Em was evacuated here during the war," Mrs. Heron said, putting her arm around the girl. "Five lovely years. We do miss her terribly. She's come back for the weekend to see us."

Em looked uncomfortable, but pleased. She slid a sketchbook into her bag and ran a hand over her gleaming bobbed hair. "Bye, Mrs. Heron," she said gruffly. "I'll see you soon, I hope."

"You'll pay us a visit in the autumn?"

"I don't know about my classes yet. I'll write to you." Her smile grew warm as she kissed the older woman's cheek. "Thank you again, for everything."

She was so self-possessed; how had she learned to be like that? He wiggled a finger through the hole in his stinking, grubby trousers, aware as never before that day how dirty and ragged they were. She must think he was a tramp.

"Anytime it suits you, please come and stay, my dear girl." Mrs. Heron smiled at her. "We do miss you."

"I miss you. And I miss Winterfold. How could I not?" She turned to David. "It was my home, you know. Only home I wish I'd ever known."

He wanted to give it to her then, to pluck it out of the land like a wizard, shrink it down, hold it out to her in the palm of his hand. *Here.*

"Look, I have to make this train and I'm walking to the station. So I'd better go."

"I'm going to the station too, yes," he said, hearing his own voice, shrill and silly. "Where are you going? Bath?"

"Yeah," she said, squeezing Mrs. Heron's hand and setting off at a pace down the drive. "Well?" she added over her shoulder. "You coming or not?"

He ran after her, waving good-bye to Mrs. Heron, who called after them, "Good-bye, dears, good-bye. . . ."

He pulled on the worn hat. It fitted like a glove, the weave cool against his forehead. David looked back and smiled at her, tipped the brim in a comic fashion, and she nodded, pleased.

He never saw her again, but he never forgot her. The large, looping wave she gave them, as they turned the corner and she disappeared from sight.

When they reached the top of the lane, by the sign that said WINTER-FOLD, the girl stopped and faced him. "What's your name again?"

"David," he said.

"Ah. Well, I'm Martha. That's my name, but I like to be called Em for short. Just want to be clear in case you attack me and I have to report you to the police."

He wasn't sure if she was joking. He was unused to any kind of light-hearted conversation, much less flirting. "I wouldn't—it's not—"

"I'm just being funny. Don't look so alarmed," she said, smiling at him. "It's a nice place here, isn't it?"

"Yes. It's lovely. Didn't know there were . . . places like this in real life. I want to sketch it."

"You like drawing too, then?" she asked curiously, as if registering him for the first time.

"I do. You?"

"I love it," she said, clutching the bag with the sketchbook. "I'm going to try for a scholarship next year. Chelsea School of Art, or the Slade. I'm going to be a famous artist, I reckon. Paint anything you want, have a stand set up on Sundays in Hyde Park, and make all my money in one afternoon. I can copy all sorts, see? I copied this last month."

She pulled out a picture. "That's *Bubbles*!" David was amazed. "Right there! You did that? Is it pastels? Where'd you get them from?"

"Joint birthday and Christmas present. My dad saved up for ages. My birthday's in November, you see. Early birthday present." She rolled the sketch back up. "Told you I was good. You any good?"

"Not like that," he said. "More . . . I don't know." He shrugged. "S'difficult to talk about."

"Oh, he's a proper artist." She walked alongside him, head bowed, lip drooping, in imitation. "Oh, he's too good for all that. He can't talk about his art!" She laughed. "Dearie me."

He stopped and smiled, pushing the hat back off his face. "Oh, get off. Don't really talk to other people much about it." About anything. About anything at all.

"All right, I get it." Somehow he knew she did, without having to say more. "I came down here to sketch. I love it. Get all the best ideas down here."

He stared into her dancing eyes again, thinking that he'd never seen anyone so beautiful. "I can see why."

"It suits you, that hat," she said suddenly, and then added, "You'll have to come back here one day too."

"Yes, I think I will," he replied, trying to sound nonchalant, though his heart was hammering. They walked on together, the afternoon heat shimmering in front of them, golden shafts of light falling on the hazy, leafy road that lay ahead.

ACKNOWLEDGMENTS

Thanks to:

My friend Jo Roberts-Miller, who I miss and who I don't see enough and who one day called me on the phone and with whom I had this epic conversation that led to the idea for *A Place for Us*. Thanks, dear Jo-Jo.

Chris, because without you I wouldn't be able to do anything at all and nothing would be worth it. And Cora, my beautiful girl, you make my day every day.

Fred and Tugie for boyztalk. Maura Brickell for cultural information. Olivia Bishop for Italian chats and Victoria Watkins for French chats, though any mistakes are definitely my own. Very special thanks to Richard Danbury for talking me through the grislier legal aspects of the novel—no spoilers, but suffice it to say he totally saved me from being buried under a mountain of legalese, and I must once again make it very clear that any mistakes are very much mine.

Lucia Rae (Lucia for President of the World), Melissa Pimentel, and everyone at Curtis Brown. And Jonathan Lloyd, a massive thank-you for Everything, very much with a capital E, these last few months.

My beautiful Gallery Ladies and Gents on the Avenue of the Americas—thank you to everyone at Simon & Schuster. Karen! Alex! You left, but I still thank you! Paige! Becky too! Jen! Oh, Jen. Louise! I am a lucky English mutha. And a mighty thank-you to Kim and David at Inkwell for always being there, and for always being right.

Finally, thanks to everyone at Headline for your welcome energy, professionalism, and the fact that I wake up every morning so happy that I'm with you!!!! Oh, good times. Thanks to Jamie, Jane, Barbara, Viviane, Vicky, George, Elaine, Frankie, Liz, Frances, Louise, Justin—I wish I had space for everyone. Most of all, though, thank you to Mari Evans.

Acknowledgments

Whatever happens I will never forget the faith you had in me when I had none in myself. I feel like a different person now, thanks to you. (Bit heavy to lay that on you, but there it is: deal with it.) I am completely in awe of your skills at editing slash publishing slash life.

This book is for Thomas Wilson and Bea McIntyre, because if I have an amazing story, I always want to save it for you two, and there comes a point when you realize that you have been friends with someone for so long they are, sort of really by now, your family.

A Place for Us

HARRIET EVANS

Introduction

WHEN MARTHA WINTER sits down one late summer morning to invite her family to return home for her eightieth birthday celebration, she knows that what she is planning to reveal at the party could ruin the idyllic life she and her husband, David, have spent over fifty years building.

As the family returns to Winterfold, their rambling house in the heart of the English countryside, each character reveals the secrets, joys, and tragedies with which they are wrestling. And when Martha finally unburdens her secret, the family's foundations threaten to crumble.

Topics & Questions
for Discussion

1. The majority of characters in *A Place for Us* are women, and consequently this book addresses many women's issues. What are some of the defining moments for the women in the novel, and how do these events impact their character development? What kinds of arguments do you believe the author is ultimately trying to make through her female characters about women's experiences? How do you relate to these experiences?

2. Martha says, "Women weren't supposed to think we could have both, back then. Do the job we loved, have the family we wanted" (p. 208). "Back then" to Martha would be the mid-twentieth century. Do you think the attitude of society today has truly progressed to encourage women to have both? Discuss.

3. The author takes the reader through the story from the perspective of multiple characters, focusing on some more than others. Do you believe all the characters play equal supporting roles, or would you argue that some are more pivotal than others? Do you think there is a main character? Who, and why?

4. Why do you think we see certain scenes from the point of view of a particular person? For example, the neighborhood party is told from Lucy's point of view. How would it have been different if seen through the eyes of Joe, or Florence?

5. The book is divided into four parts, each beginning with a quote or lines of poetry. How do these epigraphs relate thematically to the section they introduce? To the book as a whole?

6. Why do you think David and Martha never told Florence that she was adopted? Do you think they were justified in not doing so?

7. When Martha comes to Paris to take Cat and Luke home to Winterfold, Cat says she recognizes the "feeling of half sadness, half happiness that stalked her all the time lately" (p. 343) as love. Have you ever felt this way? How would you define love?

8. At the family lunch, when Martha makes her announcement, she says that she and David "went wrong, somewhere along the way," and that "it begins with Daisy. It ends with her too" (p. 209). Do you agree with Martha's perception that she and David as parents are somehow at fault? Do you agree that Daisy is the primary catalyst for the problems that affected the family?

9. Do you think that Martha was right to handle Daisy's death in the way that she did? If not, how should she have handled it differently, and what repercussions do you think it might have had?

10. When Karen and Bill separate, both feel that the other is at fault for the damage to their marriage. Who do you believe played the primary role in hurting the relationship, Karen or Bill? Do you believe that one person can be more at fault than the other when a relationship fails? The birth of Bella is a crucial moment for Karen and Bill; how significant do you think it was in their journey to healing? Do you think they can overcome their differences in the future? Do you see them together in, say, ten years' time?

11. Many characters, from Joe and Karen to Florence and Cat, wrestle with their place among the Winters and the idea of whether they truly belong. Consider the argument of nature versus nurture: How much of a person's identity is defined by one's origins, and how much of it is shaped by one's surroundings and the people in one's life? Are blood ties really the strongest and most binding of all?

Enhance Your Book Club

1. Author Harriet Evans's debut novel, *Going Home*, is also about a family coming together at their house in the countryside where secrets and controversies arise. Read *Going Home* with your book club and discuss the similarities and differences of these two novels. How do they differ in tone? What do you believe Evans is trying to say about the role of family in our lives with these two novels?

2. Each of the four parts to the story has its own title:

   • Part I : The Invitation
   • Part II: The Party
   • Part III: The Past and the Present
   • Part IV: The End and the Beginning

   Come up with your own title for each section, and then discuss why you chose that title.

3. Select a major event in the story, like Martha's announcement at the party, or an argument between two characters, and write it from the perspective of a different character than the one the author chose. Read it to the group, then discuss the scene you chose, the character you chose, and what you hoped to emphasize through this alternative point of view.